3

4

4

DUBLIN
DEAD

GERARD O'DONOVAN

sphere

SPHERE

First published in Great Britain in 2011 by Sphere

Copyright © Gerard O'Donovan 2011

The moral right of the author has been asserted.

A CIP catalogue record for this book
is available from the British Library.

Hardback ISBN 978-1-84744-530-8
Trade Paperback ISBN 978-1-84744-407-3

Typeset in Plantin by M Rules
Printed and bound in Great Britain by
Clays Ltd, St Ives plc

Sphere
An imprint of
Little, Brown Book Group
100 Victoria Embankment
London EC4Y 0DY

An Hachette UK Company
www.hachette.co.uk

For Angela

Prologue

The door. All he had to do was get to it. The breath burned in his lungs as he ran. Each rasping, aching heave of his chest was all he could hear above the thud of his feet on the sun-dried grass, the scuff of his trainers kicking up the powdery earth beneath, and the baleful thumping tread of the man pursuing him through the dark, fifty, maybe only forty metres behind, gaining with every stride. No way would he risk glancing back. He already knew what death looked like.

Ahead, the boxy white walls of a low-slung house stood out spectrally against the dark slopes and shadowed gullies of the hillside behind and the moon-bright sky above. *The door.* That was all that mattered. *La puerta.* He had to focus on it. *De duer.* The door to his own house. Stout, defensible. In his mind he brought it forward, saw every detail, every swirling knot in its stained oak planking, the black wrought iron handle, the macho studwork so beloved of the Spanish, the twisted black metal of the grille, through which, even now, she would be staring, waiting.

Sweat crawled like spiderlegs down his face, his limbs grown soft from too many years away. In his mind he was back on the streets of Dublin in the early eighties, pissing ahead of Tommy Hanrahan and his bunch of vicious little pricks. Eleven years old, quick as a switchblade and twice as sharp, he was laughing, cursing, taunting them over his shoulder, feeling the chill air run across his arms and legs like a pulse of power, the walls and balconies of the flats towering above, funnelling them all towards the corner alley where Sean Carmody and his gang, the ones who changed his life by taking him in, waited with bats and bricks to spring a savage surprise.

A different world, a different time, a different life. Who would ever have guessed skinny little Dec would come so far? And for what? To end it here, with his face kicked flat in the Spanish dust? Fuck off. He felt his lungs expand to greet the extra oxygen he needed and a new surge of energy flood into his calf muscles, into his thighs. The heaviness of his doubt fell away and his speed picked up even as he reached the patio. The door was only five metres off when the crump of the shotgun reached his ears and he felt the first shower of pellets whistle past, then ... *Shit, oh shit* ... the scalding twist of pain in his right hip wrenched him round, sent him spinning like he'd been shoved by the hand of God, and he stumbled, wheeling, somehow still upright, clawing the air in front of him, throwing himself out towards the door.

And he was there, slamming into the hard wood, and the door opened and he pushed through, falling, the shredded muscle of his thigh burning like a rod of molten iron, hope alive in him again. But where was she? Nowhere to be seen, and a wave of cold fear smashed into him as he heard the feet pounding up behind, the double click of hammers being cocked, and he turned, saw the dark man above him, face blank, eyes expressionless, just a halo of blond hair burnished by the moonlight behind and the gun glinting level at his waist, trigger finger tensing.

Oh shit, oh fuck, where in the name of—

Suicide estate agent a 'financial casualty'

Siobhan Fallon,
chief reporter

The mystery surrounding the disappearance of millionaire Irish estate agent Cormac Horgan was solved yesterday when remains washed up on the banks of the River Avon in southwest England were identified as his.

Horgan, 29, of Gorteen House, Skibbereen, Co. Cork, who vanished last week, was said to have been in despair after suffering catastrophic business losses in the downturn.

His body was discovered by a dog walker two miles from the Clifton Suspension Bridge in Bristol, a well-known 'magnet' for would-be suicides.

Mr Seamus Horgan, an uncle of the deceased, said his nephew Cormac was 'a pillar of the local community'.

A business associate, who did not wish to be named, said Mr Horgan was under 'unbearable pressure' to repay debts of €6 million following the collapse of the family-run Horgans chain of estate agents.

'Cormac was under fierce financial and emotional strain. The banks were turning the screw and he faced losing everything. I think it was just too much for him.'

A spokesman for the Irish Property Association, Colm Donegan, said Mr Horgan's death brings to 26 the number of 'financial casualties' from the property and construction industries to have taken their own lives in the past two years of economic turmoil.

The Bristol Coroner's Office will release Mr Horgan's remains tomorrow, with a formal inquest to follow. Mr Horgan, who was . . .

Turn to page 3

– *Sunday Herald,*
12 September 2010

Monday

20 September 2010

1

'The ads are up next and then you're on, Siobhan.'

Siobhan Fallon glanced up from the monitor showing a live feed from TV5's main studio and nodded at the bored-looking runner. It was a little after seven forty in the morning and her spot on the *Full Irish* breakfast show was slated for seven forty-five. She had been on the show before and knew the ropes, arriving with plenty of time to get through make-up. Still, a pang of unease clawed her stomach as she heard presenter Carl Magner giving viewers a run-down of the wonders awaiting them on the far shores of the next ad break.

'Coming up in a few minutes we have Siobhan Fallon, chief reporter at the *Sunday Herald*, talking about her new book, a gripping account of her shocking encounter with the Dublin serial killer they called "the Priest", and how she very nearly *didn't* survive it.'

A blare of brassy theme music, then a shot of the book cover filled the screen. It was all lurid reds and golds against a background of the Papal Cross, with the title screaming out in stark white, '*Crucified: How I Crossed the Priest and Lived to Tell the Tale.*'

God, she loved that cover. Underneath it, in smaller print, was her byline, or, rather, her name. Despite weeks dictating the book onto her digital recorder while she was in hospital – and long months revising and rewriting, getting it lawyered and correcting proofs – she still hadn't got used to the idea of being an *author*. It sounded so much better than chief reporter, and her agent said there was even a chance Hollywood could come calling.

'Through here,' the runner said, pulling back a corner of heavy, black soundproof curtain and guiding Siobhan into the dark fringes of the studio, indicating that she should sit on a straight-backed chair and wait to be called. It was nice and cool in the wings, away from the lights, and oddly calming. She watched as the presenters larked about off air at the far end of the studio, rehearsing in her own mind the points she wanted to get across about the book.

'How're ya, Siobhan? Two minutes now.' The floor manager's silhouette loomed out of the glare of the studio lights to shake her hand. Then he invited her to move over to the curving red sofa on which *Full Irish* guests were interviewed. By the time she sat down, Magner and his co-presenter, Denise Redmond, were there, too, sleek and welcoming, giving it the full mwah-mwah, the pally shoulder-squeeze, settling her in with practised ease.

'Twenty seconds, guys,' came the call from behind the camera.

The two presenters kept up the chit-chat as the floor manager counted them down, asking how long she'd been back at work, whether she was still having to do the physio, whether she'd mind if the camera guy did a close-up of her hands . . .

Her hands. She looked down at them, clasped in her lap. On the back of each was a raised starburst of dead white flesh, indelible reminders of the night that bastard Sean Rinn had hammered huge homemade nails through them into a cross made from old wooden planks and hoisted her aloft, trying to rip the life from her. She had scars on her feet and ribs, too. Horrible, ugly stigmata that even now made her shudder every time she showered or had to rub moisturiser into them. But it was the hands that bothered her most. She hated the way other people obsessed over them, wanted to see and touch them, like some awful talisman. No matter how much she'd excised the trauma of her nightmare experience over the intervening months, nothing sapped her spirit like these physical, visible relics of that night.

'Look, I'd prefer if you—' she said, but it was too late. The floor manager had run out of countdown fingers and both presenters were swivelling their knees, faces and full attention towards the camera.

'So, what would *you* do if a serial killer chose you as his next victim?' Magner asked his viewers chummily. 'Well, with us this morning is a woman who, amazingly, can answer that question.'

'Yes,' the lovely Redmond took up the theme. 'Last year Siobhan Fallon, one of Ireland's best-known newspaper reporters, had an extraordinarily lucky escape after she was attacked and almost died at the hands of the savage serial killer known as the Priest. Welcome, Siobhan. You're looking amazingly well for someone who only fourteen months ago was nailed to a cross . . . '

'Drugs lord, my arse,' Ford said, flicking a dismissive hand at the newspaper.

Detective Inspector Mike Mulcahy looked up from his *Irish Times*, marvelling at Liam Ford's ability to materialise from nowhere. At six foot one himself, Mulcahy was no midget, but his detective sergeant was a good three inches taller than him, and a few inches wider as well. On that dull September morning, the rain outside sucking all the light and life from the day, he'd rolled up to Mulcahy's desk as silently as a fogbank furling in off the sea.

'Somebody thought him important enough to spend money on,' Mulcahy replied. 'It looks like a professional job.'

Up against a dreary tribunal report, a factory in Tuam gone bust and yet more stormy economic forecasts for the stumbling Irish economy, the headline they were talking about was not the biggest on the front page. But for two members of the Garda drugs squad's International Liaison Unit in Dublin Castle, it was the only one likely to be of any real interest: DUBLIN DRUGS LORD SLAIN IN SPAIN

Mulcahy stood up and handed the newspaper to Ford, who held it at arm's length as he read the report of how thirty-seven-year-old Declan 'Bingo' Begley, a career criminal from Crumlin, had been discovered dead on waste ground in the southern Spanish resort of Fuengirola the day before.

'Where did they get all this stuff about Russians?' Ford asked, an eyebrow raised in scepticism. He scratched the back of his neck, frowning as he read how the assassination was rumoured to have been carried out on behalf of an expatriate Russian mafia kingpin living in the Marbella area. Begley, allegedly, had beaten up the man's nephew in a bar fight a couple of weeks earlier. Big mistake.

'No idea,' Mulcahy said. 'That story's the first I heard of it. Probably the local journos getting inventive.'

The supposed Russian connection was the only part of the story that wasn't already familiar to Mulcahy. The day before, within hours of the body being discovered, he had received a call at home from Javier Martinez, an old colleague from his years with Europol in Madrid, urgently requesting background information from the Garda Siochana. The dead man, Begley, had been a mid-ranking dealer in one of Dublin's more vicious drugs gangs before he'd retired, or more accurately – being only twenty-seven at the time – fled, to the balmier criminal climes of the Costa del Sol a decade earlier.

'But over a bar brawl? It's not exactly the Bingo we used to know, is it? He'd have got some eejit to have the brawl for him.'

Mulcahy came round the desk, thinking back to the late 1990s, when he and Ford had fancied themselves the scourge of Dublin's drugs gangs, heading up a task force to tackle the city's out-of-control heroin epidemic. He'd encountered Begley more than once back then and knew that the man's reputation, as more of a ladies' man than your typical Dublin hard case, was well deserved.

'A man can change a lot over the years. Anyway, like I said, Madrid didn't mention anything to me about a Russian angle.'

'How come they're so positive it was professional?'

It was a little too early for Mulcahy to appreciate Ford's dog-with-a-bone act. Not that it was to be discouraged generally. Friendship aside, that belligerent inquisitiveness was the main reason Mulcahy had asked Ford to come work with him when he set up the unit twelve months previously. But there were times – like first thing on a Monday morning – when it wasn't the most welcome of personality traits.

'Martinez emailed me the preliminary report,' Mulcahy said, 'and some of the crime-scene photos. Here, have a look for yourself.'

He sat down behind his desk again and swivelled his monitor so that Ford could see the screen as well. He opened a folder of JPEGs and clicked on the first.

'Ah, Christ on a bike,' Ford said, recoiling from the image: a close-up of a blackened, distorted, blood-caked mass of something that, apart from one open eye, was barely recognisable as a face. Not least because half the lower jaw was missing, exposing several inches of spinal column attached to a gore-spattered torso. 'Are you trying to make me lose my breakfast?'

'Sorry – wrong one,' Mulcahy laughed, closing it down and drawing the cursor across to the next photograph. 'This is what I wanted, the long shot.'

This image was less repellent to the eye, initially at least. At its top was a clear blue cloudless sky, and at its base what appeared to be a dusty, abandoned building site. Smashed-up red clay roof tiles, rust-streaked chunks of concrete and peeling slabs of plasterboard were scattered all around a patch of scrubby, sun-baked ground. Here and there a yawning fridge or disembowelled washing machine added blocks of stark white to the scene, but the main focus was on a hummock of seemingly ordinary household waste, a metre high and no more than four or five across. It was at the centre of this that Declan Begley's body was splayed, on its back, fully clothed, with what was left of his jaw hanging loose and seemingly crying for justice to God in heaven above.

'It's an illegal dump, on an abandoned building site off the coast road between Marbella and Fuengirola, a few kilometres from where Begley lived,' Mulcahy said. He zoomed in closer to the rubbish pile, pointing at the dead man's domed abdomen. 'Bit of a shock for the fly-tipper who found him. The body had been there a couple of days already, badly bloated – it averages thirty degrees Celsius there this time of year. Some pretty horrible rodent and insect damage as well.'

'Nice.' Ford grimaced. 'Shotgun, yeah?'

'Yeah, old-style – both barrels in the face and chest.'

'But he wasn't done there?' Ford asked, circling his finger round the body. It was all a bit too neat, not nearly enough blood and debris around for the incident to have occurred where the body was lying.

'Right. The shooting took place at his house. Early hours of Thursday morning, they reckon.'

'And they know all this how?'

Mulcahy sat back, beginning to enjoy the inquisition, despite himself. 'Well, ID was easy: he had a wallet, cards on him, and he's well known locally. When they got to his address, they found the door open, the rest of his face decorating the hall.'

'Stylish,' Ford quipped. 'No witnesses, then?'

'He lived alone. The house is in the hills, on its own parcel of land, no near neighbours.'

Ford nodded, getting the picture. 'So whoever did it wanted him found quickly. And who's going to risk dragging a corpse to a dump unless they want to make a point, right?'

'That's what they reckon: classic gangster job. It's a message, a warning.'

'So maybe the Russian-mafia thing isn't all that far-fetched, then?'

Mulcahy put his hands up. 'Obviously that's what the press reckon, but our friends in Spain are more interested in Bingo's past troubles here in Dublin, and seem to think it could be drugs-related. No surprise there, really.'

'But that was all ten years ago or more. He's hardly been back here since.'

'Yeah' – Mulcahy nodded – 'but maybe they know something we don't. Either that or they're in denial. I mean, look at the name on these JPEGs.'

He pointed at the picture thumbnails in the folder on his computer screen. Each one had the tag 'muertodedublin', followed by a number.

'What's that supposed to mean?'

'*Muerto de Dublin*,' Mulcahy said in his best Spanish accent. 'Not to put too fine a translation on it, "Dublin dead".'

'Fuck's sake.' Ford shook his head. 'They're just trying to push the work on us.'

'That may be so. Either way we've had an urgent request to send a full background report to the murder team in Malaga, plus any "relevant current intelligence".'

'Like whether any of our bozos are out there topping up their tans just now?'

'You got it in one,' Mulcahy agreed. 'So don't bother hanging up your coat. I thought we could go have a gander at who's where this morning, see if we can stir up some sleeping beauties.'

'Did you see yer one on the box this morning?' Ford asked, as they trotted down the stairs.

'Who's that?' Mulcahy pulled open the heavy door.

'Yer one – *your* one,' Ford emphasised. 'That reporter Siobhan Fallon. She was on the breakfast show, promoting her new book – y'know, about Rinn and her. And you, too, by the sound of it.'

It wasn't the cold whip of rain in his face as he stepped out that made Mulcahy feel like he'd been slapped. He'd been dreading this news for months, ever since Siobhan Fallon had phoned him and asked him to work on the book with her. It was his story just as much as hers, she'd insisted. He was the one who'd caught up with Rinn, saved not just her life but others' as well. But he had flatly refused to have anything to do with a book, or her, still messed up in his own mind over the case, still smarting over how she had so casually betrayed him for one of her precious stories.

'She was looking good, I'll say that for her,' Ford rabbited on, 'but, Jaysus, she can't half talk. Said your name should be on the cover as well, y'know, that you were the real hero that night but you wouldn't take the credit for it. Is it true? Did she ask you?'

'I didn't even know the book was coming out,' Mulcahy

said, sidestepping the question. He'd heard nothing from Siobhan since that call. He'd buried it away at the back of his mind, praying she might forget about it, too.

'I reckon she's still got the hots for you, boss,' Ford laughed, elbowing Mulcahy. 'You'd better hope Orla didn't see it.'

'Just shut up and get the car, would you,' Mulcahy said, pushing Ford in front of him, straining to keep a note of good humour in his voice. It wasn't Ford's fault; nobody knew what really happened between him and Siobhan Fallon the year before. He hoped to Christ they wouldn't find out now either, and that her damned book would be discreet. He wanted to believe it, but going on her past form, it wasn't entirely likely.

'It's that one over there,' said Ford, clicking the key fob and getting an identifying flash of lights from one of the pool cars, a blue Mondeo, parked at the base of the castle's brooding medieval Record Tower.

They climbed in and Ford reversed out and turned, then waited a moment for the barrier to rise at the massive stone gateway before heading out onto Ship Street, the dark cobbles rattling the car's stiffened suspension. Then it was straight into the mid-morning traffic, a slow crawl up through the Coombe and Dolphin's Barn, the rain getting heavier the further out they got.

Mulcahy forced himself to push all thought of Siobhan Fallon from his mind. Where he and Ford were heading, you couldn't afford distractions. For years now, a vicious turf war had raged between the gangs that controlled the drugs trade in the blighted inner suburb of Drimnagh and rivals who ran the similarly grim Crumlin estates bordering it to the south. The deepening recession had only made matters worse, the dwindling market for recreational drugs sparking off outbursts of vicious gang violence. So far the dispute had cost twenty-two lives in tit-for-tat killings, nearly all of them kids in their teens and early twenties. A terrible waste, some said, although the most any of them ever aspired to was waste, anyway.

The hypnotic whump of the windscreen wipers filled the car as Ford slowed to a stop and waited for a break in the traffic to turn into Gandon Road. It looked like any other grey residential estate in Drimnagh, ranks of ill-kempt council houses staring soullessly at each other across the street, but no one who knew the area would venture in there without good reason. Mulcahy spotted three youths in hoodies in the porch of the corner house opposite. As Ford eased the car across the junction and past them, one of the boys raised his right arm and took a sight along it – index and middle finger extended, thumb cocked – and loosed off an imaginary round at them.

'Even this feckin' downpour doesn't keep them off the street,' Ford muttered, more by way of acknowledgement than anything else.

Mulcahy noticed that another of the boys was on a mobile, doubtless letting Tommy 'the Trainer' Hanrahan know that the boys in blue were on their way. That was par for the course. Hanrahan was one of the biggest players among the loose coalition of drug-dealing thugs who ran Drimnagh, and nobody got anywhere near without him knowing about it in advance. He had secured his position not only by engaging in more psychotic levels of savagery than anyone else around him, but also by running an extremely efficient network of dealers, enforcers and informants. His nickname referred not only to his obsessive working out in local gyms but also his ability to bring out the brutality in everyone he brought into his circle, teaching them how to bend the world to his will through threats and physical persuasion.

'Over there, number twenty-seven,' Mulcahy said. 'On the right, behind that wreck.'

Half on the pavement and half off, a burnt-out car was angled slightly out and away from the scrubby patch of bare earth and dismantled engine parts that passed for a front garden. It resembled nothing so much as a tank trap.

'Do you think he's worried about a ram raid?' Ford snorted, as he pulled in across the road and cut the engine. 'It's not for the Dublin in Bloom judges, anyway.'

A flurry of wind brought the rain spitting full force into Mulcahy's face as he got out of the car and cursed, gathering the collar of his coat to his neck as he crossed the road. Before their feet hit the footpath, the front door of number twenty-seven opened and Tommy Hanrahan appeared in the entrance.

He was a tall man, about Mulcahy's height, but bigger around the shoulders and chest from all the working out. Black hair cropped close to the skull lent his brow a primitive cast, accentuated by heavy eyebrows, a square jaw and a neck that looked thickened by steroid use. His other facial features were correspondingly broad, apart from two small, close-set brown eyes, which held absolutely no warmth.

'It's yerselves, is it?' Hanrahan said, as if he'd known them all his life. 'It's been a while since we had youse lot out here.'

The door may have been open, but the wrought-iron security gate in front of it stayed shut, forcing Mulcahy and Ford to huddle up, backs to the elements, under the porch's tiny canopy.

'Aren't you going to invite us in, Tommy?' Ford asked.

'Ah, y'know, the place's a bit of a mess and the missus would only be getting embarrassed.' Hanrahan smiled back. 'If you'd phoned ahead, now, the lads an' me might've had a chance to tidy up a bit.'

A chatter of moronic laughter leaked from the three goons lined up in the hallway behind Hanrahan. If it'd been a movie, they would've been big guys, muscle, proper apes, but this lot made a pathetic-looking crew. In their knock-off trackies and thin Dunnes sweaters they could have passed for any of the string-of-piss junkies they made their living off. Their eyes, though, had an edge you never got in a smack-head's dead-eye stare. These creeps would knife you as soon as look at you.

'You heard about Declan Begley?' Mulcahy asked.

'Good riddance to bad fuckin' rubbish.' Hanrahan scowled. 'That low life was begging for a vent in the head a long time ago, and if I'm honest, I'd've been happy to put it there myself. But you don't need me to tell you that, right?'

'We know you put the word out on him,' Ford said.

'Yeah, well, that was years ago and the yellow gobshite went and done a runner, didn't he? So, like I said, I'd love to take credit for it, but I can't. I had nothin' to do with Bingo being topped. True as God.' Hanrahan folded his arms and adopted an expression of innocence that could have graced

15

an angel's face in church. One of the fallen ones, next to Lucifer.

'And none of your lads just happen to be out in Spain this week, getting in a bit of autumn sunshine?' Mulcahy asked.

'Not that I know of. But, fuck me, with all that high-tech surveillance at the airports nowadays, youse fellas'd probably have a better idea about that than me, eh?' Hanrahan laughed and looked behind him again, eliciting another round of whooping from the crew.

'Glad to hear it, Tommy,' Mulcahy said, 'but, just to let you know, I'm calling in on Martin Lynch on my way back from here, and if he says anything to the contrary, we might have to come back and get you in for a proper chat.'

Hanrahan's expression darkened. 'You wouldn't want to believe a word that wanker says. And I wouldn't bother comin' back, either.' He unfolded his thick arms and grabbed the wrought-iron gate, rattling it. 'I've got bars on all the downstairs windows and doors. To prevent unwelcome intrusions, y'know.'

'Makes you feel at home, Tommy, does it?' Ford asked.

Hanrahan didn't like that. Despite being hauled into Garda stations and courtrooms all his adult life, he had only been convicted twice on minor charges and on both occasions the sentences had – all too typically – been suspended.

'Fuck you, copper,' he snarled. 'You know I've never done time.'

'Yeah, I know,' Ford said, bending forward, his face glowering over Hanrahan's through the grille. 'But with those three monkeys you've got in there with you, Tommy, it wasn't prison I was thinking of. It was the zoo.'

16

2

'It's awful warm for that get-up today. How do you stand the heat in it?'

Siobhan Fallon tugged at the damp collar of her cashmere twinset in a futile effort to cool herself, and silently cursed the elderly Cork woman who'd made the remark. Of course she was too bloody hot. She'd nearly passed out in the church during the mass. And it was no better now that they were all outside, waiting for the hearse to depart, the sun all but cracking the flagstones of the old churchyard they were standing in.

It had been cold and lashing rain in Dublin when the taxi collected her from the TV5 studios at a quarter past eight and raced across the city to deposit her at Heuston Station, just in time to catch the train to Cork. *That* was the weather Siobhan had dressed for. How the hell was she to know it would turn out to be one of the hottest days of the year in Cork, just a hundred and sixty miles to the south? And how could a small island like Ireland even encompass two such ridiculous extremes of weather, anyway? There wasn't much she could do about it, short of strip off right here in the churchyard. She'd love to see the old woman's face if she did that.

Instead Siobhan closed her reporter's notebook and stuck her pen into the spiral of white wire along the top. 'I think I'll be getting off now, Mrs . . . eh?'

'Burke,' said the woman. 'Teresa Burke, with an "e".'

'Yes, goodbye,' Siobhan said, amused the woman could think she'd said anything worth quoting. She walked away, circling the crowd of mourners still milling outside the church doors. A fine turnout, as they say. Cormac Horgan, the young Cork estate agent whose suicide in Bristol she'd reported in the *Sunday Herald* a week earlier, was getting as good a send-off as could be expected. She scanned the faces: bereaved relatives and friends, the parish priest, local politicians and a smattering of former colleagues. She'd spoken to most of them and collected some decent, if uniformly uninspired, quotes. She'd only hung around to see if the cranky old priest would say anything out of the ordinary in his sermon, but he hadn't, just the usual dull obsequies. She'd spent most of the long, stiflingly hot ceremony fanning herself with the order-of-service booklet and putting the piece together in her head, ready to knock it out quickly on the train back to Dublin.

Why Paddy Griffin, her news editor at the *Sunday Herald*, had thought Horgan's funeral would be worth her while going all the way to Cork for, she had no idea. He knew as well as she did that funerals rarely make good copy, and he could just as easily have put a stringer on it. Yet he'd been utterly resistant to her argument that it was a waste of her

18

time. Much as she loved the old tyrant, he'd been a complete pain in the arse since she started back at work, clucking around like a mother hen, watching her every move.

She took one last look around but saw nothing of interest. By now the crowd was clumping into small groups of five or six, shaking hands, chatting in hushed tones as the coffin was loaded into the long, black hearse for its slow procession to the 'new' cemetery, a couple of miles down the road. The old graveyard around the church probably hadn't seen a burial in a hundred years.

It was definitely time to get out of there.

She was making her way along the gravel path through the graves to the gate when her mobile rang – Griffin's caller ID.

'Paddy, what's up?' she said, praying that something more exciting had appeared on the horizon.

'Ah, nothing,' Griffin said, the rasp in his voice betraying a lifetime's devotion to cigarettes and coffee. 'Just wondering how you were getting on, whether that Midas touch of yours had worked its magic down there.'

'It's a funeral, Paddy. How exciting could it be? I've got some okay quotes, but it's not going to be worth more than a couple of pars. I'm on my way to the station now. There's a train in half an hour. If I catch that, I can be back in the office by four o'clock and—'

'There's no need for that,' Griffin interrupted. 'Why don't you just head on home from there? Take it easy. There's nothing going on in here, and if anything comes up, I can get Cillian to do it.'

Siobhan stiffened at the mere mention of that name. She knew Griffin meant well. For all the years she'd been at the

Sunday Herald she'd been his favourite, his star, but this wasn't the way things were supposed to be. She was supposed to be indispensable, his *chief* reporter. Telling her to go home wasn't just patronising, it was worrying, like he'd forgotten completely who she was in the months she'd been laid up. And as for that weasel Cillian O'Gorman, who'd been covering for her while she was off, he'd got his feet too firmly under the desk for her liking. His tongue was lodged up Griffin's arse as well. The last thing she needed was to give Paddy an excuse to keep him on a moment longer than necessary.

'Listen, would you take off the kid gloves, Paddy, for God's sake?' she groaned. 'All this molly-coddling, it's complete bollocks. I don't need it, and it's not really you, either, is . . . ' She searched for the next word, but it wouldn't come to her, tiny as it was. She felt the sun on her neck again, as if all its vast cosmic density were bearing down on her. At once a prickle of cold perspiration broke out on her forehead and an overwhelming weariness enveloped her, every scrap of vitality she possessed draining straight from her legs into the ground below. Next thing she knew, she was clawing at a granite headstone for support, her knees going slack, the mobile falling from her grasp, tumbling through a slow arc as it bounced from a mossy mound onto the gravel path.

A second or two of black void. Then, through the numbness that was swamping her, she heard Griffin's voice again, tinny and distant, crackling concern from the phone on the ground.

'Siobhan, are you there? Siobhan?'

Somehow, she recovered herself. With a will she hardly

knew she possessed, she bent and snatched up the phone, forcing a semblance of calm into her voice.

'Sorry, Paddy. I'm here.' She was fighting back the emptiness, straining to keep the trembling in her voice, her arms, her legs under control. 'Bloody graveyard. I tripped and dropped the phone. No panic. Like I said, I'm fine. I'll see you later. No argument. Okay?'

She didn't wait for his response, couldn't afford to. Instead she killed the call with a jab of her thumb and bent over the gravestone again. She leant into it, allowing its polished stone-coldness to seep into her forehead and temples, embracing its solidity while waiting for the dizziness to pass. Focusing on her breathing, forcing normality to return. Everything she was wearing felt clammy against her skin, a chill had settled between her shoulders, and her stomach felt hollowed out. She remembered that she hadn't had anything to eat all morning, just a cup of foul-tasting coffee before the *Full Irish* interview.

'Excuse me. Are you all right there? Do you need a hand?'

The question from behind was accompanied by a gentle touch on her elbow. Siobhan straightened up and turned, embarrassment now added to the stew of emotion inside her. A kindly-looking woman in her late fifties, tall, with short, greying hair and a plain black suit was staring at her, concerned.

'I'm fine,' Siobhan said, struggling to adopt an air of normality. 'Just catching my breath, thanks.'

The woman glanced over her shoulder to where the funeral procession was finally getting under way, then back at Siobhan, sympathy in her expression.

21

'I used to get that way sometimes, when I was having mine. Is it your first?'

It took Siobhan a moment to understand what the woman was getting at, confirmed when she saw the forefinger pointing at her belly.

'Jesus, no,' Siobhan gasped, horrified by the very idea. A child was the last thing she needed in her life. For now, at any rate. 'I'm not ... '

'Oh, I'm sorry,' the woman said, looking a little mortified herself now.

'God no, no.' Siobhan stumbled, recovering a little, half laughing now. 'I mean, I'm not pregnant. I just felt a bit light-headed. I didn't have any breakfast and I'm dressed all wrong for this weather. But I'm fine, honestly. Thanks for asking.'

The woman smiled shyly back at her. 'I saw you, at the mass and ... Well, I suppose now's probably not the best time.'

'For what?'

'I was hoping to have a word, if you could spare me a minute.' Again the woman seemed to hesitate. 'You *are* the one who wrote that article about Cormac in the *Sunday Herald*, aren't you? I saw you on the television.'

Siobhan nodded, trying not to look too inviting. She hadn't seen this woman inside in the church and was beginning to find the encounter a little bizarre.

'It's about my daughter,' the woman said. 'Gemma. Gemma Kearney?'

'I'm sorry – do I know this ... ?' The name meant nothing to Siobhan. 'Was it Gemma you said?'

'Yes, Gemma – she was Cormac's girlfriend.'

That brought Siobhan up sharply. Her brain lurched back into focus. Nobody had mentioned a girlfriend. Quite the opposite in fact. Everyone she asked had said Horgan was single. She was sure of it. No way would she have missed a crucial detail like that.

'Cormac, as in ...?' Siobhan looked back towards the church. The hearse was gone now, a long trail of cars streaming out of the car park in its wake.

The woman nodded sadly, but said nothing more.

'Look, Mrs ... eh?' Siobhan took a closer look at her, trying to judge her plausibility.

'Kearney.'

'Yeah, Mrs Kearney. Don't get me wrong' – Siobhan shook her head, desperate to word her next question properly – 'but I was told Cormac didn't have a girlfriend. Is Gemma here? I mean, was she at the mass? I'd really like to talk to her.'

'No,' the woman said, a desperation creeping into her voice. 'That's just it. She's disappeared. I can't find her. Not since weeks back, when she said she was going away for a break to England with him. I can't get anyone to look into it.'

Offering to listen to Mrs Kearney's story was the emotional equivalent of unblocking a drain. Beside herself with worry, the woman's bottled-up fears burst out in a bitty, half-digested rush: how she'd been to the Gardai, but they were useless; how Gemma and Horgan had gone out while they were at university together, but they'd split up, got together again ...

It was too much for Siobhan to take in. Standing there in the graveyard, the sun still pounding like a piston on her head, she knew if she didn't find somewhere to sit down soon, she'd probably begin to feel faint again. Yet every professional instinct told her to stay where she was. She scanned the parade of shops across the road from the church and spotted a café.

Mrs Kearney seemed relieved when Siobhan suggested going for a coffee, like it was confirmation that she wasn't going to be fobbed off.

'I'm sorry, I really am, but I'm at my wits' end,' the woman said. 'I have no one else to turn to. I just don't know what to do.'

'Come on, now,' Siobhan said, steering Mrs Kearney through the gate. 'I'm sure we'll be able to think of something.'

The café was a neat place with red gingham oilcloths and sprays of yellow freesias in vases on each of the tables. They were the only customers. Siobhan sat Mrs Kearney down at a table by the window and went to the counter to order a couple of cappuccinos, and a plain chicken sandwich for herself. She asked for a glass of tap water while she was waiting and stood there sipping, feeling the chill revive her as it trickled down her throat, using the time to run back over what had just occurred – to reassure herself that she wasn't suffering some kind of post-traumatic breakdown. Or, for that matter, that Mrs Kearney wasn't some fantasist who'd just wandered into the churchyard from the local mental-health facility.

She reminded herself again that she had researched Cormac Horgan's background thoroughly when she wrote her original piece and 'no' had been the unanimous reply from friends and family to the question of whether a broken heart might have been part of his decision to end his life. Even so, Mrs Kearney clearly knew what she was talking about. Much more than anyone could have picked up casually at the funeral, or even by reading about it in the papers. Siobhan glanced over at her again: the prim suit, the neat hair, the slightly haggard look. Of all the instincts Siobhan relied on for her job, it was her feel for people that she trusted most. And there was no denying that there was something terribly 'right' about Mrs Kearney, this lonely-looking woman, staring out the window lost in thought, struggling to keep her emotions under control. Somehow, Siobhan was already convinced it would be worthwhile trying to get to the bottom of this.

She brought the coffees over and sat opposite Mrs Kearney. 'I hope you don't mind if I eat,' she said, tucking into her sandwich.

Mrs Kearney shook her head politely and seemed consciously to avert her gaze from the back of Siobhan's hand as she munched. Again Siobhan took in the woman's demeanour, noticing how her short hair was growing out of a style that needed regular cutting, how the skin at the sides of her eyes was crowed into tight furrows, how even a heavy layer of concealer couldn't disguise the dark half-moons like bruises beneath her eyes. Mrs Kearney was a worried woman.

'It might be best if we start at the beginning again, Mrs Kearney,' she said, automatically checking that the red recording light was showing on her tiny voice recorder on the table. 'Can you tell me again when you last heard from Gemma?'

'It's been over three weeks now,' Mrs Kearney said, swallowing hard.

'And you've heard nothing since? What about friends and colleagues?'

'I've tried everyone I could think of. Nobody's heard anything from her.'

'And did *they* sound concerned for her, as well?'

Mrs Kearney looked Siobhan in the eye for the first time. 'She didn't have many friends. Nobody seems to know anything, or care for that matter.'

'Couldn't any of Cormac's family help?' Siobhan asked, nodding back towards the church, the car park out front empty now except for one or two stragglers.

'No,' Mrs Kearney snuffled. 'They have their own grief to contend with.'

By the looks of it they had never been aware of her existence, Siobhan thought, but decided against going down that route.

'And the Gardai?' she asked, taking another nibble of chicken. 'You said you'd been to see them. Weren't they any help?'

Mrs Kearney gave a small sigh of exasperation. 'All they did was write down her details on some forms and say they'd look into it. That was over a week ago, and when I phone, all they'll say is that they're doing everything they can.'

Which wasn't necessarily much at all. Siobhan knew the stats on missing persons: over six thousand cases reported every year. One for every two Gardai in Ireland. Most resolved themselves without intervention. Unless a child was missing, or someone was clearly at risk, the chances of a serious investigation were minimal.

'But the last time you heard from Gemma, she was okay then?'

Mrs Kearney nodded. 'She rang me at home to say she had news that I'd be pleased about. It was the first time we'd talked in a while and I was delighted to hear her voice.'

'Weren't you in regular contact with Gemma?'

Mrs Kearney stiffened. 'She was never the easiest of girls. Two or three months ago I said a few things to her – you know, motherly things, caring things. About the way she was living, her values. Like how she seemed to think money was the only thing that mattered, that sort of stuff. It didn't go down well with her at all. I didn't hear from her for a while after that.'

'But something happened to change that,' Siobhan said. 'What was this "news" she wanted to tell you?'

'Gemma said she'd been seeing a bit of Cormac again. She might've had a drink or two taken. She was sort of giggling, or trying not to laugh, when she said it, like she was interested in him again – you know, romantically. She knew that I always liked Cormac – approved of him, if you want – and that I was disappointed when they broke up. I was so relieved to think they might be, y'know, an item again.'

'So what made you suspect she went to England with him?'

'I didn't. I mean, I'm not sure she did.' Mrs Kearney hesitated, running the conversation back in her head. 'She said they were thinking of going away for a few days together. I can't remember exactly. And then, a couple of weeks later, I heard about Cormac on the radio, and I saw your article in the paper. I was desperate to get in touch with Gemma, but no matter how many times I tried, I couldn't reach her. That's when I started to get really worried.'

'You don't think,' Siobhan suggested gently, 'that maybe she might have heard about Cormac's death herself and had trouble handling the news? That she might have just gone off somewhere to be on her own?'

'And done what?' Mrs Kearney asked, the desperation alive in her voice now. 'Isn't that exactly what I'm afraid of? That the girl's gone off and done something stupid to herself, like he did. How could I not think it?'

Something about the way she said it made Siobhan wonder if Mrs Kearney didn't have more reason than most to worry, but now was not the time to ask. She was already beginning to crumble, opening her handbag and rummaging in vain. Siobhan reached across to the chrome dispenser on the table, pulled a paper napkin from it and handed it to her.

'You don't live in Cork yourself, Mrs Kearney?'

'Not the city, no.' She sounded relieved to be talking about something tangible again. 'We're from Dunmanway, about forty miles west of here. Do you know it?'

'Only by name.'

'It's lovely but very quiet, especially in winter.' Mrs Kearney gave a final snuffle and stuffed the crumpled tissue into her cuff. 'All Gemma ever dreamt of was getting away from there.'

Siobhan glanced at her watch, knowing she'd have to leave soon to catch her train. All she could do now, she thought, was get the rest of the basics and follow it up later.

'Can you tell me how old Gemma is?'

'Thirty-one.'

Siobhan struggled to hide her surprise. From the way Mrs Kearney had been talking, she'd had in mind somebody younger, mid-twenties maybe, especially as Horgan, she knew, had only been twenty-nine when he died.

'Thirty-one?'

'Yes,' Mrs Kearney said. 'She'll be thirty-two next month.'

At least she's thinking she has a future, Siobhan reflected. 'And what does she do for a living?'

'Same as Cormac, an accountant. A very good one, so I'm told.'

'But Cormac was an estate agent,' Siobhan said. 'I mean, that's why he committed . . .'

For some reason she couldn't bring herself say the word 'suicide'. Perhaps because her mind was racing off down another path, her belief in Mrs Kearney assailed by doubts again.

'That's right,' the woman replied quietly, 'but he trained as an accountant, at UCC, at the same time as Gemma. That's where they met. When he graduated, they both started working in Cork, but then he went to Skibbereen to join the family firm, Horgans estate agents and auctioneers.'

Siobhan already knew that Horgans was one of the longest-established estate agents in West Cork, and that Cormac had been a nephew rather than a son. The whizz kid drafted in to give the old family firm a new lease of life. She'd even wondered if that had made its collapse more unbearable for him.

'And does nobody from Gemma's work have any idea where she might be? I mean, you've spoken to them, right? Aren't they worried about her, too?' Siobhan imagined the fuss Paddy Griffin would kick up if she failed to turn up for work for a couple of days, let alone for three weeks.

'That's just it,' Mrs Kearney said. 'There is no "they". Gemma works alone. She owns and runs her own practice, Kearney Accountancy, here in Cork. I mean, she has a secretary, an assistant, but when I call, there's never any answer now.'

'She has an office, then?'

'Yes, off Patrick Street in town. I went there again this morning before I came out here, but it's all locked up. I asked the people next door, but they only moved in a week ago and haven't seen any comings or goings.'

'No sign of her assistant, either?'

Mrs Kearney shook her head.

Siobhan drained her coffee cup. It all sounded too weird. Deliberate almost, although there was no way of judging from such a small amount of information. Baffled, all she could think of was the obvious question again.

'And you've told the Guards *all* of this?'

Mrs Kearney nodded, looking more lost now than ever. 'I know what they're thinking: that Gemma's just gone off on holiday without telling me, that it's all in my imagination. Do you know what they said to me? That they'll let me know "if anything turns up".' Her bottom lip quivered as she battled to keep her fears at bay. '"Turns up,"' she repeated, her voice a whisper of disbelief. 'It's like they don't even think she's a person any more. My poor girl, like she's just some *thing* that might be lying out there, waiting to be turned up.'

3

Another street, another row of grey, close-packed council houses looking all the greyer for the rain. Mulcahy and Ford walked back to the car and got in, the two of them slicking the rain from their hair and unbuttoning their coats in unconscious unison. This was the fifth address they'd visited, each with a different cast of hardcore Dublin scumbags, but exactly the same script.

'This is hopeless,' Ford said. 'These eejits have no more clue what happened to Begley than we do.'

'Looks like it, all right.'

It had been looking that way since they'd had the chat with Hanrahan, but Mulcahy hadn't wanted to admit it: the atmosphere on the doorstep, the posturing, the bluster, the craic. If there had been anything to play for, it would all have been a lot stiffer, stupider, more defensive. But it was the same everywhere: no tension, no spark. Nothing. Like it or not, Declan Begley, former pillar of the Dublin underworld, had been out of sight, out of mind in Spain. None of his former cronies gave a damn about who had blown his head off or why.

'Is that it, then?' Ford said. 'We go back and tell the Spanish that there's no obvious connection this end?'

'Maybe.' Mulcahy checked his watch. What had started as an early morning diversion was beginning to eat into their afternoon.

Ford was restless. Almost a year on, he was still getting used to the ebb and flow of the liaison job. He missed the action, the adrenaline, the short-term gains on the streets. And this kind of trawling around for crumbs of information for other people only reminded him how many nasty little shitehawks were out there, begging to be banged up. Sometimes Mulcahy worried that Ford felt he had made a mistake coming over to the unit, that he would have been better off staying where he was, pulling bottom-feeders off the street, where his bulk came in handier than his brain. As far as Mulcahy was concerned, though, Ford was still, as he had been when they worked together ten years before, the best detective sergeant he had ever come across, street-smart and with a razor-sharp brain beneath all the laddish play-acting.

'I just didn't want to go back to them with nothing, Liam.'

'But it's not nothing, is it?' Ford said irritably. 'I mean, we know more now than we did when we came out this morning. And we have a ton of other stuff to be getting on with. You know, these Spanish cunts, they're probably just being lazy. They need to be looking locally, concentrating on Begley's known associates out there. There's nothing for them here.'

Mulcahy's mobile rang. He listened, grunted, finally said, 'That's fine. Be sure to tell Aisling, too. I'll be back as soon as I can.' He hung up and turned to Ford. 'That was Aidan. Murtagh just called. The Rosscarbery Bay meeting has been brought forward to tomorrow, so I'll have to prepare for that when we get back. Did you sort out that final report from MAOC we talked about on Friday?'

'On my desk, just waiting for me to hand it to you,' Ford sighed. 'So we can get the fuck out of here now, can we?'

'Yes.' Mulcahy grinned. 'But there is one other person I think we could talk to before we head back.' He laughed as Ford responded with a groan. 'A guy I used to run years back. Incredibly well connected, not your typical hard man. Knows all the old faces out in Spain. He's useful. You could do with knowing him.'

On the train back to Dublin, the first thing Siobhan did was write up the notes on her conversation with Mrs Kearney. She had every word of it on the voice recorder, but she wouldn't listen to that again unless she was stuck, or needed to check some detail. What she wanted to get down immediately were her impressions of the woman and what she'd said, while she still had the feel for it.

It took half an hour to get it all into bullet points and short paragraphs. She worked at it furiously, undisturbed, glad that at the railway station she'd walked up the platform, avoiding the busier carriages, and gone for a table in the empty dining car. 'Peace for the price of a sandwich,' the steward had said, although he hadn't insisted on her ordering food. A smile and a request for a Diet Coke with ice, that seemed to keep him happy. She'd been nursing it ever since.

She was more convinced than ever that something weird

was up with this Gemma Kearney girl. Whether it was serious, though, something that would reward her involvement, remained to be seen. She felt sorry for the mother, of course she did, but Siobhan wasn't the Gardai and had no interest in doing their job for them. Not unless there was a story. And despite her gut saying this was worth pursuing, there were still things that didn't stack up for her. Principal among them being the great hulking fact that nobody she'd spoken to before had even mentioned Gemma's existence, let alone suggested a relationship with Horgan.

On the other hand, one thing that did convince her there was something more to Gemma Kearney's disappearance was this locked-up office. Siobhan couldn't imagine any accountant being flaky enough to just up sticks and bugger off like that. It didn't fit the stereotype, and it kept on nagging at her until she picked up her mobile and called Tom Fahy, the guy who did her tax returns every year; but she only got his answerphone.

'Hi, Tom. It's your favourite hack here. Who do you contact if your accountant pulls a fast one and does a runner? Is there an official body or council to complain to? Call me back, would you?'

She hung up, frustrated. She'd told Griffin that she would file the funeral piece by the end of the day, but with the best part of a week to go before deadline, he'd hardly worry about keeping her to that. In any case, Dublin was still two hours away, and knocking out the 500 words he asked for wouldn't take up more than one of those. At least, not the story she'd originally envisaged filing. But this Gemma thing, that made it a whole different ballgame.

She grabbed her mobile again, opened the contacts book on her laptop and dialled. 'Is that Paddy Rowan?'

'Yeah. Who's this?' came the subdued answer, the voice suspicious. In the background she heard a low rumble of conversation, the scrape of cutlery, the clinking of glasses.

'It's Siobhan Fallon. We talked the other day about Cormac Hor—'

'Fuck's sake,' the voice came back angrily. 'The man's barely an hour in his grave. Can't you leave us in peace to give him a decent send-off?'

There was a click and the line went dead. She checked her watch, sucked a breath in through her teeth. Maybe that was a little insensitive. Anyone who attended Horgan's funeral would probably still be in the pub for the traditional 'bite and a jar afterwards'. To try contacting any of them now would be too intrusive. She'd have to wait. But what to do in the meantime?

Siobhan sat back in her seat, a dull ache at the back of her neck reminding her of how Mrs Kearney had come upon her in the graveyard. She shook her head at the thought of it. What must she have looked like? It wasn't the first time she'd felt light-headed since returning to work, but it had never overwhelmed her like that before. It *was* just the early start, the lack of a breakfast, wasn't it? She'd have to be more careful, that's all. Putting a hand up to her shoulder, comfortingly, she breathed deep, willing herself to think of something else, and looked out the window at the lush green landscape rolling by. In the far distance, a long chain of jagged blue-grey mountains rimmed the horizon, then gave way to a clear expanse of cloudless sky. Something about the mountains, the flat blue colour of them probably, made her think of maps and classrooms, and she struggled to resuscitate her schoolgirl geography. Which mountains were they? The Galtees, or the Comeraghs? Or Slieve Blooms, maybe? She hadn't a clue, really. Her dad would have known. He was the mountain man, the outdoorsy one. She wished he could have seen her on television earlier, seen her name on a book cover. She'd been wishing that kind of thing for the past twenty years.

A well-built woman bustling awkwardly down the carriage towards the bar snapped Siobhan out of her reverie. Her gaze came to rest on the laptop again, on the folder she had opened to retrieve Rowan's number. One result of Griffin's pain-in-the-arse molly-coddling since she got back to work was that she had been doing more from home instead of always being in the office. Seeing the folder open, she remembered she had all the info she'd gathered for her piece on Horgan stored right there on the laptop, notes and everything.

She opened a file containing her unsubbed final version of the story and began reading it. Objectively speaking, it was run-of-the-mill stuff, worked up into a recession-tagged human-interest story on a slow news day. It was just about good enough for the page-three lead, with a big picture of the Clifton Suspension Bridge to give it some punch. If there had been anything doing on politics, crime or the sleazy-scandal front, Horgan's death wouldn't have got more than a mention in 'News in Brief'. But, on the day, with a deadline looming and nothing else to fill the slot, Griffin had told her to take it and run with it.

It had not come as a complete surprise when, the following day, it caught a wave of genuine public sympathy. The government's official line was that the recession had eased its grip in recent months, but everyone knew the banking crisis had never really been sorted out, that the toxic-debt time bomb ticking away could detonate at any moment and scupper the entire economy. Thousands of people around the country still found themselves in situations not so far from Horgan's, albeit on a smaller scale – up to their necks in debt, waiting for the axe to fall, terrified of losing their jobs or businesses, facing the yawning gulf of failure and shame.

And the way Horgan did it? Well, there was something so symbolic about throwing yourself into an abyss. The photo of the bridge was a beauty, suggesting the full horror of that plunge, the gorge, below, yawning open. Readers looked at *that* and imagined themselves, in their worst nightmares, up there on the metal gantry, the wind whistling around their ears, trying to make that decision. It was impossible not to imagine it. Jesus knows what awful stuff must have rushed through his head to make him go through with it.

Siobhan reached the end and gave herself a mental pat on the back for a job well done. Then she began opening each of the other files she had on the story, reading through them systematically – records of phone calls made to Horgan's family and friends, psychologists, economists, spokesmen for estate agents and property developers, and the police officer she'd liaised with in Bristol for details of the post mortem and the repatriation of Horgan's remains. Nowhere was there any mention of Gemma Kearney.

She was just about to close the folder when a name on one of the files leapt out at her: a good friend of Horgan's, supposedly, to whom she'd spoken at some length, but hadn't seen at the funeral. She thought about it for a second, then tapped the number into her phone. Her call was answered almost instantly. Cathy Barrett sounded a bit harassed at first, but remembered Siobhan and was willing to talk again.

'You weren't at the church this morning,' Siobhan said.

'No, I couldn't. The baby's not the best. I couldn't leave her with the sitter, poor thing. I'll have to send a mass card.'

She didn't sound too upset about her absence, Siobhan thought. So much the better. 'I wanted to ask you one more thing about Cormac, if that's okay. A name came up. I thought you might know it.'

'Oh yeah? Go on, then,' the woman said, only half curious, still distracted by something at her end of the line.

'Gemma Kearney. Do you know her?' The dead silence with which the question was received was enough to tell Siobhan she'd touched a raw nerve. 'Cathy? Are you still there?'

She was there all right. 'You're not seriously telling me she had the gall to turn up at Cormac's funeral? That *bitch*?'

'Eh, no,' Siobhan said, thrilled by the response but not wanting to say too much. 'But you obviously know her. Were she and Cormac—'

'Look,' Cathy broke in impatiently, 'whatever she said to you, don't believe a word of it, okay? She messed Cormac around something terrible, but that was years back. And if she's saying she had anything to do with this now, well, it's a lie. And a bloody disgusting one at that. He told me so himself. He got over her. Completely.'

You clearly haven't, Siobhan thought. There was such venom in the woman's voice. 'Sounds like it was pretty serious at the time, though,' she said. 'Why are you so convinced he wasn't seeing her again?'

'After what she did to him?' Cathy Barrett scoffed. 'No chance. She screwed him over good and proper. He'd never have been stupid enough to go back to her; nobody would. And if she's saying any different, she's lying. That's what she does best, by the way, lying.'

4

It was as if all the fight had gone from the day. The wind had dropped off completely, the rain settled into a persistent grey drizzle. Only the recurrent sweep of the wipers and occasional crackle of the Garda radio broke the silence. Mulcahy, his stomach yawning, gazed out of the car window, across the empty car park of the Gables restaurant, where they were idling. Ford was staring at the succession of big, flashy cars negotiating the junction of Torquay Road and Westminster Road, most of them gleaming Audis, Mercs and Lexus four-by-fours, driven by permatanned, dyed-blonde women of child-rearing age.

'Not much sign of the recession biting out here.'

'No,' Mulcahy agreed. 'We forget how much some people squirrelled away during the good times.'

Few places in Dublin had better form for squirrelling than the elegant, tree-lined avenues of Foxrock. This was the land of the long-term wealthy, of old money or the unfathomably quickly acquired, of fine Victorian and Edwardian mansions, and gardens measured by the half-acre rather than the square

40

metre. Some new money had moved in during the boom. Rambling old plots had been subdivided, fine old houses pulled down, and shiny, high-tech modern structures shoe-horned into the capital's most desirable address list. But there was no sign of Foxrock getting any less exclusive than it always had been. Restricting the foreign holidays to two a year rather than three was probably the toughest the belt-tightening got around here.

The clunk of the door handle behind made Mulcahy turn in his seat.

'Is it okay if the dog comes in, too, lads?' the man said, squeezing himself in through the Mondeo's nearside rear door. He was short, prosperous-looking, in his early fifties and balding. Raindrops streaked his nut-brown pate, and beneath the dripping blue raincoat, with its red Ralph Lauren logo, he was more than a little overweight. From his right hand a green and black tartan dog lead stretched out through the car door. If a dog was attached to the other end, Mulcahy couldn't see it.

'Fuck's sake,' Ford muttered.

'What else is he going to do with it?' Mulcahy said. He turned again towards the man. 'Go on then, Eddie.'

Eddie McTiernan made a clicking noise with his tongue and a terrier-sized bundle of brown and black fur shot in through the door and onto his lap. As soon as the door closed, the interior was filled with a fug of wet dog.

'If that thing shakes itself in here, I'll put a bullet in it,' Ford said.

'Sorry,' McTiernan said, addressing the apology to Mulcahy. 'I'll keep him off the seat. We had to come all the way

41

across Leopardstown Golf Course to get here. It was the only way to get away from the missus, y'know, to say I was taking Charlie here for a walk.'

Ford glanced across from the driving seat at Mulcahy. 'Did he seriously just call it what I think he did?'

'What else would Eddie call his best friend?' Mulcahy laughed.

'Ah, now, don't be going on like that,' came the protest from the back seat. 'That's all in the past. I've been out of the game for as long as you've known me, Mr Mulcahy. You know that.'

Mulcahy cast him a sceptical look. He had known Eddie McTiernan for fifteen years or more. In his early days with the Garda National Drugs Unit he had bagged him as an accessory on a cocaine bust and, as soon as he got him in the interview room, spotted his potential as an informant: his large circle of acquaintances, his love of his own voice, his gift for sly pragmatism, always hankering to do deals, hedge bets. Back then Mulcahy made it clear the price of letting him off was gratitude of a tangible variety, and McTiernan had come up with the goods, in time becoming one of his most reliable snouts. But for favours, not money. That was always the deal with McTiernan.

'Which would explain all those trips you've been taking out to Spain lately, would it?' Mulcahy said.

'Spain?' McTiernan echoed, a little weakly.

'Come on, Eddie, you didn't get that tan in this weather, and a little bird tells me you've been spending way too much time out there in the last couple of months. Six trips. Four to Malaga, two to Alicante. Giving Ryanair a lot of business there. Doesn't sound like retirement to me.'

'Jesus, talk about the surveillance state,' McTiernan said. 'Is there nothing you fellas don't know about?'

'Plenty,' Mulcahy said. 'Which is what you're doing here. Tell me about Spain.'

'Yeah, well, I suppose I can see how it might look,' he said defensively, 'but I wasn't bringing anything in, if that's what you're thinking. I'm not that desperate. It's just my investments, like. The Spanish property market's been hit worse than we have by this crash. I was trying to get a couple of places off my hands, reduce my exposure on that front, y'know?'

'Sell one to Bingo Begley, did you?' Ford cut in, the aggression in his voice attracting even the dog's attention.

'Ah,' said Eddie, realisation at last dawning. 'Okay, I get the picture now.'

'So, did you see him?' Ford asked, the growl an octave deeper this time.

The dog gave a whimper and buried its head in the crook of its master's arm.

McTiernan turned towards Mulcahy, a forced look of outrage on his face. 'Are you going to let this galoot talk to me like that, Mr Mulcahy? You know I didn't have to come out here today, especially not in this weather.'

Mulcahy shrugged. The last thing he was going to do was interrupt Ford's well-honed routine. 'Just answer the question, Eddie. I'll say "please" if it helps.'

The bald man sighed and shook his head, then gave the dog's head a stroke for good measure.

'Well, no, as it happens. Not as such. Neither did anyone else for that matter. And before you ask, no, I had nothing to do with any shooting.'

43

'We know that, Eddie,' Mulcahy said. 'Not your style. Like I said, we just want the word on the street.'

'Yeah, well, I wouldn't want to get too much of a rep for that, either.'

'So when did you hear about the shooting?' Ford broke in impatiently, refusing to let up.

McTiernan sighed. 'Like everyone else, I suppose, on the news this morning.'

'Come as a surprise, did it?'

'Well, no. That's what I was just saying, really. I didn't see Bingo, 'cos nobody had for a couple of weeks when I was out there last. The word, as you have it, was that Bingo was a marked man.'

'The word according to who?'

'Just around, y'know. It came up in passing. I was out having a meal one night with some pals, alfresco, like, and I thought I saw Bingo go by in his Lexus. I mentioned it to the guy sitting next to me and the whole bleedin' table went quiet. Then one of them said, "Dead man walking," and the others said it couldn't've been him and that was all they'd say about it. When I asked Frankie Delahunt later, he said Bingo'd got himself into some deep shit that nobody reckoned he'd be able to pull himself out of.'

'What sort of shit?'

'Well, that's just it. Nobody would say. To be honest, I didn't think they knew themselves. Just that it was major.'

'Anybody mention Russians?' Ford asked.

'In connection with Bingo?' McTiernan looked genuinely surprised. 'No way. Why? Is that what they're saying now?'

'It's what the papers are saying, Eddie.'

'Well, it could be true, I suppose. That Moscow lot are deadly out on the Costas. Have you heard what their latest scam is? Kidnapping rich Spanish banker types and injecting them with—'

'Forget that, Eddie,' Mulcahy interrupted. 'What about Bingo? What's this "dead man walking" stuff?'

'Like I said, that's what they were calling him.'

'Who's "they"?'

'The lads – y'know, the fellas in the game out there.'

'Irish?'

'Yeah, and English, too. There's so many of them lot out there you can't help knowing a few.'

'So what *exactly* were they saying?'

'Just that Bingo had got in over his head, with some really dangerous fuckers this time. Made the Dublin mob look like Barbie dolls.' McTiernan rolled his eyes for effect, then gave a little shrug. 'Beyond that I really couldn't say.'

'Come on, Eddie, you know more than that.' Mulcahy knew that when it came to the hard stuff, the solid stuff, McTiernan always had to be reeled in, made to feel he was the one making the running. 'What is it you're after?'

'Well, there is something, now you mention it,' he said, as if the thought had never before crossed his mind. 'A pal of mine, his son, up for possession. Only a couple of grams, mind. Purely personal, I promise.'

Mulcahy looked at Ford, playing the game. 'Can we do anything, Liam?'

'A couple of grams?' Ford said begrudgingly, giving McTiernan a baleful stare. 'Depends. Do you know who pulled him – were they in uniform?'

'No, plainclothes, couple of 'em, in a club. He was taken to Santry Station.'

Ford nodded. 'Probably our lot, so maybe. What's his name?'

'Get the details later,' Mulcahy cut in. 'You spill first, Eddie – if it's good, we'll do what we can.'

McTiernan tried to look like he was thinking about it for a second or so, then nodded. 'Okay. It's only a rumour, like, but you know that English fella Ronson? Got topped a few weeks back, across the water?'

'The guy in Liverpool?' Ford asked.

'Yeah, big player.'

'Trevor Ronson,' Mulcahy said, uneasy at the mention of that name. Ronson had been gunned down outside a pub on one of Liverpool's roughest estates a few weeks earlier. Tagged by the British as a major wholesaler of cocaine and other narcotics, the hit had sent shockwaves through the criminal underworld. The enforcement community's secure intelligence sites and blogs had been ablaze with it, too, although in all the digital chatter Mulcahy hadn't picked up on any Irish connection. He wasn't disposed to believe there was one now, either.

'Come off it, Eddie. What the hell's that got to do with any-thing?'

McTiernan smiled to himself and gave a little snort of sat-isfaction before answering. 'I would've thought you lads'd know all this already. Bingo and Trevor Ronson got fierce friendly over the last few years. They were always hanging out over at Ronson's waterfront place in Puerto Banus, y'know. Living it up, like.'

46

Mulcahy and Ford exchanged glances.

'Bingo?' Ford was the first to get it out. 'Fuck's sake, Ronson was major league. What the hell was he doing messing around with a low life like Bingo?'

'Ah, but that's just it.' McTiernan smiled. 'You're thinking of Bingo as he was when he left Dublin. But, y'know, he was doing very well for himself out in Spain. Got himself seriously well connected, went pretty much from low life to high life. Too high by the looks of it – over his head, maybe?'

'Bingo?' Mulcahy and Ford chimed, still exchanging looks of disbelief.

'Yeah, I know what you lads think,' McTiernan continued, 'but he wasn't like that any more. Bingo changed out there. Made a real go of it, like. He was always a smart cookie, y'know, just played his cards close, stayed under the radar. These last few years out there he was stashing it away big time. Nothing too showy, but he was into something big, no question. Like I say, I'm kinda surprised you fellas don't know about this yerselves.'

McTiernan chuckled to himself and licked his lips. 'To be honest, fellas, I went out there kinda hoping Bingo might want to take one or two of my places off my hands, for cash, like, on the quiet. But then some of the lads warned me off, told me it was all blowing back on him. Just as well, eh?'

He paused for effect, then leant forward in a still more confiding manner, pushing the dog aside so as not to squash it with his belly as he moved. 'It's only a guess, like,' he whispered, 'but, if you ask me, Ronson and Bingo both getting whacked in the space of a few weeks wasn't much of a coincidence. And you can be bloody sure there's plenty more out in Marbella thinking exactly the same as me right now.'

If he did know more, that was as much as McTiernan was willing to give. Mulcahy zoned out while Ford took down the details of the arrest he wanted them to sort out. Then they sat and watched him tramp heavily away, back towards the golf course, the dog waddling damply behind him on its lead.

'Those two could do with getting out for walks more often,' Ford snorted, before switching on the engine and turning the car towards the city. 'That feckin' dog looks like a slug on stilts.'

Mulcahy said nothing, still trying to get his head round the bomb McTiernan had dropped about Trevor Ronson. There was no doubting Eddie would know the impact of what he was saying, and his info was nearly always spot on, but a link between Ronson's murder and Begley's? It wasn't that it was inconceivable – not if what he'd said about the two of them being so pally was true. Theirs was a dangerous world and people often got caught in the crossfire. The real question was, were there wider implications? It might be worth having another, quieter word later.

Unusually, Ford also kept quiet for most of the journey back into town. Still more unusual was the fact that the traffic flowed, some sweet spot having opened up between the school run and the early evening outrush of workers from central Dublin to the suburbs, and they made good time. Even so, it was getting on for a quarter past five by the time Ford turned the Mondeo into Dame Street.

'This thing needs a fill-up,' Ford said, tapping the fuel

warning light on the dashboard. 'I'll drop you off at the gate and swing round to the pumps. Doesn't seem fair on the next lads to leave 'em with the stench of dead dog *and* an empty tank.'

'Damp dog,' Mulcahy corrected.

'Smells the same to me.'

Ford pulled up outside the Olympia Theatre. Across the street, between the swaggeringly ornate Allied Irish Bank and the accusingly plain Sick and Indigent Roomkeepers' Society, a narrow gateway led into Dublin Castle's lower yard. Mulcahy looked at Ford but didn't move.

'I didn't like the sound of what Eddie was on about,' he said at last.

'You and me both,' Ford said, a grimness in his expression. 'More like a bloody fantasy if you ask me. You sure he's still reliable? Sounds like he's been out of the game a while.'

Mulcahy shook his head. 'That's the thing about Eddie. He's never either in or out completely. All his pals are up to their necks in it, though. You heard him – a trip out to Marbella and he's boozing and schmoozing with some of the main players on the Costa. Irish, English, Dutch ... doesn't matter – he knows them all. Even a few of the East Europeans, despite what he says.'

'So are you going to get in touch with the Brits, then?'

'I'm not sure,' Mulcahy said. 'I don't want to stir anything up if I can help it. Most of my contacts over there are with the Serious Organised Crime Agency, and they tend to do stuff by the book. Official channels and all that. I'm not sure it's worth going down that road at this stage. The Brits will be throwing some serious weight at the Ronson killing. It's a question of whether we want to get caught up in it. Even if there is something in what Eddie says, I'd need something more substantial than his word to bring it up with them.'

'Maybe we could try the local lads, in Liverpool.' Ford scratched his head. 'What would they be? Merseyside Police?'

'Yes,' Mulcahy said, turning to Ford like a light had gone on in his head. 'That's not a bad idea. They've got their own Level Three op there, the Major Crime Unit. Weren't they on that Operation Trinity thing you worked on a couple of years back?'

'Operation Triton, yeah,' Ford said. He thought for a second. 'Actually, there was a really good guy on that, Paul Solomons, a DS that I got on well with. His missus is from Dublin. He'd be up for some share and share alike, I'm sure – if he's still there.'

'Could you dig out his number and give him a call when you get a chance?' Mulcahy suggested. 'You know, nothing too specific – just get the inside track on the Ronson thing and drop Bingo's name in passing. You don't have to tell him he's dead. They may not even be aware of that yet.'

'Sure,' Ford said. 'You don't want to speak to him yourself?'

'No, you know him, you call him,' Mulcahy said. 'It'd only arouse his suspicion if I called him.'

'Why are you worried about that?'

'Like I said, I don't want to get us tangled up in a multi-jurisdiction investigation unless I know what's in it for us. If we need to get involved, fair enough, in which case we'll go in prepared, and at a level where we have some proper input.

If we stumble into something the Brits are already running, we could end up chasing our tails on some bullshit investigative carousel and get nothing out of it.'

'You should know,' Ford said.

'Yeah, well, if I learnt anything from seven years with Europol, it's that you never go into anything like this blind if you can help it.'

'Solomons will be solid, I'm sure. He's a laid-back guy. Great on Triton, only interested in getting the job done, whatever it took.'

'Good,' Mulcahy said. 'I've got a couple of calls to make before I finish, but you might as well get straight off after you drop the car back. There's nothing more we can do today.'

'You sure? You don't fancy a quick pint in the Long Hall?'

Mulcahy shook his head. 'Can't. I've got this Rosscarbery thing to work through and I'm meeting Orla out in Monkstown for dinner afterwards.'

Ford swung an arm round the steering wheel and leered over at him.

'I'm telling you, boss, you got a fit one there. Nothing like a physio to get physical with, eh?'

'Go to hell, Liam.' Mulcahy hooked his fingers into the handle and pushed at the car door. When he was out, he turned and leant back in. 'And do me a favour, find a woman of your own and get your mind off mine, would you?'

'I'm only taking an interest,' Ford said, doing his best to look offended.

Mulcahy stared him down. Sure enough, the look of injury quickly reverted to a leer as Ford lifted both hands off the wheel and cupped them in front of his chest. Mulcahy slammed the door as Ford, cackling like a complete headcase, revved the engine and pulled out into the traffic.

She heard them laughing as soon as she stepped out of the lift. As ever on a Monday, the *Sunday Herald*'s newsroom was mostly deserted. There was none of the hum and hassle and stink of stress and sweat that you got on Fridays and Saturdays as deadlines loomed and the great task of building a Sunday newspaper from scratch every week got seriously under way. Now there were just the advertising and IT guys, plus some subs and editors working the soft-end stuff, the arts, travel and TV pages, which were all got out of the way before the news operation got into full swing later in the week.

Siobhan thought the laughter was coming from the news desk, felt sure the wheezing chortle of one of the two loud voices was that of Paddy Griffin. She frowned as she heard the wheeze become a hacking cough, thinking he must've had a skinful, although he'd recently been warned to go easy on the drink. Paddy never was one for taking advice, medical or otherwise, she thought, as she rounded the corner and stopped, disconcerted by the sight of Griffin, rocking in his chair, helpless, holding his hands up as if begging the man sitting opposite him for mercy. Every hair on her neck stiffened as she realised who it was: Cillian O'Gorman, the horrible little slimeball. What in hell's name was he doing in today?

As if she'd pricked the bubble of their mirth, both men stopped laughing instantly, turned to her open-mouthed, then looked back at one another and exploded into paroxysms again. She tried to suppress the creeping suspicion that it was herself who'd been the butt of their joke, and shrugged off her jacket and hung it up before walking up to the desk. Griffin was pulling a handkerchief from his pocket, still spluttering. O'Gorman kept his small eyes fixed on her as she approached. He was lounging back, elbows out, hands clasped over his belly and his right leg propped blokishly on his left knee – in her chair, at her desk, beside Griffin's.

'Paddy, how're you doing?' she said, and nodded at O'Gorman, who smiled back up at her but didn't budge an inch. 'Could you shift, please, Cillian? I need to get to my desk.'

'Oh Christ, I've usurped the seat of power again,' O'Gorman said in mock horror, throwing up his hands and giving Griffin a knowing look. He made a meal of getting up and standing beside the chair, bowing and muttering, 'Your throne, madam.'

Siobhan ignored him, pulled the chair out so viciously he had to jump to avoid a crack on the ankle, then sat down. She was about to log on when she felt a weight on the chairback and realised O'Gorman was standing behind her now, looking over her shoulder. No way was she going to let the little weasel see her password. She turned and glared up at him.

'Do you mind?'

'Not at all, darling – you go right ahead.' He smirked, turning his attention back to Griffin. 'I'd better be getting off, Paddy, before I get us into any more trouble. But thanks for this, and for the jar. It was good to catch up. Call you tomorrow, soon as it's done. Be seein' ya, yeah?'

Without a word of farewell to her, he was gone, strutting down the passageway like the complete cock that he was.

'All right, Scoop?' Griffin said, giving her an avuncular smile, a stale whiff of stout on his breath. He nodded towards the departing figure, shook his head. 'Bloody mad eejit.'

'What was he doing in?' she asked.

'Ah, nothing.' Griffin gave his eyes a last wipe with the handkerchief before putting it back in his pocket. 'Something that came in this afternoon – I asked him to follow up on it.'

'Comedy job, was it?'

Griffin gave her a sharp look, like she'd crossed some line. 'No. Political, actually, and urgent. Jimmy Duggan's off sick and this needs to be done tomorrow.'

A stab of unease ripped through her stomach. Duggan was the *Herald*'s political correspondent, and it was usually she who covered for him when he was off. 'I could have done that – I'm around tomorrow.'

'No, you couldn't,' Griffin said gruffly, 'and you're not in tomorrow, anyway. I told you to take the day off in lieu of today, remember?'

Siobhan widened her eyes. 'Of course I do, and I remember just as clearly telling you I didn't want to take it, not when I was already wasting one day of my week slogging down to Cork and back for a useless fucking funeral.'

She instantly regretted saying it, knowing there was too much aggression, too much complaint in her tone. It would be hard enough to argue the case for chasing up Gemma Kearney's story when she'd so resisted covering the funeral in the first place. On the train back, she had envisaged joshing Griffin a little, flattering him, telling him he'd been right all along, that Horgan's funeral had dug up an interesting new angle – how it would all just fall into place, and she'd get what she wanted, as usual. From the furious look on Griffin's face she could tell she'd blown any chance of that now. He was shaking his head again, but not in a good way. In fact he was looking completely pissed off with her. She decided to try a more conciliatory tack.

'Look, Paddy, I'm sorry. The thing is—'

'No, Siobhan,' Griffin interjected, the slur in his voice from the drink instantly more audible. 'You look, because I'm getting tired of this. I agreed to have you back from sick leave early on the understanding that you'd take it easy, for your benefit, not mine. But you're just not playing ball. You're either grabbing at every stupid bit of work that comes in, without even knowing what it is, or arguing the toss over what I actually want you to do. It's not on, girl. I mean, I told you to go home this afternoon, but no, here you are, dragging yourself in at half past five, and for what? So you can get on my back again for sending you out on a story that, in my professional opinion, had legs for a bit more. And which, by the way, I still think has. And which it's your bloody job to make sure does, okay?'

'But that's what I'm saying, Paddy.' She paused, trying to find the right words, but they wouldn't come to her. It was too late, anyway. Griffin was already on a rant.

'I don't care what you're saying, Siobhan. I don't want to hear it, okay? I don't want to hear it now, and I don't want to hear it tomorrow. In fact, I don't want to hear it anytime this week.' Griffin had got out of his chair and was towering above her, stabbing an insistent forefinger in her direction. 'Last time I checked, I was still the news editor here. I make the decisions about who does what and what's best for everyone, and I'm deciding now: I don't want to see you in here again this week, Siobhan. File that story when you get a chance and take the rest of the week off.'

'Jesus, Paddy, what in hell's the mat—'

But Griffin just put the flat of his hand in front of her face to shut her up. 'I'm serious, Siobhan,' he said, grabbing his jacket and folding it over his arm. 'I'm going home now and I'm telling you to do the same. Get some rest, or go do some promotion for that book of yours. Anything. But don't come near this office again before next week or there'll be trouble. I mean it. You're not fit for it.'

5

Head down against the rain, Mulcahy crossed the castle's lower yard, the sky darkening into dusk. The lights were going on early behind the wide plate-glass windows of the Stamping Building, casting a soft yellow glow onto the wet tarmac at his feet and up across the grey stone walls and carved Gothic pinnacles of the Chapel Royal opposite. Rounding the corner, he spotted Detective Garda Aidan Duffy, and another man he didn't recognise, exiting the fine Georgian doorway of the Garda National Drugs Unit.

'Hold the door there, lads, would you?' He ran the last few yards, grabbing the heavy oak door from Duffy, who had a large sports bag slung over his shoulder and was looking a little sheepishly at his watch.

'I waited as long as I could, boss, but I have to head off for training now, okay? I told you last week, yeah?'

Mulcahy stopped. Duffy was short for a cop, five ten or so, but powerfully built and ideally made for the position of scrum half, which he occupied on the Garda Siochana rugby 'A' team, the sort of major achievement that brought plenty of in-job admiration with it. Mulcahy was sure Duffy considered himself desperately unlucky to be working for the one cop in the entire country who had no interest in any kind of football, let alone rugby, and few other sports for that matter unless they involved water and sails. The guy was always apologising for going off for training, although in truth Mulcahy didn't mind. He only cared about Duffy's other, even rarer talent, which was for following the intricacies of paper trails and money. For that he'd be willing to put up with pretty much anything. 'No problem, Aidan. I'll see you tomorrow. Is Aisling up there?'

'Yeah, still holding the fort.'

Inside, Mulcahy flicked the rain off his hair and coat sleeves, and made his way up the stairs to the International Liaison Unit's office at the back of the building. There were still quite a few people working in the open-plan space on the first floor, but he ignored most of them, raising an amiable hand to one or two but making it clear he wasn't stopping for a chat. Despite what Duffy had said, his other colleague, Detective Garda Aisling Sweeney, was nowhere to be seen, although her computer was still on and he could see a bag on the floor beneath her desk. In the glass-walled sanctuary of his own office, he shrugged off his jacket and logged on to his computer, his free hand picking up the phone on his desk.

He went straight through to voicemail. 'Eddie, it's me, Mulcahy,' he said. 'Couple of things you said earlier, I got the impression you didn't want to elaborate with Liam there. Give me a call when you get a chance, yeah?'

He sat down, exhaling a long breath. On screen he double-clicked a folder called 'Rosscarbery Bay' and shook his head on seeing the mass of subfolders inside. This was what he had been avoiding when the Begley thing came up: preparing for a Joint Task Force meeting on what should have been by far the biggest anti-trafficking success of the year – the seizure of almost a tonne of cocaine on a yacht off the southwest coast of Cork. Yet it was proving one of the most frustrating investigations he'd ever worked on, not least because both the Garda Siochana and the government were getting a regular pasting in the press for not having sewn it up.

He heard a noise in the outer office and looked up. Aisling Sweeney was back at her desk and he called her. She turned, waved and pointed at the mobile phone she was holding to her ear, then at his computer, mouthing the word 'email' at him, before turning away again to speak to her caller.

In his email queue he saw a message from her – 'Thought this might help you catch up' – with a document attached called 'Rosscarbery Bay: Summary.'

Mulcahy's heart lifted. Sweeney had a gift for concision, and as he opened and read through the document, he was momentarily lost in admiration at how she had covered, in just a few brief paragraphs, all the salient points quickly and efficiently. In early June, an ocean-going yacht, the *Atlantean*, had been spotted rolling in the swell, smoke belching from her engine, a mile off the coast of West Cork outside Rosscarbery Bay, by the Irish Navy's patrol vessel *LE Niamh*. Thinking the *Atlantean* might be in distress, the skipper of the *Niamh* had changed course, approached and hailed, only to see the *Atlantean*'s crew immediately abandon ship and speed off past the Galley Head lighthouse on a powerful rib that had been tied up, unseen, on her starboard bow. Forced to secure the yacht rather than pursue the rib, the navy made the most spectacular discovery of the drug-enforcement year: ninety ten-kilo bales of cocaine stowed in the living quarters, street value in excess of €100 million.

It was a terrific coup, which had kept the media bubbling over for days, but a major disappointment, too, as the massive Garda manhunt launched to find the smugglers was an abject failure, and the subsequent investigation had completely stalled due to the lack of any evidence aboard the *Atlantean* as to who was behind the smuggling operation. Even the yacht's GPS navigation system had been taken by the fleeing crew, meaning investigators couldn't so much as say for sure where she had come from. Or rather, they hadn't been able to until Mulcahy received some tantalising intelligence from a colleague in the Dutch police force just a few days previously.

He heard a cough and looked up. Sweeney was standing in the doorway, head and hip cocked as she leant her shoulder against the frame. In her late twenties, she was five seven or so, and slightly built, her tawny hair framing a narrow face dominated by big, intelligent green eyes. The first time he'd met her, Mulcahy thought she could be stunning if she wanted to be, but got the impression that she most definitely didn't. Which wasn't so unusual among women cops. He hadn't really thought about it since. As with Duffy, he was more interested in her other talents – IT and languages.

'Liam not come back with you?' she asked.

'No, I let him off the leash for the evening.'

'Lock-up-your-daughters night, is it?' she smiled. 'I think I'll be staying in. Not worth the risk, being out there with him on the streets.'

Mulcahy laughed. 'Thanks for doing that background paper. It's great. Would've taken me hours.'

She smiled again and nodded. 'Make any amendments you want, and when you're happy, just press "send" and it'll be cc'd to everyone on the list.'

'Great. Thanks,' Mulcahy said.

'Got an interesting lead on that while you were out.' She hesitated. 'Well, not a lead exactly, not like your Dutch thing, but interesting.'

Mulcahy sat back in his chair. 'Go on.'

'The Bundespolizei in Heidelberg, their liaison passed it on. Some local German woman was watching a TV doc on drugs last night. Her ears pricked up at a mention of Rosscarbery. Turns out she rented a holiday cottage there the first week in June, knew nothing about the seizure until now, but says the night before she left – i.e. our night – she saw a Land Rover towing an empty trailer down to the pier at about ten in the evening.'

That was interesting. Much of southwest Cork's jagged coastline was a smuggler's paradise, packed with isolated coves and rarely used piers. Rosscarbery was especially tempting for the smuggler, a wide, easily navigated bay offering a choice of gently shelving beach on one side or a solid pier and slipway on the other. Most importantly, both had good roads down to them and were at least a mile away from the village and prying eyes. Any evidence they could get to pinpoint where the gang had intended landing the drugs could help build a case against them should any arrests be made further down the line.

'They must get a fair few cars going down there, for fishing and that,' Mulcahy said. 'Why would she take any notice?'

'I'm not sure. The Bundespolizei guy didn't go into that much detail, but apparently the woman did say that the fella driving had trouble negotiating the trailer round one of the bends, so she guessed he probably wasn't local. And it was getting dark, so she just thought it was weird. Then, about three hours later, she saw it coming back again. Trailer still empty and going at a hell of a clip, in the dark. Made her think of the Drugs Watch signs down on the road.'

Mulcahy tutted. 'And it took her how long to phone?'

'Well, to be fair, boss—'

'I'm not being serious,' he said. 'We're lucky to get anything new at this stage. I don't suppose we can hope for details – number plate, anything like that?'

'No, nothing like that.' Sweeney smiled. 'But I thought I could maybe give her a call myself, see if I can dig anything else out of her.'

'Absolutely.' He was sure that if anyone could, Sweeney could. 'But tomorrow, yeah? You might as well get off now.'

Sweeney nodded and turned to go. He looked on a moment while she switched off her computer and began gathering her belongings. Soon his attention turned back to his screen and the report, and what she had written about the new Dutch lead he had unearthed. It was one of the few real breaks the investigation had had in months. An information request sent out via Europol had turned up intel that a yacht identical to the *Atlantean*, but sailing under a different name, had put in for repairs at a boatyard in southern Holland and had vanished four nights prior to the Rosscarbery Bay seizure. From what he'd seen, and given the timings, there was a more than strong chance that she was the *Atlantean*. The question now was, did the smugglers take the drugs on board there, or had they been en route from elsewhere? A trio of detectives from the main investigation team in Cork were flying out to follow up, with Mulcahy's contacts smoothing the way with the Dutch, who, like most police, resisted letting outsiders onto their precious patch for fear of being shown up.

He made a few minor refinements to Sweeney's document and circulated it to all the attendees. Then he opened a new document, this one for his eyes only, and began making notes for his presentation, suggestions as to paths the investigation might take now, others relating to the worrying prospect of a new trafficking route opening up between mainland Europe and Ireland. It was a good hour and a half before he looked up again. Sweeney was long gone. Most of the lights in the office outside were off, just a few blooms of illumination here and there above the ranks of filing cabinets, shelves and storage units that divided up each individual GNDU fiefdom.

Peaceful, quiet, he felt a yawn begin to grow in his chest and sat up and stretched, determined to concentrate, but his mobile phone rang, shattering the silence. He grabbed it, thinking it must be Eddie McTiernan getting back to him, but it was Orla's caller ID that flashed up. Probably checking that he was still on for dinner. She'd been doing that ever since he'd left her waiting in restaurants twice running, when he'd been delayed on urgent jobs. He thought about letting

63

her go through to voicemail, putting in another half-hour, but his eye wandered to the clock on the phone screen. That would probably be stretching it.

She knew in her heart it was stupid, that it verged on the downright crazy, but Siobhan spent the whole of the taxi ride home to Ballsbridge fretting, convincing herself that Cillian O'Gorman had turned Paddy Griffin against her and that he was just one step away from ousting her from her job at the *Sunday Herald*. By the time she was upstairs at the door of her apartment, the rush of paranoia had peaked. Hands shaking, head numb with anxiety, she felt tears brimming on her eyelids as she fumbled to get the key in the lock and blinked rapidly to get rid of them. No way would she give in to that.

She shoved the door shut behind her and leant back against it, folding her arms and digging her chin into her chest, squeezing her eyes shut, taking in bigger and bigger gulps of air until she felt her head clear a little, the pressure in her temples ease, and her eyes become ready for the light again. Looking down the corridor towards the comfortingly familiar chaos in her living room, she felt a flood of relief run through her. A picture of Griffin came to her as he'd been in the office: eyes red-rimmed and rheumy from laughing, the smell of stout on his breath. He'd been half pissed, she reasoned to herself. Maybe in a bad mood to begin with. He probably didn't mean half of what he'd said. For as long as she'd known him he had been nothing other than a good boss and better friend to her. Why would he change now?

In the living room, she pushed aside a pile of magazines on

the sofa, sat down and started thinking it through, forcing herself to be rational. Looking back over the past few weeks, maybe Griffin did have reason to be annoyed. She had been grabbing at work, she realised. Throughout her career she'd always been keen, but never desperate. And perhaps she had been questioning his judgement a lot, but she'd always done that. It was one of the reasons he was fond of her: she challenged him. But had she been more arsey than usual, lately? She couldn't see it, but felt a flush on her cheeks as she realised she hadn't had a proper chat with Griffin in weeks, and knew nothing about what was going on with him that might be affecting his mood at work. That was bad, when they'd always been close. But was he at fault for it, or her?

She went to the fridge, took a gulp of chilled still water to try and quell the anxiety firing up inside her again. She was going to have to sort things out with Griffin. In the short term, that meant not pushing against him. He was the most stubborn person she'd ever met, apart from herself, and though she could often wrap him round her little finger, once he'd made a firm decision he rarely went back on it. Even so, the thought of spending another week at home, doing nothing, was out of the question. She had to stay busy working to keep the churning in her mind at bay. The only way she'd got through the past year was by writing her book, writing that evil bastard Rinn out of her system and onto the page.

Could she maybe kill two birds with one stone? She picked up her bag and went to the dining table by the window overlooking the gardens. She cleared a space amid the books and papers and bits of clothing strewn upon it and opened her laptop. Her head was buzzing again with thoughts of Gemma

Kearney. That was the story she wanted to follow up, and if Griffin wouldn't let her work from the office, then she'd damn well do it from home.

She quickly scanned her notes to see what might be her next move. Cathy Barrett, the young mother who'd expressed such hatred for Gemma over the phone, was an obvious place to start. And tracking down that assistant, or anyone who could tell her about Gemma's accountancy practice in Cork, wouldn't hurt. But going back to the beginning of the story might yield more in terms of a story. To Cormac Horgan. What could possibly have happened to Gemma if she really had been with him in Bristol? Actually, Bristol might well be the best place to start. She called up the contact details for the police in England, the ones she'd dealt with when Horgan's body was found. She checked her watch. It was a bit late, but the cop had given her a mobile number; she might as well try it.

'Hi. Is that Sergeant Walker?'

'Yes, that's me.'

She remembered the voice now, open, friendly, unlike most of the cops she spoke to. Maybe they bred them differently in England. Maybe it was just the fact that she was dealing with a woman.

'It's Siobhan Fallon, from the *Sunday Herald* here in Ireland. We spoke a couple of weeks ago regarding—'

'About Mr Horgan. Yes, of course, I remember. How can I help?'

That was very promising. 'Well, I was wondering – you said there were some loose ends to be tied up, like where he was staying and all that. Did you ever figure that stuff out?'

'You must be psychic,' Sergeant Walker laughed. 'We actually made some progress on that today. We located Mr Horgan's car over near the bridge.'

'His car? I thought he'd taken a flight to Bristol.'

'It was a hire car. He left it parked in a side street near the suspension bridge. It's been there a while, obviously, but was only reported to us by an irate resident yesterday. There were some of Mr Horgan's belongings in it. I was just about to inform his family and arrange to have the items forwarded. There was some documentation, too.'

'Anything important?' Siobhan jumped in. 'A suicide note or something?'

'No, nothing like that. Other things – tickets, hotel and restaurant receipts, an overnight bag. They might help build a picture of his movements before he jumped, but I haven't had a chance to go through them in detail yet.'

Walker was being remarkably open for a cop, but the case was pretty much wrapped up as far as she was concerned. Siobhan wondered if what she was going to say next would change all that.

'Was there any indication he might not have been alone?'

'No, not that I saw.' Walker sounded surprised. 'Why?'

'I just spoke to a lady here today who says Horgan was in Bristol with a girlfriend, an Irish girl, called Gemma, who's gone missing. It came as a shock to me because I thought I'd looked into the circumstances of his death pretty thoroughly.'

'You say her name was Gemma?' Walker asked, but not with any sense of recognition.

'Yeah, Gemma Kearney.'

'I don't remember seeing anything, certainly not in the car, but I can check for you when I'm going through the items tomorrow, if you like.'

'That would be great, thanks.' Suddenly a jolt of possibility hit Siobhan. It was a good friend, that feeling, and for the first time in months she felt the dead hand of anxiety release its grip and something else come to life inside her: the old familiar ache, the thirst, the longing for a story. She didn't even think about it, just knew she was going to dive straight in.

'Look, Sergeant, I know this probably sounds mad, but if I were to come over to Bristol tomorrow, would you have time to show me what you've got?'

There was a pause, whether of surprise or suspicion Siobhan couldn't tell.

'Why would you do that?'

Siobhan was about to say it was because she was convinced there was more to the story, but she knew that wouldn't wash with a cop, however nice. She wondered did Walker have kids herself. A daughter, maybe. It had to be worth a shot.

'Because Gemma's mother, the lady who contacted me earlier, is absolutely frantic with worry. She's desperate to get some information about her daughter.'

'But if this girl is missing, you should let the police handle it. I mean, your Garda people, over there in Dublin.'

'They are handling it,' Siobhan said, 'but it looks like I'm the only one asking questions. I promise I won't get in your way. Will you help us?'

Mulcahy was parking the car outside the restaurant when his mobile rang. He pulled on the handbrake and answered without looking.

'Hi, I'm just coming,' he said.

'Lucky you,' came the response from the earpiece. 'It's a marvel you can talk at the same time.'

He hadn't heard her voice for months, but recognition hit him like a sucker punch, out of nowhere.

'Siobhan?' he said, feeling himself flush instantly hot, glad he was in the dark, in the car, not with Orla yet. 'Is that you?'

'The very same,' she said. 'Like the bad penny, just when you think I'm gone for good, I turn up again. How's it going, Mulcahy? Sounds like you're not dying of loneliness, anyway.'

'No, not so far,' he laughed, despite his surprise. She sounded like the Siobhan of old: the wisecracks, the challenge. Not like the last time they'd seen each other. He relaxed a fraction, felt the breath easing out of him, the fabric of the car seat cushioning his shoulders.

'But you couldn't possibly comment, right?'

He could hear the smile in her voice, all but see the light dancing in her blue eyes.

'You said it. But look, how are you? How's the—' He broke off, unable to find the word for it. 'I mean, are you back at work full-time yet?'

'Ah yeah, I've been back a couple of months now. I'm still trying to get my head around it, to be honest, but it's okay. How about you?'

'Yeah, good,' he said, grinding to a halt again. What should he say to her? He cursed himself for being so nonplussed.

'Look, Mulcahy,' she broke into his silence, 'I know I probably should have told you this before, but the book's coming out. You know, the one I was—'

'Yeah, I heard,' he cut in. 'Liam said he saw you on TV this morning.'

'Oh yeah? And did I do okay?'

'He didn't say.'

'Ah, right.' She coughed. 'And you didn't ask.'

He let that one hang in the air, not wanting to confirm it, not willing to deny it.

'Look, eh, you've obviously got somewhere to be, Mulcahy. I just thought I should tell you myself, you know, not to worry – I didn't put anything in about . . . well, you and me. I know you weren't keen on the idea, anyway. That much was—'

'It's okay, Siobhan. It's not a problem. It's what you do. I just didn't want to be a part of it. The book's fine, I'm sure.'

'Oh, okay, great.' She sounded more surprised than relieved.

'And thanks for letting me know. I appreciate that.'

'I'm just sorry I didn't get to you first,' she said. 'The book's not even out until next week, but the TV slot came up out of the blue and I didn't want to pass it up. I'll get the lads to send you a copy, yeah?'

'That'd be grand,' he said, not meaning it, but there was no need to be rude about it now. She'd made the effort, after all.

'Look, while I'm on . . . ' She hesitated, then seemed to think better of it. 'Ah, it doesn't matter.'

'No, go on. What is it?' He couldn't have admitted it even to himself, but he knew what he was hoping she'd say; wanted her to be the first to say it. But that wasn't to be.

'Okay, it's only just occurred to me this minute, I swear,' she said, all business. 'I need a contact, somebody in your

70

area of expertise. The international side, I mean, not drugs. I'm trying to help a woman whose daughter's gone missing, over in England, she thinks.'

Mulcahy tried to follow the sudden switch into work mode, but it wasn't really working for him. 'Have you tried Missing Persons, up in the Park?'

'Ah, come on, Mulcahy,' she laughed softly. 'Surely you can do better than that? I mean, this girl Gemma's mother reported her missing over a week ago and all they'll say is that they're doing everything they can.'

'They probably are.' Mulcahy felt obliged to say something in their defence, but the truth was, Missing Persons were always swamped with more cases than they could handle, especially since the recent cuts had hacked staff numbers to the bone.

'Don't suppose they can do much if she's out of the jurisdiction,' he continued. 'Did you say you're not even sure England's where she went missing?'

'Well, not entirely, but the mother thinks the girl went there with a boyfriend of hers. To Bristol, we think.'

'And what does the boyfriend have to say about it? Did they ever get to Bristol, I mean?'

'That's just it. The guy came back in a box. Suicide. Threw himself off the Clifton Suspension Bridge. That's how I heard about the girl. It might be the story you saw my byline on.'

Mulcahy grunted, noncommittal, said nothing.

'The whole thing's fucked up, anyway,' she continued. 'The first I heard of this girl was earlier today at the funeral. The mother is convinced she was with him. Daughter's been missing since then. You can appreciate why she's worried, right?

Any ideas on who might help me out with this, on the British side I mean?'

Mulcahy scratched his ear. 'Not off the top of my head, but look, let me have a think about it and get back to you tomorrow. Is this the best number to get you on?'

'Yeah, that hasn't changed. Thanks, Mulcahy. Talk tomorrow.'

The line went dead. She was gone, and something inside him already felt empty. Mulcahy shook his head to get rid of the feeling, but it wouldn't shift, perhaps because it wasn't in his head, but buried deeper inside him. He sat there staring blankly at the phone in his hand. When he eventually resurfaced, it was the time that startled him. Shit. Another ten minutes gone by. He stabbed at the phone, scrolled to Orla's number.

'Hiya. Look, sorry, I'm just parking the car. I'll be with you in a second . . . '

Tuesday

6

Siobhan had flown out of Dublin many times for work and holidays, but she'd rarely seen the city reveal itself in such beauty as it did that morning. Below was the usual patchwork of green fields, grey industrial estates, endless ranks of close-packed houses and trailing black ribbons of road; only now the entire scene was bathed in the shimmering pink sheen of a cloudless dawn. She watched the world fall away, feeling the engines' immense power pulling her up into the crystal-clear air. The plane banked sharply and the sea rose to meet her, bringing with it the wide sweep of the bay as the curving city met glinting steel-grey water all the way round from Howth to Killiney. Then they were level again, and as soon as the safety-belt sign was turned off she stretched out on the empty seats beside her and slept. Fifty minutes later a steward woke her as they began the descent into Bristol.

Sergeant Walker told her to take a taxi straight to the Clifton Suspension Bridge, that she would meet her by the toll booth on the Clifton side. On the road in from the airport, Siobhan kept catching glimpses of the bridge, high above the city, gleaming creamy white in the soft light, like a fragment of antique lace stretched between distant cliffs. The Asian cab driver kept up a constant patter about how nice a city Bristol was to visit, but the traffic was terrible, housing too expensive and the local authority utterly incompetent. She might as well have been in a taxi at home, even if the swear words 'politician' and 'banker' never once passed his lips.

She tuned out, taking in the form and feel of this city so unknown to her, forgot all about the bridge until the taxi began a straining climb up through narrow, twisting streets and then, all of a sudden, there it was again, almost on the same level as she was, arcing out across the gorge, more beautiful than she'd ever have guessed a bridge could be. The taxi looped round a sloping area of grass and trees, and drew up short of the toll booths where cars were queuing to cross. As she got out and paid, Siobhan saw a tall, trim black woman approaching confidently, her hand outstretched.

'Hi, it *is* Siobhan, isn't it? I saw your photo online. I'm Andrea Walker.'

Siobhan had encountered her fair share of women detectives in the Garda Siochana, but she could count on the fingers of one hand the number of black officers, of either gender, she'd come across in Dublin. Or, for that matter, cops who were as good-looking as Walker, with her lean figure, high cheekbones and a pearl-grey trouser suit that enhanced her long limbs.

'I hope you don't mind me dragging you out here,' Walker said. 'I thought if we came to the bridge first, you'd get a better sense of it all.'

'I'm glad you did,' Siobhan said, shaking Walker's hand warmly. She turned to take in the vista spread before them.

The taxi had come up some pretty precipitous streets on the way, but she hadn't been prepared for the sense of great height she was experiencing now. Off to her left, the ground dropped away vertiginously, revealing a sprawl of grey city spreading out along one bank of the curving river below, a busy motorway folding it in like a cradling elbow along the distant western edge. Beyond that again was a ring of low, sparsely populated hills.

'This is stunning.' Siobhan walked further out and looked across the bridge towards the steep, tree-covered slopes on the far side. It was impossible not to admire the structure as much as its setting. The huge brick towers at either end, like the great, white, wrought-iron suspension chains that hung from them, were so solid and reassuring, their arches like stout legs planted on the massive brick piers either side of the gorge, braced to take the strain of the two-lane roadway that hung between them.

'I've only seen it in photographs,' she continued. 'They don't do it justice, do they? It looks so much more impressive in real life.'

Walker smiled indulgently, strolling alongside her. 'Especially on a sunny day like today. I suppose I get used to it, living here – you know, when you see it plastered on every second sign and business card, not to mention all the tourist tat. Personally, I'd love the bridge a lot more if people would stop chucking themselves off it.'

'Yes, well, when you put it like that, I guess you would.' Siobhan smiled, liking the sergeant's abruptness. 'I suppose we'd better get down to business.'

'Yeah, let's.' Walker turned and pointed towards a terrace

of elegant Georgian villas snaking down the road on the rim of the gorge, their first-floor balconies covered by black and white striped metal canopies. 'One row behind there,' she continued, her finger pointing over the roofs, 'is a backstreet called Westfield Place, where we found the car. It more or less confirms what we suspected – that Mr Horgan came here to jump. It's surprising how many cars turn up there; sometimes we don't hear about them for months, until one of the residents complains. But in this case the hire company had reported it stolen.'

'Are there that many suicides?' Siobhan asked, surprised.

'Nothing like as many since they put the barriers on the bridge ten years ago. But every couple of months or so some bloke will still get over. Nearly always males these days.' She glanced at Siobhan to emphasise the point. 'But Mr Horgan was a bit unusual for us.'

'Unusual?' It was one of those words that, when used by officials, always got Siobhan's antennae tingling. 'I wasn't aware there was anything *unusual* about it.'

'No, not like that. Unusual, yes, but not suspicious. I only mean the fact that he went in the water. It had us confused for a while.'

Siobhan looked at the bridge, then at the river below and turned her palms up at Walker. 'I'm a bit that way myself – confused, I mean.'

Walker laughed. 'C'mon, let me show you. It's easier.'

She steered Siobhan across the road, a hand placed in the small of her back, dodging the traffic at the toll machines. On this side of the road, the view opened out into one of almost rustic tranquillity. No sense of the city behind them now. Just the gorge, all green wooded slopes on the far bank, all sheer scrub-covered cliffs on this side, and between them the toffee-brown river winding away into the distance. Walker followed the footpath round the tower, on the side of which a prominent embossed metal sign announced, 'Samaritans care,' with a phone number underneath. Siobhan looked around, wondered if there'd been a phone box, too, in the days before mobiles. She strode over to where Walker was waiting by the stone wall edging the pier. Siobhan rested her arms on the parapet, stood on her toes and peered over the edge, her eyes instantly swimming at the near-vertical drop to the bottom, where a surge of heavy traffic was screaming along the riverside road below.

'Jesus, I wasn't expecting that,' she said, stepping back. 'I thought you said there was a barrier.'

'On the bridge itself, yes.' Walker pointed out across the span, where a network of thin steel wires stretched up above the Victorian ironwork of the bridge, discouraging anyone with thoughts of climbing over it. 'But not here on the piers.'

Siobhan risked another look, this time keeping her body pressed tight against the wall. Hundreds of feet below, out beyond the traffic, the river was so still and narrow it seemed not to flow at all but ooze from the vast mudbanks shelving down on either side. 'That really is creepy,' she said, shaking her head to dispel the dizziness it induced. 'How far down is it?'

'About two hundred and fifty feet to the road,' Walker said. 'A bit more to the water, depending on the time of day. The Avon has a big tidal range, a difference of at least thirty feet between high and low tide. That's why you see those mudbanks now, but in a few hours' time they'll be completely submerged again. It's another thing that helped us place your guy.'

'How do you mean?'

'Like I said, Mr Horgan's case was a slightly unusual one for us. Nobody saw him go over. When his body was washed up at Nelson Point, a couple of miles downriver, we knew he had to have come off a bridge because of the injuries he sustained. Virtually every bone in his body was ...' She hesitated, then came back at it from another direction. 'You know, hitting the water from this height is like smashing into a brick wall at speed. People think they'll drown, but it's the sudden stop that kills them.'

Walker let out a long breath and rubbed her eyes like she was about to explain something even she found complex. 'It's almost impossible to get over those wires without attracting attention. Even then you need to be a bit of a gymnast. The CCTV on the bridge is good, and there are guys on duty in the toll booths at either end, but the thing is, generally, if you don't go over the wires, you don't go in the water. The only other option is to jump from one of the piers, but as you can see, there's no water below us here. And you'd be amazed how off-putting that can be. Before they get here, people imagine a nice clean end in water, and instead they're faced with rocks, bushes, concrete and cars.'

Siobhan glanced back at the Samaritans sign, then over the wall again, cautiously. She noticed now the trees, scrub and rocky outcrops on the cliff face beneath her. Most of all, she took in the significance of the roadway running noisily below. The river was at least thirty or forty feet further out than it at first appeared to be and, directly underneath the brick pier,

80

the road was covered by a wide, grassed-over concrete canopy. To prevent suicides from falling on road users, Siobhan imagined, and causing death and havoc down there, too.

She smiled wanly. 'So, what – Horgan jumped from the other side?'

It looked like the water ran right underneath there.

But Walker shook her head again. 'It's deceptive, isn't it, but that's even further back from the water. See the railway line running along the bottom over there? And there's a footpath outside that again.'

Siobhan squinted, adjusting her eyes to the perspective, stomach turning at the thought of the leap, the falling body, and saw that Walker was right.

'So what did happen?'

'That's just it. We're only guessing, but we reckon that he must have actually jumped from exactly where we're standing now. There was some temporary scaffolding blocking the CCTV camera here that week, so we could have missed him that way. We think he must have hit that shoulder of rock sticking out down there.' She leant out over the wall, pointing, and Siobhan had no choice but to look over again, determined not to let the vertigo get the better of her.

'The guys reckon if he hit it at just the right angle, it could've sent him spinning out over the road and into the river. It's, like, a million to one and the only place where the angles would work. Even at that, he'd have to have done it at high tide, and there was one, around eleven p.m. that Saturday. Otherwise he'd have landed in the mud on the bank and been visible there for hours. His body would have been spotted by someone for sure.'

'Jesus, are you serious? Is it even possible?'

'There's no other explanation for it,' Walker said. 'The dates and tides work. And if you look hard at that spot on the rock, you can see a patch of discoloration, a smear maybe, that could be some tissue deposits, but we haven't been able to organise a climber to go down and get a sample. Suicides don't come high on the list of priorities where resources are concerned, I'm sorry to say.'

The thought of someone hanging on a rope above that void, scraping bits of human flesh off a rock made Siobhan's stomach squirm again.

'So you're saying there's definitely nothing suspicious about his death?'

Walker gave her a confidently affirmative smile. 'Nothing at all. Everything adds up: the injuries, where the body was found, all that. Matches the pathologist's report, which says the body featured the kinds of injuries – blunt-force trauma, tissue abrasion and multiple minor fractures – consistent with precisely this kind of fall.'

Walker looked out over the wall again, down along the river to where it disappeared behind a distant bluff. 'The balance of probability always pointed to him jumping from here, but with no eyewitness or CCTV to confirm it, we couldn't be certain. They get jumpers off the Severn Crossing, too, a few miles up the Bristol Channel, and if the tides are right, the bodies float back up this way sometimes. Finding Mr Horgan's car here was the last piece in the jigsaw. It pretty much clinches it.'

7

Sweeney was already at her desk, looking buffed and fresh from the gym, when Mulcahy got in to the office at an hour even he considered early. She was deeply involved in a phone conversation, which he took to be personal, his unexpected appearance eliciting an embarrassed grin and a waggle of her fingers as he walked past her and into his office. He'd heard rumours of a boyfriend, currently out on the west coast of America, Santa Barbara or somewhere, working in the kind of IT job it was no longer possible to find at home in Ireland. It had to be getting on for midnight out there, he reckoned.

Mulcahy switched his computer on, struggling to shake off the torpor of a bad night's sleep as he waited for the screen to boot up, the coffee refusing to have any reviving effect on him despite the extra shot he'd had them put in it. Things hadn't gone well with Orla the night before. He'd been twenty minutes late, not ten, and he'd had to spend at least half that time again apologising for leaving her waiting alone in the restaurant. He couldn't blame her: the place had been absolutely heaving with couples and gangs out for a good night. Sitting on her own at the table, she'd looked as solitary as a lighthouse when he'd walked in.

It hadn't helped, either, that he'd been more than a little unsettled by Siobhan Fallon's call. Orla had guessed something was up almost from the start. Some instinct in her awakened, she had switched from hurt at his lateness to concern over his inattention, more than once asking if he was okay, if there was anything wrong. Not exactly a recipe for romance. They'd struggled to keep the conversation going over dinner, and it had stalled into complete silence in his car. Then, when he dropped her off at her house in Dalkey, she'd hit him with the big one. She wanted to take a step back, she said, take things a little more slowly. She wasn't sure they were as compatible as she'd first thought. She'd given him a long, meaningful look then, and he got the impression he was supposed to be arguing the toss with her, making a case for togetherness. But all he felt was tiredness. Or was it numbness? And right at that moment, in the dark outside her house, the only honest emotion he felt was that she was right. It probably wouldn't hurt to pull back a bit, and if it did, they'd know they shouldn't be apart. Then he'd driven home, thinking not of Orla but of Siobhan Fallon, the entire way.

Knocking back the last of his coffee, he tried to push all that from his mind as he got to grips with the upcoming Joint Task Force meeting. Rosscarbery Bay wasn't the only case they would be reviewing, and there were a number of policy issues up for discussion that also required his input. It was getting on for ten thirty when a knock on the glass partition wall made him look up.

Sweeney, looking pleased with herself.

'Boss, I just had a long chat with that German woman I told you about last night, name of Erica Farber. Everything she says checks out. She was definitely there the night of June seventh because she flew back to Frankfurt the following day for her eldest daughter's birthday. She'd even gone to the trouble of digging her plane ticket out after seeing the TV programme, so she could read me the flight number to check it myself.'

'How very Teutonic and efficient of her.'

'That's what I thought,' Sweeney replied. As ever, irony glanced off her like a ricochet.

'So did you get anything useful from her?'

'I'm not sure, but maybe, yeah. I was thinking about what you said last night – you know, about why she took any notice of this vehicle going down to the pier in the first place. So I asked her and she said it was because the trailer was so new-looking.'

'And?'

'She said she was sitting out on the verandah, enjoying the last sunset of the holiday, when a flash from the road caught her eye. It was this shiny trailer being towed by an ancient green Land Rover. Seems she was amused by the contrast between the manky Land Rover and the spotless aluminium trailer. Then she noticed how long the thing was – about five or six metres, she reckoned – and she could see it was completely empty. Why go to the pier with a big, long, empty trailer? Especially when he almost got stuck going round the next bend.'

Mulcahy had been out on that road to Rosscarbery Pier.

The day after the *Atlantean* was seized he had driven down to Cork and out west along the coast to Baltimore, the harbour to which the seized yacht had been brought by the navy. He wanted to inspect the yacht for himself and witness the extraordinary quantity of cocaine that had been retrieved. All the time thinking this could have been his gig, how he could have been the senior investigating officer on the biggest drugs seizure in Irish history – *would* have been, if it hadn't been for getting caught up with Sean Rinn and Siobhan bloody Fallon the year before. Then he'd driven back to Rosscarbery with a couple of lads from the Cork investigation team, taken a look around the wide, scenic bay they reckoned was the intended landing place, with its pretty beach on one side and pier and slipway on the other. A perfect, secluded spot for offloading a large consignment of narcotics.

'Couldn't the trailer have been for a boat?' he said to her. 'There's a slipway down by the pier.'

'Well, no, that's just it. She was very specific. Said it wasn't a boat trailer but more of a flatbed type. A "*landwirtschaftliche Anhänger*" was the phrase she used, meaning "agricultural trailer". Which, again, you know, is weird, because there is no farm along there. She says hers was the last house out on the pier road.'

'It'd have to be one hell of a coincidence, that night of all nights, especially with the light failing when she saw it. The *Atlantean* was sighted just before dusk.' Mulcahy rubbed a contemplative paw around his chin. 'And it definitely came back empty?'

Sweeney nodded enthusiastically. 'That's what she said.'

'Christ, they'd never be cheeky enough to transport the

best part of a tonne of cocaine on an open trailer, would they?'

'Why not?' Sweeney shrugged. 'It's not like anyone would have recognised what it was. Those bales off the *Atlantean* could've been anything. Lots of fertiliser goes out wrapped like that – peat moss, manure, silage. It all looks the same wrapped in white plastic. And anyway, he could've had a big tarp in the back of the Land Rover for all we know.'

'Or maybe they weren't planning on moving it very far,' Mulcahy added. 'You keep saying "he". Did this woman get a look at the driver?'

'No. That's just how she put it. I did ask, but she said she didn't see who was driving. There could have been others in the Land Rover for all she knows. She couldn't say either way.'

'Damn.'

'Yeah.' Sweeney nodded. 'There was one other thing, though.'

'There's more?'

Sweeney grinned. 'She said when the guy got stuck going round the bend, she went into the house to get her binoculars for a better look.'

'Are you serious?'

'Yeah, but don't get too excited. By the time she came out he was on his way again. All she got a look at was the back of the trailer. She didn't get a number plate, but she did say there was some kind of logo on it – a big red "H", with a name across the middle.'

'Which was?'

'She couldn't remember. But I was thinking, if it was

printed on the trailer, it could be some kind of brand name, or distributor, maybe. In which case, it shouldn't take too much tracing. I mean, how many people make and sell that kind of trailer? Not many, right?'

'Absolutely,' he said, getting out of his chair now. 'And if it was that new, maybe it was bought locally. If we trace a dealer, they might have a payment record.'

He brushed his fingers through his hair, thinking hard, then looked over at Sweeney standing there, grinning back at him. 'Jesus, well done, Aisling. This could be really useful.'

On the way to Walker's office, Siobhan stared out of the car window at the Georgian terraces and ornate Victorian mansions lining so many of the residential streets. It wasn't all that different from some of the nicer parts of Dublin, she supposed, except that more of these houses were on a grander scale. She had flicked quickly through an in-flight magazine while the plane was landing, read the intro to a dull piece about how Bristol had become enormously wealthy, centuries before, on the back of the slave trade and the Industrial Revolution. On this evidence, the entire population must have been loaded.

'These houses are something else. Is all of Bristol like this?'

Walker laughed. 'You must be kidding. Most of Bristol's a tip, with a few nice parts scattered in between, mostly around here – Clifton, Redland and Cotham. What's Dublin like?'

'Oh, much the same. There's good and bad in it. You've never been?'

'Always meant to. I hear Ireland's a lot of fun.'

'Maybe if you're visiting,' Siobhan said, less enthusiastically than she intended, and they both laughed.

For the rest of the short journey Siobhan filled Walker in about Gemma Kearney. The policewoman listened attentively and nodded or shook her head now and then, but said little other than that she'd had a look through the items found in the car but hadn't come across any reference to Gemma, or any indication that Horgan hadn't been alone. The paperwork relating to his flights and hotel contained nothing to suggest he'd been travelling with someone else. As far as Walker was concerned, she'd found nothing to suggest the case needed further examination, but of course if Siobhan could present her with evidence to the contrary . . . For the first time, Siobhan wondered if maybe she wasn't the one being played here.

Five minutes later Walker's opinion of Bristol appeared to be borne out when they got to the bottom of a steep hill and drove into what felt like the centre of the city – an ugly, bustling, traffic-choked, mishmash of every kind of building imaginable, with the exception of anything fine or pretty. They pulled into a yard at the back of a hulking grey 1960s office block.

'Home sweet home,' Walker said, locking the car and punching a security code into a numerical keypad beside the building's steel-reinforced back door. Inside, she signed Siobhan in at reception and took her up to the fifth floor, then asked her to wait in a small interview room while she went off to get something.

Almost immediately, as Siobhan sat there in the empty, airless room, with nothing to distract her, a creeping sensation of tiredness began to overtake her. The early flight, like the journey to Cork the day before, had sapped her energy. It was like all the vitality was earthing out of her, straight into the floor. She thought of how much energy she used to have, how it was what had marked her out from her fellow journalism students in Rathmines. Her determination, her persistence . . . Her eyelids were beginning to flutter when the door opened and Walker entered with a small cardboard evidence box in one hand and a leather holdall in the other, both of which she placed on the table.

'Are you okay?' she asked, scanning Siobhan's face. 'Can I get you some water or something?'

'No, I'm fine. It's just the early flight. I'm not . . . I mean, it's okay, honestly.'

'I'd get you a coffee from the machine but you might not survive it. It's pure swill.'

Siobhan smiled, amused by the thought of swill in a cop shop, and began to feel livelier just imagining what might be in that bag, that box. 'I'm fine, really. Don't think you have to be nice to me. The Gardai never are.'

'I'm not usually this helpful, either,' Walker said, 'but after we spoke, the first time, I looked you up online. Just to be sure of who I was dealing with, you know? And I saw what's up there about you. What happened to you, I mean. On the cross and all that. Are you sure you're okay?'

Siobhan lifted her head. The last thing she felt like talking about now was that. 'Thanks, honestly. It was just the early start. We gotta move on or we get nowhere, right?'

Walker didn't take the hint. 'I read your articles on the Net. It's a horrific thing to happen to anybody. I just wanted to say that, as a woman, I think you're extraordinary. To have survived it, I mean, and to be back at work so soon.'

That took Siobhan by surprise. The ball of stress that was lodged in her gut clenched momentarily, then eased noticeably. 'Thank you,' she said, with a gasp, almost laughing from the relief, 'but to be honest, I didn't have much to do with the surviving of it. That was down to the guys who rescued me and the doctors and nurses in the hospital.'

'No way. *That* I do not believe,' Walker said, jabbing the air with both hands. 'Most people I know, man or woman, would be off work for ever after something like that. A colleague of mine was stabbed three years ago, nothing like what you went through, and she's still out. No, you were the one who got you back on your feet. You were the one who decided not to let it stop you.'

Siobhan had to think about that one. She'd spent every day for a year now promising herself that she wouldn't let what Rinn did to her ruin her life, but at this precise moment she wasn't so sure she hadn't been fooling herself all along. 'Maybe you're right,' she said, 'but it's not what I want to be remembered for, you know?'

'You wrote a book about it, didn't you?'

Siobhan shrugged, unsure whether Walker was being sarcastic or not. 'Yeah, I did. It's out next week. I thought it might put the lid on it for me.'

'Closure, like?'

Siobhan nodded. 'That was the idea. Sometimes I think the door's still wide open.'

'No, no, it's not.' Walker reached over and placed a hand on Siobhan's. 'I see victims every day. Most of them grab the stick they've been hit with and hold on to it like it's their most precious possession. It beats them up from inside. That's so not you – I know it. Seriously, I'm going to be first in line to buy your book when it comes out over here.'

Siobhan smiled and pulled her hand away as politely as she could.

'No, don't go buying it,' she said. 'I'll send you a copy myself.'

'I'd really like that,' Walker said, taking a step back and smiling. 'Anyway, enough of the sisterhood stuff, yeah?' Instantly her voice was more brusque and businesslike, and she turned towards the table and swept her hand over the leather bag and the evidence box. 'Like I said, I absolutely wouldn't do this normally, but I've got a meeting to go to, so I'm going to leave you here for half an hour while I'm gone and you can look through this lot, if you like. I'm only doing it 'cos I've already gone through it carefully myself and I know there's nothing personal in here that you shouldn't be seeing, okay? And because I know you're not going to rat me out by writing that you had unsupervised access to these items – which you won't, by the way.' Walker pointed a long, confident finger at a CCTV camera mounted just below the ceiling in one corner of the room. 'It's on, so nothing leaves the room, Siobhan. Not even for a second. Right?'

'Right,' Siobhan said. 'Whatever you say.'

Walker went back to the door and smiled again as she opened it. 'So long as that's understood.'

8

The sun beat pleasantly warm on his back as Mulcahy hurried through the newly opened Garda Memorial Garden at the back of Dublin Castle, past the high glass entrance to the Chester Beatty Library of Oriental Arts and round the corner to the doorway of the old Ship Street Barracks, a pre-boom-time restoration project that had produced the only offices in the castle complex considered swish enough for Assistant Commissioner Donal Murtagh. As head of the Garda National Drugs Unit, Murtagh was the closest Mulcahy had to an immediate boss. He was also, to all intents and purposes, Mulcahy's saviour.

It was Murtagh who, on being promoted to his current eminence the year before, had rescued Mulcahy from suspension and the threat of being stuck in a dead-end Sex Crimes post. It was he who had insisted that the GNDU should have a dedicated International Liaison Unit, and who had appointed Mulcahy to head it up. Why squander the talent of the only Garda inspector ever to spend seven years with Europol's Narcotics Intelligence Agency, Murtagh had argued to a resistant Garda review board. Just because he'd had one lapse in judgement? Amazingly, the review board had agreed with him.

Mulcahy trotted up the stairs to the second floor, just in time to meet Murtagh emerging from his outer office, still rattling orders to his PA inside. He was a man who radiated authority in uniform despite his comparatively short stature and narrow, acetic frame. He couldn't have been more than five ten, but the bristling sense of energy that emanated from him always seemed to add a couple of inches in sheer presence. He shot his hand out as soon as he saw Mulcahy approaching, giving him a brisk but warm handshake.

'Good man, Mike. Come on, we'd better get inside. The rest of them are here already. But remind me I need to talk to you about something afterwards, okay?'

Murtagh's office adjoined a massive meeting room that had a table long enough to seat all twenty-two regular members of the Joint Task Force on Drugs, as well as the video-conferencing facilities needed to cater for members who, inevitably, couldn't always make it in person. This was the monthly forum in which all the news, enforcement strategies, policy initiatives and major drugs investigations were debated by senior members of the Garda Siochana, the Revenue Commissioners and the Naval Service, the main objective being communication, intelligence-sharing and just plain keeping everyone up to speed.

Today's meeting, though, was to be a more intimate affair, a Garda-only offshoot dealing specifically with the Rosscarbery Bay case, a number of other policy matters raised as a result of it and a string of more minor seizures made along the south coast over the summer. Mulcahy's role would be to provide an update on the intelligence he'd received from the Dutch regarding the identification of the *Atlantean*. It was a role the Southern Region investigation team could have fulfilled just as easily, as they were doing the follow-up, but for some reason Murtagh had insisted on him being present. As they entered the meeting room, the hum of conversation dropped as Murtagh did the rounds and sat down at the head of the table. There were only nine people present out of the usual cohort, plus, Mulcahy noticed, a couple of faces from the Cork team sitting in via the video link on the wall.

He pulled up a chair and zoned out momentarily as Murtagh embarked on the preamble, concentrating instead on what he was planning to say and wondering whether to share Aisling's discovery regarding the trailer on the pier road or, as instinct nudged him, to wait and let her make something more of it herself. He looked up and cleared his throat as he heard Murtagh mentioning his name.

'Okay, moving on to the first item, gentlemen. I've asked DI Mulcahy from the International Liaison Unit to give us an update on some potentially exciting intelligence he's received from our colleagues in the Netherlands regarding the Rosscarbery Bay seizure. And while we're at it, thanks, Mike, for the briefing paper you sent around last night. If only all our colleagues would show such consideration and concision, we'd get through these meetings a hell of a lot quicker.'

A ripple of hearty laughter rumbled through the room, undercut somewhat by the steely glare Murtagh swept around the table, leaving no one in any doubt that despite the smiles, he was making a serious point. Mulcahy, meanwhile, was doing his best not to look mortified for being made to look such an arse-licker, especially when most of the work that went into it hadn't even been his.

'Okay,' Mulcahy said, leaning forward in his chair and waiting for everyone to look up again. 'Those of you who read the brief will be familiar with this. Those of you who didn't but want the details, you'll find them in there. The main point is this: when the *Atlantean* was seized off Rosscarbery Bay back in June, the initial assumption was that she'd sailed up from either the Caribbean or West Africa, just like the other seaborne cocaine consignments we've intercepted in recent years. However, over the succeeding months not a single shred of evidence emerged to back up that assumption. Not from the Maritime Analysis and Operations Centre in Lisbon, or the US Drug Enforcement Administration, or the Caribbean port authorities. Not even from our good friends in Interpol. In fact, this was possibly the coldest trail ever left in the wake of such a major seizure, and certainly in terms of our experience. Fortunately, though, thanks to the work of our colleagues in Southern Region, a partial serial number retrieved from the *Atlantean*'s engine, which we circulated a few weeks ago, has now led to what could be our first major lead in this regard.'

Mulcahy went on to explain how one of his contacts in the Criminele Inlichtingen Eenheid – the Dutch criminal intelligence service – by giving the matter considerably more than the usual effort, had traced the engine's serial number, partial as it was, to a private boatyard in the southern Netherlands port of Vlissingen, where an identical yacht, sailing under a different name, was laid up for a couple of months, only to set sail again a few days before the *Atlantean* was spotted off the Cork coast.

'We are pretty *confident* now,' Mulcahy emphasised, 'for the technical reasons I've detailed in the brief, that this was the same thirty-six-foot ocean-going yacht that we all know as the *Atlantean*. And, as a result of further information retrieved last week regarding specific damage that appears on the *Atlantean*'s engine casing, Southern Region will now be sending members of the Cork investigation team over to requisition the relevant supporting documents and take statements with the help of the Dutch authorities. Probably the most interesting single item of information we've unearthed so far, but not yet confirmed, is that the Dutch manager of the boatyard had the impression the owner of the yacht, who he didn't deal with directly, could well have been Irish. And he knows someone he thinks can provide us with a description.'

That was the bombshell Mulcahy *hadn't* put in his briefing paper and he was gratified by the murmur of surprise and interest it elicited around the room. He let it linger for a moment or two longer, before looking up towards the screen on the wall, at the now irritated-looking individual whose face occupied the right-hand side of the video-conferencing link. Detective Superintendent Sean O'Grady was the senior investigating officer on the Cork team. He was also the man who'd got the head of Southern Region job, and the promotion, when Mulcahy had been forced to withdraw his candidacy the year before.

'Is there anything you'd like to add to that, Sean?' Mulcahy smiled, knowing he'd scored a direct hit with that one.

*

The leather holdall was expensively made, as were the few items of clothing it contained, bearing labels from design houses like Zegna, Boss, D&G and Guest. Horgan certainly liked his clothes. The same could be said for his brogues. Beautiful, barely scuffed tan leather, they looked to be hand-made and Siobhan wondered idly what he'd had on his feet when he stood on the parapet wall at the suspension bridge, contemplating his end. There was nothing else in the holdall, nothing of any interest at any rate, not even a toilet bag. So she moved on to the evidence box, tipping its contents carefully out onto the table. These were the loose items taken from the car. A pair of aviator-style Gucci sunglasses, a burgundy passport with the Irish harp in gold on the cover, a small Moleskine notebook, a couple of blister packs of paracetamol, an unopened can of Red Bull, some road maps and a bundle of receipts and printouts held together with an elastic band.

Siobhan was immediately drawn to the passport, which was clean, smooth and unmarked externally, and obviously of fairly recent issue, or re-issue, more likely. She opened it and stared for a while at the photo of Cormac Horgan. He'd been a reasonably good-looking guy. His face was nicely made, the eyes blue, the hair a sandy blond in a nondescript, estate-agenty, country-barber cut. If it hadn't been for that and the slightly receding chin, he might have been almost handsome in a wet, Robert Pattinson kind of way. There had been a nicer shot of him, younger, smiling, published alongside her story in the *Sunday Herald*, but he hadn't looked particularly happy in that, either, despite the smile. She studied the passport photo again and for a second saw his features morph into a scream, felt the air rush over his skin and hair as he fell, as she had fallen, then shuddered and looked away. She focused on the other details on the page: his date of birth – 17 November 1980; his place of birth – Cork; his middle name – Patrick. Finally, she flicked through the pale blue, empty visa pages before putting the passport aside, a vaguely sick feeling in her stomach.

She picked up the notebook, hoping it might be some kind of diary, but she was disappointed. Its pages were unused apart from the first two, which were covered in lists of letters and numbers. She flicked through the book of road maps for the British Isles and Europe. It looked to be fairly well thumbed. He certainly hadn't bought it just for this trip. There were notes and addresses scrawled in his indecipherable handwriting on the inside covers, front and back. Tucked in between the pages were AA Route Finder printouts of journey instructions, one from Amsterdam south through Belgium and France to the ferry terminal at Calais, another describing the route from Cork to somewhere called Liscannor in County Clare. But there was nothing relating to Bristol, or anywhere else in the UK.

Except for the four loose leaves of paper, folded and tucked under the cover: three printouts and a car-hire agreement. The first two were electronic boarding passes for round-trip flights from Dublin to Bristol, outbound on Friday 3 September, returning on Sunday 5 September. She wondered whether that in itself, the return flight, wasn't an indication that he had never actually planned to kill himself, but then decided it probably meant nothing; people with suicide on their minds probably weren't the most rational to begin with, anyway. The third piece of paper was an online hotel reservation for the Lennox Hotel, Berkeley Square, Bristol. Pre-paid, for two nights, Friday 3 and Saturday 4 September. Nothing strange there. But when she opened and examined the last item, the Avis car-hire agreement, one thing did strike her immediately. It was an original docket, not a printout like the others. Which meant he probably hadn't decided to rent the car in advance, that he must only have decided to do so after arriving in Bristol, and at considerably more cost than booking online.

She looked more closely again at the agreement, saw that the car had been picked up at eleven o'clock on the Saturday morning at Avis's 'Bristol Centre' office. That chimed with the last-minute idea: if he'd planned to hire a car, why hadn't he done so at the airport the night before? She turned her attention to the bundle of receipts. The man had clearly been an accountant to the core, asking for and keeping paperwork for every expense. She rummaged through them, looking for one that might be a taxi fare for the journey from the airport into town. There was one taxi slip, but obviously it had been only a short hop. Nothing like the amount she had paid to come in from the airport that morning. Horgan didn't seem like a man who'd contemplate using public transport, but even if he had, there was no bus ticket, either. Had someone collected him from the airport?

She stared at the pile of receipts, looking for a revelation, but all she saw were a few restaurant bills and corner-shop purchases, and a scattering of others for items she couldn't readily make out. On top was a bar bill from somewhere called the Gold Bar. It looked a bit pricey for drinks for one person. She checked her watch. Already twenty-five minutes of her allotted half-hour had elapsed. No time for taking notes. She pulled out her phone, flattened the receipt on the table between her outstretched finger and thumb, took a snap of it and then moved on to the next, framing each with her fingers, working her way through them.

'I know none of ye need me to tell you that this stretch of coastline has been targeted for years as an easy route for narcotics into the EU, but having worked the frontline down there for a decade myself, I can honestly say we've made some real, tangible headway in recent years. Thanks in large part to this Task Force's strategic initiatives in relation to effective naval patrols, better intelligence-gathering on the ground and, more than anything, increased awareness and cooperation from the public.'

Assistant Commissioner Murtagh was winding up the meeting with some motivational spiel. 'So, while it's important not to forget that Rosscarbery Bay represents a significant victory for us in prevention terms, it's equally important from a public-perception viewpoint that we don't allow the organisers of such high-profile smuggling ventures to be seen to escape justice.'

Murtagh drew a long breath as everyone around the table nodded in agreement. 'Right, that about wraps it up for this session, unless anyone has anything else to contribute?'

There was a murmuring of negatives from around the table, then the usual commotion of coughing, sniffing and chatting as everyone stood up to leave. Mulcahy was pushing his chair back in place when he saw Murtagh break off from greeting the deputy head of the Criminal Assets Bureau.

'Mike, hang back. In my office for a minute, yeah?'

'Sure.' Mulcahy nodded, remembering what Murtagh had said to him before the meeting about wanting a chat. He ambled down the corridor and into the large, comfortably appointed office, past Murtagh's stony-faced PA.

'I'm going to wait for him inside,' he said to her, giving her no chance to object as he strode into the inner sanctum and over to the window beside Murtagh's impressive carved oak desk. He stared out at the sun-drenched view the window afforded of the Memorial Garden, wondering if the good weather would last until the weekend. All that talk of boats and coastal waters had fired him up to get over to the marina in Dun Laoghaire and take *Seaspray* out on one last run before laying her up for winter. For the first time since early morning he thought of Orla, how at home she'd been on the boat, loving the wind and salt sea air almost as much as he did. In memory he could even taste it on her skin. Why hadn't they done more of *that* over the summer? Why hadn't the urge for fun and tenderness won out against this obsessive need to work?

'Thanks for waiting, Mike.' Murtagh gusted into the office like a sudden squall, pulling out his desk chair and bouncing into it like he was testing its hydraulics. 'You'll never make a politician, anyway, that's for sure. You couldn't resist giving O'Grady a poke with that thing about the Dutch boatyard man, could you?'

'O'Grady's big enough to take it,' Mulcahy countered.

'But not thick enough to just laugh it off. He's an okay lad, Mike. And you, above all, should appreciate the value of having friends in high places. It's not his fault he got the job you wanted.'

'I know, Donal, but Liam and myself had to work the Dutch damn hard to get that lead. I didn't want him taking the credit for it.'

'Hmm, maybe you have a point,' Murtagh conceded. 'That's actually what I wanted to talk to you about, sort of – about showing people that the International Liaison Unit is doing something worthwhile.'

Mulcahy almost choked. Where the hell had that jab come from?

'I'd have thought that was obvious to everyone, given that we've just made the first break the investigation's had in weeks.'

'I'm not talking about the Rosscarbery case, or even us on the Joint Task Force, for that matter. I'm talking about the people higher up. Does the commissioner know it, or the minister . . . ?' Murtagh trailed off, scratched distractedly at the back of his neck.

'You'd be in a better position to know that than me, Donal.' It sounded a bit glib, a bit arsey, and he instantly regretted saying it, but he also wanted to know where this was going now.

'Look, I'm not trying to get at you, Mike. I'm just trying to warn you. About that meeting that took place last week, over in the commissioner's office?'

Mulcahy said nothing, baffled but unwilling to admit it. He'd heard the rumours about some big-brass pow-wow in the Phoenix Park, but he'd been too busy, head down, working, to take much notice.

Murtagh cursed beneath his breath. 'It was a budget meeting, *the* budget meeting, the one about the cuts.'

'Okay,' Mulcahy said, although he was definitely thinking now that it wouldn't be.

'You've seen the news. They've doubled the deficit-reduction targets – €15 billion instead of €7 billion off public spending over the next four years. Christ, that's you and me, Mike, and it's not like there's anything left to cut.'

Murtagh sat back in his chair, and for the first time ever Mulcahy thought he looked almost defeated. 'I thought I'd have some clout when I was promoted. Instead I step into the job just as the whole country's going bust, and all I end up with is an axe and instructions to lay waste all around me.' He broke off again, wiped his palms and fingers down over his cheeks and jaw before bunching his fists and quietly but firmly striking the leather on his desk. 'We're not talking thin slices, Mike. All the fat's gone already. Now it's amputations. And before we even got in the room last week, some fucker had convinced the commissioner that the Drugs Unit could take more pain.'

'But that's bullshit,' Mulcahy said. Staff numbers were already so depleted much of the time the GNDU offices looked half empty.

'Of course it is. And like a complete novice I made the mistake of trotting out the line about false economies. The commissioner totally lost his rag. Had a real go at me, said even he knew of examples of where "substantive economies" could be achieved. Which is when he mentioned the ILU.'

'What?' Mulcahy was staggered. 'But we've only been up and running nine months.'

'Which, from his point of view, makes it all the easier to shut you down again. Look, the economy's fucked and we're all fighting over the same dwindling pot of cash. There're no easy decisions left. Your problem is that you're not the most visible of presences. Like you said yourself, other people get the credit for your hard work. And axing an entire unit looks great on the balance sheet. The minister won't even know there's only four of you in it. All he'll see is the headline figure.'

'Is that it, then? We're finished? Jesus, Donal, you're talking like it's a done deal.'

'No, I'm not. That's what I'm saying. Nothing was settled. Everyone else at that meeting got it in the neck as well as me. And yours was far from the only unit mentioned. I know how valuable your work is, Mike. For me, that's not an issue. What I'm saying is, if you ever had a back-of-the-drawer plan to convince the big boys you're a vital cog in their machine, now's the time to dust it off and put it into action, okay?'

9

'Any idea what this is about?' Siobhan asked, holding up the Moleskine notebook, open on its two used pages, when Walker came back into the room.

The sergeant peered at it like she hadn't really given any thought to it before, then shrugged. 'Road directions, looks like. There's "M4" and "M32" written there – those are the main routes into Bristol.'

Siobhan looked again. It made sense: roads, junctions, directions. Horgan had hired a car, brought his map book. Maybe he planned a journey. She could check it out later, see if he'd gone anywhere interesting. She took a picture of the two pages and did her best to look confused when Walker raised an eyebrow.

'When I said nothing leaves the room, I meant it,' Walker said, irritated.

'Oh, of course, yeah, sorry,' Siobhan said, feigning a well-practised innocence. 'I only took a couple. I'll delete them if you like.'

As if.

But Walker didn't seem to be listening to her, like she was

distracted, making her mind up about something else. Siobhan slipped her phone into her jacket pocket. Out of sight out of mind.

'So that was it?' she asked, as much to fill the silence as anything. 'There was nothing else in the car?'

'I wasn't going to show you this,' Walker said, holding out something that Siobhan hadn't noticed she'd been clasping in her hand all along. Something rigid, oblong and black, wrapped in a clear plastic evidence bag. Siobhan's heart leapt when she recognised what it was: a mobile phone. She shot her hand out to take it, but Walker pulled back.

'No way, Siobhan. I can't let you have this. We found it in the side pocket of the car, out of power, but I charged it up overnight. Everything's on here since Mr Horgan died, or went missing, which is what most of these people thought he was. Missing as in a he'll-turn-up-soon kind of way. Emails, phone messages, texts. There's some distressing stuff on here.'

Siobhan was suddenly conscious of the fact that she was salivating. She could visualise it already, laid out across a cracking two-page spread. The story of a suicide's phone. All the pain. All the heartache. All the grief. It would be such a shit-hot story. She could see Paddy Griffin getting a hard-on just hearing about it.

'And *way* too sensitive and personal for any journalist to get hold of,' Walker said, smashing that fantasy to smithereens.

Siobhan could barely contain her disappointment, but she could see from the set of the policewoman's jaw that there was definitely going to be no wavering on that point. Walker had no intention of walking out of the room and leaving her alone with this one.

107

'So why show it to me?' Siobhan said, not quite pouting but the implication was there.

'Because I had another look, just now, and there was one thing on here that I thought you should see.'

'What?' Siobhan asked, eyebrows rising, clouds parting again. 'Something from Gemma?'

'Not as such.' Walker was peering through the plastic, tapping at the screen on the phone. 'Just this.'

She held it up so that Siobhan could see the backlit screen through the evidence bag. It looked like a page from the phone's contacts book, but what she saw made Siobhan's hopes die as quickly as they'd risen again. All that was there were Gemma Kearney's name, address and phone details, exactly the same ones Mrs Kearney had given her the day before.

This time Siobhan didn't bother concealing her feelings. She tutted loudly. 'I've got all that already.'

Walker ignored the display of petulance. 'I thought you wanted proof that they were still in touch. That's it, isn't it? The phone's a recent model. He can't have had it for very long.'

'Yeah, I guess,' Siobhan said, thinking that was actually a good point. But it didn't get her any further, did it?

'That's just for starters, anyway,' Walker said, smiling again. 'What you really want to see is this.'

She tapped at the screen and again held the phone out for Siobhan to see. This time the page was from the phone's built-in organiser, from the diary section, and headed 'Saturday 4 September', the second night of Horgan's stay in Bristol. But it was what was written beneath the date that took Siobhan's breath away.

'Fuck me,' she whispered, almost to herself. 'Does that say what I think it says?'

Walker came round and stood beside Siobhan, so the two of them could look at the screen together. Siobhan squinted through the plastic again. There was no doubting what it said: 'G – CSB, 9 p.m.' And beneath it was a phone number.

'"G" for "Gemma",' Siobhan said. 'What do you reckon "CSB" stands for?'

'Well, if it's what *you* are thinking, that would have to be "Clifton Suspension Bridge", wouldn't it?'

'And what are you thinking?'

'Nothing. I'm keeping an open mind,' Walker insisted.

'Do you think maybe she didn't turn up, and that's why he . . . ?' Siobhan trailed off, thinking it through.

'It might be one possibility.'

'A possibility? Come on. I mean, that's definitely around the time he died, right?'

Walker held her pale palms up in a gesture of surrender. 'Roughly. The pathologist's estimate for time of death was twelve hours before or after noon on Sunday 5 September. That's slightly outside the timeframe, but the body was in the water for a long time, and TODs are difficult at the best of times.'

Siobhan looked at the phone again and then at Walker. 'Meaning?'

'Meaning nothing.' Walker was sounding a little exasperated now. 'Meaning anything. I just thought you'd want to see it. It doesn't make any difference to me. No skin off my nose if you tear off on a wild goose chase; but if you do track this Gemma girl down, and it turns out she was in the area at the time, obviously I'd like to talk to her.'

'What about the number?' Siobhan said. 'Have you tried it?'

Walker shrugged. 'Do you recognise it? It looks like a UK number to me.'

'It's not the one Horgan had in his address book for Gemma.'

'So, odds on, it's not even her.'

'Maybe we should just try it,' Siobhan said, and, fast as a gunslinger, drew her phone from her pocket again and started tapping in the number.

'No way. Don't you dare,' Walker said, snatching Horgan's phone away. 'Leave it. I'll do it. But not on this. I don't want to give anyone a heart attack, calling from a dead man's number.' She took her own phone out of her pocket and dialled, waiting, head cocked, for an answer.

'Anything?' Siobhan whispered impatiently.

Walker shook her head. 'Nothing. It just rings and rings. It's not even connected to an answering service.'

'Can't you trace it? With GPS or something?'

Walker treated Siobhan to a withering look of scepticism. 'No, Siobhan. That would take time and money, and, like I said before, I see no good reason to spend any more of Avon and Somerset Constabulary's resources on this. Or mine, for that matter. This is as much as I can do for you. It ends here.'

'Jesus, what a waste of time this has been,' Siobhan said, frustrated with herself as much as anything else.

'Thanks a bunch,' Walker said. 'But I did try to warn you last night. It's just one of those sad stories. Finding the car was never going to tell us much more than we knew already.'

'There was one thing, though,' Siobhan said, clutching at

110

straws. She pointed at the reservation form on the table. 'It told us the hotel Horgan stayed in, didn't it?'

'Sure. The Lennox. Very chic, very boutique, very pricey,' Walker confirmed. 'What about it?'

'Have you spoken to them there yet?'

'Earlier,' Walker said. 'Horgan paid in advance online, so they didn't even notice he hadn't checked out until one of the maids found some things of his still in the room. They said they emailed him, but, obviously, he never got back to them, so the few bits he left behind were just stuck in a cupboard for the last couple of weeks. I'm going over there in a minute to pick them up and send everything back to the next-of-kin together. But don't get your hopes up. They said there's nothing much there: a wash bag, a sweater, some other odds and sods.'

'Can I come over with you?'

'I don't think so, Siobhan,' Walker demurred. 'This is still official police business.'

But she hadn't said no. Not as such.

'All I want to do is see the place for myself,' Siobhan pleaded. 'I've come all the way over here and got nothing. Can't I just join you if you're going over anyway, rather than having to find the place for myself? I promise I won't say anything to anyone. I won't even come in with you, if you don't want me to.'

Walker puffed out her cheeks and shook her head slowly, the long waves of her hair moving stiffly. 'Shit, Siobhan, you're really pushing it here, but okay, all right, I'll show you where it is. But that's it. Then you go home, and none of this appears in your story, or I'll be in crap up to my neck. Okay?'

'You've got nothing to worry about on that score,' Siobhan said, pouting. 'Far as I can see, there isn't going to be any story.'

The Lennox Hotel was exactly as Walker had described it: small, stylish and expensive, tastefully remodelled from two large Georgian houses facing a lovely garden square. In the end, Walker didn't insist on Siobhan staying outside, providing she kept her mouth shut. Not that it made any difference. All they did was wait at reception while the manager went and got a carrier bag from her office. Walker's prediction regarding what would be in it also proved accurate. Nothing of interest: a brown leather wash bag containing shaving kit and a selection of half-used traveller's requisites, a rain jacket and a few more loose papers and receipts, including a torn Aer Lingus boarding pass. It was the latter that made Siobhan do a double-take when they took a closer look once they got back to Walker's car.

'I think I'm going mad here,' she said to Walker, who by now looked ready to believe it. 'This boarding pass, it's for Cork to Amsterdam.'

'What's the date on it?'

'Same date as he flew here, but half an hour earlier. Six thirty in the evening.'

'You're sure?' Walker was sounding more weary than sceptical.

'Of course. Look.' Siobhan leant across, holding up the scrap of paper. 'Friday 3 September, it says.'

Walker glanced at it and tutted as she pulled out into the traffic. 'There isn't even a name on it, Siobhan.'

She scanned the boarding pass again. 'That bit's been torn off.'

'So why assume it's his?' There was a definite note of irritation in Walker's voice now, but Siobhan wasn't really listening. She was too busy thinking.

'Why would anyone check in for a flight they weren't going on?'

'Who says he did?' Walker sighed. 'Believe me, Siobhan, I checked his flights as part of the ID process. He was on the seven p.m. flight out of Cork that evening.' She checked her mirror, then switched lanes in the heavy traffic. 'Maybe someone dropped it in Cork and he picked it up.'

'But why?' Siobhan was still staring at the boarding pass, specifically the word 'Electronic' printed along the top. Why would Horgan have picked up someone else's boarding pass? It just didn't add up.

Beside her, Walker sighed like this was the last thing in the world she wanted to be thinking about. 'Look, Siobhan, if there's one thing no one can dispute' – the implicit 'not even you' was left hanging in the air – 'it's that Horgan was here in Bristol. I helped pull his body out of the river, remember? And that's his shaving kit you're holding in your hand.'

Ford was sitting back, rocking his chair on its back legs, feet on his desk, tucking into what looked like a double-sized Mars bar in one hand, and a can of Fanta in the other. On seeing Mulcahy, he took a long swig from the can and swallowed noisily.

'That went well, then,' Ford said. 'You look like you've been shat on from a height.'

'Something like that,' Mulcahy said. 'Is Aisling around?'

'Still at lunch.' Ford stuffed the last of the Mars bar into his mouth and tossed the wrapper at the bin on the far side of the desk, punching the air when it dropped in dead centre. In one fluid movement he lowered his feet to the floor, dusted some crumbs from his T-shirt and swivelled his chair round to face Mulcahy straight on.

'Is that it for us on Rosscarbery Bay now? Do we just let the Cork lads sort out the rest of it and move on to something else?'

Mulcahy looked at him. Did everyone, even Liam, really think that other people always got the credit for the work done by the ILU? Had he been thinking it himself, albeit subconsciously, when he gave O'Grady that poke earlier? He considered telling Ford what he'd just heard from Murtagh, but dismissed the idea. Ford had passed up what might have been a career-making move to the Armed Response Unit to become his second in command. He'd go straight to the bottom of the pile again if the ILU shut up shop. And the same went for Sweeney and Duffy. Mulcahy knew it was up to him, and only him, to find a way out of the mess. If there was one. Best to proceed as normal for the moment.

'No, we'll need to have another word with the Dutch,' he said. 'Make sure they're completely up to speed before the Cork team get there. Aisling's come up with some interesting info about a vehicle going to the pier on the night of the seizure. If we leave her to follow that up, I think she'll make something good of it. There's plenty more mileage for us in Rosscarbery Bay. In the meantime we've got to get back to the Spanish about Declan Begley. Have you done up the draft memo on that?'

'I emailed it to you.' Ford grinned. 'It's only the one para-graph, telling them we conducted enquiries this end, as requested, but found nothing to indicate a Dublin connection to Begley's murder. Basically, giving them the old heave-ho, politely.'

'Okay, I'll have a look,' Mulcahy said. Ford's idea of polite didn't always accord with his own. 'Anything else?'

Ford dropped his voice to a lower register. 'That guy I was talking about last night, Solomons, I gave him a call while you were at your meeting. About Begley.'

'Oh yeah?' Mulcahy gestured at Ford to follow him into his office. He leant on the edge of his desk while Ford shut the door. 'So, what did he have to say?'

'Well, he's still with the Merseyside Major Crime Unit, all right, but he's going on secondment in a couple of days.'

'Lucky you caught him.'

'You can say that again. He's actually been working flat out on the Ronson murder this last couple of months, as local liaison for the SOCA team who're officially heading up the murder inquiry. So he was a bit jumpy even talking to me about it. It's a big deal for him, I suppose. SOCA's like the FBI for them, isn't it?'

'I suppose so,' Mulcahy said. 'So did you get a chance to run what McTiernan said about Begley past him? Did any of it check out?'

'He hadn't heard of Begley himself, not in terms of a con-nection with Ronson, but, like I said, I got the impression his focus was local, so I didn't push it. To be honest, what he was telling me about the Trevor Ronson inquiry was more inter-esting. You wouldn't believe the half of it.'

'Try me,' Mulcahy said, intrigued.

'A lot of it was about how big Ronson was and how much gear he was bringing into England.'

'They called him "King Cocaine",' Mulcahy said. 'That much I do know.'

'Right. So after a bit more chat Solomons starts telling me that SOCA are following a definite line of enquiry. He wasn't hugely forthcoming about it, but, to be honest, what he did say sounded mad, anyway.'

'How so?'

'Brace yourself,' Ford said. 'According to him, SOCA are working on the theory that one of the Colombian drugs cartels, the one based in Cali, had Ronson whacked.'

'They what?' Mulcahy wasn't sure he was hearing properly. 'Come off it, Liam. He's taking the piss.'

'That's what I thought, but he said it was absolutely straight up. And after I put the phone down, I was thinking, your man McTiernan said yesterday that Bingo had got himself into a hole he couldn't climb out of, and everyone was calling him a dead man walking. And I wondered, what if his death and Ronson's *are* connected? I mean, you're the one who said the way Bingo's body was left on that dump was a message. Well, maybe it was a message from the Cali Cartel – "Don't fuck with us."'

'That's a hell of a leap, Liam.' Still, Mulcahy's thoughts zapped straight to the conversation in the car with McTiernan the day before. What hadn't he been telling them? And why hadn't he returned his call?

'I know, but it would be just like the Bingo of old, wouldn't it?' Ford chuckled. 'He finds himself going up in the world,

116

plenty of dosh, powerful new friends and bang – it all blows up in his face. Literally, in this instance.'

'Say you didn't put any of this in your memo to the Spanish.'

''Course not,' Ford said. 'It wouldn't be for us to say, would it? It'd be up to the Brits and the Spanish to sort it out.'

'We'd better hold off on sending it for now, anyway, until we find out some more. You didn't mention McTiernan to Solomons, did you?'

'No, I thought you wouldn't want me to.'

'Good,' Mulcahy said, relieved. 'Christ, why would the Cali Cartel have wanted to kill Ronson? He must've been one of their best customers.'

Ford put his hands up. 'Like I said, Solomons wouldn't go into it, not on the mobile.'

'So what are we supposed to do if we want to know more? Go over to Liverpool for a chat? Couldn't we phone him on a secure line or something?'

'No, boss.' Ford was grinning again. 'Better than that – he's here in Dublin.'

Mulcahy glared at him suspiciously. 'What is he doing over here?'

'Don't worry,' Ford laughed. 'It's nothing dodgy. Remember I said his wife is a Dub? So she got him to take a couple of days off before he starts his new gig. They've come over for some family do, a wedding or something. Tonight's a write-off, but he'll meet us tomorrow morning if you want. We'd be doing him a favour, he said, get him away from the in-laws for a couple of hours.'

117

10

By the time Walker dropped her off in the city centre, Siobhan reckoned that for all her earlier professions of admiration, the policewoman's patience with her had run completely dry. Such was the look of relief on Walker's face as she smiled and pulled away into the traffic, Siobhan experienced a sensation not unlike satisfaction. It never did any harm to keep officialdom on its toes. No matter how nice its face.

What she wanted more than anything else now was to find somewhere to sit down for a bite to eat and a cold drink, and to take stock. For all intents and purposes, her trip to Bristol had been a miserable failure. She'd found no trace of Gemma Kearney except, possibly, an initial 'G' and an unanswered phone, and that was barely a trace at all. Moreover, regardless of what Walker said, the circumstances of Horgan's death didn't seem quite so cut and dried as she'd been led to believe originally. All that stuff about falling or not falling in the water – what was all that about? In terms of a story, though, it still added up to nothing.

Walker had let her out on a bustling paved concourse full of fountains, metal sculptures and benches. But unlike a European piazza, it was surrounded not by nice shops, cafés and restaurants offering succour and sustenance but by three lanes of roaring traffic on every side. The only refreshment available appeared to be from a parked-up van selling hot-dogs, burgers and soft drinks. Not quite what she had in mind. Then, in the distance, she spied what looked like a restaurant with tables outside in the sun, so she set off in that direction. As she walked, she took out her mobile, checked there was plenty of time before her flight and then, on a whim, tapped in the number for 'G' that she had memorised from Horgan's phone. There was no reason why Gemma Kearney couldn't have two mobiles. Lots of people did, for home, for business, for having affairs. But again it just rang on endlessly, like it would never be answered again.

The restaurant she'd spotted had no tables free, so she carried on, emerging into a redeveloped docks area: rows of waterside restaurants, drinking sheds, gallery spaces and ware-house apartments with balconies over water. She found a nice place with shady umbrellas over the tables outside and sat down, ordered a Caesar salad and a large glass of sauvignon blanc. The lunchtime crowds were beginning to thin out, people heading back to work for the afternoon, looking like they wished they could stay out and enjoy the fine weather. Feeling tired again, Siobhan sat back and stared vacantly at the rippling movement of light on the water, the glint and sparkle of the sun triggering a long-dormant memory of other oven-hot days, even hotter nights in a canal-side room in Amsterdam, ten, fifteen, could it really be almost twenty years before? Smoking strong black dope with a blond and sun-tanned Dutch boy called ... what? Try as she might, she couldn't remember his name, only randomly vivid details of that moment, like the flex of his muscular arms as he pulled her in to him.

Amsterdam? She kicked back up to the surface. That's what was bothering her most. It *was* bizarre. There was something not right about Horgan having that boarding card for Amsterdam in his possession, no matter how easily Walker dismissed it. Maybe he had picked it up, but in that case why keep it? She pulled her notepad and pen from her bag, jotted down what details she could remember from the slip of torn paper – the flight number, the time, underscoring the word 'Electronic' that had been printed across the top. Maybe that was it. It's all done online these days. You check in and print off the boarding pass yourself. Maybe he originally had other plans, then changed his mind and decided to come to Bristol instead. There was another part to this puzzle, she felt certain, and it simply wasn't revealing itself.

She sat back, took a long sip of wine, a crunch of salad and tried to see the case from Walker's point of view. For all her helpfulness, the policewoman was never likely to have wanted to start unpicking a case that she'd already wrapped up neatly and put to bed. Not when she probably had new cases piling up all the time. Still less so when the victim was a non-national who was already buried in another jurisdiction. And then of course there was the small but unavoidable fact that there was no evidence whatsoever that anything untoward had occurred. Wasn't that fair enough?

She ate another mouthful of salad, arranged her knife and fork beside each other and pushed the plate away from her. No, it wasn't. Not when applied to a man who, only twenty-four hours later, killed himself, and whose girlfriend – former or otherwise – had subsequently disappeared. That wasn't 'fair enough'. It was a provocation. Something kept nagging her about the car hire as well, but what? Her thoughts swung back to the airport. She checked her watch again. An hour and a half remained before the flight. There wasn't much she could do in the meantime, except maybe have another drink, and sit and think. She called the waiter over, ordered a small glass of wine and the bill, and asked him to book a taxi for her in about twenty minutes. Sitting back, the warm sun on her shoulders, she felt the tension in them ease a little. There was probably nothing much she could do about any of it, full stop.

The departures lounge in Bristol Airport was heaving, and the queue for Ryanair flight FR175 to Dublin was about as orderly as a queue for UN food relief in a disaster zone. Siobhan stayed seated at a table in the Soho Coffee concession, sipping a lukewarm cappuccino, reading a copy of the *Irish Independent* she'd picked up at WH Smith, absorbed in a follow-up story about an expatriate Irish drugs gangster who'd been shot out in Spain. There was no point joining the general melee; she'd rather wait it out in comfort for priority boarding to be called and then fight her way through when the time came. When it did, she elbowed and excused her way to the front and handed the steward her passport and boarding card. Only then, as she idly watched him scanning and tearing the piece of paper she'd printed out the night before, returning the upper portion for her to keep, did it hit her – like a lightning strike – what it was that had bothered her about Horgan's boarding passes.

Siobhan felt herself jostled from behind as people pushed past. She was physically rooted to the spot by the realisation. Of course, that was it! It wasn't the Amsterdam boarding pass that was wrong. It was the Bristol ones. But she hardly had time to think about it, swept forward as she was by the crowd stampeding through the terminal door and onto the airfield towards the waiting plane. Only when she was queuing again at the bottom of the steps to board did she get a chance to fish out her phone and flick back through the photos she'd taken of Horgan's paperwork. She cursed, realising she'd only snapped the loose receipts, not his flight and booking information, but it didn't matter. What she had comprehended didn't have to do with the detail of the passes, but the mere existence of them. And if she was right, it would clear up some of her other doubts about Horgan's movements as well, not least the question of the car hire.

She looked up the steps at the shoulders, rear ends and hand luggage of the people in front of her, fighting the frustration of knowing she wouldn't be able to do a thing to prove herself right until she got back to Dublin. Back home, she'd have a broadband connection to confirm some things online, and the space and privacy to make one or two discreet calls. Whether they would bring her any closer to finding out what had happened to Gemma Kearney, she really didn't know, but she could feel in her stomach the gnaw that always came with the start of a good story, when the knot of perma-stress dissolved, leaving a yawning hollow demanding to be filled.

Mulcahy spent every spare minute he had that afternoon trying to get in touch with Eddie McTiernan, but the fat man's mobile went unanswered, and every message he left went unreturned. The number Mulcahy had for him at home in Leopardstown just clicked from dial tone into silence as if it had been disconnected. Eventually Mulcahy rang a contact of his, Paddy Halloran, in the Communications Unit and called in a favour. It was after half past six when Halloran rang back to say McTiernan had recently changed broadband providers and got a new number, but it was unlisted, and he wouldn't be able to get the details until the following morning. Mulcahy looked at his watch. With a little imagination, Leopardstown could be thought of as on the way home, and with luck most of the rush-hour traffic would be gone.

'In one hundred and fifty yards, turn right.'

Mulcahy slowed and indicated, then did as he was told by the sat nav, turning the Saab across Brewery Road and into the pleasant, tree-lined estate of large, detached houses where, according to his contacts book, Eddie McTiernan resided. In some splendour, too, by the look of it, but that was hardly a surprise. He continued slowly down the road, squinting at the numbers on the doors until, a hundred yards or so further on, he pulled up outside number seventeen. Like all the other houses on the street, it had been extensively refurbished in the boom years, and extended right across the generous plot. The garage had been converted, with an extra floor on top, and a massive porch entrance had been added to the house, running two-thirds the width of the façade. The former front garden had been obliterated, reduced to a few strips of flowerbeds bordering the obligatory expanse of block paving. On which, Mulcahy noted, there was no sign of McTiernan's car, his beloved Bentley Continental GT.

An electronic peal of church bells greeted his ears on pressing the buzzer, but the temptation to genuflect withered the instant the door was opened by a formidable-looking woman in her forties, or maybe cosmetically enhanced fifties, with bleached-blonde hair and a permatan to match her husband's. From behind her legs, the terrier McTiernan had been accompanied by the day before peered out at him accusingly, as if Mulcahy had interrupted some event of major canine significance.

'Mrs McTiernan?'

'Yeah. What do you want?' she said. Not a fan of niceties.

'I'm actually looking for your husband, Eddie. Is he in?'

'No.' She folded her arms beneath her substantial, probably enhanced chest and stared at him. Her impression of a brick wall was clearly well practised.

'Any idea where I might find him?' Mulcahy persisted.

'I wouldn't know. He never tells me anything,' she said huffily. Her accent had the harsh clip-clop of once-rough Dublin in it, softened by money and years of living among the more rounded vowels of the suburbs. 'He just takes off whenever he feels like it. Far be it from me to interfere.'

'So what time are you expecting him back?'

'I'm not,' she said. 'What's it to you, anyway?' She looked

at him assessingly, then over his shoulder at the ancient Saab and pursed her lips. 'Are you a cop?'

Mulcahy nodded, bracing himself for a tirade, but none came.

'The one he gets favours off of?'

'That's one way of putting it, I suppose,' he said, taken aback. 'Mulcahy's my name. I thought you said he never tells you anything?'

'Some things, y'know, stay between a husband and wife,' she said cryptically, but the stony set of her face seemed to ease a little. 'You let my kid off once, years back, gave him a chance. Turned his life around, that did. Scared him. He's in the civil service now.'

Mulcahy did his best to look noncommittal. If he had helped her son, he didn't remember it. More likely, McTiernan hadn't wanted to admit that it was his own flesh and blood he'd asked a favour for. Pride worked in weird ways. The wife didn't look too happy about it now, either. She was looking away, chewing her bottom lip like she was ruminating on a major moral quandary.

He decided to leave her to it. 'Tell Eddie it's important, Mrs McTiernan. I really do need to talk to him tonight.'

'I can't,' she said, looking first at the ground, then the fanlight, then straight at him, her eyelashes blinking rapidly, like she literally couldn't believe what she was about to do. 'He's taking the evening ferry to Holyhead,' she said in a rush. 'You'll have to hurry if you want to catch him.'

And with that she stepped back and slammed the door in his face.

11

By the time Siobhan shut the door of the flat behind her, she was bursting to get on with the job, but there were other things she needed to do first, practical things, mundane things, like checking emails and having a restorative half-hour soak in the bath. Nothing was so urgent it couldn't wait for that. Keeping one ear on the gush of hot water in the bathroom, she used the laptop to quickly deal with the more urgent emails that had piled up, mostly ignored, on her phone during the day. Then she gave her publicist, Maura, a quick call to finalise the arrangements for some book signings that had been set up towards the end of the following week. Ten minutes later she was leaning back in the steaming-hot bath, letting the skin-prickling heat overwhelm her and leach away the ache of the day. There had been times in the previous twelve months – cold, heavy days of loneliness, hatred and crippling physical pain – when she'd have given anything to feel the weariness of a day like she'd just had. There is nothing so soul-sapping as the nothingness severe injury brings with it, the inability to think of anything but pain.

Intense and frustrating as her day in Bristol had been, it was life; it was work. It was everything she had craved.

It didn't take long for her to have her fill of relaxation and for her mind to swing back to the brainstorm she'd had in the queue at Bristol Airport. She had gone over and over it again on the hour-long flight, and during the slow journey home through rush-hour Dublin. More than ever now she was sure that she was right: it wasn't only the return leg of Horgan's flight to Bristol that had gone unused; the outward one hadn't been used, either.

She cast her mind back to when she had seen both of the boarding passes, outbound and return, in the interview room at Walker's offices. She'd held them in her hand, and they were both exactly the same: both on fresh sheets of A4 paper, obviously printed out at the same time, presumably on Horgan's printer. Exactly the same. Folded, yes, but otherwise pristine, unsullied. Neither of them had been rent, torn or otherwise interfered with. Understandably, for the homeward leg. But on the outbound pass the lower portion that should have been retained by the airline for security and immigration control was still there, still intact. It had not been torn off by the ground staff; it could not have been used to board the plane. Which in turn meant Horgan couldn't have flown to Bristol on the evening of Friday 3 September, or leastways not on the flight he had booked and checked in for online. And she was convinced now that the explanation for that lay in the other boarding pass, the one to Amsterdam.

But how could that be? As Walker had forcefully pointed out to her in the car, there could be no doubting that Horgan had turned up in Bristol at some stage in the following twenty-four hours and met his death there. Had he just missed his flight and caught a later one? Siobhan didn't think so. Wrapping herself in her heavy white cotton bathrobe, and turbaning her hair in a hand towel, Siobhan went back out to the dining room. Sitting down at the table with her laptop, she Googled rapidly through to Aer Lingus's online flight timetables.

Within seconds she established what she had guessed would be the case: that there was only one flight from Cork to Bristol on Fridays, or on any other day of the week for that matter. It was a niche route; why would they need any more? What she had to do now was check departure times for Saturdays. She noticed that she was holding her breath waiting for the page to load – then she gasped with satisfaction and slapped the table with her hand on seeing that the only flight to Bristol on Saturday 4 September had departed in the early afternoon. In which case, how come Horgan had managed to pick up his hire car in the centre of Bristol at eleven o'clock that morning? There was definitely something dodgy about this, and it had to do with that flight to Amsterdam. She *knew* it did. She could taste it in her mouth like a metallic tang.

Mulcahy saw the boxy white bulk of the Stena Line ferry berthed at the terminal in Dun Laoghaire as he crossed the narrow bridge onto Harbour Road. A cloud of dark smoke belched from one of the stacks at the stern. She was getting ready to sail. He swung the Saab to the right, past the lantern-like glass and steel drum of the Irish Lights building and down onto the terminal approach road. Behind the security gates, the concrete apron was crowded with cars, vans and lorries, two hundred at least, maybe more, lined up bumper to bumper in the numbered lanes, waiting to board for the trip across the Irish Sea to Holyhead.

He pulled over as a security guy in a cap and yellow hi-vis vest emerged from a cabin at the gate, gesturing at him to stop and show his ticket.

Mulcahy held up his warrant card. 'Garda Siochana. I need to talk to one of your car passengers. Don't want any fuss.'

'You'd better get a move on. They've already starting loading the lorries.'

The steward raised the barrier and let him through. Mulcahy parked the Saab and walked towards the ranks of cars, trying to spot McTiernan's distinctive ride. There were plenty of big cars, Mercs, hulking Range Rovers, BMWs and Porsche SUVs, but it wasn't until he hoisted himself up on the chainlink fence to gain a better view that he saw the sleek silver Bentley over near the back of the second last row. He looked towards the loading area. The open bow section of the ferry was yawning like a hungry whale, already sucking in cars like so much krill. Running over to the Bentley from behind, he saw a fat elbow clad in a familiar blue jacket crooked out of the open window, a trail of tobacco smoke leaking from within. As he drew alongside, a pudgy, tanned hand emerged and tapped a grey stool of ash from a fat cigar onto the concrete.

'Taking a trip across the water, are we, Eddie?'

McTiernan whipped his face round as fast as its folds of

flesh would let him, choking on his smoke. 'Christ, Mr Mulcahy,' he coughed, the whirring of his brain all but audible. 'You nearly put the heart crossways on me. What in the name of Jaysus brings you down here?'

'I left you lots of messages, Eddie, but you never got back to me.'

McTiernan looked flustered and held up his hands. 'Ah, sure, it must've slipped my mind what with the trip coming up and all.'

'A bit urgent, is it?' Mulcahy put his hands on the sill and leant into the interior of the two-seater car. Plush, with plum-coloured leather upholstery and brushed-steel fittings, it was as roomy as a small aircraft hanger inside. He looked into the passenger area and the footwells, noticed McTiernan's eyes following his gaze and flicking anxiously behind towards a red plaid car rug that was covering something in the gap between the passenger seat and the rear chassis.

'Ah, y'know yourself – opportunities arise and you have to grab them. Something came up on the retail front and I'm just popping across to have a look-see. At least, that's what I told the wife, anyway, eh?' McTiernan winked lasciviously at Mulcahy.

'What were you holding back on me yesterday about Begley, Eddie? I don't have time for messing around.'

'Holding back? Ah, c'mon now, Mr Mulcahy, you know me better than that. Didn't I do my best to help you out?'

'Eddie, I know you're not giving me the full picture. You said as much yourself.' He stood up straight again and looked over at the ship. The loading was unbelievably quick and efficient. Already two lanes of cars had been directed up into the ship's maw. 'They'll be coming to this lane in a minute and unless you start talking to me I'm going to haul you off and tell Customs I have reason to suspect you're carrying contraband in this car. Then you'll have all night to tell me about Begley.'

'Contra-what?' McTiernan spluttered. 'For God's sake, there's no need for that. Why are you hassling me? I told you everything I know about Bingo yesterday.'

'I don't think so, Eddie,' Mulcahy said, leaning into the car again. 'By the way, what's under the rug?'

McTiernan threw his head back in frustration. The plum leather headrest absorbed the impact with a gently yielding hiss.

'Nothing you need to know about, Mr Mulcahy.'

'So tell me about Bingo and Ronson.'

The cars in front of McTiernan's were being called forward by the stewards now and McTiernan went to push a podgy finger at the ignition button, but Mulcahy grabbed his hand and pulled it back.

'Don't even think about it, Eddie. You're going nowhere until you tell me.'

The cars behind began hooting. Mulcahy stepped back and signalled at them to move around the Bentley. First one, then another slid out and zoomed ahead, the drivers glaring out the windows. A steward ran up to see what was causing the hold-up, but backed away when Mulcahy held up his warrant card at him with a growl of 'Garda business.'

'Come on, Eddie, out with it. What else do I need to know?'

'Fuck's sake,' McTiernan cursed, glancing round at the

stream of vehicles being directed around his car now. 'All right then, but you didn't hear it from me. I'm serious. Never more so. I don't want to draw any of this on myself, okay?'

Mulcahy nodded. 'So tell me.'

'Ever hear of a guy called Steve Hayford?' McTiernan asked with a sigh.

Mulcahy thought about it. The name rang only the vaguest, most distant bell. 'Here, or out in Spain?'

'Neither. He was a Liverpool lad.'

'One of Trevor Ronson's?'

McTiernan nodded. 'Right-hand man. Like I said, Ronson was spending a lot of time in Puerto Banus. I never met Hayford, but I know he ran the show for Ronson back in the UK.'

'And what – he decided it was time to get rid of Ronson?'

McTiernan snorted. 'No, no, that's not it at all. Hayford's dead these past six months. That's what I'm trying to tell you. He was gunned down in a bar fight in Rotterdam, by a gang of geared-up Colombians.'

'Colombians?' Mulcahy's eyes lit up.

'Yeah, exactly.'

'Over what?'

'Rotterdam, guns, Colombians . . . What the fuck do you think?' McTiernan sneered. 'Jesus, I thought you were supposed to be in the drugs squad?'

Mulcahy let that one go. All he could think of was what Ford had told him earlier about the line of enquiry SOCA was pursuing in Liverpool.

'Ronson was seriously fucked off,' McTiernan continued. 'I mean *seriously*. It was like his own flesh and blood had been taken from him. Said he was going to get his own back. Get even, you know. And Ronson had plenty of heat at his disposal, I can tell you. The problem was who he decided to take on.'

'Not just any old Colombians?'

McTiernan grimaced and nodded at the same time. 'Six months later Ronson and Bingo are dead. So go figure, as they say.'

'But what has any of this got to do with Bingo?'

'I don't know, I swear. Like I said before, him and Ronson were pretty tight. Bingo had a reputation for being good on the money side. You know, as in laundering. Maybe he got caught up in that end of things. All I know is, he was scared shitless. He was white with it.'

'Hang on,' Mulcahy said. 'You told us yesterday you didn't go to see him when you were over there. All that dead-man-walking crap. How come—'

'I didn't. Go see him, I mean.' McTiernan swallowed. 'Bingo came to me. He just turned up one evening at my place in Marbella, knocked on the window. I barely recognised him, he looked so rough. He'd heard I was looking for property and offered to sell me some of his places at a knock-down price for cash. Said he needed it quick because he had to get away.' McTiernan paused.

Mulcahy frowned. 'Go on.'

'Christ, I mean, I'd been hoping he'd buy me out. And, when I told him, the man just crumpled, went to pieces right there in front of me. So I sat him down and gave him a couple of whiskies, and he started jabbering on about how he was fucked, he was finished, and some fuckin' unstoppable greaseball loony was on his tail. He was pretty incoherent, but what I understood was he'd got caught up in some scam after Steve Hayford was murdered, something he'd got dragged into with Ronson and now some Colombian hard heads were out for his blood. He buggered off pretty soon after that. And that's all I know. That's the God's honest truth, Mr Mulcahy.'

There was a boom like a foghorn from the ferry, and a corresponding roar from the Bentley's V12 engine as McTiernan started the ignition. Mulcahy looked around. They were alone in the vast parking area now. The last of the cars had boarded and, from the activity dockside, it looked like the ferry was ready to depart.

'Wait, Eddie.' Mulcahy put a hand on McTiernan's arm. 'When was this?'

'I told you, last time I was over – two, three weeks ago. Not long after Ronson's funeral. He'd just come back from there. Now I really have to go.'

Mulcahy jumped back as the Bentley shot forward, eating up the empty acres of concrete in seconds, and squealed to a halt at the foot of the boarding ramp. At the top of the incline the bow doors of the ferry were already beginning to close. Only then, looking at the Bentley's brake lights burning bright red in the distance, did Mulcahy realise that darkness had fallen. He turned away and walked back to the Saab. For once in his life it looked as if Eddie McTiernan might have missed the boat.

Siobhan went to the fridge to get a glass of wine, and a ready meal to heat up. She was coming back to the table, glass of chilled sauvignon in her hand, an M&S seafood casserole pricked and in the oven, her mind still buzzing, when she noticed the light on her landline answer machine blinking. She stopped and stared at it. She had never really trusted the machine since the year before, when someone had left a series of creepy messages, in the form of Roy Orbison songs, on it. The weeks she'd spent in hospital had obviously put whoever it was off, as she hadn't received any more since, but she still thought of it every time she saw the light flashing. She pressed the answer button tentatively, ready to turn it off again at the merest suggestion of music. But instead, thankfully, she heard her accountant's chipper tones emanating from the speaker, returning her call from the day before.

'Siobhan, it's Tom Fahy here. Sorry for taking so long to get back to you. I was away yesterday familiarising myself with the Revenue's latest masterplan to force us poor PAYE fools to pay for the sins of others. But to answer your question, yes, you'd have to get in touch with the CAI, Chartered Accountants Ireland, to make a complaint about an errant, negligent or malfeasant colleague. Don't be surprised if they tell you there's a long queue ahead of you, though. The profession hasn't been exactly showering itself in glory since the financial crisis hit. You'll find all the CAI's details online. Anything else, give me a shout. I'm around for the rest of the week.'

She deleted the message, sat down again, put her untouched wine on the table and called up the CAI website on her laptop, copying down on her notepad the contact phone number, which she intended calling first thing in the morning. Beside it, she jotted down some other questions that badly needed answering in relation to Gemma Kearney. Just doing

135

so brought the doubts flooding back. Was there really a story in this, or was she just fooling herself? Bashing her head against a brick wall simply because it was there? And what did it matter how Horgan got to Bristol, anyway? What she wanted to know was whether he'd met Gemma there or not.

Taking a sip of wine, she Googled the Lennox Hotel and dialled the number for reception. She asked to be put through to the manager, but the person who answered wasn't the one Walker had dealt with earlier. This woman sounded younger and friendlier.

'Hi, I know it's a bit late,' Siobhan said, 'but I spoke to your colleague earlier – Ms Trenchard, was it? Is she there still by any chance?'

'I'm sorry, she's gone off duty now. Can I help?'

She felt her hopes of getting any information diminish with that response, but pressed on regardless. 'Yes, I hope so. My name's Siobhan Fallon. I came in earlier with Sergeant Walker, to pick up the belongings of a guest called—'

'Yes, of course. I remember. I'm Sally. I was just coming on duty as you were leaving. You're the Irish policewoman, aren't you?'

Siobhan vaguely remembered a smiley young woman hovering in the background when Walker had been talking to the hotel manager. Well, she wasn't going to waste an opportunity like that.

'Eh, yes, that's right,' she said. 'Sorry to disturb you again, Sally, but I forgot to ask earlier – would you, by any chance, have a record of what time Mr Horgan checked in with you?'

She repeated Horgan's details and dates, and waited as she heard the tapping of fingernails on a keyboard.

'Yes, here it is now. Mr Cormac Horgan. He was with us on the third and fourth, and his check-in time was . . . Oh, that's . . . ' Sally's voice trailed off.

'That's what?' Siobhan said, trying to keep a lid on her curiosity.

'Oh, nothing, really. A little odd, I suppose. It says here that Mr Horgan didn't check in until five a.m. on the fourth. The night porter must have let him in.'

'Five in the morning?' Siobhan exclaimed. All sorts of questions were running through her mind now. 'That's more than a little *odd*, isn't it? It's weird.'

'Well, nothing's weird in this business, as such,' Sally said, making it sound like some kind of corporate mantra. 'But, yes, it is early, or late, I suppose, depending on your point of view. Friday nights can get quite hectic here in Bristol.'

At last Siobhan saw the goal wide open for the one question she had wanted answered all along, even before she went to Bristol. 'Eh, is there any way of telling if he was alone when he checked in, Sally?'

There was a soft cough from the other end of the line. It sounded suspiciously like the shutters coming down on that line of questioning. 'I'm sorry, Officer. We charge by the room, and what guests do in them is their own affair so long as they do it cleanly, quietly and legally.'

Another corporate mantra, no doubt. Siobhan was about to thank Sally and hang up when the girl came back with one last suggestion. 'Unless this message could shed some light?'

'Message?' Siobhan might as well have felt something go pop in her head. 'Your colleague didn't mention any message.'

'Well, no. It's a check-in message. When one's left before a guest arrives, we log it and it automatically comes up on screen when they check in. It only popped up again now because I accessed Mr Horgan's actual check-in details.'

'Can you tell me what it says?'

'Yes, it's short. It says, "Well done. Told you crossing would be fine. See you later, Gemma."'

'Gemma?' Siobhan gulped. 'You're absolutely sure of that?'

'Yes,' said Sally. 'It's here on the screen in front of me.'

When Siobhan put the phone down, her mind was on fire. In a single stroke all her doubts had been resolved. Gemma Kearney *had* been in Bristol with Horgan. Before she could think about it any further, the phone rang in her hand. No caller ID, but she recognised the number as the one Mrs Kearney had given her. She'd meant to call the woman earlier, but had put it off and off again, not wanting to have to tell her that she hadn't been able to turn up any definite leads on her daughter in Bristol, that she really couldn't justify spending any more time on looking for Gemma. Well, she sure as hell had something more positive to tell the woman now, didn't she?

Wednesday

12

She woke with a start, the chill of early morning on her skin, fear like bands of steel cramping her breathing as she fought for air and prayed the blackness weighing down on her was the ordinary dark of night and not the end. She threw out her arm, fumbling, scrabbling, searching until at last she found the light switch and with a click brought reality, reassurance, relief surging into her heart along with the light. She flopped back against the pillows, struggling to regulate her breathing, pulling the duvet up to stop the cold settling on her skin, the stress in her chest ebbing away slowly, second by second. She was safe; she was in her own bed; she was alone.

Even as a shudder of relief ran through her body, she tried to laugh it off. The dream had been so literal, so stupid, like something out of *The Wizard of Oz*. How could she have been so fooled, so terrified by it? Had the trip to England prompted it, maybe? She'd been in a boat, one of those long, flat skiffs you see in period dramas, laid back on a bed of silk cushions, one hand trailing in the water, luxuriating in the warmth of a beautiful day. She closed her eyes and drifted off but knew something wasn't right, and when she next looked up, the sky was black, the world around had changed utterly, and she was on a sea of dark water, no land in sight. The boatman, in his striped jacket and straw boater, was no longer behind her but at the front of the boat, thrusting the long wooden punting pole in and out of the water with a remorseless slurping, slapping rhythm, pushing them on towards some awful looming threat. But of what?

She reached for the red hardcover notebook she kept by the bed to record the nightmares that, thankfully, came less and less often now, for the therapist who, even more thankfully, she saw only once a month instead of the twice weekly it had been for so long. This was what they called progress. She jotted down the details as she remembered them: how she tried to call the boatman but he didn't hear her, or ignored her; how she sought desperately to crawl forward and make him turn round, make him turn back; and when she reached him, when she tugged at the bottom of his white linen trouser leg and looked up, how all her hope had fragmented into razor-sharp shards of horror as he turned his head and she recognised the face seared onto her memory the year before, the scar on his neck burning like a purple flame . . .

Rinn. Who else could it have been? Who else was it ever going to be? She shook her head, wished for the thousandth time she could train her subconscious to recognise her fears for what they were: stupid, irrational. And what right did that evil bastard have to supplant every other thing in life that had ever frightened her, to become the sum of *all* her fears. Was there nothing else left in her imagination? Couldn't it rustle up something new, more original than Sean fucking Rinn?

She wrote it all down, wrote it all out of her, the fear, the fury, the frustration, and, when she'd finished, saw she'd covered six full pages in the untidy scrawl her handwriting became when she was angry. Ever the reporter, she looked back over it, correcting solecisms, striking out repetitions here and there, noticing that she'd used the same word time and again to describe the setting and the nature of the journey she'd been on. The crossing. Like she'd been on some kind of Stygian journey with Rinn the ferryman pulling her from life to death. How boringly predictable was that for a woman who'd been crucified?

She shut the notebook, lay back against the pillows, closed her eyes, thought of the conversation she'd had with Gemma Kearney's mother before she went to sleep. The woman had been drinking, she was sure of it. Probably to numb the pain of not knowing. Was there anything worse, Siobhan wondered, than the pain of not knowing whether your child was alive or dead? The child you'd loved and nurtured half your life, whose every hope and dream became your own. Jesus, at least you got closure with the grave.

A memory drifted in now of her own mother, a sad, unfulfilled, hopeless alcoholic whose love, in later years, had always been contingent on the proximity of a vodka bottle. So much for closure. Siobhan had stiffened like a board when she heard the slur in Mrs Kearney's voice, half a childhood's dread and resentment rushing automatically to the surface in that flash of recognition. But as Mrs Kearney started telling her about what a difficult child Gemma had been – so bright, so pretty, so gifted, yet always dissatisfied with what she had, with what Mrs Kearney and her husband could give her – it became evident that it was Gemma, not her mother, who was the unstable personality in the Kearney family.

Siobhan yawned, turned over on her side. The clock on the bedside table read 3.47 a.m. Exhaustion at last engulfed her.

Mulcahy woke early, surprised to find the first thing on his mind was precisely what had been occupying it the moment he fell asleep the night before: Orla. The deep green irises of her eyes, flecked with brown, and the freckles on her cheeks that weren't visible until you got so close there was no going back. He hadn't really thought of her in that absorbed, longing kind of way since they'd first got together, six months back. She'd called him the night before, late, at about eleven thirty, while he was lying on the bed reading the paper, and they'd talked. Not about *them*, but about the day, the news, some television show she had been watching. It was gentle, easy, teasing chat – both of them knowingly keeping it light, and all the better for that.

It left him feeling restless and keyed up by the time he got into work that morning. Eager to get on with things, to make some headway. And it made Liam Ford's announcement that he'd arranged to meet Paul Solomons, the Liverpool cop, for a late breakfast at the Clarence Hotel all the more welcome. Mulcahy had half expected he would be dragged along for a couple of rushed lunchtime pints in the Long Hall or the Stag's Head, and then have to leave Ford and Solomons to get trashed for the afternoon in the name of 'catching up'. Which he would have gone along with for the sake of hearing what Solomons had to say about Trevor Ronson's murder – of even more interest to him now, given what

Eddie McTiernan had hinted about a possible criminal connection between Begley and Ronson. Money laundering was the ultimate bastardy as far as he was concerned. It was what enabled dealers and drug barons to think they could wash not only their dirty money but the blood from their hands as well.

During the five-minute walk from Dublin Castle to the Clarence, Mulcahy filled in Ford on how he had caught up with Eddie McTiernan at the Dun Laoghaire ferry terminal the night before.

'I'm amazed you believe anything that fat windbag tells you,' Ford said, as they crossed Dame Street and stepped into the narrow funnel of Sycamore Street, and headed down past the stage door of the Olympia Theatre into the heart of Temple Bar.

Mulcahy shook his head. 'You've got to understand how Eddie is. He's straight most of the time. Sure, he might exaggerate, or pass on something he's swallowed whole himself, but he wouldn't sell me a deliberate lie. I've known him too long for that.'

'Not so long you can't enjoy putting the wind up him, though, eh?' Ford chuckled. 'Jesus, I'd love to have seen his face when he realised he'd missed that boat. I've never seen blubber go purple. I've a feeling that might be the last you see of your arch-informant for a while.'

Mulcahy wasn't at all sure he shouldn't be feeling more guilty about that, but he managed a laugh. 'Well, he can't have it all his own way. Whatever he had under that rug in the car, there's an even chance it shouldn't have been leaving the country.'

Turning the corner by the Purty Kitchen, they passed the

blue front wall of the Project Arts Centre, then crossed Essex Street, making for the angular rear entrance of the Clarence.

'This always reminds me of going into a courthouse,' Ford said as he went up the steps, like he was some kind of regular. They walked through to reception, but there was no sign of Solomons, so they went back to the Tea Room and were seated at a table beside one of the big windows, the sun beaming in like it was still mid-summer. Ford began reading out the menu, offering his recommendations and suggesting, with a punch on the shoulder, that Mulcahy might enjoy 'the full Irish' – a laboured reference, he eventually understood, to Siobhan Fallon's appearance on breakfast TV the day before. Just at that moment Mulcahy's mobile rang and, bizarrely, it was her name on the screen.

'Siobhan,' he answered. Across the table Liam Ford raised a curious eyebrow at him. Mulcahy turned away. 'We were just talking about you.'

'Really?' She sounded surprised. 'I hope it was good.'

'Good enough. What's up?'

He strained to hear her as the line broke up then cleared again. It sounded like she was outdoors somewhere.

'I know it's short notice,' she said, 'but is there any chance you'd be free around lunchtime today? I need to see you about something.'

Christ, that was all he needed. Yet something deep and unacknowledged clawed at him to say yes. Only then did he realise he'd completely forgotten to run down that Missing Persons contact she'd asked him for.

'Look, I haven't had a chance to get that name for you yet, Siobhan. I've been kind of busy.'

'Don't worry,' she said quickly. 'It's not that. I wanted to pick your brains. It won't take long. It's such a beautiful day I thought we could meet in Stephen's Green by the—'

What she said next was partly drowned out by a loud whoop of greeting from Ford. Mulcahy turned and saw him standing, hailing a stocky, crop-haired man in jeans and a black leather jacket walking towards their table, a hand raised in greeting. Solomons, he presumed.

'Look, Siobhan, I've got a meeting now, but yeah, okay, I'll see you there. Half past twelve, yeah?'

He clicked off and stood up as Solomons reached the table, accompanied by a strong whiff of something soapy and astringent, like he'd just stepped out of the shower. Solomons apologised for being late, saying he'd had a heavier night of it with the in-laws than expected – and loudly trotted out all the usual cracks about the Irish and alcohol, drawing one or two critical looks from nearby tables. He didn't even notice. In his early to mid-thirties, his eyes were red-rimmed and his skin had a sallow, liverish cast to it, probably from the depredations of the night before. His voice had the nasal singsong of the native Liverpudlian. They chatted easily enough while ordering, Mulcahy leaving Ford to explain again that Ronson's name had come up in connection with a case they were working. Solomons seemed happy enough to oblige and really got into his stride once the food was served.

'One thing you got to remember about Ronson,' Solomons said, smothering a thick slice of black pudding in bright yellow egg yolk, 'he'd been around a long time. Canny enough to keep in with the old-style Merseyside villains as well as the gang kids that took over the street trade in the late

1990s. But he stayed in the shadows while he built up his power base. We almost caught him in 1999 for a two-hundred-kilo load we pulled over, but it was his partner who went down for it – leaving the field open for Ronson to become even more powerful. That's when he started spending more time out in Spain, putting as much distance as possible between himself and the product but still keeping hold of the reins back home.'

'My source said as much,' Mulcahy said. 'Everything was low key.'

'Spot on,' Solomons nodded. 'None of your bling and Hummers for him. He was too smart for that. He kept it at the wholesale level, as well. He was ordering coke by the tonne from Cali long before we realised how big he was. By the time we did figure it out, he'd made himself pretty much untouchable – everything he did was arm's length. SOCA reckons there were times his network brought in between fifteen and twenty thousand kilos of powder a year – that's nearly two-thirds of everything that was coming into the UK then. And he did H, blow, meth and everything else in the sweet shop as well. He was wholesaling all sorts, but mostly he was King Cocaine. No one else had links like his with South America, and he was getting into Mexico, too – we reckon he was the first UK importer to spot the potential there and start building up contacts. No one else came near him in terms of his network.'

For Mulcahy, that raised one question more than any other: 'So how come he was caught out?' he asked. 'From what I've seen online the shooting was a cinch. From the back of a motorbike?'

'Yes, but not your standard two-hander job – just the one

bloke, no one on the pillion. So even if Ronson had spotted him coming, he probably wouldn't have thought he looked dodgy. Ronson was coming out of this gym in Speke that he owned, with a couple of his lads. Shooter drove the bike right up, shotgun came out of nowhere, and boff – both barrels in the chest. Cool as you like. Before you know it, the shooter's roared off and Ronson's minders are scraping what's left of him off the pavement.'

Solomons sat back in his chair, pushed away his empty plate and poured himself another coffee.

'Like the boss says, it sounds too easy,' Ford said, holding out his cup for a refill. 'A guy that powerful – you wouldn't think he'd leave himself open to it.'

Solomons leant over with the pot and poured. 'Some parts of Liverpool, Ronson would've thought were safe. Speke was home turf, even if he didn't spend much time there, and he was with a couple of his heavies. I doubt he'd have thought anyone would have the balls to try it there.'

'Sounds like a set-up,' Ford said.

'Yeah, well, obviously we looked into that possibility ourselves, but we're fairly confident it wasn't. Both of the minders took some shot when they tried to dive for the shooter, so it's not like they stood back and let it happen. And the word on the street was against it—' Solomons broke off and held his hands up. 'Never say never, like, but there would definitely have been something on the jungle drums if it was a local job, especially if it was any kind of gang hit.'

'So what's the thinking your end, then?' Mulcahy said.

Solomons turned to Mulcahy. 'Liam must've told you about the line SOCA likes – the Colombian angle?'

149

Mulcahy scanned Solomons's face for any hint of amusement, but there was none. The man was being serious. 'Liam mentioned it, yes. I must admit it sounded a bit far-fetched to me, but then I don't know the detail. This source of mine suggested it was all over some guy. What was he called, Hayford or something?'

'Steve Hayford?' Elbows on the table, Solomons gave Mulcahy a long, level look over steepled fingers before replying. 'That's one hell of an impressive source you have, Inspector. Did he tell you any more?'

Mulcahy rolled his shoulders, not wanting to say too much. 'Not really, no.'

'They're just names to us, Paul,' Ford broke in, sensing some tension. 'We have no clue who's who or what's true. That's why we came to you – so we could get an idea of how it fits together without having to go through all the official rigmarole. Who was this Hayford guy, anyway?'

Solomons looked back to Ford, relaxing again. 'He was Ronson's top lieutenant. Chief disciple, too. Modelled himself on the boss, kept the profile low but wasn't slow to stick his neck out when needed. He was, like, manager to Ronson's chairman, took care of the day-to-day stuff, sorted out the bash-up and distribution.'

'There's no chance Ronson thought Hayford was getting too big and had him done?' Ford asked.

'No, nothing like that. Those two were tighter than Madonna's arsecheeks. We're pretty sure they had some kind of king-maker deal between them – Ronson wanted out of the game, but risk-free. So he was training Hayford up to take over the gig in return for a quiet retirement abroad and protection, plus a percentage of the ongoing profits, of course. Another few months we reckon it would've happened. Ronson had stopped doing everything bar the deal-making. He was spending more and more time in Spain, only popping back for the occasional meet. You with me?'

Mulcahy nodded. It squared with what McTiernan had told him. 'So what *did* happen to Hayford?'

'All we really know is that Hayford got tapped in a bar fight over in Rotterdam back in April. Drilled, fifteen rounds, three or four different weapons.'

'That's some bar fight,' Ford said.

'Right,' Solomons agreed grimly. 'Anyway, it was a complete clam-up job: nobody saw nothing, nobody heard nothing, the usual thing. But the fact is, they were in Rotterdam, and the bar was owned and run by Colombians. The Dutch threw a decent team at it, but all they managed to scrape together was that Hayford had been getting bevvied all afternoon with a gang of Colombians – we assume to wet the head on a successful deal – when all of a sudden everything kicked off. The pearl-handled pistols came out and bam-bam – that was the end of Steve Hayford. He probably insulted somebody's mother by accident or something. You know what they're like.'

Solomons paused to take a sip of coffee, but Ford wasn't content to wait even that long to get to the end of it. 'So, what – Ronson decided to get his own back and it all went wrong?'

'That's what we hear, or something like that, but not exactly.' Solomons wiped his upper lip with the back of his hand like he'd been glugging Guinness. 'You know these guys – loyalty and friendship matter, but life's still cheap.

Money's the only thing they care about at the end of the day. The problem for Ronson was to do with what Hayford and the Colombians were celebrating over. Because, as we hear it, Hayford had just taken delivery of a huge load of coke from them, come in through Rotterdam Container Port. We're talking massive: a tonne at least – street value £70 million, minimum. That's what, 100 million in euros? Like I said, Ronson was one of maybe three guys in the whole of the UK who commanded that kind of credit with the Colombians. But this time he refused to cough up the cash, supposedly.'

'Because of Hayford?' Mulcahy was astonished.

'A bit, maybe, but mostly because he claimed the coke was never delivered.'

'I thought you said Hayford had taken delivery.'

'I did, and, as we hear it, that's what the Colombians said, too, but Ronson reckoned that didn't count. It never got to him, so no way was he stumping up for it. Said he had no idea where it was, or any proof that it had ever been handed over. Threw it back at his suppliers in Cali, said it was their fault for blitzing his man.'

'So what happened to the cocaine?' Ford asked. Mulcahy glanced across at him, wondering if he was thinking the same thing as himself.

Solomons put his hands up. 'No one knows. Rotting away in some lock-up in Rotterdam would be my guess, location known only to Steve Hayford, deceased.'

He chuckled as both Mulcahy and Ford cursed in astonishment.

'Meanwhile these Cali boys are majorly out of pocket and can't afford to take it lying down. Sends out the wrong message, doesn't it? Especially with the Mexicans muscling in on all their markets right now. Nothing else for it but despatch a man to take out Ronson and teach everyone the lesson – don't think you can pull a fast one on us.'

'So it's true,' Ford gasped. 'They actually sent someone over to whack Ronson? Jesus, I've never heard anything like it.'

'That's the theory, anyway. Proving it is a different matter.' Solomons sat back in his chair and folded his arms.

'There must be some evidence to back it up?' Mulcahy prompted. No way would an investigation go down that route without being pushed.

'We're getting it from the ground up,' Solomons said, 'from a number of different sources. But it makes a weird kind of sense. The shooter was definitely alone and a pro. He left no trace of himself anywhere.'

'Sounds like he did you a big favour,' Ford said.

'No, not as far as we're concerned,' Solomons said, a pained expression on his face. 'Hayford's death was bad enough, but Ronson's leaves us with three years' work down the drain on our books. Not a single shittin' arrest to show for it. Meanwhile we've barely been able to keep a lid on things back home. Ronson was a stabilising influence on Merseyside. He had such a tight grip nobody dared upset the applecart. Something like this, the whole house of cards comes down and all the other dickheads pile in looking to take a slice. It's complete chaos on the streets: rumours flying, a major turf war kicking off with all the johnny-come-latelys trying to grab what they can and fill the vacuum. It's murder. And I mean *murder*. Four dead already, and there'll be more.'

'I'm still not seeing how Bingo fits into this,' Mulcahy said, turning to Ford. 'Why would the Colombians go after him as well?'

'Is this your Begley guy?' Solomons broke in. 'I checked him out like Liam asked. We had nothing on him locally, not even a known-associate file. So there won't have been a Liverpool connection. I had a look at a couple of other databases, too, and he popped up on the UKBA side – that's our Customs guys – who had him down as a possible drugs trader, but only in Irish–Spanish terms. So nothing there. You're sure it's not just a coincidence?'

'We're not sure of anything at the moment,' Mulcahy said. 'It's only this one source pointing us in that direction.'

'Well, remember back in Liverpool everyone who knew Ronson is jumpy as fuck right now. Could it be somebody adding things up wrong, maybe?'

'It looks like it, doesn't it?' Mulcahy said. 'Except Begley was supposedly living in fear of his life.'

'Yeah, but that could have been for any reason,' Solomons said. 'You know these guys. They're never happy unless they're ripping somebody off. But, like I told Liam, I was only handling the local liaison side of things for Merseyside. The SOCA guys are who you should be talking to. Commander Gavin Corbett's the lead on the inquiry. You should give him a shout. He'd be bloody keen to hear about this source of yours – sounds like a live one.'

'I'll have a think about that, sure,' Mulcahy said, pushing his seat back. 'I'm not sure how much further this gets us, but thanks for filling us in, anyway.'

'No worries.' The Liverpudlian grinned. 'Anything to escape the dragon-in-law for a couple of hours.'

13

'I told you I didn't want you here for the rest of this week.' Paddy Griffin glared at Siobhan. She examined the stern face, the cracked, mottled and thread-veined skin on the cheeks, the flabbiness of the jowls from decades mining at the coalface of news in bars, restaurants and after-hours drinking holes, and knew the look instantly for what it was: one of his fake, don't-you-know-the-meaning-of-the-word-deadline glares, which he dished out daily to reporters and sub-editors who were dragging their heels. She knew then that things would probably be all right. If it had been the sizzler, the one that made you feel you were having boiling tar poured all down your head, neck and chest, the one he reserved for real fuck-ups, her response might have been different.

'I didn't say I was staying, did I?' She ventured a half-smile at him and saw a twitch of response on his lips, a hairline crack in his resistance. 'So be quiet for a minute, please, Paddy, and hear me out. I need to talk to you about something.'

Griffin puffed his cheeks out, pretended to curse under his

breath, but he stayed sitting in his chair – another sure sign he was open to compromise. He even went so far as to swivel her chair round and point for her to sit in it.

'Go on, then, what is it? But be quick – I've got an eleven-o'clock meeting with Harry and the lawyers about that NAMA lead we did a couple of weeks ago. Bloody developers have issued proceedings.'

She raised an eyebrow. It wasn't unusual for the *Herald*'s editor, Harry Heffernan, to be meeting the paper's lawyers, or for people to threaten to sue for libel. But to actually set the legal wheels in motion was unusual, and costly, too. The story Griffin was talking about was one of Cillian O'Gorman's. She had thought some of the quotes smelt a bit whiffy from the off. She'd even said so on the day and been disregarded. Had the weasel O'Gorman cocked up? Was he about to get them hammered for a fortune? She resisted the urge to indulge her curiosity, knowing that if she went down that road, Griffin might get defensive about his own role in the story and pull the shutters down on her completely. She was so caught up in the thought she didn't notice him shifting in his chair impatiently.

'Siobhan, what do you want? Like I said, the clock's ticking.'

'I need a contact in Aer Lingus, someone high up who can access names on a passenger manifest.'

Griffin raised a grey and bushy eyebrow, an eye fixing on her like a hawk spotting a flicker of prey far below. 'I thought you had good people at Aer Lingus. You did that piece a couple of years ago, the one about the union ballot rigging, didn't you, with what's-her-name? Damn good story that.'

'Eileen Daly, yeah. I tried earlier. She doesn't have the right clearances. I don't think her career's exactly flourished

156

since that story. I need somebody higher up, with access to the security side of things.'

'I told you to take a rest,' Griffin growled.

'Yeah, and we both knew that was never going to happen. So do you know anyone or not?'

Griffin rubbed his chin, intrigued. He knew Siobhan wouldn't risk humiliating herself by coming in and begging a favour unless she was on to something. He knew her well enough for that.

'I might do, but it's not someone I'd approach lightly. I'd have to know what it's in aid of first.'

Siobhan beamed at him, knowing she had won the first round – getting her foot in the door. Some shameless flattery wouldn't go amiss now. 'Okay, so you were right. I did get something at Horgan's funeral in Cork. So, please, don't come over all "I told you so", but I met this woman, or at least she approached me ... '

They left by the main entrance, stepping out onto Wellington Quay, where a stream of heavy traffic thundered by between them and the granite quay walls. Solomons was walking back towards the Ha'penny Bridge, so they did their goodbyes and backslaps outside the hotel, and headed off themselves in the opposite direction. Across the river, beyond Grattan Bridge, the sun was melting the green copper dome of the Four Courts into the pale blue of the sky.

'Were you thinking what I was thinking in there?' Mulcahy asked Ford, checking over his shoulder that Solomons wasn't coming after them for any reason.

'What?' Ford said. 'That there's some mad Colombian

cunt going round blowing chunks out of kingpins and the Brits can't pretend to be even a little bit happy about it? Too feckin' right I was.'

'No, I mean about this massive load of cocaine that's supposedly gone missing in Rotterdam. Didn't you think that's a bit weird?'

'Well, yeah. I'd have thought we would've got wind of a story like that before now, from the Dutch if nobody else.'

'Maybe they're doing an ostrich on it,' Mulcahy said. 'Pretending it doesn't exist. Nobody's actually seen it, have they? And the Brits obviously want to play the Ronson hit close to their chests, too. Probably to prevent all-out war in Liverpool with the gangs.'

'I suppose,' Ford agreed warily.

'Didn't you think anything about the coke itself?' Mulcahy asked again, trying to prompt the right response from Ford. 'That size load, I mean.'

Ford scowled as a lorry thundered past too close for comfort, its slipstream swirling exhaust fumes and grit into their faces. 'You mean in terms of the *Atlantean*, Rosscarbery Bay?'

'Yes, that's exactly what I mean.'

'Sure, I thought it.' Ford shrugged, stopping on the corner and turning to Mulcahy. 'A tonne of coke goes missing in Rotterdam. A couple of months later the *Atlantean* turns up off Cork with not an awful lot less than that on board. Bit handy that, I thought. If it did happen. But that's the problem, isn't it? We don't even know for sure it did happen.'

'Oh, come on, Liam – you know as well as I do that the Brits wouldn't be pursuing that line of enquiry if there wasn't some solid evidence for it.'

'So why didn't the Brits make the connection with the *Atlantean*? Why didn't they come to us with it?'

'Why would it even occur to them?' Mulcahy said. 'It is Ronson's murder they're looking into, not a smuggling operation. And, anyway, they don't know what *we* know.' Mulcahy tapped the lapel of Ford's jacket with his index finger. 'They don't know that the *Atlantean* sailed from Holland. We didn't know it ourselves before last week.'

'Neither do we now. Not for certain,' Ford reminded him. 'The Cork team haven't even got there yet. And what are you suggesting? That we should tell the Brits about this?'

'God, no,' Mulcahy said. 'We don't even know if there is a link yet. We need time to think this through, and then go and prove it.'

'Prove it?' Ford snorted. He was getting irritable now. 'How do you propose we go about that? You know the stats better than I do, boss. Sixteen million containers a year go through Rotterdam Port, with upwards of what – a hundred, two hundred tonnes of coke smuggled in among them? What are we going to do, try and identify which one it was? And what good would it do us, anyway? Even if it was the same coke, it won't tell us anything about who was behind the job.'

'It would be a bloody good start.'

'*If* there is a link,' Ford said grudgingly.

'And if we think there could be, then we have a duty to investigate it.'

Ford's expression contained everything Mulcahy needed to know regarding his opinion of investigations initiated for the sake of duty.

'You were the one accusing me of leaping to conclusions

last night, boss. And if you don't mind me saying so, you're going in for a bit of pole-vaulting here yourself. Let me get this right. You're seriously thinking Bingo could be linked to the *Atlantean* now, as well as the Ronson murder? Bingo fuckin' Begley?'

Mulcahy held his hands up placatingly, knowing he'd have to get Ford on board if he was going to take this any further. 'Look, one thing's for sure – you and me have been caught on the hop here, assuming that Declan Begley was still the same small-time little shit he was when we knew him ten years ago. Come on, that's got to have crossed your mind, too.'

'Okay,' Ford said. 'Maybe it did.'

'And you've got to admit there's *something* going on here. I don't claim to know what it is, or whether it links to Rosscarbery Bay, or if any or all of those threads will come together when we examine them, but it's got to be worth having a look at least, yeah? I mean, if there was a link, it would be massive. Don't you agree?'

'I suppose so,' Ford nodded. He looked like he was about to add a rider, but Mulcahy cut in ahead of him.

'Right, in which case the first thing we need to do is get on to the murder team in Malaga and get their victim profile of Begley. That should give us an up-to-date idea of what he had his sticky fingers in recently, and the extent of any money laundering he might have been suspected of, yeah?'

'Maybe,' Ford said, with a little more enthusiasm. 'But what about SOCA? Shouldn't we talk to them about Ronson and Begley?'

'Yes, we should, but I'd like to have this other info in place first. To get both sides of the equation, you know? When we get back, could you get in touch with someone on the Dutch end and find out what they have to say about Hayford's murder and the missing cocaine? That's what we really need to know.'

'I could give that Dutch intelligence guy a call, the one we're liaising with about the boat. I'm sure he'd fast-track me through to whoever we need to talk to.'

'Great. I'm sure he could.'

Across the road, over Ford's shoulder, something caught Mulcahy's eye and he looked up. On the corner of Parliament Street, the sunlight falling on the Italianate arcades and painted terracotta frieze of Sunlight Chambers made the building look, for once, perfectly at home on the banks of the Liffey. It was the sort of low, bright light that used to fill his heart with warmth on cold winter days in Madrid, its intensity so unexpected and welcome. It made his heart lift now, too.

'While we're at it,' he said, 'why don't we get Aisling and Aidan working on this, as well, throw everything we've got at it for a couple of days, see what comes out the other end?'

'A couple of days?' Ford said, his eyebrows like steeples. 'Are you sure you're feeling all right? Even if there is something to this, don't you think we'd be better off passing it on to O'Grady and the lads in Southern Region to chase up? I mean, they've got a hell of a lot more resources than we do.'

'No, not a chance,' Mulcahy said, a glimpse of the possibilities, the bigger picture, coming together in his mind now. 'Look, Liam, trust me on this. I've got my reasons. If it comes to nothing, so be it, but if we do pull the lid off something big, I want it to be all our own work, and nobody else's.'

*

Mo Sheeran was the name he gave her, a source from way back, when Griffin had been halfway to making managing editor on the old *Irish Press* and Sheeran had been climbing the ranks of the CID. Unlike Griffin, though, Sheeran had switched vocations in his late forties and left his hardcore anti-terrorism job with the Garda Siochana to become a senior member of the national airline's security staff.

'Don't piss him off,' Griffin warned her. 'He'll find a way to hurt you.'

She rang Sheeran at Aer Lingus, wondering whether Mo stood for Maurice or Moses and deciding she'd better not ask, in case the guy thought she was hoping to quote him on anything. Just from the way he answered the phone – quick, abrupt, not a scintilla of warmth or hesitation – she could tell he was a serious player, imagined him as a tall, broad-shouldered man with a sharp suit, a firm jaw and close-cropped grey hair.

She explained who she was, what her connection to Griffin was and what she wanted. He made no comment other than to take her number and tell her he would call her back in five minutes. When he did, she could tell he was in a different space, smaller, quieter, more private, she guessed.

'Is this for Griffin or yourself?' Sheeran asked.

'For the paper,' she said.

For some reason he seemed to like that, the snort he made sounding marginally more positive than negative.

'This is confidential information. It's not to be published, recorded or broadcast in any way. I will refute any attribution. Understood?'

'Yes, understood.'

'Okay. What flight was it? Have you got a number?'

'That's the thing,' Siobhan said. 'There were two flights, both from Cork, both on the same night, Friday 3 September. I think the guy checked in for both but only got on one.'

She gave Sheeran the details, glad now she had double-checked the flight numbers online beforehand. He didn't sound the type to tolerate fumbling vagueness. She heard him inputting something on a keyboard, a pause, then the same again.

'Is this a drugs story?' he asked.

'Drugs? No, a missing person.' She made a poor job of concealing her surprise. 'Why would you think it was drugs?'

'I don't think it's anything,' he said sharply. 'It's your story. Bristol and Amsterdam were the destinations, yes?'

'Yes,' she said, feeling the tension coil in her stomach.

'You're right,' Sheeran said. 'He checked in online for both flights but only boarded one. *Could* only have boarded one as they departed within half an hour of each other. The flight Mr Cormac Horgan actually boarded on Friday 3 September was the earlier of the two, EI844 to Amsterdam.'

'And the Bristol flight?'

'Seat went empty.'

14

St Stephen's Green was busier than usual: hundreds, maybe thousands of optimistic souls venturing out from shops, offices and assorted other workplaces, streaming into the great park on the southern fringe of the city centre to soak up one last blast of late summer sunshine over the lunch hour. Mulcahy arrived a few minutes early, entering via the imposing stone arch on the Grafton Street side. Siobhan had said she would meet him by the O'Donovan Rossa memorial, but the benches there were already taken, and the patch of grass around it was filling up with sun-worshippers, too. He looked around, saw an elderly couple get up from a bench overlooking the lake and hurried over, feeling a ridiculous sense of frustration when two girls in grey bank-teller's uniforms got there and nabbed it before him. Why was he even thinking about getting a seat? All he wanted was to get the encounter over and done with.

He checked his watch again. Still a couple of minutes to go and he really didn't feel like hanging around. His phone rang: Siobhan's caller ID.

'Mulcahy, it's me – are you there yet? I'm going to be a couple of minutes late. You okay to wait?'

'Yes, okay. But it's packed here. I think we should find somewhere else, somewhere to sit—' He stopped himself, wondering where this sudden obsession with sitting had come from.

'You could try the Yeats garden,' she said. 'Do you know it? Over by the lake. It's always quiet in there.'

He had an idea, but she told him where it was, anyway, tucked away behind a tall screen of shrubbery on the far side of the pond. Like she said, it was fairly empty, no more than a dozen people scattered around, sitting, reading, munching on salads or sandwiches. It was all paved, more like an amphitheatre than a garden, with lots of steps and different levels all in cut stone. He sat down on one of the low slate ledges that doubled as seats, feeling the day's accumulated heat radiating into the backs of his thighs, put his head in his hands, smoothing his hair at the sides.

A green metal sculpture, two, maybe three metres high, stood on a circular pedestal in a far corner. A vaguely human shape but more like a sheet of canvas ripped by a gale. Was it supposed to be something to do with Yeats? All he could recall from school was something about treading softly on dreams, and a title that stuck in his mind, 'The Circus Animals' Desertion', though he couldn't remember a word of the poem or even what it was about. Siobhan would proba- bly know it, he reckoned, smiling at the easy assumption and realising, or maybe just admitting, for the first time, that he actually wanted to see her.

*

165

The minute she laid eyes on him – sitting there, oblivious, his big frame slouched over, hands clasped under his chin, elbows on his knees, smiling to himself as he stared at the Henry Moore bronze of W. B. Yeats at the far end of the garden – she knew that, for her, it was going to be the same as before with him. The same as always. Even now, when things were totally different.

'Hiya,' she said, forcing life into her voice, smiling the professional smile and mwah-mwahing either side of his big rough-hewn face, careful not to touch. He looked more perplexed than pleased to see her, but moved his jacket off the wall so she could sit.

'I love this place,' she said. 'It's like a secret garden, so tucked away and quiet.' She felt his eyes examining her as she placed her bag between them and sat down. For some reason she couldn't meet his gaze.

'You look different,' he said, eyes still combing her. 'You changed your hair.'

'I did that a while back.' She touched the top of her head self-consciously, smoothed her hand over the crown, down the nape to her bare neck. She hardly ever thought of how it was before. But, of course, he would remember it as it was back then – the mop of black curls, cropped now. 'A new start, a new look, you know?'

But he couldn't know. He could have no idea of how, almost from the moment she'd woken up in the hospital, she'd wanted to tear the whole filthy mass of it out by the roots. No one could know. It defied reason. For months, even after the pain of her other injuries had eased, she'd felt the prongs from the barbed-wire crown Rinn had scraped

166

through her hair, into her scalp. No matter how many times they washed her hair, no matter how often they told her the skin beneath had healed, she felt the sharp points of it digging down, pressing in. Until one day she took a scissors to her locks herself, and it was as if the cold sting of steel got swept away with the curls.

'It looks great. I mean, *you're* looking great. Being back at work must suit you.'

'You're not such a fright yourself,' she said, and surprised herself by putting out a hand and touching his shirt, the merest whisper, above the elbow. 'It's good to see you, Mulcahy.'

'You too. For a while there I thought you'd gone off me.'

It was such a ridiculous thing to say, she looked up at him, into his eyes and his teasing smile, and they both laughed.

'Here,' she said, opening her handbag and digging out the brown paper bag inside. 'I brought you this.'

He took it, but this time she saw his eyes take in the scar on the back of her outstretched hand and glance quickly away again. Embarrassed. Disgusted maybe.

'What's this?' As if he didn't know already. He untwisted the paper at the top and pulled the book half out, then stopped.

'Ah, your book,' he said flatly, taking in the title, the cover. '"*Crucified.*" Nice. I mean, congratulations. And thanks. I'll ... uh ... I'll save that for later.'

He pushed it back in the paper bag and put it down on the ledge beside him, like he was afraid he'd get infected if he held on to it any longer.

'Look, Mulcahy, about that ... ' She breathed deep, hadn't

intended getting into it so soon, but it was there now between them.

He was putting his hand up. 'It's okay. We said everything that needs to be said the other night. So let's just leave it at that, yeah?'

It annoyed her that she felt any need to apologise to him for the book. She wanted him to listen to her defend it like it deserved, but what was the point? It was obvious where he stood on the subject, that nothing she could say would change his mind. And there was no point setting out to upset him. Not when she needed a favour from him. 'Okay.'

'What was it you wanted to see me about?' he asked. 'This missing kid you were chasing up?'

'Yeah, but she's no kid. Did you have any luck getting me that contact?'

He looked away, over towards the statue again. 'Sorry – it's been a busy week. But there is a guy I thought of this morning, after you rang.'

He reached in his pocket, handed over a yellow Post-it note with a name and number on it. 'Give him a call, mention my name if you have to. He might be able to help.'

She glanced at it and put it in the inside pocket of her bag. 'Thanks. There's something else I wanted to run by you, as well. Do you mind?'

'Missing persons isn't really my thing, Siobhan. You'd be better off—'

She held up a finger. 'Please, Mulcahy. I just want to see if you think this is weird, too. You've got good instincts. And you're here now, yeah?'

He shrugged, like he knew there was no point resisting,

which there wasn't really. She started telling him again about Gemma Kearney and Cormac Horgan, reminded him what she'd said to him a couple of nights before. He seemed to remember most of it.

'And I told you we weren't sure Gemma had actually gone to Bristol, right?'

He nodded and mumbled something she didn't catch.

'Well, she was there – definitely. I know that for a fact now. I was over there myself yesterday.'

His eyes widened. 'You went to Bristol to check this out? It must be some story.'

'It's no story at all yet, but I'm telling you, Mulcahy, there's something not right about it.'

He listened while she told him what she'd learnt from Sergeant Walker, about finding the mobile phone in the car, the appointment with 'G' and, later, the message waiting for Horgan from Gemma when he checked into his hotel. He agreed that it was all a bit strange, but he seemed more surprised about the level of access Walker had allowed her than anything else.

'Well, you know, I have a good record of charming the pants off my sources,' she said, smiling broadly – the old smile, the confident smile. Then she saw him look away, redden a little, and she realised what she'd said. Christ, how could she be so stupid? Oh well, he was the one who wanted to skim over things. She could do that, too.

'The thing is, Mulcahy, the more I look at Horgan's story, the less it makes sense. When I did my piece on his suicide, it was easy. The bridge was there; he'd bankrupted a multi-million-pound business; there were no suspicious circumstances.

169

Therefore, you know, he must have gone to Bristol to kill himself. But once you put Gemma in the mix, none of it adds up. I mean, what the hell were they doing there? It sure as hell wasn't for a romantic weekend away.'

'Who can say?' Mulcahy shrugged. 'Maybe it started out that way. Or maybe it was to do with his business. The UK economy isn't as buggered up as ours. Maybe he had some property over there, or someone he hoped would throw him a lifeline, and when that didn't work out . . . Look, I have no idea, but it strikes me as being a long way to go to kill yourself. The Cliffs of Moher would've been a hell of a lot closer, and easier. Beyond that, I wouldn't want to speculate.'

'I'm not asking you to. I've already been through the whole thing again with Paddy Griffin, my editor, this morning. The only thing we could absolutely agree on was how bizarre it is that Gemma's office has been closed up like that, without anybody but her mother creating any fuss. I persuaded him to give me two days to get something definite on it. After that he's closing me down.'

She felt his eyes on her again.

'And you haven't had any joy from Missing Persons?'

She shook her head. 'They wouldn't discuss the case with me, and when her mother tried, they just palmed her off again.'

'Well, beyond that name I gave you, I honestly don't see how I can help.'

He smiled in a semi-apologetic way and ran his hands over his thighs like he was about to stand up. 'It's been nice seeing you, Siobhan, really, but I'd better be getting back.'

170

She put up a hand to stop him. 'Hang on, Mulcahy. I haven't got to the really weird bit yet. I only found this out a couple of hours ago, and I honestly do think you might be interested.'

He aborted the move to stand up, and sat back down again, heavily, tolerantly. 'Okay, what is it?'

'Why would Horgan have checked in for two simultaneous flights but only taken one of them, and not to the city he ended up in?'

He looked at her like she'd addressed him in a foreign language, and paused as if translating it to himself before replying with a sigh. 'I have no idea, Siobhan. The laws of physics, maybe?'

'No, seriously, Mulcahy,' she said. 'This was the day before he died. He went to Amsterdam. How he ended up in Bristol I have no idea, now.'

She told him everything she knew about Horgan's boarding passes, how her informant in Aer Lingus was adamant Horgan had taken the flight to Amsterdam, not Bristol. Mulcahy thought about it, agreed that this too was peculiar, but beyond that?

'Why would you think I might be able to throw some light on it?'

'Because the guy who gave me this information seemed to think it might have something to do with drugs.'

'Didn't you ask him why?'

'I did, but he wouldn't talk about it.' She looked away. 'Getting anything at all from him was like milking a stone. I can't tell you who he was, but let's just say he's in a position to know what he's talking about. I thought maybe you – being the great drugs expert and all – might have an idea. I mean, why would he put boarding passes and drugs together?'

Mulcahy drew a deep breath. 'There's only one reason I've heard of anyone doing that deliberately. And, with Amsterdam as the destination, I can maybe see why someone in security might think of it. But, honestly, I think this guy's given you a bum steer there, Siobhan.'

'Why do you say that?' For some reason she didn't want to admit that Sheeran hadn't given her any steer at all.

'Because what he was probably thinking of was an old druggie trick that used to be common enough a few years back. But this Horgan character? I just don't get how it could be relevant to him in any way. He sounds completely clean to me.'

She couldn't resist a lead in like that. 'But what's the trick? Go on, tell me, please.'

He looked at her like he was weighing up whether she deserved to know or not, then gave in. 'Back in the 1990s when Ryanair and the other low-fare airlines started expanding everywhere through Europe, some of the bigger drugs guys who travelled around a lot, doing the really shady deals, they came up with this idea to mess up intelligence-gathering operations. They'd buy two or three cheap return air tickets to different places whenever they were flying anywhere, to confuse any surveillance operations regarding their ultimate destination until the very last moment. It made keeping a continuous eye on them extremely difficult for us, and it undermined the chains of evidence we relied on in court to establish patterns of movement in big drug-trafficking cases. Do you follow?'

'Sort of, but I sense a "but" coming,' Siobhan said.

'You'd be right. As I was about to say, that was then. We've since come up with ways of countering that kind of dodge. It's also much easier to monitor people's movements electronically nowadays. I mean, do you have any real reason to suspect Horgan was involved in drugs, as opposed to someone with odd travel arrangements?'

Siobhan wished she could come up with some riposte to that, but she felt pretty much shot to ribbons by it. Her one potential lead of the morning lay in tatters.

'No, not really,' she said with a big sigh. 'It just seemed to tie in with something I heard about Gemma, that's all – about how she got into trouble when she was younger. I rang her mother last night to tell her what I'd found in Bristol. She'd had a few drinks, I think, and she started telling me all sorts about how Gemma had been this bright but difficult kid who ran off to Dublin as soon as she finished her Leaving Cert. This was a few years before she went to college and met Horgan. Mrs Kearney said Gemma got a job up here as a receptionist for a record company, Klene Records. They used to do all that retro-punk stuff in the late 1990s, had a few good bands – the Reeraws, the Ballgags and some others. Do you remember them?'

'It rings a bell,' Mulcahy said, looking like he didn't like the sound of it but couldn't think why.

'They were an edgy sort of crowd, anyway,' Siobhan continued, 'and it sounds like Gemma embraced the sex'n'drugs even more than the rock'n'roll. She got herself involved with some scumbag manager who did the dirt on her. I mean properly, got her hooked on all kinds of drugs and shit, then kicked her out when he got sick of her. Brought her very low, suicidally so, by the sound of it. Anyway, Mrs Kearney let slip that Gemma got into serious trouble with you lot during that time.'

'And?'

'And nothing. As soon as Mrs K realised what she'd said – or who she'd said it to, more like – she got upset. Gemma's career, good name and all that. She wouldn't tell me any more, insisted it had nothing to do with Gemma's life now, but it was obvious she was thinking exactly the opposite, that it was at the root of all her worries, really. Which is why I called you this morning – you know, drugs. And then, when I heard this airline security guy talking about drugs, I thought—' She broke off, looked up at him and shrugged.

'You thought what?'

His mood seemed to have changed now, his expression critical, like he knew what she was going to ask him but he wanted her to say it, anyway. Not that that was ever going to be a problem.

'I thought you might look up your database for me, see what it was she was done for – whether it was more than once, whether it ever came up again, whether Horgan had any drugs connections in his past. It doesn't seem so far-fetched, does it?'

She could see his face going red as she said it, but wasn't quite prepared for the blast of heat that came at her when he answered.

'Jesus, I don't believe you, Siobhan. The first time I see you in over a year and within five minutes you're asking me to hand you over confidential information about drugs offences from Garda records.'

'Oh, come on, Mulcahy, lighten up. It's probably all in the public domain, anyway.'

'So you can get it yourself, then.'

'Not easily, like you can. You know that. All I'm asking is for you to look up your computer. It wouldn't take you more than a minute and it would at least fill in that blank for me. Nobody needs to find out. Christ, it's not like I'm trying to bring down the government or anything. I just thought, you know, if there's a drugs element to this, then maybe you might get some mileage out of it as well.'

'I don't think so.'

'For God's sake, it's just a little crumb of information. It could never be traced back to you—' She broke off, tried to up the level of pleading in her eyes. 'I need this, Mulcahy, please. I don't even know why, but I need to do this story.'

'Fine, but you'll have to do it without me. Christ, Siobhan, you of all people should know how I feel about crossing that line.'

She shook her head in disbelief and smiled at him bitterly. 'You cop, me hack. Is that it?'

'That's not fair, Siobhan. You know what happened last time. I nearly fucked up my career for good over what happened with you and Rinn. How can you forget that? How can you think that's just gone away?'

'Gone away?' She choked on that, felt a glob of dark emotion bubble up from somewhere she hadn't fathomed in a long, long time. 'Nobody remembers better than me, Mulcahy. Believe me.'

Without even really realising what she was doing, she held up her hands in front of his face, turning them so he could see the scars on both sides. 'I saw you looking earlier. Don't you think I see them, too? Don't you think they remind me every minute of every fucking day? And what about my career? Don't you think I might have lost more than you? Don't you think I would give anything to have the last year of my life back, to have things the way they were before?'

She grabbed her handbag and stood up, overtaken by fury, stabbed a finger out at the brown paper bag on the ledge by his leg. 'Do you think I *wanted* to write that? Jesus, what a bloody fool I was, thinking it might mean something to you, too. That you might actually want to help me salvage something from all this shit that would get me back where I was before. Nice to fucking see you again, Mulcahy.'

She turned on her heel and stormed away. How could she have been so stupid and delusional as to think that he might actually care? Did he seriously believe she wouldn't give anything, *anything* in her power to forget the past year of hurt and misery, and have her life the way it was? And what does he do? Spout rules and fucking regulations at her. Christ, to think there was a time when she thought that he might be the one, the one who actually got her.

Behind her she heard a rushing noise, a heavy tread of feet and felt something pulling at her elbow. Muffled by the billowing clouds of anger, a voice said, 'Hang on, Siobhan.' But it was a whisper compared to the rush of blood pounding in her ears as she felt herself pulled back, just as she'd been pulled back fourteen months before as, in the darkness of a garage in Rathgar she saw a claw hammer swing out from behind her and strike her photographer, Franny Stoppard, on the back of the skull with a sickening crunch. A prelude to her own night of terror.

Everything went quiet. The world stopped. She knew she had screamed, and when she opened her eyes, all she saw was Mulcahy taking a step back from her, his face pale, his hands up, palms out, a look of shock and deep concern in his eyes.

'It's okay, Siobhan,' he was saying. 'It was me. Everything's all right. It was only me.'

In her confusion, she was looking around, seeing every face in the small stone garden turned to her, agog, sandwiches and plastic forks frozen midway to mouths, wondering what was going on, fearful they might be expected to intervene. With a snap of realisation she came back. Knew where she was. Knew what had happened. She felt something tear inside her.

'Siobhan, look at me,' Mulcahy was saying. 'Everything's all right. It's okay. You're safe here. Look at me.'

So she did look at him, and she watched him lower his right hand and hold it out to her. 'Only if you want to,' he said.

And she found she did want to, because everything was beginning to fall apart inside her now. Her legs were shaking, and her lungs were heaving with something that wouldn't be contained, so she held her hand out, felt it folded into the bigness of his and found herself sitting down with him again, allowing him to put his arm around her shoulders as, for the first time in as long as she could remember, she felt the consoling warmth of another human being press against her, and the tears fall from her eyes.

*

Such was the clamour of emotion in Mulcahy by the time he got back to Dublin Castle, he stormed up the stairs and stomped through to his office and flung the glass door shut behind him, logged on to his computer and sat there staring unseeingly at the screen. What the fuck had all that been about? Jesus. The intensity had overwhelmed him. Sitting there with Siobhan in Stephen's Green, his arm around her, it had all come flooding back: the Phoenix Park the year before, Siobhan blood-drenched, hanging from the Papal Cross, and Rinn, screaming at him to get back, get back or he'd ... Fuck. He'd pushed so much of it out of his mind. Especially his own failure afterwards, after all the fuss died down, after she'd rebuffed his attempts to see her twice, was it three times? And he'd just accepted it. Turned round and tried to forget her, like she deserved it. And when she'd come to him about the book, told her to take a hike. Like a petulant child. Christ, how could he be such a prick? No wonder she'd gone spare at him.

How long they'd sat there for, he didn't know. But not very. Her pulling herself together, embarrassed, him saying the little he could think of to make her feel okay about it. After a few minutes she'd pulled away from him again, sat stiffly apart, apologising for being such an idiot, for losing it. She said things still crept up on her occasionally, got the better of her. She hadn't slept well and ... she was sorry. That was the gist of it, anyway. He'd asked her if she was okay, if she was well enough to be back at work at all, but she said work was the only thing that kept her going, and that she'd better go do some. Then she'd apologised again, for calling him, said it had been a stupid idea after all that time. He'd never seen

178

anyone look so lonely as when she walked off towards Dawson Street.

He heard a knock on the glass door and looked up to see Ford, leaning in round it, his expression one of superficial concern masking far greater curiosity. Behind him, still sitting at their desks, he saw Duffy and Sweeney staring in after Ford, their faces full of unabashed, almost gleeful interest. The boss in a state – what a laugh. Christ, had Ford said something to them about who he'd gone out to meet?

'You okay, boss? You look like you've seen your nana in the nip. Is everything okay?'

'Everything's fine, thanks.' He said it in a low growl and turned back to his computer screen, only looking up again when he realised that Ford hadn't moved but was still standing with his head round the door, looking in expectantly.

'What is it?' Mulcahy barked, more a challenge than a question.

Ford looked like he was about to lob that one back at him but, for once, decided that the smart-arse remark was not the way to go. 'It's five past three, boss, and you did say we had to have this brainstorm session at three o'clock. Do you want to cancel? Will I tell the lads to get on with something else?'

Shit. He'd completely forgotten about that. This was what he should have been thinking about on the way back. Not spent every step of the way, head down, fretting about whether Siobhan would be okay. What sort of idiot must he have looked like to the others storming in like that? He rapped his fingers on the edge of the desk and stood up, going over to the door, pulling it open as Ford stood back.

179

'No, Liam, thanks,' he said with as much authority as he could salvage. 'I was ... uh ... checking something. I'll be with you in a couple of minutes, okay? I'm just going for a quick ...' He jerked a thumb towards the bathroom down the corridor.

'Okay, boss, whenever you're ready.'

He went in and turned on the tap, scooped up a double handful of water and buried his face in it. He repeated this three times, letting the cold shock of water on his forehead and eyes calm him and bring him back to earth. He grabbed a paper towel and stood up straight, staring at himself in the mirror, seeing a man with a jaw that was too big to be handsome and a nose with a kink on the bridge from where *Seaspray*'s tiller hit him full in the face during a squall when he was thirteen. He wiped his face again and got his hair in order. A man, he said to himself, as if his father's hand was resting there on his shoulder. He took a deep breath and cleared his mind of everything but what Solomons had told them earlier at the Clarence. If Donal Murtagh thought the ILU needed some sort of coup to ensure its survival, then finding the source of the cocaine on the *Atlantean* would be the best chance they were likely to get of delivering something spectacular. That's what he had to focus on now. If they could establish that link, maybe they would be able to push it even further. *If* the link was there.

15

As soon as Siobhan got round the corner onto Dawson Street, she had started looking out for a taxi. No way was she going back to the office again, despite what she'd said to Mulcahy. She wasn't fit for anything after that scene, and it wasn't like she'd be missed at the *Herald*. Eventually she saw a cab coming and hailed it, climbed in and slumped in the back like a stringless puppet, slack, spent, oblivious to the driver's line in amiable jabber. Fifteen minutes later she was back in the safety of her apartment, feeling cold, pulling a blanket from the box at the end of the bed and wrapping it around herself. Looking for excuses. Mulcahy had been a bit of an arse, sure, but it wasn't like she hadn't provoked him. She met worse than him most days and it didn't plunge her into full-on meltdown mode. What the hell had happened there? Was it the nightmare? The lack of sleep? Was it because Mulcahy was the only tangible reminder she had – the living proof in so many ways – of exactly what she had allowed Rinn to take from her?

She went into the kitchen, poured herself a glass of wine,

went back to the living room, wrapped the blanket tight around herself again and turned on the laptop. Anything to stop dwelling on herself. What had happened to Gemma? That was all that mattered now. She was determined to get somewhere with it, but the problem was that the woman herself remained like a ghost to her. She had gathered all this information on Horgan, yet Gemma was as elusive as ever. So far everything she'd learnt about her had come from either Mrs Kearney or the one or two of Horgan's friends who'd been willing to talk to her. Even the accountancy governing body hadn't returned her call. The only thing for it was to go back down to Cork again, she decided, put some old-fashioned legwork into it, track down that PA of Gemma's. Surely she would know what Gemma had been planning. There had to be someone around those offices who knew who the PA was. Or she could get in touch with the landlord, maybe, find out if they knew why the office was closed up. If he was the right type, or aggrieved, he might even let her have a poke around. It had to be worth a try, anyhow, didn't it?

Buoyed up with enthusiasm for the task, she set about making plans for a trip to Cork the next day, cursing herself now for wasting so much time going to Bristol. But even as she did so, her thoughts snagged on Horgan again, and what Sheeran had said earlier about him flying to Amsterdam. How could he have flown to Holland and then ended up checking into the hotel in Bristol at five the following morning, less than twelve hours later? Had Gemma ever really met him in Bristol?

She went over to her bag on the sofa and got out her mobile, remembering the photos she had taken in Walker's office the day before. Maybe that bar bill would yield some sign of Gemma, some indication of a female presence. She opened the photos on her phone. As she flicked through them, they all looked just as innocuous as they had the day before. Except for one, which was very indistinct, but looked to be for a large amount: €129. The next was the bar bill she'd been looking for: £16 spent in the Gold Bar, Bristol, beverages and food . . . She looked at the photo again, then thumbed back to the one before. How had she missed that first time round? One receipt was in euros, the other in pounds sterling. She flicked through the other photos. All were in pounds except for one, for another sizeable amount in euros – €70.20. Had Horgan made some last-minute purchases before he left Ireland?

She maximised the top section of the photo on the phone screen and just about managed to make out what was printed at the top of that receipt: 'Total Belmos.' There was no indication whether it was Irish or not, but what she saw underneath it, now, in the smaller print below, made her stop: the date 03:09:10, followed by a time, 22.35. Five hours after he'd left Cork. She stared again at the name at the top of the receipt. Total Belmos. It was meaningless to her. She took a sip of wine and typed the name into Google, tutted when she saw that the top hits were all to do with the French oil company Total, then nearly choked when she clicked on the first site, anyway, which brought up a map and directions to a petrol station, a Total petrol station at Belmos, Belgium, on the main E19 route south of Antwerp – about a hundred miles south of Amsterdam.

She was sure she'd seen a reference to E19 somewhere else

in Horgan's stuff. The Moleskine notebook. The lists. Walker had said they might be road numbers, junctions. She'd taken pics of them as well. She clicked forward to those pictures, but they were illegible on the phone's small screen. She thought of emailing them through to the laptop, blowing them up on that, but before she did, another number floated to the surface of her memory. Or not just one number: A18/E40. That was it. She was sure of it. She typed it onto the screen, hit search, breathed out as she saw A18/E40 listed on various sites as a motorway in Belgium, but this time south of Bruges, heading west towards the coast and on to . . .

She sat back, felt several pieces of the jigsaw click softly, simultaneously into place. The road maps, the lists, the early morning check-in at the hotel, even Amsterdam made sense to her now. But mostly it was what Gemma had said in the message she left for Horgan at the hotel that snapped into perfect clarity: 'Told you crossing would be fine.' Jesus Christ, even her subconscious had tried to flag it up for her in that dream and she'd missed it. Crossing. *The crossing*. She clicked on the map on her screen, saw the A18/E40 highlighted in blue on it, ran a finger down the E19 from Amsterdam, to where the roads connected and then ran west to Calais, from where the ferry crossed the Channel to England.

'It had to be Ronson,' Sweeney insisted. 'Nobody else could have known where Hayford left the drugs and nobody else could have turned around such a large-scale smuggling operation in under two months.'

They were all in Mulcahy's office, sitting around his desk. They'd been going at it for over an hour, refamiliarising themselves with every aspect of the Rosscarbery Bay case. Ford had done a good job while Mulcahy was out. Not only had he been in touch with the Dutch authorities – and confirmed in essence, if not in detail, everything Solomons had told them about Hayford's murder in Rotterdam and the rumours of missing cocaine. He had also briefed Duffy and Sweeney thoroughly on what Solomons had said in the Clarence, and how it might tie in with the *Atlantean*. He had even got them to prepare quick profiles of both Ronson and Hayford from what intelligence information was easily available. All Mulcahy had to do was fill them in on what McTiernan had told him the night before about Begley's possible involvement. Then they had started in earnest by making up a timeline. With Ford writing it up in bullet points on a whiteboard he'd pinched from the Surveillance Unit next door, and Duffy using his laptop to double-check the dates using press reports and intelligence bulletins, they went through each of the key events in detail.

What quickly became evident was that a clear line of possibility did, in fact, run from Steve Hayford's murder in Rotterdam in April through the seizure of the *Atlantean* off Cork in June and on to the murders of Trevor Ronson and Declan Begley. So much for possibility. The question of probability was rather more elusive. As was the issue of who could have acquired the cocaine and arranged its shipment to Ireland in such a relatively short space of time – the subject of Sweeney's current line of argument.

'You can't just throw a sophisticated operation like that together in a couple of weeks,' she argued. 'Not unless you have the organisation in place already.'

185

'But it didn't take only a couple of weeks, did it?' Duffy objected. 'As you said yourself, it took at least a couple of months – we can see that from the timeline. And it was only sophisticated in theory. They botched the job, for Christ's sake. How often did Ronson cock it up like that? Not very.'

Duffy sat back in his seat like he'd delivered the *coup de grâce* to that particular line of argument, but Sweeney was having none of it. 'The fact remains that Ronson must've had some idea where the cocaine was left in storage,' she insisted. 'I mean, a €100 million worth – you're not going to just lose it, are you? He must've had an idea of what Hayford planned to do with it.'

'Not necessarily,' Mulcahy said. 'Especially if Hayford was running the day-to-day end of the business.' There wasn't much point reminding Sweeney how drugs organisations and hierarchies were usually structured, how the people at the top were cushioned from risk by the layers below them, how details of movement and shipment were always on a need-to-know basis – for the protection of everyone concerned. Sweeney knew more about the theory of all that than many a Garda detective with five times her experience on the streets.

'Look, we know from what Solomons said that Ronson told the Colombians he had no idea where the consignment was,' Mulcahy repeated. 'He must have reckoned there was a chance they would believe him.'

'Yeah, but he would say that, wouldn't he?' Sweeney jumped in. 'It would have had to be his starting position either way, whether he was telling the truth or lying to them. My point is, on the balance of probabilities, Ronson has to be the most likely candidate. Like Liam said, what better way could he dream up of making the Cali Cartel pay for topping Hayford than by nicking a tonne of their cocaine?'

Mulcahy squeezed his hands together in frustration and sat back in his chair. 'But why would Ronson even risk it? It doesn't take a brain surgeon to figure out that you can't get embroiled in a feud like that with the Colombians and come out ahead. And the one thing that emerges consistently from the intel on Ronson is that he was exceptionally intelligent. He must have known there was no chance he could take on a cartel and win.'

'He wouldn't be the first cokehead to get grandiose ideas about himself,' Ford said.

'Yeah, but he wasn't, was he?' Mulcahy said. 'Everything we have on him says he steered well clear of the product.'

'I thought we were supposed to be thinking outside the box here?' Sweeney broke in again. 'I mean, just supposing your guy Solomons is wrong and Ronson did know where the drugs were and decided to chance his arm with them.'

'Solomons did say Ronson wanted out of the game, boss,' Duffy joined in now. 'And €100 million worth of coke is a hell of a pension pot.'

Mulcahy had to concede that one.

'Look, I think we're getting way off the point here,' Ford complained. 'Surely the question is not why the Colombians might have killed Ronson. It's how we make the link between the cocaine that went missing in Rotterdam and the cocaine that turned up on the *Atlantean*. I thought that's supposed to be what we were about here.'

'It is, Liam,' Mulcahy said, 'but so far Ronson is the only plausible link between the two that we've come up with.'

'Sorry, boss, but I think Liam might be right,' said Duffy, who'd been looking off into the distance for the last couple of minutes. 'If we concentrate on Ronson, we'll only end up going round in circles. I think there might be an even more obvious link.'

Duffy paused and all three stared over at him. 'It's the wrapping,' he said, a light-bulb look in his eyes now. 'That's the thing that ties it all together.'

Mulcahy watched, amused, as Sweeney made an elaborate job of throwing her eyes heavenwards and tutting loudly. 'What are you on about, Aidan?'

But Duffy had turned away and started clacking furiously on his laptop as the others looked at each other. As the one member of the quartet who hadn't worked closely on the Rosscarbery Bay case, he had already made a few suggestions that elicited derisory responses from them.

'What wrapping, Aidan?' Mulcahy asked.

'The stuff the bales of cocaine were wrapped in.'

'What about it?' Ford's exasperation was getting the better of him.

Duffy swivelled his laptop round towards them. On the screen was a blown-up news photo of the ninety bales of cocaine stacked on the quayside beside the *Atlantean* in Baltimore, the day after they were seized. Mulcahy recognised the shot instantly – he was probably somewhere just off the edge of it himself.

'Don't you see?' Duffy said, like they were all as thick as planks. 'The cartel guys wouldn't have whacked Ronson straight away, because at some level they trusted him. They'd been doing business for years. And they only had proof that

Hayford got the cocaine, but not that it had ever got to Ronson afterwards. So what if – after a couple of months go by, say – they suddenly discover a really good reason to think Ronson was taking the piss all along. Like, if they found out he was trying to get the stuff out of Holland by some other route.'

Duffy looked on expectantly as he waited for the others to digest that. Ford was the first to come back on it. 'Aidan has a point, boss. If Ronson did decide to hang on to the cocaine, he wouldn't have wanted to risk bringing it into the UK through his normal channels. The Colombians might've got wind of it.'

Mulcahy nodded. It made a lot of sense.

'That's right,' Duffy said enthusiastically. 'So Ronson might have tried bringing some of it in here to Ireland, to disguise where it came from, which would have worked perfectly if the trip had gone smoothly. But it didn't. The *Atlantean* got seized and her cargo displayed for all the world to see on the quayside in Baltimore. That's what I'm trying to say. Those bales were all in their original wrappings.' Duffy looked around at them as he pointed to the address bar on the photograph. 'This is a Reuters picture. There must have been loads like it splashed all round the world. What if these Cali guys saw one and recognised their missing product? They'd have figured out for sure that Ronson really had tried to pull a fast one, wouldn't they?'

Everyone in the room went quiet. They all remembered the press frenzy that had surrounded the seizure. They'd lived through it, facilitated it, been a first point of contact for the rush of interest that had flooded in from other enforcement agencies around the world on the back of it. Mulcahy himself had stood on the quay in Baltimore and looked on as the slavering press pack – photographers, TV reporters and print journalists – were given access for the carefully choreographed press conference. The *Atlantean* moored up, the bales of cocaine stacked for maximum visual impact behind the Garda commissioner and the Minister for Justice, who'd been helicoptered in specially to share the credit for this victory in the global war against drugs, as rare as it was spectacular. Duffy was absolutely right. The pictures had been splashed on front pages, and the film footage on TV news reports, all around the world. Every publicly released detail of the operation had been written about – including descriptions of the bales and their thick, sealed white plastic wrapping, each one bound with heavy-duty twine.

'The way that twine was tied on the bales *was* distinctive,' Ford said to Mulcahy. 'You said so yourself at the time.'

He had. The packaging itself was fairly standard Colombian: each of the ten-kilo bales had been heat-sealed and waterproofed in thick industrial-grade white plastic. But the thick vegetative cord round each bale, run twice round the width and once along the length, and knotted at every intersection, was unusual. Presumably it was there to make the bales easier to carry across the mountains into Venezuela and on to whichever Atlantic port they had been shipped out from. The investigation team had sent samples of the twine to the DEA in the US for testing, and they had confirmed that it was made from Colombian sisal. It was another of the reasons everyone initially assumed the *Atlantean* had sailed up direct from the region. Those bales looked like they hadn't been tampered with since leaving the jungle compound they were made up in. And the way they had been tied, every time with just one length of cord, all bound and knotted apparently by the same hand, really had been individual.

'I think we might be on to something here,' Mulcahy said quietly. 'If you'd been the person who prepared that consignment, or even handled it, one close look at that photo and you'd recognise it straight away. I've no doubt about that.'

'Jesus, that's got to be a possibility all right,' Ford said in a low voice. 'They waited until they had the feckin' proof.'

Sweeney coughed and drew their attention towards her. 'And if everything between Ronson and Begley really was as your pal McTiernan described it, boss,' she said, running with the idea now, 'you know, all super-pally and that – well, it could give us the Begley connection as well.'

'You're right,' Mulcahy said. 'If Ronson wanted to get stuff in through the back door via Ireland, who better to turn to for help than his new best pal, Declan Begley.'

16

Mulcahy was sure they were on to something, but doubts lingered about whether it could ever tie up quite so neatly in reality. Few major investigations could be wholly resolved by a two-hour brainstorm, and they still hadn't moved beyond the point of pure speculation. But it was a start. He told Sweeney and Duffy to devote all their efforts to it: her priority to liaise with the Spanish murder team and get everything they had on Begley, Duffy's to work the Dutch angle and gather as much info as he could on the fallout from Hayford's murder in terms of the missing cocaine. Meanwhile, Mulcahy said, he and Ford would approach SOCA regarding Ronson. They could all reconvene the following day at the same time, and he wanted tangible progress made, no matter how hard they had to push it.

As the others got up to leave, he asked Ford to hang back, waiting to speak again until Sweeney had pulled the glass door shut behind her.

'Before we get into all this, I wanted a quick word about something else that's come up.'

Ford cocked an eyebrow at him. 'Oh yeah? Like our lives aren't exciting enough already?'

'I'm sure this won't do anything to push you over your thrill threshold. It's just a name I came across. Klene Records? Ring any bells with you?'

'Klene with a "k" and two "e"s?'

'Could be,' Mulcahy said. 'They were some punk-music outfit, so they probably couldn't spell. Did they come up in anything we've been looking at recently?'

'Not recently,' Ford said, 'but you'll have heard the name all right, years back. Around the time you went off to Madrid, or just after, maybe. Yeah, you probably would have been gone by then. We shut down a place with that name, or at least the Criminal Assets Bureau did, with our help. The place was a total front. Drugs money in one end, CD sales and supposedly legitimate profits out the other. It was Klene ha, ha – as in laundry. The CAB confiscated the lot – property, recording equipment, even the stock of CDs and master tapes or whatever you call them. There was a massive shit-storm about it at the time – you know, suppressing the creativity of the nation's youth, all that liberal bollocks. I suppose we did deprive a few lousy bands of their fifteen minutes of fame.'

Mulcahy couldn't help wondering why Siobhan hadn't mentioned anything about that. Was it possible she wasn't aware of it? It wouldn't be like her to not be fully in the know, but then she hadn't been firing on all cylinders, had she? He thought of the haunted look in her eyes again. Christ, how had she even recovered that much from what Rinn had done to her?

193

'You okay there, boss?'

Ford was staring at him with that look on his face again.

'Yeah, sorry, Liam. Did you work on the Klene job?'

'No, it was GNDU all right, but before my time. I was still over in A Division then. But I know some lads who did work on it. Do you need some background? It'll all be in dust-wrappers in the archive by now.'

'Can you pull the file on it for me?'

'The file?' Ford snorted. 'Jesus, there's probably hundreds of files. Like I said, it was a major deal at the time. Was there anything in particular you were interested in? Could you give me a name or something to concentrate on?'

Mulcahy rubbed his forehead, the frustration building up in him again. There were far more important things to be getting on with, and no way should he be involving Ford in this as well.

'This has to stay between the two of us, okay?'

'Fair enough,' Ford tutted, clearly insulted. 'Who else would I tell?'

'Look, I only say that because it's important for *me* to keep it quiet. I need to find out about a woman called Gemma Kearney, DOB October 1978 or thereabouts. I think she worked at Klene Records around the time it was shut down, or before that, maybe. I'd really appreciate it if you could have a squint at what we have on her – you know, arrests, mentions in dispatches, anything at all. Apparently she was picked up by us at some stage. I need to know when and what for. Okay?'

Ford couldn't let it go at that. 'Can I at least ask what it's in connection with?'

'I'd prefer if you didn't, Liam. Like I said, it's between you and me for now. If anybody asks, say you're pulling the files in connection with Rosscarbery Bay. That should shut them up. And if there's a problem, refer them straight to me, okay?'

'Sure, if it's that important.'

'Thanks, Liam,' Mulcahy said, turning to his computer screen and clicking on his contacts book. 'I'll crack on with the SOCA side of things while you're doing that and get the ball rolling. What did Solomons say the SIO's name was? Commander Gavin Corbett, was it?'

'That's right,' Ford said, getting up. 'I don't know whether he'd be London- or Liverpool-based.'

'Probably a bit of both—' Mulcahy broke off, and looked up as Duffy rapped on the glass door and opened it far enough to stick his head into the room.

'Boss, are you done there? It's a call for you. Sounds urgent.'

'Who?'

Duffy winced like he'd been caught out. 'Some detective inspector, says she has to talk to you right now. Not sure of the name, she said it so quick. Gogan or Grogan or Brogan, I think.'

'Brogan?' Mulcahy exclaimed. 'Claire Brogan?'

For the second time that day Mulcahy found himself completely at a loss. He'd worked with Brogan the year before on the Priest investigation, or at least until she had used the case as an opportunity to leap-frog over him and get herself a transfer out of Sex Crimes and into the Murder Squad. He hadn't seen or heard from her since, save for a whisper on the grapevine that she had left her husband and taken up with

195

the head of Murder, a guy called Lonergan. Hearing Brogan's name out of the blue just hours after meeting Siobhan, it was all getting a bit too weird for him. What in the name of God could Brogan want?

He shook himself out of it. Both Ford and Duffy were giving him that perplexed look again.

'Did she say what it was about?'

'No.' Duffy grimaced, like he was being accused of something,

'Okay, put her through, thanks,' he said, finally regaining some of his composure.

He picked up the phone. 'Claire, how can I help you?'

She told him exactly how he could help, and in no uncertain terms. He began to feel sick in his stomach, too shocked by what she was saying to do anything more than mutter occasional single-word responses and assurances. As he put the phone down his hand was trembling, his entire body numb with anxiety and disbelief.

'What's the matter, boss? You've gone grey as bone.'

Mulcahy looked up at Ford. He hadn't even been aware that he was still in the room. 'Fuck's sake,' he whispered, more to himself than to Ford. 'It's Eddie McTiernan . . . '

It took Siobhan just another hour or so to put flesh on the bones of Horgan's itinerary the night of Friday 3 September. He had flown from Cork to Amsterdam, she knew. At some point he must have picked up a vehicle, driven it south through Holland on the E19 for two hours or so before refuelling somewhere near Rotterdam, then driven on for another couple of hours down through Belgium and France, before taking the midnight ferry across the Channel to England. All this she gleaned from the two receipts for purchases in euros. The first must have been for fuel, she surmised, when the second revealed itself – enlarged on her laptop – as both a receipt and ticket for the 11.30 p.m. SeaFrance ferry from Calais to Dover: €120 for one *van utilitaire* and one *passager*. She didn't need to be a genius at French to figure out what a *van utilitaire* was: a van. And from Dover, Horgan had driven it another 200 miles on to Bristol, arriving at around 5 a.m.

There was only one reason Siobhan could think of why anyone would do all of that, and try to cack-handedly cover up the fact by booking another flight to Bristol at the same time. There was one big question in her mind now, too: why would anyone go to the enormous trouble of doing all that and then kill himself twelve hours later? Shortly after meeting Gemma Kearney.

Eddie McTiernan lay slumped against the bodywork of his silver Bentley, the heavy driver's door gaping open, a pool of viscous brown blood congealing around his legs and hips, and seeping away behind him beneath the car. His face was a horror show, eyes and mouth frozen open in shock, the leathery brown of his features drained to a dull grey. Behind and above him, the coachwork of the car was peppered with shot and plumes of dark dried blood, spattered about with gobbets of flesh and bone ripped from the football-sized hole in his chest by what could only have been a shotgun discharged at very close range.

Mulcahy stepped out of the stifling forensics tent, both hands covering his nose and mouth, the bitter stench of blood, hot air and what must have been McTiernan's spontaneous terminal bowel movement threatening to overwhelm his stomach. He pushed back the hood of the thin, papery coverall he was wearing, to get some air on his forehead. Turning towards the slew of Garda cars and Technical Bureau vans parked up on the road outside McTiernan's house, he walked over to the low wall at the front of the garden and bent over it, trying to catch his breath, determined not to throw up.

Guilt sat on the back of his neck like a dead weight, shooting darts of pain between his shoulders as he straightened up again. All the way out to Leopardstown, he had been unable to staunch the suspicion that, if it hadn't been for his intervention, McTiernan would have caught the boat to Holyhead the night before and been safely out of the country when his killer came calling. Again and again he replayed in his head the look of panic that had flashed in McTiernan's eyes when he realised he might miss the ferry, and felt a sharp twinge of shame every time for having laughed about it with Ford earlier – maybe at the same time poor Eddie had been lying there, rasping out one last breath. He felt an even greater wave of it crash in when he recalled why McTiernan's wife had given him the information. Christ, what must she be feeling now? And what the hell had McTiernan been running from? The evidence of his eyes forced him to wonder if it hadn't been the same thing as Begley. And Ronson for that matter. All three of them ripped apart by shotgun blasts. But what the hell could McTiernan have had to do with all that? He had said he was out of the game. Could he really have been lying about it all these years?

Mulcahy turned round and took in McTiernan's house, the extensions, the swagger of it, in a markedly different light now. A huge white plastic forensics tent covered at least half the expanse of block-paving drive, shrouding the corpse, the car and anywhere the gunman might have stepped, all the way up to the front door. The silver Bentley, he remembered, was on a 2009 registration plate, so McTiernan hadn't traded up to the current year. Still, what was it worth – €120,000, maybe more? And McTiernan had been moaning about having to offload properties in Spain?

He was stepping out of his coverall and bagging it up for one of the lads from Technical Bureau when he saw DI Claire Brogan emerge from round the side of the tent where the front door of the house was. She stopped briefly to say something to one of the uniforms, raising a hand to Mulcahy to indicate he should hang on, that she would be over in a second. She looked just like she had the year before, when he had first met her, in St Vincent's Hospital – her red hair plaited at the back, her suit dark grey and clearly expensive, her shoes sporting a bit of a heel despite her height. As she walked over to him, he detected even more confidence in her stride than she had possessed before.

'Seen everything you wanted?' Brogan asked.

'Too much,' Mulcahy said. 'Like I said before, I knew him for years. He was a terrible chancer, but you couldn't help being fond of him all the same.'

Brogan nodded. 'I just had a word with one of the lads in the Organised Crime Unit over at Harcourt Place. He confirmed more or less everything you told me about Mr

199

McTiernan and his criminal acquaintanceships. It looks like I'm going to be spoilt for choice on this one.'

Half an hour earlier Brogan had been professional rather than friendly when Mulcahy had turned up uninvited at her scene. On the phone she'd only said stiffly that she needed to interview him urgently because Mrs McTiernan had said an Inspector Mulcahy from Drugs had been looking for her husband the night before. Obviously Brogan was intrigued to hear what Mulcahy had to say about that, but she had insisted on him leaving any explanation until the interview. Yet while she hadn't been overjoyed, exactly, when he arrived at the house, nor was she as suspicious as he thought she would be. As she would have had every right to be. Instead, she had listened carefully as he set out exactly what his connection with McTiernan had been, and filled her in on the events of the night before – without going into too many specifics. She had asked a few smart questions, satisfied herself for the moment that his presence wasn't obviously suspicious, and repeated her wish to interview him on a formal basis at a time more convenient for her. She had even relented when he asked to see McTiernan's body for himself. Something he wasn't sure he would have allowed her to do if their positions were reversed. But he had been quite insistent. As soon as he'd heard a shotgun was involved, he had to see it for himself.

'Was there anything else you thought of, inside?' she said, inclining her head towards the forensics tent. 'You know, as to why or who?'

'One thing did cross my mind,' he said, rubbing his eyes tiredly. 'When I spoke to Eddie last night, he had something wrapped in a plaid rug behind the car seat. He seemed kind of desperate to keep it to himself. I had a squint inside the car just now and it's not there. Do you know did it turn up in the house at all?'

Arching an eyebrow, Brogan looked a mite more suspicious than she had before, like she was wondering if his interest in the item was more for himself than for her. 'Why would that be important?'

'I don't know that it is, but, looking back, he seemed scared of it somehow. I just wondered if it might have had something to do with this.'

'I didn't come across anything like that.'

Brogan called over a uniform and asked him to send the head of the search team out to her. A minute later a man clad in a proper tech's blue antistatic coverall emerged from the house. Mulcahy repeated the question for him.

'I thought that was a bit weird,' he said to Brogan. 'It was in the hall. An old oil painting wrapped in a rug. As soon as I saw it I thought of that break-in at Kanteeley House a few weeks back – you know, the big art and antiques theft over in Mayo.'

Mulcahy had read something about it in the papers.

Brogan nodded as well. 'Maybe he was trying to shift it across the water last night, get it off his hands,' she suggested, turning to Mulcahy. 'The guy in OCU said McTiernan had a rep as a high-end fence.'

'I wouldn't put it past him,' Mulcahy sighed. 'I did hear about him being involved in that kind of thing. Not so much fencing the stuff as brokering its return.'

'Same thing, these days,' the search officer said. 'They get more from the insurance companies for giving it back than they ever would on the black market.'

'Was it hidden away?' Mulcahy asked. 'Inside, I mean.'

'No, it was propped up against the hall table,' the search guy said. 'It was the first thing I saw when I walked into the house.'

'In which case,' Brogan said, 'unless our gunman was blind, I think we can probably rule it out in terms of motive.'

'Unfortunately, I reckon you can,' Mulcahy replied.

17

Mulcahy turned the Saab in at the Ship Street gate and held up his warrant card for the uniform in the security cabin. Mulcahy looked at him, saw a man in his early fifties, greying hair, sagging skin around the jowls, sitting in a wooden box and waiting for retirement. The barrier began to rise and the uniform waved him on. As he put the car into gear Mulcahy felt a rush of weariness come over him, wondering what it must be like to spend an entire working life on the lowest rung of the ladder, but nothing came to him beyond a vague, unwelcome sense of passiveness and bad luck. He shrugged off the thought and cursed to himself when he saw that all the GNDU's allocated parking spaces were full.

He pulled up outside the dungeon-like door of the Garda Museum at the base of Dublin Castle's massive medieval Record Tower. The museum was locked up for the night, so he wasn't going to be blocking anyone's access, and he wasn't intending hanging around for long, anyway. He crossed over to the GNDU building and was running upstairs when his mobile trilled. Ford, wondering whether he was coming back to the office or not.

'I'm just coming in now – where're you?'

'Over in the Companies Office. Hang on there a few minutes, would you? I won't be long and you'll want to see this.'

Ford hung up before Mulcahy had a chance to say anything else. He looked at his watch, wondering if he hadn't misheard Ford. It was past seven. How could he be in the Companies Office? It was a public building and should have closed hours ago. And what the hell was he doing over there, anyway?

He shrugged off his jacket and logged on to his computer. Duffy and Sweeney had already gone, so he had the ILU to himself. Getting a few notes down about McTiernan and the events at the ferry terminal, while they were still relatively fresh in his mind, would not go amiss. He started bashing away on the keyboard, but the work didn't come easily. Every time he thought of McTiernan in the car the night before he got a corresponding image of his slaughtered face hanging grey against the Bentley's bodywork, and a strong sensation of a large, judgemental finger pointing at himself. Christ, how in hell was he ever going to live with that? He could imagine all too clearly his dreams being haunted by McTiernan for months, just as they had been by Rinn the year before. He was so caught up in it he nearly jumped out of his skin twenty minutes later when Liam Ford materialised beside him.

'Jesus, Liam, you nearly gave me a heart—' He exhaled heavily rather than complete the sentence, or the thought.

'Sorry, boss,' Ford said. For once the sentiment seemed

genuine. 'You look shattered. Was it that bad out in Leopards-town?'

'Brutal.' It was the only word he could think of to sum it up.

'They on to anyone for it?'

'Not a clue as far as I could tell. No witnesses, anyway, but it's early days. Brogan's a good detective. I'm sure she'll get to the bottom of it.'

'It's too fucking weird he was done with a shotgun, though, isn't it? After everything he was saying to you. Don't you think?'

Ford shook his head ruefully, but his heart didn't seem to be in it. Mulcahy wondered whether it was because he didn't give a damn one way or another about McTiernan, or because he was thinking of something else.

'What is it you wanted me to hang on for? Is it something to do with the *Atlantean*?'

'No, I left Aidan and Aisling to get on with all that like you said,' Ford said, pulling up a chair. 'They rang me before they left, said they'd come up with some interesting leads. I actually got the impression the two of them were heading off together to do some more work on it, over a drink or something.' He paused, smirking at Mulcahy, as if to say he wouldn't mind being in Duffy's position, getting up to extracurricular activities with Sweeney. Then he brightened again and smacked a fist enthusiastically into the palm of his other hand.

'To be honest, boss, I was totally caught up with this Gemma Kearney bird. How did you pick up on her? It's mental.'

'How do you mean?'

'Gemma Kearney – how did you know about this whole Klene Records connection?'

Ford's face was more animated now than Mulcahy had seen it all day. He looked like a man bitten by a bug – an infectious one. Mulcahy sat up, energised himself now, or at least intrigued. 'I told you earlier. She worked there.'

'No, no. I mean the connection with Bingo.'

'Bingo?'

'Well, yeah, I kind of assumed you knew that when you asked me to look into yer one.'

'No,' Mulcahy said, flabbergasted. 'I mean, all I heard was that she worked for Klene Records.'

'Jesus, you're going to love this, then.' Ford beamed. 'I think her and Bingo might have been an item at some stage. Look.' Ford held up the sheaf of A4 documents he had in his hand. 'From what I've been able to gather, Begley was up to his neck in Klene.'

'I don't bloody believe this.' Mulcahy stood up, gripped by a new anxiety. Had Siobhan Fallon been playing him again? Was her real interest in Begley? In the murder? Had she been feeding him info about one thing hoping to get something on another? But that was ridiculous, surely? There was no way that could even begin to make sense. Siobhan hadn't so much as mentioned Begley in passing, and she'd seemed genuinely concerned about the Kearney girl, and this other guy, the one in Bristol, whatever his name was. It had to be a coincidence. He shook himself out of it, looked up, saw Ford staring at him like he was waiting for permission to continue.

'Well, go on,' Mulcahy said.

Ford grinned. 'Okay, so I was rooting around over in the archive trying to get some info on this Kearney wan from the case files on Klene and getting nowhere. There were a couple of notes about her, but only saying that she was a receptionist there back whenever.'

'That's what I heard,' Mulcahy agreed.

'Right. So I logged on to see if we had anything on her, in her own right, and it turned out we did – an arrest ten years or so ago, right from the time she was working at the record company. So I requested that file, too, seeing as I was over there, and fuck me if it wasn't right there on the first page of her arrest sheet – the person she asked to be made aware of her incarceration was one Declan Begley of St Theresa's Terrace, Drimnagh, Dublin 12.'

'When was this?'

Ford thumbed through to one of the photocopies. 'On 12 October 2000, booked into Kevin Street Station, one thirty in the morning.'

'Did it say what their relationship was?'

'No, but is it too much of a stretch to think boyfriend? I mean, you're not very likely to call your boss or your dealer to come get you out, are you? She's a bit of a looker, too. You could see Bingo wanting to have a bit of that.'

Ford pulled another page from his sheaf of photocopies. It was a grainy, very poor copy of a mug shot of a young woman Mulcahy assumed was Gemma Kearney. He immediately found himself wondering what she looked like now because despite the poor reproduction it was clear that, back in 2000, she had been very good-looking indeed: a dead ringer for the model Cindy Crawford, right down to the beauty spot on her upper lip.

Ford had obviously noted it, too. 'Them birthmarks can look revolting on some women,' he said, 'but on her it looks like a come-on.'

Mulcahy decided there was no point correcting him. 'Her dealer, did you say? It was definitely drugs she was picked up for, then?'

'That's the thing. Remember, this was months before ourselves and the CAB closed in on Klene. And her arrest didn't take place on the Klene premises. It was in some music club on Wicklow Street, closed down long since. She was arrested under Section 2 of the 1996 Act, charged with possession of controlled drugs – cocaine, ketamine and Es – significant quantities thereof.'

'Seriously?'

'Yeah, more than enough for an intent-to-supply charge.'

'For Christ's sake,' Mulcahy said. 'That doesn't make any sense at all. Are you absolutely sure it's the same woman?'

'You're the one gave me her details.' Ford held up the arrest sheet for Mulcahy to see.

'But this woman's an accountant now, with her own practice,' Mulcahy said. 'You can't qualify for that if you've got a conviction for dealing, can you?'

'I wouldn't think so. But it doesn't apply here, anyway. That's what I was about to say. She wasn't convicted. It never went to trial. She was let off with a slap on the wrist.'

'For possession with intent?' Mulcahy looked at him sceptically. This was getting stranger by the second.

Ford shrugged and flicked forward a few pages through his

photocopies. 'Some meathead came forward and said he'd put the gear in her bag without her knowledge. He got twenty-six months. She was never even charged, only given a strong warning. There's a note on the file from the desk sergeant at Kevin Street about her being administered a caution.'

'What they're really saying is someone took the rap for her?'

'Yup, a guy called Ciaran Stock, a right scumbag, loads of form. Dead now, actually. OD'd while he was banged up in the Joy. Not on that conviction, the next.'

'Why would he take the fall for her?'

Ford shrugged. 'Why do they ever? Paid to, or made to? Writing off a smack debt? Either way, you can be sure Begley was behind it.'

'Sounds like his style all right. But it's a lot to read into one line on a charge sheet, and I can't see where his connection with Klene comes in.'

'Not in relation to her, no, you wouldn't.' Ford fixed Mulcahy with a grin that screamed, *Go on, ask me, ask me.*

'To what, then?'

'Well, like I said, I hadn't seen any mention of her in the later Klene files, or Begley for that matter, so I dived back in, looking back before the date of her arrest, and there I saw his name again, early on. Like I said, you have to remember this was a good eighteen months before the CAB managed to close the place down, okay?'

Mulcahy nodded. 'So?'

'It looks like our lads were on to them from fairly early on. About the drugs, anyway. The extent to which it was a laundering outfit only became clear later. In the early stages

209

we did a surveillance op on the Klene premises, down off Sir John Rogerson's Quay. Sure enough, Begley gets regular mentions in their logs, but while the lads clearly know who he is, they never actually mention what he's doing there. Like it was so obvious it didn't need to be said. Annoyed the fuck out of me, that did. So then I started really digging.'

Mulcahy knew what that was like. When Ford got the bit between his teeth, he was like a force of nature: unstoppable.

'And what did you turn up?'

'Not so much, actually,' Ford said, still grinning. 'Until I came across this.' He pulled another photocopied document out of the sheaf in his hand and brandished it in front of Mulcahy.

'What am I looking at?'

'A certificate of business registration from the Companies Office.'

Mulcahy glanced at the document but nothing of interest caught his eye, other than the fact that it had been issued in the name of Klene Records on 15 February 2001.

'What am I supposed to be looking for?'

Ford pointed at a column of names on one side of the document. 'That's the list of registered partners in the business at the time the CAB moved in on Klene.'

The list was like a rundown of the top-ten ringleaders in the Drimnagh gang at the time.

'It's a wonder they ever got it off the ground with that gang of gougers in charge.'

'They weren't so well known back then,' Ford said. 'Anyway, a business only has to be registered with the Companies Office, not the Gardai. Anyone can set one up.'

Mulcahy shook his head impatiently. 'Obviously, but I don't see where any of this is going.'

'Look at the date. It's a good five months after the date of Gemma Kearney's arrest.'

'So?'

'So, by this time Klene's been running as a proper business for a couple of years. A front, but a properly incorporated one, according to our own surveillance notes. So how come this document suggests that the company was only registered more than two years after it was set up? That's just not possible. Legally, getting the cert is the first thing you have to do with any business. Therefore it must have been changed or altered or something.'

'Fair enough,' Mulcahy said, still baffled. 'And your point is?'

'Jesus,' Ford sighed theatrically. 'I thought you were supposed to be the bright one. Look, my point is, I have a pal who works in the Companies Office, so I called her and asked her how that could've happened. She says some companies re-register if there's been a major change to structure or ownership – like if a sole trader sells out to another business that then absorbs or incorporates it. So I asked her to check this one out for me. And by the time I get over there she's found out that, sure enough, there *was* an earlier certificate issued, and she'd done a copy for me. Here.' Ford presented Mulcahy with the photocopy. 'As you can see, none of the business particulars have changed – still Klene Records, registered office Creighton Street, blah, blah – but just look at the ownership details on this one.'

Mulcahy did. And then he looked again. Far from the

gallery of grotesques listed on the other certificate, there was just one owner's name on this sheet – 'Klene Records, sole trader and proprietor: Declan J. Begley.'

'Well, fuck me,' Mulcahy said, not entirely sure what to make of it. 'Bingo the businessman.'

'Precisely. But look – here, my lady friend gave me this as well. Stamped the same date.' Ford arched his eyebrows, handing him another sheet, this time with a ta-dah flourish. 'This is the attachment to the cert, where the applicant has to set out the commercial aims and activities of the company in more detail.'

As soon as Mulcahy had it in his hand Ford started stabbing a finger at one line in particular. 'Look there, yeah?'

This time Mulcahy couldn't even offer an expletive in response to the information contained there: 'Company secretary and treasurer: Gemma C. Kearney.' He just stared at it, gobsmacked.

'Good, eh?' Ford said. 'Her name's been removed from the later cert, as well, see,' Ford added, jabbing his finger at the re-registered certificate. 'And you won't believe whose replaced it.'

Mulcahy read the name he was pointing at: 'Thomas Francis Hanrahan.'

That could only be one person: the ape they'd visited out in Drimnagh first thing Monday morning. 'Tommy the Trainer?'

'You got it in one.'

'Jesus, Liam. That's some digging you've been doing.' After the day he'd had, though, Mulcahy couldn't even begin to get his head round it. The one thing that was crystal clear, though, was that it couldn't be ignored.

'Puts paid to one mad delusion I had, anyway,' Ford said, looking pleased with himself.

'What's that?'

'That *you're* the feckin' genius in this outfit.'

Mulcahy laughed. 'Right, and I'll be more than happy to acknowledge your intellectual superiority if you could tell me what any of this means. In terms of today, that is.'

Ford looked askance at him, not at all happy with that response. 'I was kind of assuming you'd be the one telling me that. You were the one who brought the Kearney bird's name into it. Who is she?'

'I'm not even sure myself, Liam. All I know is she's gone missing.'

'Missing? How do you mean, missing?'

Mulcahy gave a long sigh and put his hands up to his eyes, hiding behind them for a few seconds, before rubbing them hard with the flats of his fingers.

'Look, Liam, don't get pissed off, but I haven't got anything like all the facts myself. She's just a name I heard from someone else.'

'In connection with Begley?'

'No, not at all.'

The look Ford gave him now married scepticism with exasperation. 'You're the one who's not making any sense now, boss. Why would you send me off looking up the Klene files if you didn't have a reason?'

'All I'm saying is, I genuinely didn't know Kearney had any connection to Begley when I asked you to look her up. But now you tell me they were lovers or business partners or something at one time, I honestly don't know. It's just hard to ignore the fact that she's disappeared off the face of the earth in the last couple of weeks.'

Ford scratched his head, as confused as Mulcahy by now. 'You think she might've got caught up in this mess with the Colombians?'

'Who knows, Liam. But I didn't think there was any connection between McTiernan and Begley, either, beyond a passing acquaintance, and now he's lying dead out in Leopardstown, too. I can't help thinking there's a bigger picture here that we're not seeing. And maybe Gemma Kearney was part of that, as well. Otherwise, why else would this come up, right here, right now?'

Ford was nodding his head vigorously. 'I told you there was more to that fat fucker than you thought.'

'Yeah, and I'm beginning to think you might be right – just this once.'

'Glory be to fuckin' Jaysus,' Ford said, raising his hands in a mock hallelujah.

Mulcahy laughed, and tried to stifle a yawn that escaped at the same time.

'I'm too shattered to get into it now, Liam, but tomorrow let's have another, proper look at this. We'll leave Aisling and Aidan to get on with the Rosscarbery Bay end, and we'll run with this for a bit, see where we get to. All right?'

'Great, can't wait.' Ford jerked his head towards the door. 'Are you going to buy me a pint now or what?'

Mulcahy frowned apologetically at him. 'I'll get you next time. I have to check out one or two more details about Kearney, make sure we're not hightailing off on a complete wild goose chase. Speaking of which, do you know if Aisling got those details of Begley's movements from the Spanish yet?'

Ford shrugged. 'Actually, she did mention that some shit-for-brains on the Spanish end wouldn't play ball with her over sharing Begley's flight details.'

'Okay, that's got to be a priority for the morning, then. I'd be very interested to know if Begley was in Cork at all recently. That's where Gemma Kearney's been based for the last few years.'

'Cork?' Ford grinned. 'She can't be all bad, then.'

'I've never known it to be a recommendation myself.' Mulcahy laughed. 'Okay, you get out of here now. I'll see you in the morning.'

'Yes, boss.' Ford gave a mock salute and loped out through the door, looking pretty happy with himself. Mulcahy put his elbows on the desk, cupped his forehead in his hands for a good minute, the tiredness of the day catching up with him. Then he turned to the computer, clicked into the GNDU intranet and scrolled through the contacts book until he found the number he was looking for. He dialled it from the desk phone.

'Hi. Detective Inspector Mike Mulcahy here. I know it's late but is there anyone still on duty in Missing Persons?'

18

'Siobhan?'

A silence first. 'Mulcahy?'

'Are you at home?'

More silence, then, 'Why?'

He was on his mobile, standing at the entrance to a gated development in Ballsbridge, just off the main drag on the Merrion Road. It was dark and funereally quiet, and while his memory of waking up in one of the swanky apartments inside, once, a year or so before, was as strong as it could be in the circumstances, he had no idea what number it was, or any recollection whatsoever of the tall, white iron gates that refused access to anyone who didn't know the security code.

'I'm outside your gates. I need to talk to you.'

The silence was deeper and longer this time. 'I'm not sure that's such a good idea, Mulcahy. I'm sorry about earlier, genuinely. I should never have asked to meet you. It was stupid of me to think . . . ' She trailed off, left it hanging.

'I want to talk to you about Gemma Kearney.'

'Look, Mulcahy, it's late. I'm not dressed. The place is a mess.'

'That's fine. I'll go down to Crowe's, get a drink and wait for you. Like I said, it's about the missing girl, not us. If you're not there in twenty minutes, I'll know you're not coming.'

'No, wait,' she said, grabbing at it now, thinking about it. 'Okay, but not Crowe's – it's always manic in there on a Wednesday. Go into Madigan's, the Horse Show House – you know it? Opposite the RDS. At least we'll be able to hear ourselves think in there. I'll come as soon as I've put some proper clothes on.'

He left the car where it was and walked back up the street. Turning left, he saw a huge Guinness ad painted on a gable end, and a pub sign beyond. He'd never been in the place before, but it was okay, quiet like she said, though probably mobbed whenever there was a show on across the road at the RDS. He sat at the bar, realised he hadn't had anything to eat since lunchtime and ordered a steak baguette and chips along with his pint. He was halfway through it when she came in the door. A flicker of anxiety in her big blue eyes as she glanced around the room. She had delayed long enough to put on some fresh make-up, as well as the clothes, he reckoned. Now he was used to her hair short like that, he couldn't help thinking it made her even more beautiful than he remembered.

He put that thought away, waved at her, left the food on the bar and ushered her over to a corner table before going back to order the gin and slimline tonic she asked for.

'I'm only staying if you promise not to bring up lunchtime again,' she said when he got back.

'Fine. I meant what I said. I came to talk about Gemma

217

Kearney. You were right. We did have some information on her.'

She looked interested, took a sip of her drink and sat back. 'You as in the Drugs Squad, or you as in the Gardai generally?'

'Both.' He looked across the table at her assessingly. 'Did you already know about this before you asked me, or were you fishing?'

'Fishing?' she repeated, insulted. 'I told you everything her mother told me. The only reason I asked you was because if Gemma had been in trouble over drugs before, the Missing Persons guys might not bother pulling out all the stops. You know how it is. I don't suppose you got in touch with them for me, did you?'

'Not for you, no,' he said.

'But you did get in touch with them?'

'Yes.'

'And?'

'And you were right. She's not on anyone's priority list.'

She looked at him expectantly, and he knew his plan to avoid giving her any direct answers was hopeless. He remembered now how trying to palm her off about anything she'd homed in on was like trying to wrestle a shark. No way should he have come out to see her tonight. He was too tired and she was too sharp. She seemed to have put the incident at lunchtime entirely behind her, seemed like a different person altogether. He could see who was going to get more out of this conversation.

'I could do with another drink,' he said, and asked her if she wanted one, too, but she had barely touched hers.

'So, are you going to keep me in suspense all night?' she said when he got back from the bar. She flashed him the old smile, the one he recognised from a year before. 'Why are you here?'

'I wanted to ask if you could help me out.'

'Me, help you?' she said. 'Jesus, you've changed your tune. How?'

'Tell me what the story is with Gemma Kearney. Why are you so interested in her?'

Siobhan stared hard at Mulcahy, as if wondering whether he was suffering short-term memory loss. 'I told you, she's disappeared. As for why, I told you that, too – her mother approached me.'

'And that's the only reason?'

'Sure. What other reason would there be?' She stopped, narrowed her eyes. 'You've found something, haven't you?'

He was all too aware he hadn't got her to commit to staying off the record, but he knew if he didn't hold out some kind of tangible lure, she wouldn't anyway.

'Look, I shouldn't be telling you this, but when I was checking her out for you, I found out that her name had also arisen in relation to another investigation I've been working on. I need to ask you some questions about her and I don't want you asking any back. Will you do that for me?'

'What's in it for me?' she said, putting her drink down and fixing him with a look that suggested she was more at home with this kind of negotiation than he was.

'Well, if you're willing to play the long game, you might get a bigger story out of it.'

'How much bigger?'

He glanced around again and this time came back with his voice pitched a little lower. 'Look, Gemma's involvement could be a complete coincidence. If it comes to nothing, you'll be the first to know.'

'Jesus, Mulcahy, you'll never win deal-maker of the year. What if it *does* come to something?'

'Same thing, but you get the inside story, without mentioning my name. My bosses would be down on me like a ton of bricks if they knew I was talking to you. I know it was nothing compared to what you went through, but they really did haul me over the coals for letting you get to Rinn. If they thought I was feeding you a story—'

'That's ridiculous,' she broke in, the colour rising in her cheeks. 'You didn't "let" me do anything. I tracked Rinn down on my own.'

'Let's not get into that now,' Mulcahy said. 'All I'm saying is that I have to be really careful. They won't let me get away with it again. And, whether you like it or not, your name is still poison as far as some in the force are concerned.'

She sat back, and he felt the full heft of her blue eyes on him again. 'Okay, tell me what you want.'

'Everything you've got on Gemma, past and present, but there's one thing in particular I want to know.'

'Is it about Horgan?'

'Horgan?' Mulcahy asked, surprised. 'No. Why do you ask?'

'Just a thought,' she said, moving on quickly. 'This is all about drugs, yeah? I mean, your interest in Gemma's past. That's why you're asking?'

'Yes, I think she used to hang around with some pretty

rough types when she was working for Klene Records. Gangster types.'

'And by gangsters you mean drug dealers?'

'I think one of them might have been her boyfriend for a while. You said something earlier about her being involved with some hard case who got her into drugs. Can you tell me more?'

She shrugged. 'Like I said, Mrs K wouldn't go into it.'

'She didn't mention a name?'

Siobhan shook her head. 'She just said Horgan was the one who helped Gemma put that part of her life behind her.'

'Do you think you could ask her again? I need to find out if Gemma might have met up with this old boyfriend recently. Do you think her mother might know? Do you think you could get it out of her?'

'What was this guy's name?'

'That's what I'm not sure of,' he lied, 'but if she comes up with the right name, I'll know.'

He scratched his ear and immediately pulled his hand away, glad he wasn't in a game of poker. Siobhan didn't appear to have noticed.

'They weren't close, but it's possible she might know, I suppose,' she said. 'This was all years ago, though, wasn't it? Why do you think it could have anything to do with Gemma's disappearance now?'

'That's just my point, Siobhan. I don't know.'

'Why not ask Mrs Kearney yourself?'

'You said you were having a hard enough job getting anything out of her about it, and she trusts you,' Mulcahy said. 'Anyway, if I did that, there'd be no chance of a story in it for you, would there? Like you said, fair's fair – it was you who brought her to my attention in the first place.'

Siobhan cocked an eyebrow at him. 'One thing I do know, Mulcahy, is that you're not doing this for my benefit.'

'Mutual benefit,' he said. 'Will you help me?'

She looked away, like she was weighing up each pro, each con separately, knowing that for now at least he would be getting the better part of the bargain.

'Okay, on one condition,' she said. 'If the name I get matches the one you're thinking of, you have to confirm it straight away and tell me why he's of interest to you. No waiting. Is it a deal?'

He thought about it for a second, then reached his hand across the table and shook hers. 'Deal.'

Thursday

19

The clouds were slabs of slate, low in the sky, pelting the city with warm rain. Rain that trickled down the windscreen without fogging it up inside. Rain that carried the ghost of sunny days past. A 'soft day' they'd call it down the country, but that just didn't fit when you were stuck in a traffic jam in Ranelagh at a quarter to eight in the morning. And the entire economy was threatening to expire and take the rest of Europe with it. Or so they were saying on the radio. The reports on *Morning Ireland* were relentlessly negative: yet more forecasts of savage budget cuts and years of austerity to come. Mulcahy looked across the road at a four-foot-high scrawl of red paint screaming WANKER BANKERS from a hoarding around an abandoned building site. But that wasn't even half the truth. For all that the bankers were at fault – and they were – they couldn't have ruined the country without the developers, who in turn couldn't have done it without the government, who couldn't have done anything at all without the people who kept voting them back into power so everyone could keep pretending the Irish were the only people on the planet who could have wealth without responsibility. Maybe they were all wankers to some extent, if only for their blind optimism.

He switched the radio off, but there was no escaping the gloom. His mind immediately drifted to the one subject he'd been trying to keep at bay: Siobhan Fallon, and the nagging sense of loss he'd felt on his way home to Milltown the night before. It was as if seeing her again had raised a ghost that had been haunting him all those months without his even realising it. He had wanted her so much the year before, been so intoxicated with her during the Rinn investigation that he'd made a couple of really stupid mistakes, putting both their lives at risk. Even now, when everything was different, irretrievably so, there was still something animal between them. It crackled across the gap between their thighs when he sat beside her. It hummed in the fraction of a second longer that she always held his gaze. Even now, when it was perfectly evident that pain and circumstance had taken her beyond the point where she could even see him in that light, it was still there, taunting. And what killed him, what really put the tin hat on it, was the realisation that this was precisely what was missing from his feelings for Orla. That urge. That need. Not if he spent ten lifetimes with her, could he imagine feeling that kind of intensity for Orla.

The lights were green again and the traffic into town shifted forward even fewer metres than before. Mulcahy slipped the Saab into gear and covered the gap that had opened between him and the car in front. Cursing himself for being so down on everything, he hooked up his hands-free kit and put in a call to Javier Martinez in Spain. At least Martinez would be in the office already: they were an hour ahead in Madrid.

'*Ola, caballero! Cómo estás?*' Martinez's voice, sunny as ever, lifted his spirits immediately. They bantered on in an old, familiar blend of Spanish and English for a couple of minutes before Mulcahy cut to the chase.

'Look, Jav, sorry to push on, but you know this case we were talking about at the weekend – do you have any good contacts on the team down in Malaga?'

'*Por supuesto, hombre.*' Martinez sounded almost offended at the suggestion that his network might not extend so far. 'You know me. What do you need?'

'One of my people here was trying to get some information about the victim's recent movements in and out of Spain. She keeps getting the brush-off from some lazy *cabrón* who thinks formalities are more important than urgency, you know?'

Martinez knew all right, and when Mulcahy finished outlining the basics of Begley's murder for him, he said he would find out who was in overall charge of the case and call straight back.

'Actually, I'm in the car, Jav. Could you drop me the details by email? And if you were a real pal, you might give the guy a call and tell him to be nice to me.'

'Butter him over for you, you mean.'

'That would be "butter him *up*", Jav,' Mulcahy snorted. 'Buttering him over might compromise all our careers.'

Martinez was still hooting when he hung up.

The lights turned green ahead again, but this time the queue didn't move an inch. There must have been an accident ahead. He rapped out a beat with his fingers on the steering wheel. Like a guilty conscience his thoughts stole back to Siobhan, but this time in terms of what more she'd had to say about Gemma Kearney.

Which was not a huge amount, really. From what the mother had said, Kearney seemed to live a pretty solitary, work-oriented existence. Siobhan had made enquiries with the appropriate institutions and Kearney's academic and professional qualifications had checked out. Her practice appeared to be legit, although it had a reputation for catering for only a small and very select clientele. As far as he could see, Siobhan had spent most of her time chasing around after this dead guy Horgan, with nothing much to show for it. He had the impression she would have said some more about that but then his phone had rung – Orla – and in the time it took to say he'd call her back later, Siobhan had decided she was tired and was going home.

The cars in front shifted forward minimally and Mulcahy was following suit when his mobile pinged: voicemail. Someone must have phoned while he was talking to Martinez. It was Claire Brogan, asking him to call her, as soon as he got a chance, with regard to Eddie McTiernan's murder. Her team had turned up a witness and she needed to check a couple of things with him. He considered leaving it for later, but he couldn't, too intrigued. Again he checked the queue ahead. Through the veil of raindrops the traffic was solid for as far as he could see.

He got straight through to Brogan, who explained that, the previous evening, a Chechen woman who was working illegally as a live-in maid in one of the houses opposite McTiernan's had come forward. She had witnessed the shooting from an upstairs window but been terrified she would be deported if she said anything – until she confided in the woman of the house and was made to go to the Gardai.

'It took us a while to track down a translator for her, but—'

'I hope you got a better one than last time,' Mulcahy interrupted, laughing. It was because he could speak Spanish that he got involved in her case the year before.

'Ha, ha, very funny,' Brogan said, not meaning it, like a teacher ticking off a naughty child. 'The point is, this girl saw the entire thing, start to finish, and gave us a good rundown, including a description of the shooter.'

'Do you reckon she's reliable?'

'Sure. It all rings true. She said she saw McTiernan coming out of the house and walking over to his car, leaning in to get something. Next thing a small, green car – a Golf or a Jazz or something that size – zooms up and stops outside. Shooter jumps out of the driver's side, walks up to McTiernan with a shotgun straight out – proper job, not a sawn-off – there's two loud bangs, and, well, you saw the result. McTiernan didn't even have time to react. He's thrown back against the car with a crater in his chest, and the shooter turns, walks calmly back to his car and drives away.'

'There was just the one guy? No driver?' Mulcahy's thoughts leapt to what Solomons had said about the hit on Ronson in Liverpool. The motorbike rider there had been on his own. Cool, too. And he'd used a shotgun. For that to happen once was strange enough, but twice? It was one of those dumb criminal conventions held over from the old days – when vehicles are used, there has to be a dedicated driver.

'As far as we can tell, unless the car was a left-hand drive, which seems pretty unlikely. The vehicle details are vague beyond size and colour, no reg number or anything. I think our girl was mesmerised by this guy holding the shotgun. As you would be, I suppose. But her description of him was good: tall, at least six foot, not young, thirties she reckoned, thin and wearing a black coat or jacket. So far so general, but then she says he had very blond hair, quite long – shoulder length – and, get this, he was heavily tanned. We're getting her together with an e-fit artist this morning to pin that down, but those are the essentials and I just wanted to see if it rang any bells with you.'

Mulcahy was lost for words. Heavily tanned? Christ Almighty, surely it wasn't actually possible? A Colombian hit man making his way around Europe shooting people? Here in Ireland? It just refused to make any sense. And why would they have come after Eddie McTiernan? There had to be another explanation.

'Mike, are you there still?'

'Yes, Claire. Sorry – the signal must have dropped off.'

'Well, do you have any ideas?'

He cursed to himself. Sure he had ideas, but he didn't want to admit them, let alone share them. It was just too stupid. And he knew from hard-won experience that Brogan didn't have a good record for being open to conjecture. If he started telling her about Colombian assassins on the loose without any hard evidence to back it up, she'd most likely laugh in his face. And anyway, half of McTiernan's circle probably had deep suntans. They all spent most of the year out in Spain. Better to be as noncommittal as he could, and say just enough so it couldn't come back to bite him further down the line.

'Eh, not on the specifics, no,' he said, 'but you know McTiernan had lots of connections out in Spain, don't you? He owned properties out there, spent a lot of time there with his wife, and socialised with some seriously dodgy types, so probably did a bit of business with them, too.'

She was way too good not to have established that information already, but her interest was aroused nonetheless. 'You mean drugs business?'

'Eddie always insisted he was out of the game, but some of the guys he hung around with were in it up to their necks. One of them was gunned down recently, over in Spain. We're actually doing some digging around on it for the Spanish at the moment. Do you want me to send the details over to you?'

Mulcahy didn't want to have to commit himself beyond that. He heard the angry beeping of a car horn from behind, looked ahead and saw that the traffic had moved five or six yards forward. Salvation. He waved a hand at the rear-view mirror and put the car into gear. 'Look, Claire, I'm in traffic. I've got to go, but I'll get back to you as soon as I get into the office, okay?'

He didn't wait for her to respond. He hung up and moved off. All the cars ahead were doing the same now. Whatever the blockage had been, it was unplugged. A gap opened up in the lane beside him and he moved into it, the flow marginally freer thanks to vehicles turning left onto Canal Road. He could get to Dublin Castle by that route, too, maybe even more quickly. And for some reason he was keener than ever to be sitting at his desk, getting on with his day.

*

231

Siobhan Fallon was also on the road, although by now she was already an hour and a half out of Dublin. She was making good time in her ancient yet still serviceable red Alfa Spider. Although the windscreen wipers were only barely adequate and the fabric roof had a tendency to leak around the seams, it could still just about manage the occasional long excursion. And the recently completed M8 motorway made all the difference. Once, when she was a teenager, it had taken her four hours to drive down to Cork. Now they said it could be done in two and a half. She wondered what the record was.

Since she'd left Mulcahy at the gates to her apartment block the night before, she'd been wondering if he had any real idea how much he'd let slip to her about Gemma Kearney. He was a bright guy, but way too straight for his own good – although that was also the thing she'd always liked most about him. It hadn't even occurred to him that by confirming Gemma Kearney's past involvement with a drugs gang, he'd encouraged her to think she might be on to a bigger story than she'd imagined. Bigger even than he imagined, she suspected. She wasn't sure why, in the end, she had changed her mind and not told him what she'd discovered about Horgan's pre-Bristol trip to Amsterdam. She'd played it cool, hadn't given too much away. After all, Mulcahy was the one who'd set the terms of the 'deal'. He was the one who said he didn't want her asking questions. Well, he could hardly expect her to provide him with unsolicited answers either then, could he? Big idiot. She smiled to herself, recalling how he had stammered when he took that phone call and turned away, embarrassed. Must've been the girlfriend, though he never said so.

Flicking the indicator, she moved out smoothly past a slow-going Toyota, peered through the smear of rain on the windscreen, saw there was no traffic whatsoever on the straight road ahead and was struck by an urge to put her foot down. Fuck the weather. She pushed the pedal to the floor, felt the muscles in her thigh stretching, the surge of speed press her back into her seat, the knot in her stomach easing as her jangling thoughts were left behind in the slip-stream and all she could hear was the rain buffeting the bodywork and the engine screaming as it strained to meet her expectations.

Inspector Jefe Hernan Ferrer was the Malagan lead investigator working on Begley's murder. Martinez had supplied not only his office and mobile numbers but delivered on the introduction as well. '*Por supuesto* . . . ' Ferrer began, when Mulcahy got through to him. Of course he would be honoured to take a call from an Irish colleague of Comisario Martinez. As so often in Spain, someone who might otherwise have been defensive to external enquiries became entirely, almost obsequiously facilitating once an official introduction came into play.

Mulcahy explained that he was bypassing the formal liaison procedures at this stage solely in order to expedite matters on another investigation he was pursuing. The chief inspector understood entirely, said he would handle the matter personally. Mulcahy got the impression the man was not too hard pressed anyway, perhaps because as soon as they started discussing the progress of the investigation into Begley's murder, it quickly became clear that it had gone nowhere in the past few days. A series of nationwide anti-austerity strikes by public-sector workers in Spain had left half his support services, his civilian administrators and forensics personnel, backed up for days. Mulcahy's hopes of getting the information he needed anytime soon began to recede.

'I was wondering, Chief Inspector, if your team had made any enquiries into Señor Begley's movements in the weeks prior to the shooting. Specifically air travel.'

Mulcahy assumed this would be standard procedure, but you could never be sure how much effort would be put into investigating the murder of a non-national, especially a scumbag non-national like Declan Begley. The coastal fringes of Spain were awash with foreign criminal vermin of every kind, splurging their ill-gotten gains in the sun. But it seemed Ferrer had not been sparing the horses on Begley, and one reason for that soon became clear.

'We already had this request, from colleagues in Britain, from the Serious Organised Crime Agency,' Ferrer said with satisfaction, like he'd been dealing with the FBI or something. 'So yes, we have this information already. One moment, please, Inspector.'

Mulcahy was staggered. SOCA? What the hell were they doing investigating Declan Begley? Paul Solomons said they hadn't even come across his name. Had he tried to score some brownie points with SOCA by calling them from Dublin after the meeting in the Clarence?

'*Si, si,*' Ferrer said as he came back on the line, pausing and audibly sifting through some papers. 'Señor Begley made many flights in and out of Spain in the last six months. A total of ... eh ... fourteen, yes, fourteen.'

'Where were they to?'

'To many places. To Gatwick, Eindhoven, Frankfurt-Hahn, Marseilles . . . these places.'

'What about Cork? Did he fly to Cork, here in Ireland, at all?'

'Eh, no. Not according to this list. Not to Ireland anytime, in fact.'

'You're sure about that?'

'Yes, of course.' Ferrer bridled a little. 'Or if he did, it was not from Malaga, not direct.'

'And what about to the UK – you mentioned SOCA?'

'I told the officers in London that Señor Begley did take . . . eh . . . three flights to the UK in this period. Most recently on the first weekend in September. This was the occasion they were interested in. It corresponded with the funeral in Liverpool of Mr Trevor Ronson, another of our local property owners who, as you may know, was murdered recently – though not in the Malaga region, thank God.'

Mulcahy felt a tingle at Ferrer's use of the word '*asesinado*', the standard Spanish usage for 'murdered', but so much more redolent in the context of a possible hit man on the loose. Was Ferrer being deliberately indiscreet? Was he trying to see whether Mulcahy had already heard of a Ronson connection?

'Really?' Mulcahy said, hoping the inflection of surprise didn't sound too fake. 'Did SOCA suggest a link between these two murders?'

'Not as such, no,' Ferrer said carefully. 'I had the impression they were more interested in eliminating a connection than establishing one.'

'Eliminating a connection?' Ferrer was full of surprises, it seemed. 'How so?'

The chief inspector cleared his throat before replying. 'They mentioned a name and asked if this person might have been in the Marbella area at the time. I tell them we have no record of this person.'

'Who was this?'

'A Colombian national by the name of Guttierez.'

'Colombian?' So SOCA really were pursuing the hit-man theory vigorously.

Ferrer was just as keen to tell him the rest. 'Yes. I told them we have no record of this person in the Malaga region. Or of entering Spain at all, according to our border authority.'

'That's very interesting, Chief Inspector.'

'I thought you would think so.' The Spaniard said this with some satisfaction.

'And when did you have these discussions with SOCA, can I ask?'

'Only yesterday.'

'Right,' Mulcahy said, feeling certain now that Solomons must have been their source. It was fairly understandable from Solomons's point of view, trying to win some credit for himself, but he doubted whether Ford would be impressed. He was about to say thanks and hang up when a loose end tickled the air in front of him, the niggling sense that there was more to all this than he had fully grasped. 'One last thing, Chief Inspector, can you tell me again – what date was Begley's last flight to the UK?'

A finger rustled on paper as Ferrer consulted his file. 'Mr Begley departed Malaga Airport on Saturday 4 September and returned on Tuesday the seventh. I believe Mr Ronson's funeral was in Liverpool on Monday the sixth.'

'To London Gatwick, did you say?'

'No, not on this occasion,' Ferrer said chummily. 'I too thought this strange. There is, after all, a direct service from Malaga to Liverpool and Mr Begley did not use it. But our UK colleagues, they did not think it significant.'

'Hang on,' Mulcahy said, beginning to think he'd misunderstood. 'I thought you said Begley *didn't* fly to London?'

'That is correct,' Ferrer grunted.

'So if he didn't fly to Liverpool, either, where *did* he fly to?'

What next emerged from Ferrer's lips could not have surprised Mulcahy more if Begley had risen from the grave and bashed him on the head, in person. Not only did it answer the question of why those dates had been bothering him, it opened up a whole new world of possibilities.

'Are you certain about that?' Mulcahy asked Ferrer. 'There's no chance of a mistake?' But he knew there could be no mistake. Ferrer again insisted he had double-checked it for the Brits.

'Thank you, Chief Inspector. If I give you an email address, could you get someone to send copies of those flight details through to me?'

He gave Ferrer the address, thanked him again and put the phone down. Looking out to see if Ford was anywhere around, he saw him steaming slowly through the open-plan office like an Arctic ice-breaker, his massive head and shoulders above the sea of white room dividers.

Mulcahy gesticulated at him through the glass wall. 'Liam, in here, quick. I've just heard something really, really weird.'

20

'Bristol?' Ford scratched his head, took a slug from the grande latte he was holding in his hand. 'What the fuck was Bingo doing in Bristol?'

Mulcahy shook his head impatiently. 'No, no. The question is, what the fuck was Bingo doing in Bristol the same weekend as Cormac Horgan killed himself there and Gemma Kearney disappeared?'

'I suppose it couldn't be a coincidence?'

'Come on, Liam. What are the odds of Begley and his squeeze from ten years back coincidentally flying into the same UK city from different parts of the world on exactly the same weekend?'

'No more than in the millions, I imagine.' Ford's frown of concentration made him look like he was actually doing the calculations. 'But it doesn't necessarily mean they were up to anything funny, does it?'

'What, and the fact that this other ex-boyfriend of hers who happens to be in Bristol at exactly the same time and ends up dead – that's a coincidence, too, is it?'

'How should I know?' Ford shrugged grumpily. 'I grant it's a bit strange, but is it any more reasonable to assume that, just because Begley was in the city at the same time as the other two, he must've had something to do with the death of one and the disappearance of the other?'

'Bloody right it is,' Mulcahy snorted. 'You know Bingo as well as I do.'

'That's just it, though, isn't it, boss? We don't know Bingo at all any more. From what your pal McTiernan said, he was a bigger fish out in Spain than he ever was back here. Jesus knows what filth he was up to his neck in. And even assuming these lot did meet up, the coroner's report said this Horgan guy's death was suicide, didn't he? Isn't that what you said?'

'I think so,' Mulcahy said, allowing himself at least that doubt, 'but I haven't got the details. I'm not even sure there's been a formal inquest yet. We'd better get on to them and check. Make sure it all ties up.'

'No problem. I'll do that.' Ford leant over the desk for Mulcahy's message pad, scrawled a note on it and tore out the page. 'Look, you know how tricky it would've been for Bingo to set foot in Dublin again. Maybe he wanted to see them, for whatever reason, in neutral territory, and here was an opportunity as he was going over to England anyway.'

'So why not meet in Liverpool, or even London? Why go to somewhere as out of the way as Bristol?'

'Maybe it was the only place they could get direct flights to – you know, from both Cork and Malaga.'

Mulcahy scratched his head. Could the reason really be as prosaic as that? 'I doubt it, but I suppose it's worth checking.'

Ford took another slurp of coffee and something sparked in his eyes. 'Aren't you kind of overlooking one obvious thing?'

'What's that?'

'Well, you're assuming Bingo was in England that weekend because he was on his way to Ronson's funeral, but do we even know he went to it? I mean, if I thought some assassin had it in for me, the funeral of the last guy he'd shot is probably not where I'd want to be showing my face. You know?'

Ford had a point. There was only one way of finding out whether Begley was in Bristol to see Kearney or if he was just stopping off on his way somewhere else. It was time to stop pussyfooting around with regard to the Brits.

Siobhan pulled shut the door of the small quantity surveyor's office behind her and would have punched the air had it not been for a smug-looking man in a loud suit walking towards her on the landing. He was leering at her as it was; she really didn't want to encourage him to open his mouth. Jesus, what was it with these Cork guys? She hurried past him and ran down the three flights of stairs to street level. Outside, she looked back up at the rickety five-storey office building on Academy Street, delighted she had stuck to her guns and come to check the place out in person.

Her progress earlier had not been so encouraging. A meeting on the other side of the city with Pat Delaney, owner of the Academy Street building where Gemma Kearney rented a two-room second-storey office suite for her accountancy practice, had yielded little or nothing. She had hoped that, as an individual landlord rather than some faceless management firm, he might know some other people Kearney dealt with, but he didn't. As soon as she felt his eyes rove over her when she brushed the back of her thighs to sit down, she knew he was going to be useless. Things were fine for as long as he was trying to impress her, telling her how much property he owned and how lucky he was not to have been hit too hard by the downturn, but when it came to Gemma he was hopeless, admitting he hadn't even been aware her practice had been closed up for weeks until Siobhan told him so.

'I hardly ever go over there,' Delaney said. 'She's been in that suite for years now and the rent's always paid on time, quarterly in advance. There's still a couple of weeks to run before it next falls due.'

Not for the first time Siobhan had to remind herself that Gemma had only been gone for a little over three weeks. For some people, that was a holiday. And as far as Delaney was concerned, in terms of Gemma being missing, it was clear his rent was all he cared about. As for the rest, he just didn't want to play ball. Delaney couldn't take more than a stab at the name of Gemma's assistant. And, for reasons of 'commercial confidentiality', he refused to say who Gemma's referees had been when she took out the lease. Siobhan's attempts to charm him only resulted in him asking whether she was staying in Cork overnight, and if she had already made arrangements for dinner. When she noticed that his gaze had graduated from her legs to the back of her hands, and seemed to have become stuck there, she stood up and left before anything too sick could evolve in his mind.

Going over to the building itself on Academy Street hadn't yielded much, either. Initially. As Mrs Kearney had found, the other tenants on the first and second floors said they hardly knew who Gemma Kearney was, and none had either friendly or commercial relationships with her. It wasn't until Siobhan tried the quantity surveyor's office on the third floor that she hit paydirt – a young, dark-haired receptionist who liked to sneak out for a smoke in the yard behind the building and who'd got friendly with Gemma's PA, who used to do the same.

'It was turrible,' the girl said in a lilting Cork accent. 'Ali came in four mornings running and the place was all shut up. The bitch owed her three weeks' money, and she hasn't seen or heard from her since.'

But this Ali was clearly resourceful, because she had left a mobile number so her pal could let her know just as soon as 'the bitch' showed her face in the building again. Siobhan glanced at the Post-it note in her hand and dug her phone out of her bag. It was one of the basic tenets of tabloid reporting: you rarely, if ever, get better than an aggrieved ex-employee when it comes to dishing dirt. Ali McCarthy, she just knew, was going to be the big break she'd been hoping for.

Routed through the UK liaison office, Mulcahy's request to speak to Commander Gavin Corbett of the Serious Organised Crime Agency was fulfilled within the hour. Corbett turned out to be a lot less stuffy than any of Mulcahy's previous SOCA contacts, although that wasn't necessarily saying much. After the introductions and explanations,

Corbett was happy to get straight down to business, asserting that his interest in Declan Begley had been purely in the context of 'known associates', people who fraternised with Ronson and might have borne a grudge against him – for whatever reason.

'We had been aware that Mr Begley and Ronson were friends out in Spain,' Corbett said, deftly sidestepping the question of how he'd heard about Begley, 'but once we ruled out his presence in the UK at the time of Ronson's murder, we lost interest in him, more or less. Until we heard about him being gunned down the other day, when we thought we should take another look. But in terms of what the Spanish investigators were able to give us, and what we've been able to ascertain ourselves, we uncovered no evidence of any criminal relationship between them here UK-side. Unless you're going to tell me something different, of course.'

There was a mild challenge in Corbett's voice. Mulcahy wondered was the man trying to play him, but as he'd seemed perfectly straightforward so far, he decided it was probably just his imagination.

'A source of mine here in Dublin suggested the two murders might be connected, but not how,' Mulcahy said, choosing his words carefully. 'So from what you said, can I take it that you're not linking them?'

'We have no reason to,' Corbett said. 'Not at this stage.'

That was a strange way of putting it, Mulcahy thought. 'We were wondering if you might be able to tell us whether Begley attended Ronson's funeral. Did you run a surveillance operation at it?'

'Well, we couldn't miss a chance like that, could we?'

Corbett chuckled and for the first time Mulcahy got a flash of fellow feeling, of joint purpose, with the man. 'It's not often we get such a gathering of the clans, and it can be very illuminating to see who's talking to who. As I recall, there was an individual we initially thought might be your Mr Begley, although he was indistinct on our video capture. That was one of the main reasons we went back and took another look at Begley when we heard what had happened out in Fuengirola. But then, at more or less the same time as we were making our renewed enquiries, it emerged that the individual in our video was actually a mourner down from Newcastle for the day, very well known to some of my colleagues from that part of the world. So no, no sign of Mr Begley, I'm afraid.'

'You're sure about that?' Mulcahy asked.

'Absolutely. There was quite a crowd there, so it took us a while to sift through them all, but we're now confident we have identified everyone who attended both the church and burial. As far as we're concerned, Mr Begley was not present. Having said that, if you're talking to the Spanish, I'd appreciate it if you didn't go telling them about our friend from Newcastle. We put something of a squeeze on them to procure the information on Begley in a hurry.'

'I spoke to Chief Inspector Ferrer in Malaga this morning. I got the impression he was more than happy to help you.'

Corbett fell silent as he considered the import of that. 'Ah, you've spoken. Well, that's good to know.'

'Just one last thing, Commander,' Mulcahy said, deciding to go all in. 'This source of mine also hinted at another link, which I initially thought was just fantasy but I'm now being forced to reconsider. Something about a missing shipment of cocaine in Rotterdam, and a Colombian hit man out for vengeance.'

'That's an impressive source you have, Inspector.'

'Yes, Commander, very impressive. And now also very dead, unfortunately.'

This time the silence at the other end of the line was more in the way of a plunge than a gentle fall. 'Ex – excuse me?' Corbett spluttered. 'Did you say dead?'

With a bitter smile Mulcahy realised that his earlier suspicions about Solomons must have been correct. Corbett had assumed that Mulcahy's 'impressive source' was Solomons, too.

'Yesterday, point blank with a shotgun, in much the same way as Ronson and Begley.' Mulcahy left it a second or two before relieving the commander of his fears. 'At his home, in Dublin.'

'His home, you say?' Corbett said.

'Yes, Commander. My source was a part-time crook and property developer with links to Begley in Dublin and Spain. He was also an acquaintance of Trevor Ronson, though exactly how well he knew him I couldn't say.'

'I see. Yes. Okay.' Corbett was doing a spectacularly poor job of disguising his relief. 'And now you're thinking these . . . these three murders could be related, is that it?'

Mulcahy thought he might as well push for all the information he could while he had the Englishman on the back foot. 'Well, obviously, I have no evidence for that as yet, but I wouldn't discount the possibility, either. When I was talking to Chief Inspector Ferrer, he led me to believe that you had a suspect in mind for Ronson's killing. A Colombian national?'

'Ah yes, Guttierez,' Corbett said, keen to let the focus shift. 'As you clearly already know, the possibility that a hit man may be involved is a theory we're working on, though not the only one.'

'And you're giving serious credence to that idea?' Mulcahy made no attempt to disguise his scepticism.

Corbett hesitated, as if trying to make up his mind. 'It's the theory that is most favoured by those on the ground here. By that I mean among the local criminal population on Merseyside, rather than ourselves necessarily. To be honest, it's not a belief we're seeking to discourage. It keeps the locals from each other's throats if they can blame an external force. A *deus ex machina*, you know. Or a *deus ex Colombia*, if you see what I mean.'

'Well, my Latin's a bit rusty, but yes.'

'Unfortunately, the question of credence, as you put it, is complicated by this Guttierez chap. He popped up on our radar just before Ronson was killed and, not to put too fine a point on it, disappeared. He's known to be a heavyweight with the Cali Cartel and comes with a reputation fearsome enough to merit a warning from our Colombian colleagues that he was boarding a flight out of Bogota for Heathrow.'

'You had him tracked?'

'Yes, or rather my colleagues in security and immigration thought they did.' Corbett coughed. 'Rather embarrassingly, when I say he disappeared, I mean into thin air, quite literally. We know he boarded the plane at Bogota, but somehow he slipped through immigration this end without making a mark. Possibly by using a different passport. He must have disguised himself, somehow, before passing through immigration. How, we don't know. Even our facial-recognition software failed to identify him – to be fair, there were a great many flights coming through at that time. We now fear he may have been waved through on an EU-issue passport and be travelling freely within the European Community on it.'

'Christ, that's a bit unfortunate all right.' Even Mulcahy felt he was understating the case.

'Yes, so I'm afraid we have no idea of his current whereabouts,' Corbett said, exasperated. 'Other than that the Colombians assure us he hasn't gone home, which means we can't rule him out for Ronson's murder. Not with that background dispute over the cocaine and so many rumours about a hit man going about. Luis Guttierez, as we understand it, is one of the Cali Cartel's most brutal enforcers. He's also proving one of the most elusive, despite his nickname – "El Güero", they call him over there.'

'Are you serious?' Mulcahy had to stop, take a breath, unsure from Corbett's anglicised pronunciation whether he'd heard correctly or not. He'd only ever heard that term in the feminine form before: *la güera*. But there was no reason why it couldn't be applied to a man, was there?

'Did you say "El Güero"?' Mulcahy asked, staggered. 'The Blond?'

It was exactly how Brogan's witness had described McTiernan's killer.

'I see your Spanish is better than your Latin,' Corbett said. 'But yes. You'd think it would make him stand out rather too much to be good at his job over there. Not so noticeable here in Europe, though.'

'I wouldn't be too sure about that,' Mulcahy said, the pounding in his chest beginning to move up into his head.

In the couple of hours before Ali McCarthy could take a coffee break from her new job, Siobhan managed to fill in a few more pieces of the Gemma Kearney jigsaw. Out in suburban Douglas, she met up with Cathy Barrett, the young mother who had been so outraged at the thought of Kearney going to Cormac Horgan's funeral – a russet-haired, emerald-eyed young mother whose life was now focused almost exclusively on her three-month-old infant daughter. As they sat in the kitchen of her large detached house, the baby gurgling happily in a stroller between them, Cathy told Siobhan that Kearney and Horgan had been together for four years and that Kearney had lived with – or sponged off, as Cathy put it – the comparatively wealthy Horgan for much of their time at university and while they were doing their professional examinations.

'First sniff of a job of her own, though, and she was off,' Cathy said. 'She just dumped him, from nowhere. Poor Cormac was devastated. She never told him why, just told him to F-off, and when he tried to persuade her to come back, she got some thug to threaten him. Can you believe it? Told him to stay away or he'd get his legs broken. We were all horrified, but it shouldn't have come as a surprise. We always knew she was scum. She couldn't hide it for ever. I wanted Cormac to go to the Guards, but of course he refused. Why he felt any loyalty to her I'll never know.'

All of which had been, partly at least, behind Horgan's decision to leave Cork and go to work in Skibbereen. Cathy hadn't seen so much of him since that time, especially not since she'd got married, but her incandescent hatred of Kearney hadn't dimmed by so much as a single lumen over the years. Its precise cause never did come out, but seemed to be based on a towering snobbishness and an unshakeable belief that Kearney was the most selfish and manipulative woman in all Cork.

'Closest I've ever met to living, breathing poison,' Cathy confirmed, 'and you can quote me on that.'

Siobhan fully intended to, just as soon as she had a story to quote her in. It was all good background, and maybe even went some way to account for the fact that, hard as she tried, she didn't manage to turn up anyone else in Cork who knew Kearney well. A couple of people at the local Chamber of Commerce said they knew *of* her, sure, but to socialise, have a meal or do business with? Nothing. The most interesting suggestion they made was that Siobhan should try some of the estate agents around the city, as Kearney was known for brokering lucrative property deals on behalf of clients – and there weren't many of those going these days.

By the time Siobhan headed back into the city centre, she felt she had lots of scraps of information but still no big picture. Happily that was something Ali McCarthy looked very likely to provide when she sashayed into Gloria Jean's coffee shop on Patrick Street, overbrimming with indignation and attitude. No taller than Siobhan but with haystack blonde hair, denim cut-offs over leggings, and a short green tailored jacket over a logo-emblazoned T-shirt, she didn't look like someone who'd ever be happy stuck away in a second-storey office licking envelopes.

'The only reason I stayed was because the money was good,' the girl said, once she got settled with her skinny latte. 'She treated me like dirt. Treated everyone like dirt, actually. But she wasn't there half the time. She was away a lot.'

Ali's job, it seemed, was mostly just to sit by the phone and refuse business by telling any enquirers that the practice had no space on its client list at present.

'That's exactly how she told me to say it: "Miss Kearney has no space on her client list at present." And then I had to ask them for their contact details and tell them we'd be in touch if a vacancy came up. But even she said that was only to stop them from calling us again.'

'Did she seem that busy?'

'Well, yeah, really busy. She was always working when she was around. I asked her why she kept spending money putting the ads in the local papers. She said it was "a matter of perception".'

I'll bet it was, Siobhan thought to herself.

'She did a lot of business over the phone,' Ali continued. 'Most of it seemed to involve moving money around the place, all over the world, like. She always kept the door to her office shut. Locked it when she was away. But sometimes when I went in with a coffee or something, I'd see her computer screen and there were all these accounts in the Cayman Islands and the Virgin Islands and places I never even heard of. I often wondered if what she was doing was even legal.' Ali paused and gave Siobhan a look so replete with insinuation it might as well have been a nudge in the ribs. 'I used to put a lot of calls through to her from abroad, from Spain mostly. She used to buy and sell property for clients living out there, but there was this one bloke in particular she was always on the phone to. He was just as big a shit as she was . . . '

Leaning back in the chair, as close to horizontal as he could go, Mulcahy opened his eyes wide, blinked rapidly at the white blur of ceiling, then closed them again and massaged the lids with the tips of his index finger and thumb, feeling the tension leach away down his spine. El Güero, for Christ's sake. It sounded like something from a Tarantino film. Comical. But not inconceivable. And that was the problem. Now that Corbett had provided a direct link with the Cali Cartel, the hit-man theory became that bit more plausible. With the high-level contacts a South American drugs cartel could furnish, and pay for, it would be all too easy for a man like that to fly from city to city and get tooled up wherever he went. Ditching his weapons and moving on, possibly even changing passports wherever he went. In and out. Clean skin. No dirt. No shadow.

He was reminding himself again that he had yet to call Brogan back when a shadow moved across his eyelids. He sat up. Ford was in front of the desk, another sheaf of papers in his hand.

'I spoke to one of the coroner's officers over in Bristol, a very helpful guy,' Ford said, brandishing the documents. 'The post mortem on Horgan showed typical features of a fall from height, nothing incongruous, entirely consistent with other deaths of that type, although . . . ' Ford paused and ran a finger down the top sheet. 'Here it is: he didn't fall straight in the water. Poor bastard hit some trees and rocks on the way down, "sustaining major head wounds, broken

251

bones, contusions and large lacerations that *could* have masked any pre-existing injuries". In other words, it's impossible to determine what killed him apart from the fall, so they can't rule anything out.'

Ford handed the paper over to Mulcahy before continuing, 'He said it's not uncommon for the coroner to reach an open verdict in this kind of case where they have no witnesses to the jump. Comes down to the "balance of probabilities", he said. Given the location, the fact that Horgan's business was in the crapper and no other compelling factors, he reckons they'll decide it's a reasonable assumption that he took his own life.'

'Nothing conclusive either way, then.' Mulcahy quickly read the document before handing it back. 'The thing is, it turns out your hunch was good. According to SOCA, Begley never went to Liverpool – or not to Ronson's funeral, anyway. They filmed the whole thing covertly and spent the last two weeks identifying everyone who turned up. Begley wasn't one of them. And they've got good reason now to think this Cali hit man's not as daft an idea as we thought it was.'

He updated Ford on what Corbett had said about the missing enforcer known as El Güero.

'Christ on a bike,' Ford exclaimed. 'They're fuckin' serious, aren't they?'

'Looks like it,' Mulcahy agreed.

'Still, that's no reason to think this Horgan thing's dodgy, is it?'

'No, but I think it's worth having a closer look at him.'

Ford gurned a smug smile at him. 'Actually, I got there

before you, boss. I put him through PULSE while I was waiting for you to come off the phone, ran a detailed check.'

'You're a smartarse of the highest order, Liam.' Mulcahy chuckled. 'What did you get on him?'

'Not a feckin' thing. Cormac Patrick Horgan of my own fair county of Cork was as clean as a whistle. Not so much as an illegal download. A proper sparkler. Almost too good to be true, actually.'

'Fuck that,' Mulcahy said. 'There's got to be something more. Who do we know in Skibbereen?'

21

Half an hour talking to the local CID man, Detective Sergeant Pascal McCann, at Skibbereen Garda Station set Mulcahy some of the way straight at least. Cormac Horgan had been a popular and successful man around town. A newcomer, he'd moved the fifty miles southwest from Cork city to 'Skib' six or seven years previously, to take over the family firm from his ageing bachelor uncle. He settled in to the close-knit market town quickly, joining all the appropriate local clubs and commercial associations. A regular churchgoer, he fundraised enthusiastically and donated generously to a wide range of local charities. The only conventional thing he hadn't done was marry. Most of all, though, he'd turned round the Horgans chain of estate agents in a matter of months after taking over, and just in time to make the most of the boom. At the same time he branched out into property investment services and, initially at least, did wonders for local property developers, farmers and small-time investors while adding considerably to his own fortune in the process.

A paper fortune, as it transpired. In line with the crazed conventional wisdom of the Celtic Tiger, which refused to recognise even the possibility of a rainy day, however distant, it seemed he had salted virtually nothing away and instead ploughed everything he earned into onward investment. And he had convinced half the town to throw their nest eggs in with him, advising high-rollers and risk-averse alike to plough every spare penny into an evermore elaborate series of development ventures at home and abroad, which one day – he claimed – would pay out a bonanza beyond their wildest and most avaricious dreams. His speculating frenzy peaked at more or less the same time as the global money markets collapsed, Lehman Brothers went splat, and the Irish property bubble imploded. That he'd lost so many people's life savings as well as his own was rumoured to have hit him hard, said the sergeant. Not that there was much sympathy among his fair-weather friends in Skibbereen.

'I'm sure that's why the family decided to bury him up in Douglas,' DS McCann said, his accent thick with the melodious rhythms of West Cork. 'There might have been a graveside riot down here. A lot of people felt he took the coward's way out. All that stuff in the papers about him being universally missed? Not around here, I can tell you. Lost too many people a bloody fortune.'

There was such an air of vehemence in McCann's voice, Mulcahy had to wonder if the CID man himself might have taken a not-so-crafty punt on one of Horgan's property investment schemes.

'Some people said he didn't even care so much about the property businesses any more,' McCann said, really getting into his stride. 'He must've thought he'd set himself up for life. I was talking to a pal of his only the other day who said he'd confided as much in private to him, that the estate agencies were only shops, and he didn't take their loss so much to heart. It was the other stuff that affected him. Losing everyone else's money. And the other business, of course. He was mad about that. Couldn't stay away from the water.'

It was as if McCann was engaged in a private reverie, not even bothering to supply details of what he was talking about. But Mulcahy's curiosity was aroused by the reference to Horgan's other interests.

'I don't follow,' Mulcahy said. 'What other business?'

'Oh, himself and a pal had a nice auld sideline down in Glandore,' McCann said. 'They must've made a fortune out of it from the tourists in the summer. Boating and sailing, dolphin-watching and fishing – anything to do with the water. Anytime you went into the estate agent's looking for him, they'd tell you he was down there. Himself and Conor must've had at least five boats in the harbour. You couldn't get on them when the sun came out, they were that popular. Doing tours, round the coast, out to Galley Head and back, down as far as Baltimore and Glengariff if the weather was right. And they did fishing, too. Big business, corporate stuff – you know, taking out these suits who'd never held a rod in their hands before, fishing for sharks and other big stuff. Pay a fortune for it, y'know, not realising they were the ones being reeled in.'

'So what happened?'

'That went, too. Overextended himself on the last couple of boats, apparently. Started out with just a couple of dinghies for the fishing, but these latest boats, Jaysus, they were like floating tour buses. Massive things. Must've cost an absolute fortune. The bank repossessed the lot. Them and all the other ones.'

'Helpful as ever, then, the banks?'

'Oh yeah, you're not wrong there. By then the boats were about the only recoverable assets Cormac had left. The uniform lads down here helped the bailiffs secure them. A couple are still down in the harbour, chained up and sealed, ready to be picked up by the new owners, but the rest were taken away after the sale. That must've been tough on Cormac, seeing them auctioned off like that. It was only a few weeks afterwards, you know, that he killed himself.'

When he put the phone down, Mulcahy felt a germ of excitement ripping through his thoughts. DS McCann's comments about boats and sea tours around Galley Head and Baltimore, in particular, were strobing like a lighthouse beam in his brain. He walked out into the outer office and over to the map pinned to the wall behind Ford's desk. As always when he looked at a map of Ireland he recalled how, as a kid in school, he'd always thought its island shape looked like a fat old man sitting in a comfy chair, arms crossed and legs stretched out, staring west across the ocean to America. He looked down now at the southernmost tip of Cork and Kerry, to where the old man's toes dipped into the blue vastness of the Atlantic. He was tracing a forefinger round the rugged coastline when Ford came back.

'This is your neck of the woods, Liam,' Mulcahy said. 'Turns out Horgan ran a boating business out of somewhere called Glandore. I can't see it. Do you know it?'

'Sure,' said Ford, waving a finger vaguely at the map. 'It's out west there, on the coast, near Skibbereen.'

'I know that,' Mulcahy said tetchily. 'But where *exactly*?'

Ford turned round, squinting at the map. 'It's tiny, barely a few houses and a harbour. Lovely spot, though. Just a couple of headlands round from—'

For Mulcahy, it was like a series of pilings sliding into place. One after the other they fell into line: the location, the boats, the desperation for money. He knew exactly what Ford was going to say microseconds before his own eyes took in the name Ford was stabbing his forefinger at on the map, their eyes meeting, a rush of disbelief and excitement on their faces.

'Rosscarbery Bay,' they both said, in unison.

22

'Boss?' It was Sweeney, head round the door, lean forearm hugging the jamb, a hank of dark hair spilling over her left eye, urgency in her expression. 'There's a guy here from Pearse Street, wanted to talk to Liam, but he's gone out again. Can you have a word? Says it's important, to do with Rosscarbery Bay.'

'He's here?' Mulcahy said. He couldn't remember the last time anyone had just dropped into the office. It was so last century. 'Send him in.'

The guy in question was Detective Inspector Kevin O'Neill, head of the B Division Drugs Unit working out of Pearse Street, one of the busiest city-centre stations. In its ambit was everything from Government Buildings and Grafton Street to the pubs and clubs of throbbing Temple Bar. Ford knew him well, having worked with him in the North Central hellhole that was Store Street Station when O'Neill was a sergeant. Mulcahy had only met him once or twice at socials, a short, dark, growling type with a brittle air and a fixed look of fury on his face. A Dubliner through and through, what he could have to say about Rosscarbery Bay was anybody's guess.

'Yeah, well, that's just it, isn't it,' O'Neill said. 'We picked this guy up during a raid on a squat over on Fenian Street, must be three, four weeks ago now, and he had twenty wraps of coke in his bag. He had no idea how it got there, naturally, so we processed him and he's been over in Cloverhill on remand since. Then I get a call from one of the prison officers saying this guy is in trouble on the wing – some scrote tried to shank him – and he's begging to see *me*, says he has some information to trade. So I was out there this morning, anyway, and he ups and outs with it – that he was one of the crew, on that boat, the Rosscarbery one, you know?'

'The *Atlantean*? Are you serious?'

'Yeah, that's what he called it.'

Mulcahy was almost dazed by the suddenness of it. 'Is there any reason to believe him? It was all over the news not so long ago. He could've got the name off the TV or the papers.'

'Well, obviously, and yer man, stupid twat, says he won't spill anything till he knows the deal. Then I remembered bumping into Liam at a match a couple of nights ago and he mentioned you guys were still circling on Rosscarbery and thinking now maybe the gear might've come over from Holland.'

'And?'

'And that's just it, isn't it? This guy – his name is Cuypers – he's Dutch. The only thing he'd give us was that the boat came over from Holland ...'

*

260

Forty minutes later Mulcahy was out in the sprawling new-build wasteland of Dublin West, turning off the M50 and approaching the drab diamond-shaped cluster of buildings that was Cloverhill Prison. For all its claims to be a twenty-first-century specialist remand facility, the prison was very much Victorian in spirit, with an old-fashioned panopticon layout at its core, and even an old-style prisoner tunnel leading to the newly built courthouse next door. All Mulcahy could see as he walked from the car park was the five-metre-high curtain wall that enclosed the complex, its continuum broken only by the bunker-like reception building, bulging out in a curving architect's fancy of red brick and glass. It did nothing to make the place look any less intimidating for visitors – quite the opposite, in fact, as the narrow, overhung windows set deep into the façade looked about as welcoming as machine-gun slots.

He showed his warrant card and was informed by a dour-faced screw that he was on the governor's list. Although no one impeded his progress, it took another twenty minutes of searches, jostled key chains, clanging doors and endlessly long corridors before he was, at last, shown into a bare-walled, windowless interview room. There, a tall, tanned, grizzled man in jeans, trainers and a pale blue sweatshirt was sitting at a table that was bolted to the floor. Mulcahy waited as the prison officer who'd accompanied him shut the door and took up position beside it, affecting a blank-eyed indifference to any words that might be uttered in his presence, short of threatening ones.

'Willem Cuypers, right?'

The man nodded, stress manifest in a muscle spasm on his

left cheek. Mulcahy could well believe the man was a yachts-man, the deep teak tan that weeks banged up inside had done nothing to pale, the thin green tattoos faded to near-nothingness by sun and salt on forearms that looked tough as bog oak. He'd met many like him on piers and slipways all over the world. Not a man to suit a prison. Not a man to be trapped indoors.

'I'm Mulcahy. You have information about a case I'm working on?'

'Yes. The big cocaine find at Rosscarbery Bay. I was there. I can tell you about it.'

The words sounded harsh, guttural in the man's heavy Dutch accent, but his English was good. What impressed Mulcahy most was the certainty in his deep voice; he wasn't surprised O'Neill had taken this man seriously.

'So tell me about it.'

Cuypers fixed him with an icy stare. 'Do I get what I want?'

'What is it that you want?'

'I told the other guy, O'Neill. I want to get out of here, now.'

'Don't be ridiculous,' Mulcahy said, lacing it with a bit of anger. He pushed back his chair and stood up.

'No, wait.' The Dutchman's glare softened. 'I don't mean release. I know you won't do that. I want a transfer to another prison, today. After that, if I'm convicted, I want a reduction in my sentence and a guarantee I can serve it in the Netherlands.'

'You're very sure of yourself, aren't you?' Mulcahy said, staring down at him.

'No, not of myself, but I am sure you will want what I know.'

Mulcahy sat down again, shook his head. 'I might be able to swing a remand transfer, but it would probably be tomorrow at the earliest. And I'd need to check the accuracy of your information first. The other stuff, serving abroad, I have no control over. It's a bureaucratic matter, decided by civil servants. All I could do would be to make a recommendation.'

'And you would do that, yes?'

'If what you say stands up, yes, sure. No skin off my nose.'

'And you will have me moved quickly?'

'Like I said, that depends on what you tell me. What are you so afraid of, anyway?'

Cuypers lifted the right-hand side of his sweatshirt, revealed a large, paperback-sized bandage pad taped to his stomach just above his waistband. There was a dark stain of dried blood spread across the centre where the wound had leaked through the thick cotton wad.

Mulcahy sucked his breath in through his teeth. 'Okay. I heard he missed you.'

'Sure, he missed my liver, my kidneys,' Cuypers scoffed. 'He missed killing me.'

'Why would anyone want to do that?'

'Who knows? Maybe I upset somebody in here, or maybe it is for what they are afraid I will tell you. But if they're trying to kill me anyway, I might as well trade with you and have a chance, yes?'

'Makes sense to me,' Mulcahy nodded. 'Tell me what you've got, and if it's good, I'll get you your transfer.'

What Cuypers had to tell Mulcahy wasn't just good. It was

dynamite. In under a minute Mulcahy had no more doubts that it was the real thing, not least because it confirmed much of what they already suspected regarding the *Atlantean.*

'We sailed out of Vlissingen – do you know it?' Cuypers began. 'The English, they call it Flushing.'

Mulcahy nodded slowly, afraid of giving away too much in his excitement. Vlissingen was the location of the boatyard they'd been told about.

'It's down south on Walcheren, near Middleburg, right out on the coast. Very quiet, but it has everything for boats, you know? They told me to get there at midnight, for leaving early in the morning.'

'They? Who are "they"?'

Cuypers shook his head. He would only say he'd asked a friend how he might make some quick cash to sort out a debt that had been called in. The friend told him someone was looking for crew for a no-questions-asked sailing trip. He knew from the amount on offer – €2,000 for a three- or four-day voyage – that it had to be illicit. A fact confirmed when he turned up at the boatyard, deserted but for a pocket of hectic activity around a ten-metre Bermuda-rigged yacht, the *Atlantean,* onto which the skipper and another crewman were busy transferring large plastic-wrapped packets from the back of a silver Mercedes van parked alongside, and stowing them below decks.

'What were they like, these packets?'

Cuypers shrugged. 'White plastic, about ten kilos each one, with some thin, you know, rope tied round them.'

'Twine.'

'Yes, twine, that's the word,' Cuypers agreed.

'You must have suspected what was in them,' Mulcahy said.

'I didn't ask, if that's what you mean.' Cuypers shrugged. 'Maybe I didn't want to know. Most of it was already loaded when I got there. I only found out how much there was when I went below later to stow my bag. Sure, I was shocked by the amount. I realised I was dealing with some serious people, but I needed the money, and I couldn't have backed out then even if I wanted to.'

Fair enough, he knew too much already by then. Again Mulcahy asked for names, but Cuypers claimed he didn't know them. Not very likely, but Mulcahy let it go for now. He was the one holding all the cards. He could wait. The last thing he wanted was for the man to give him fake names just to get him off his back.

'So what happened then?'

'The other guy drove the van away, and we made ready to sail.'

'He was the man in charge? He didn't sail with you?'

'No,' he said. 'The skipper was an English guy, but the guy with the van was the boss, for sure. He was Irish, I think. That kind of accent, anyway.'

'Describe him.'

Cuypers shrugged. 'I don't know. I was below deck most of the time. I didn't see him so much, and it was dark. So, one metre ninety, maybe, the same as me? I didn't really see his face; he had on a baseball cap, and a leather jacket.'

'Age?'

'Thirty-something? Forty maybe. But that's just a guess. One thing I do know is he didn't know boats. He never came aboard, not once. Everything was hurry, hurry, hurry with him.'

'Okay, we can go back to him later. Go on with the rest.'

Mulcahy sat back again, as Cuypers embarked on a seaman's account of the three-day voyage, how the *Atlantean* handled poorly, how they discovered her engine was pretty much on its last legs as they motored out of port, but forgot about all that as soon as they reached open water and made sail, caught some great wind and weather and pushed the boat on as hard as they could as they skirted round Ostend and Calais and down into the busy English Channel. Mulcahy let Cuypers know that he was a keen sailor himself, which seemed to relax him a little, enough eventually for him to drop a name, the skipper's name, Jenkins, which Mulcahy then used to press him for the other crewman's name.

'Go on, Willem. What's it to you, for God's sake? You've already gone most of the way down the road; you can't stop now. You'll have to tell us in the end.'

Cuypers tried to argue, but Mulcahy was obviously right. Eventually he caved in. The other guy's name was Ryan, he said, but didn't know whether that was a first name or surname. All he knew was he was Irish, from Dublin.

'He didn't say much. I didn't have much to say to him, either, because I was pissed off. He was no sailor. I had to do most of the work, with the skipper. That's not easy on a yacht that size, not when you're going hard for three days non-stop.'

Cuypers continued until he got to the point on the third day when they dropped sail in a choppy sea a couple of miles off the southwest coast of Ireland, establishing their position by GPS and an earlier sighting of the Galley Head lighthouse. They started up the engine so they could maintain position, but it gave them trouble straight away and Jenkins, the skipper, began to get nervous.

'We were sitting in the swell, the wind was getting up, and Jenkins was cursing because we were at the exact coordinates and there was nobody there to meet us. We'd made such good headway before we had to trim back most of the day. Now, the sun was low in the sky and we were supposed to make the rendezvous at dusk. Where were they? I think Jenkins, he felt exposed, sitting there, holding position with the engine coughing and belching out oily black smoke like a big signal. And we were talking about what to do when we heard a shout from Ryan up forward. We looked and saw a white rib speeding out towards us, and Jenkins said get ready to transfer the cargo.'

'You weren't surprised by this?' Mulcahy asked him. 'You're saying you knew the plan was to transfer it at sea?'

Again Cuypers gave a philosophical shrug. 'Sure. Jenkins told me sometime on the first day. I think to reassure me. He said we'd be met, they'd take the cargo, and we'd sail the empty yacht on to Kinsale and moor her up there, nice and clean, and I could catch a flight back to the Netherlands from Cork.'

'So what happened?'

'Ryan was below deck passing the bales up to me when I heard Jenkins cursing. He was pointing at what looked like a patrol vessel coming up fast, really fast – you know, maybe as much as eighteen or twenty knots. I thought it had to be a coastguard cutter or something – then I saw the big gun up front and knew it was. I also knew there was no way we could outrun it.'

'But the rib got to you first.'

Cuypers nodded. 'When they came alongside, they didn't even know there was a problem, but as soon as they tied on one of them spotted the patrol ship and he totally panicked. I mean, the cutter was still at least ten minutes off and Jenkins was screaming at them, really, saying we must take some of the cargo, but they wouldn't listen. They threatened to go without us.'

'There were two of them?'

'Yes, two.'

'Irish accents?'

'I would say so, definitely. But don't ask me who they were. The light was going by then, and they were wearing wet-weather gear, big mufflers and hoods. It was cold, you know? It was total panic. Jenkins was arguing with them, saying we'd all be tracked down and killed for abandoning the cargo, and them saying they'd rather take their chances than go to prison.'

Cuypers broke off and leant back in his chair, staring up at the ceiling, exhaling a sigh of the most heartfelt variety. 'I was afraid, too, and pretty exhausted, man. After a minute of this shouting I just jumped across to the rib. I wasn't going to be left behind. Then Ryan came after me, so Jenkins had no choice. He grabbed the GPS and jumped, too, and right in that moment the rib's two big outboards kicked in and we shot – I don't kid you, it was like being shot from the barrel of a gun – away towards the shore. It was terrifying. At that speed the waves were like brick walls and the rib was buck-ing off the top of them like a wild horse. It was all I could do to cling on for my life.'

'Sounds like a hell of a powerful boat,' Mulcahy said. 'You reckon you could have got away with some of the cargo?'

'Thinking back, for sure. We had at least ten minutes. We could have got fifteen, maybe twenty bales off. They would have saved a lot of money. But like I said, it was panic. There was no way the patrol could have caught that rib. The other ones, they must have known that, but they killed everything with panic.'

'Amateurs, you reckon?'

Cuypers gave Mulcahy a level stare. '*I* was an amateur,' he said, prodding his own chest. 'All I know is how to sail.'

'It sounds to me like the one in charge of that rib knew what he was doing. Nobody could have kept you upright at that speed without knowing how to handle her properly.'

'For sure, that's true. And he knew the coast, too. It was getting real dark when they landed us in that cove. It wouldn't have been an easy place to find, cliffs and rocks all round, tricky currents, too. They knew it well, I think.'

'And they just marooned the three of you on this beach and took off by sea themselves again?'

'*Ja*. We thought it would be where they had arranged to offload the drugs, and there would be somebody to meet us, you know? But there was nobody. After a while we realised it was just a cove; there wasn't even a road down to the beach, only a kind of track, for animals, or swimmers maybe. We hung around for a bit, but it was so cold we decided we should try to make our own way. We couldn't see our hands in front of our faces, it was so dark. All we did was fall over and get more lost.'

'I don't suppose you know which way the rib headed when they left you. East? West?'

'Look,' Cuypers said wearily, 'I have no idea. My only thought then was for getting away. For me. I didn't care about them. Just me. Like I said before, I can't tell you anything at all about those guys.'

'Oh, I don't know,' Mulcahy said, holding out the flat of his palm and starting to tick things off on his fingers. 'You've told me they were Irish, that they knew how to handle the rib pretty expertly and knew the waters, even in the dark and in a panic. And that they had somewhere to get back to themselves, and fairly quickly, so they could cover their tracks. I'd say that suggests they were locals, wouldn't you?'

23

'Liam, call me as soon as you get this, okay?'
A red Honda cut in front of him with a blare of its
horn, forcing Mulcahy to tap the brakes. He was back on the
M50 and the traffic was heaving and jostling, building
towards the late-afternoon rush. It would be just his luck to
get pulled over for not using his hands-free. He hung up and
in a fit of irritation threw the mobile on the passenger seat,
cursing as it bounced off the leather upholstery and into the
footwell. Why hadn't he just put it in the door pocket? Now
if Ford called back, he wouldn't—The phone rang even as he
was having the thought. With a fusillade of expletives, he
pulled across first to the nearside lane, then to a stop on the
narrow hard shoulder, hitting his hazard warning lights,
scrabbling on the floor to find the phone.

'Liam, where the hell have you been?' he shouted into the
phone, over the traffic roaring like a heavy sea just feet away.

He was met with a momentary silence. Then Siobhan's
voice. 'No, Mulcahy, it's me – you sound like you're driving.
Are you okay to talk?'

Shit. This was all he needed. He took a deep breath, used the wheel to pull himself upright again and decided he'd better be polite. 'Yeah, go on. I've pulled over now. What are you up to?'

'I'm down in Cork, of course, like I said I'd be.'

'Right,' he said, remembering she'd told him the night before that she was heading down there. Was that only last night? Christ. 'Did you come up with anything for me? About Kearney, I mean?'

'Yeah, quite a lot, actually. You wouldn't believe the half of it.'

'I probably would,' Mulcahy said, meaning it.

She laughed. 'Yeah, maybe you would at that. I tell you, I'm getting a very strong impression that Gemma Kearney is not quite the sweet little angel her mammy thinks she is.'

He winced as a heavy six-wheel gravel truck thundered past, just feet away, its roar deafening, a smattering of stone chips chinking on the car roof. He could barely hear what she was saying to him, something about him having to keep his side of the bargain.

'What was that?' he shouted.

'The name of the guy you're interested in – it's Begley, isn't it?'

He smiled. There was the confirmation. 'Who did you get that from? The mother?'

'No, actually, I got that from Kearney's PA, who I managed to track down this morning. I'm telling you, that accountancy practice of hers is one weird set-up. But I spoke to Mrs Kearney afterwards and asked her about this guy. She knew his name all right. I could almost hear her hackles going up. Said he was the "gangster" – that's the word she used – who did the dirt on Gemma in Dublin. Apparently, Gemma turned up with him, out at the mother's house, not long after she started up her business. Mrs K was appalled – after all he'd put the girl through – but Gemma said it was just work, and she needed all the clients she could get. Apparently, he'd asked her to help him buy some property in the area. Mrs K said they left together and she never heard mention of him again.'

'When was this?' Mulcahy asked.

'Must be four or five years ago at least. Whenever Gemma set up on her own. Mrs K said she told Gemma no matter how desperate she was, she'd never need clients like him.'

'She wasn't wrong there,' Mulcahy said, looking at his watch, thinking again about how desperately he needed to talk to Ford.

'How much do you actually know about this Begley guy, anyway?' Siobhan was asking. 'He sounds like a complete shit to me. Gemma's mother said he moved another girl into the house while Gemma was living there with him. I suppose she would have done anything for the drugs at that stage. And he sacked her and kicked her out not long after, cut her loose completely. What a creep.'

Mulcahy flinched as another enormous truck blasted past, blaring its horn, so close the Saab rocked on its axles this time.

'Jesus, what was that?'

'Look, Siobhan, I'm sitting on the side of the M50 here,' Mulcahy said. 'I'm going to cause an accident if I stay any longer. Can I call you when I get back to the office?'

'The deal was, you'd tell me about this guy as soon as I got the name.'

'Yeah, but, to be fair, I wasn't expecting to be playing dodgems with juggernauts when you called.'

She wasn't happy about it, but she agreed so long as he called her within the hour. As soon as she was gone he tried Ford again, but once more only got his voicemail. Fuck it.

'Liam, come on, I need to talk to you. This thing is really beginning to fall into place. We need to decide on a strategy. Get Aidan and Aisling together and tell them to be ready to move. We're going to have to act really, really fast.'

Half an hour later he was back in the office with Ford, Duffy and Sweeney sitting round his desk, listening with a kind of awe-filled anticipation.

'So, before I go,' Mulcahy said, 'I ask Cuypers if there's anything else he can tell me about the rib – him being a sailor, and he's been banging on so much about how incredibly fast it was.'

'And?'

'He said he thought it was a Ballistic but couldn't be sure.'

Ford put his palms up. 'The only ballistics I know are to do with bullets.'

'They're an English boat manufacturer,' Aisling said. 'I came across them when I was doing the research into the trailer.'

'Did anything ever come of that?' Mulcahy digressed, curious.

Aisling looked distracted. 'Did I not say? I found a company based in Dunmanway, called Hourihans. They import

and distribute all sorts of trailers. I looked at their website –
red logo with a big "H" on it.'

'She shoots, she scores,' Ford whispered, punching the air.

'Well done. We'll chase that up as soon as we get a chance,'
Mulcahy said. 'But to get back to the Ballistic thing . . .
Cuypers said this rib was a big one, maybe six, seven metres,
which makes sense given the weight of cocaine they were
planning to offload onto it. The important point is, it's not
the sort of boat your average day sailor would own.'

'But you might if you took corporate types out on fishing
expeditions, or tourists on sightseeing trips, is that it?' Ford
said.

'That's what I'm thinking, yeah.'

'I'd bet my right bollock this Horgan fella was up to his
neck in this.'

'I'm not sure I'd be so free with the future of humanity,
Liam, just yet.' Mulcahy laughed. 'What was really interesting was what he said about the outboards on it – two
Evinrude 225s. Now those are unusual. American imports,
really powerful. Definitely not your standard Yamaha or
Honda jobs. And of that size, there can't be more than a
handful in the whole of Ireland.'

'Can we get the Cork boys out to Glandore quick, to have
a check on Horgan's gear?' Ford said.

'Most of it's been sold off already,' Mulcahy replied, 'but
there's another way. Aidan, you get on to the bank. They'll
have a record of all the boats and other equipment that was
seized from Horgan by the bailiffs. If there's a seven-metre
Ballistic rib with twin Evinrude outboards on the list, then it's
in the bag. *Our* bag. We can leave it to the Cork lads to track

where it's gone to and whether there's anything Technical can get off it at this stage.'

'Jesus,' Ford muttered, his fists balled with excitement. 'I only wish I was down there to do it with them. Could do with a bit of action.'

'Well, I might be able to help you out with that, too.'

'Yeah?' Ford's eyes lit up.

'I told Cuypers the deal was off if he didn't give me more info about this Ryan guy. There was no way he didn't know more about him – this was the guy who got the three of them off Galley Head and away before the search could catch up with them. He obviously had some serious contacts: got them to Cork, then up to Dublin. I'd put a bet on that he's the one who's been bankrolling Cuypers in the meantime, maybe even putting him up until he got arrested.'

'You think this Ryan might've been the one arranged the stabbing in Cloverhill?' Sweeney asked.

'Who knows. If it was, he made a big mistake. No way was Cuypers wanting to give him up before that.'

'But you persuaded him?'

Mulcahy smiled. 'A secret's not much good if you're dead, is it? Ryan wasn't his real name at all. When they got to Cork, Cuypers noticed everyone was calling this guy "Marker" or something like that. Then in Dublin—'

'Marker? Are you fucking serious?'

Everyone turned to look at Ford, who had a look on his face like he'd just won the lottery, ecstasy and disbelief vying for the upper hand.

'Yeah, Marker. He gave me a description,' Mulcahy said.

'Hundred and eighty centimetres or thereabout, early thirties, cropped dark hair, gym bunny. You know him?'

'Mark "the Marker" Waldron.' Ford was looking even happier. 'It's got to be. Hard man for the Clondalkin mob. Vicious fucker. And a bloody big fan of Bingo's, as I recall. Always trying to shaft someone. Tried it on with me once.'

'Cuypers said something about his left ear?' Mulcahy said.

'That's him. A bloke bit off his earlobe in a mill years back. Oh my fucking mother.' Ford was barely able to contain himself. 'Kev and me spent months with a surveillance team trying to nail him and we got nowhere. What the fuck was he doing on a boat? Dirty scrote would barely recognise a bath.'

'I think we know what he was doing there, Liam. Keeping an eye on the cargo. Making sure it got where it was going to.'

'Yeah, and did about as good a job as usual.' Ford rubbed his hands together gleefully. 'Let's call Kev O'Neill, get him picked up, yeah?'

Mulcahy put his hands out, palms down, calming. 'Okay, set it up, but make sure you check back with me before you move on it. I need to talk to Murtagh first. And I want you to be there when they take him in. I want us to get the credit for this. That's important.'

'Just try and stop me,' Ford said. 'No way would I miss that – not for the fucking world.'

The rest of the afternoon went in a blur of frantic activity: phone calls, briefings and yet more phone calls. The first call to Murtagh was met initially with disbelief, then a torrent of questions and finally an elaborate, if slightly exasperated bouquet of congratulations.

'You know you've overstepped your brief by a hell of a margin here, Mike,' Murtagh said gruffly. 'But I suppose I can't really complain about it, given that I was the one who told you to come up with something to prove your worth.

Murtagh said he'd need an hour to call O'Grady and bring him up to date. He then suggested Mulcahy should come over and brief the Cork investigation team on the new developments via the video-conferencing facility as soon as possible. 'It might be useful for you to go down to Cork as well, afterwards, Mike, to make sure you're *seen* to share the credit for this. In the meantime I'll get O'Grady to send some lads out to Glandore and check out this Horgan character's boating business.'

Mulcahy looked up, saw Duffy waving at him from the door.

'Eh, hang on a second, Donal,' he said, and motioned Duffy in, who handed him a piece of paper with a number of items marked with orange highlighter pen, and followed it up with a huge grin and a double thumbs-up.

As soon as he saw what was on the page he grinned right back at him.

'Actually, there's no need, Donal. I've just been passed a note by Aidan here. It's a schedule of assets seized by the bank from Glor na Mara, Horgan's boating business. Among the items listed are three rigid inflatable boats, including, I quote, "one 6.5m Ballistic rib with twin Evinrude 225hp outboard engines". That's an exact match for what Cuypers told me. I think that wraps it up as far as Horgan is concerned.'

'Christ Almighty,' Murtagh muttered. 'Haven't you left anything at all for them to do down there?'

But of course he had. The second man on the rib, for instance, needed to be identified and tracked down, and an hour later, in the course of the briefing he gave to O'Grady's stunned Southern Region investigation team, Mulcahy was able to point them in a possible direction for that, too, suggesting the one person they might want to interview as a matter of urgency was Horgan's boating business partner, who the Skibbereen CID sergeant, McCann, had named as Conor Hayes.

Mulcahy was also able to outline to the Cork team the actions being initiated in Dublin to mop up the man known as Ryan, aka Mark Waldron, and to see if any trace could be found of the *Atlantean*'s English skipper, Jenkins. And Murtagh had fulfilled his promise and made sure the big man himself, Commissioner Thurlock Garvey, had been patched in to the briefing as well, so there was no question that the glory for these crucial developments was going to anyone other than Mulcahy and the ILU. To his credit, Detective Superintendent Sean O'Grady in Cork had looked only marginally less pleased than the rest of his crew regarding the breakthrough.

All of which left Mulcahy, on his way back from Murtagh's office, feeling elated but totally knackered. Walking through the Garda Memorial Garden, his mobile trilled. He looked at the screen and cursed, so loudly a woman walking past the gate outside looked up, startled, and frowned across at him. He'd completely forgotten to call Siobhan back.

'Mulcahy, you are a complete and utter cu—'

'Hang on, Siobhan,' he interjected before she could get going properly. 'I'm sorry, I really am, but I've got a major operation going on here. It slipped my mind, okay?'

279

'Yeah, right,' she said, not willing to let it go but sounding a lot mellower than he expected. 'But a deal's a deal, Mulcahy, and you promised you'd tell me more about this Begley guy. That said, I did find a bit more out myself in the meantime, anyway.'

'How did you do that?' Mulcahy asked, as ever marvelling at her ability to get hold of sensitive information.

'I just Googled his name,' she said, her tone scornful. 'It was all over the bloody *Irish Times* and *Indo* on Monday. I knew I'd seen it somewhere recently. It is the same guy, isn't it – the one who was murdered out in Spain last week? That's this mysterious "other thing" you were working on?'

Mulcahy decided he'd better calm down; the excitement of the last few hours had maybe gone to his head.

'Yes, it is, but I'd appreciate it if you could—'

'They described him as a drugs baron,' she cut in. 'Was he really that big?'

He couldn't but get the feeling he was being interviewed. 'Anything I say is off the record, Siobhan. We agreed, yes?'

'Of course. I just wanted to know if he was ever involved in bringing the drugs in himself.'

Mulcahy stiffened. It was an innocent enough question on the surface, but he knew her too well. Siobhan Fallon never 'just wanted to know' anything, and this was very specific. He drew in a long breath.

'Mulcahy?'

'Yes, I'm here,' he said, still thinking through how much he could afford to tell her, reminding himself that he had, after all, promised to fill her in.

'Look,' he said eventually, 'Begley was a sort of mid-ranking thug when he lived here in Dublin. Nothing special. But when he moved to Spain, we know he met some fairly major operators. So smuggling was a possibility, yeah, but we're still not sure. Why do you ask?'

What she said next made the hairs stand up on the back of his neck.

'Well, it's weird. I'm down here in this place trying to get some more detail on Horgan, and I've just had the strangest chat with this guy who was in business with him, and the guy just seemed ridiculously shifty. I don't know why – it's so nice around here, all these boats and stuff – but I just thought—'

'Hang on a sec, Siobhan,' Mulcahy broke in. 'What boats and stuff? Where are you calling from?'

There was a pause at the end of the line, which he assumed was Siobhan bridling at the abruptness of his question. Then she obviously decided to let it go.

'It's gorgeous, actually,' she said. 'Tiny place a few miles outside Skibbereen, like a little fishing village, on the sea. Except I don't see any trawlers. Probably mostly tourism these days. Glandore, it's called.'

'For fuck's sake!' Mulcahy thought he was saying it to himself, but somehow it burst up and escaped his lips in an angry growl.

'Excuse me?' came the indignant response from Siobhan. 'Mulcahy, what is going on up there? You're behaving like a complete arse. What have I done wrong now? All I'm doing is standing on the harbour wall here admiring the view.'

'What made you ask about smuggling, Siobhan? It can't have been the bloody view. What aren't you telling me?'

'Me telling you . . . ?' She paused, building towards anger.

'For fuck's sake, Mulcahy, you're the one who's been holding out on me. We had a deal, and you're the one who hasn't kept his side of it.'

'Who were you talking to, Siobhan? Tell me, please.' He all but shouted it into the phone in his frustration.

'His name was Conor Hayes,' she said, startled, but getting stroppier herself by the second. 'What's it to you? What the fuck is going on?'

He knew there was no point trying to hide it any more. He looked at his watch. The Cork team probably wouldn't even get there for another couple of hours. He prayed to Christ she hadn't spooked Hayes. The only thing he could do was try to get her away from there before she blew the whole thing out of the water.

'Look, Siobhan, that honestly doesn't matter now,' he said, 'but you've got to get out of there. I can't tell you why, but you have to believe me. I'll be down there myself in the morning. I'll give you an exclusive briefing, if it makes a difference, in Skibbereen, wherever, tomorrow morning. But only if you leave Glandore now and don't talk to anyone else there in the meantime . . . '

Even as he said it, he knew there would be a better chance of her going skiing in the Sahara than taking any notice of a request like that.

His head was pounding again. He got back to find the ILU office deserted. Ford had been only too happy to take on running the Dublin end of the operation with O'Neill and the B Division team – half of whom he either drank or played football with regularly at the Garda GAA Club out in

282

Westmanstown – and had obviously taken Duffy and Sweeney with him.

Mulcahy sat down at his desk, feeling suddenly very tired, and noticed two Post-it notes attached to his screen: one in Duffy's scrawl about a call from Malaga to say an email with flight details had been sent through, the other in Sweeney's more elegant hand saying DI Brogan had called and could he get back to her when he got a chance. He didn't feel much like getting into it with Brogan now. Didn't want to go sending her off on a wild goose chase, either, and despite the mounting evidence, he still wasn't entirely ready to accept the hit-man scenario was likely, least of all in relation to McTiernan, who he genuinely believed would have had nothing to do with a major drugs-smuggling operation. It simply wasn't Eddie's kind of thing. Not for all the money in the world.

In which case, who the hell had killed him?

He picked up the phone to call Ford, logging on to the ILU email queue as he did so. Sure enough, atop the swamp of policy directives and bulletins in the inbox was a mail from a name he didn't recognise with an '@policia.es' ending. He clicked into it and saw the summary he'd requested from Ferrer of Begley's flights in the previous six months. He looked at the last two of them, the Malaga–Bristol return flights, and noticed there were a couple of files attached. He put the phone down, intrigued, and clicked on one of the attachments. An EasyJet passenger manifest for the return leg of the journey opened up. Chief Inspector Ferrer had been most punctilious, it seemed, in double-checking everything regarding that particular flight. Doubtless because SOCA had taken an interest.

Mulcahy scrolled down through the list of names: Aherne, G. . . . Aherne, T. . . . Almaraz, F. . . . Almarez, P. . . . Ballagh, S. . . . Begley, D. . . .

There he was. No doubting that, then. Bingo had definitely been to Bristol and back. He had never even intended going to Ronson's funeral. Mulcahy was about to close the attachment when something snagged the corner of his eye further down the list, the proximity of a capital letter K to a capital G, perhaps, and he looked down properly, astonished at what he saw: Jimenez, P. . . . Kearney, G. . . .

Well, well. That was a turn-up. Gemma Kearney had gone back to Malaga with Begley, two days after Horgan died and two weeks before Begley himself had been murdered. He remembered now that McTiernan said something had spooked Begley when he was in the UK. Had it spooked Kearney, too? So much that she just dropped her entire life and ran off with Begley? If so, where the hell was Gemma Kearney now? Maybe Siobhan would be able to throw some light on that tomorrow. Providing she'd calmed down by then, of course.

He closed the file and looked at the list of Begley's movements again. The fourteen destinations read like an itinerary of western Europe's most popular drugs-trading cities and he cursed himself for making so many easy assumptions initially about Begley. It was obvious from the list alone that Bingo was a much bigger player than anyone had realised. Alicante, Amsterdam, Berlin, Frankfurt-Hahn, Eindhoven, Marseilles . . . The names went on until he came to one that, again, brought him instantly to a halt: Rotterdam. How the hell had he not noticed that before? He examined the dates beside the out- and inbound flights. Christ, there it was in black and white. Begley had been in Rotterdam back in April.

He got up and went out to where Ford had shoved the whiteboard against the wall, still showing the timeline they'd put together the day before. The dates of Begley's flights straddled exactly when Hayford had been killed. So that was it. Begley must have been in Rotterdam the day Hayford was shot by the Colombians. Had he witnessed something? Is that why they were after him?

Mulcahy looked at the whiteboard again, an even bigger picture forming in his head, straining to remember exactly what McTiernan had said to him down at the ferry port, thoughts tumbling and ricocheting round his brain, making connections, opening possibilities. Vlissingen really wasn't very far from Rotterdam. He ran back to his desk, swivelled his computer screen round to face him, checked once more through the list of dates and destinations. There it was. Begley had flown to Rotterdam again for five days the week the *Atlantean* had sailed for Cork. Shit!

Was it even possible? Could Begley really have found himself in the position of being the only man on the planet who knew where Hayford had stashed €100 million worth of cocaine?

His mobile rang and he snatched it from his pocket: Ford. Thank Christ for that.

'Liam, are you done yet? How would you fancy that pint I owe you?'

24

'What in the name of Christ happened to you?'

Mulcahy spotted Ford approaching from the other direction just as he was about to enter the Long Hall. He waited under the striped canopy outside, puzzlement growing with every second. Even from twenty metres away, the bruise purpling up on Ford's left cheek, just below eye level, was very, very nasty.

'Don't you start,' Ford growled at him.

'What am I starting?' Mulcahy said. 'Am I supposed to ignore that you look like a train ran into your face?'

'It's not that bad,' Ford said, touching the skin, stretching it carefully, examining his reflection in the window. 'I'll just have to disappoint the ladies for a day or two.'

'No change there, then. So what happened?'

Ford shrugged. 'Marker, the little shit. I asked Kev to, you know, let me have the pleasure of going in first. So, when they dinged the door, in I went and ... Fuck, I don't know. Marker was on his own, but completely off his face. Must've been on the fairy dust or something. It took four of us to pin him down in the end.'

Mulcahy reckoned he was probably better off not trying to visualise that, so he said nothing, just let Ford continue.

'As soon as I went in the room the cunt just picked up this plate-glass coffee table and flung it at me, like it weighed no more than an ashtray. I'm not kidding, it must've weighed a couple of stone.'

'You were hit by a glass coffee table and that's all the damage it did?'

'It didn't hit me,' Ford said, irritated. 'I slammed into the edge of the door trying to dodge the fucking thing. That's when I got really annoyed.'

'And it still took four of you?' Mulcahy had seen Ford truly angry on maybe five or six occasions in all, none of them pleasant.

'Strong as a fucking water buffalo, he was.'

'Come on, I'll buy you an extra one for that,' Mulcahy said, pushing in through the door.

Inside the pub the chandeliers and mirrors glittered a jagged low light on the half-deserted interior – a small gang of besuited office workers up the front end, the usual lonely throats at the bar and a scattering of loving couples in the back room. The barman snapped a grudging greeting at them as they passed, then told them to sit down in the back, that he'd bring the drinks over – a sure sign he was bored rigid. They grabbed a couple of chairs in the corner, and Mulcahy listened to Ford's account of the afternoon's events while they waited for the pints to come.

As soon as they did, they each took a long, cool draught

and Ford sat back while Mulcahy outlined the information that he'd uncovered in the email from the Spanish, particularly with regard to Begley's flights to and from Rotterdam.

'So what are you saying?' Ford asked, still trying to get his head around it. 'That Bingo might've done all this off his own bat? That even Ronson didn't know about it?'

'Would you put it past him?' Mulcahy asked.

Ford scratched the back of his head. 'I guess not,' he said, exhaling heavily. 'We both know the man was an opportunist of the highest order. And no better fella to stab a pal in the back. But this is Bingo Begley we're talking about. I mean, would he have had the nuts for it?'

'That's just it,' Mulcahy said, taking another pull on his pint. 'The only thing we can say for absolute certain about Bingo is that we've totally underestimated him in every other aspect of this. So why not again?'

Ford sniffed loudly and took an enormous gulping swig of his pint. 'It would make sense of one thing, anyway. Right from the minute I mentioned the *Atlantean* to Marker, he started screeching on about Bingo, how we were all a bunch of stupid cunts and Bingo would have the better of us. Ha, ha, ha.'

'Hadn't he heard the bad news, then?' Mulcahy asked.

''Course he had,' Ford grunted. 'Those two go back further than most. I just assumed he was blaming us for what happened to Bingo out in Spain. Like I said, he was off his face, raving. To listen to him, you'd think he'd been knocking back whiskies with Bingo just the other day. But this way, it kind of makes sense – gives us another link between Bingo and the *Atlantean*, right?'

Mulcahy shrugged. He wasn't so sure it made that much sense. 'Interesting that other thing about Kearney heading off to Malaga with Bingo, though. I wonder where she is now.'

'In the grave with him, with any luck,' Ford said dismissively. 'She was up to her tits in this. She must've been in touch with Bingo all along.'

'I think she probably was,' Mulcahy said, thinking of his earlier conversation with Siobhan.

'Sounds like some kind of black widow,' Ford continued. 'I'm glad she's not my fuckin' accountant.'

'No chance of that, Liam. I hear she had "a small and very select clientele". It did make me wonder, though. If Bingo really was this big player without anybody knowing it, he must've needed somewhere to salt away large amounts of cash. And it turns out this ex-girlfriend he's still in touch with is an accountant who runs a mysteriously small yet high-yielding accountancy practice in a backstreet in Cork. And she in turn has an ex-boyfriend who's making an absolute fortune in the property business. Is it really so easy to make millions from an estate agent's in Skibbereen?'

'You were there yourself, weren't you, when you went to Baltimore?'

'I passed through it,' Mulcahy shrugged.

'Skib's a nice enough place and all,' Ford said, 'but it's no Beverly Hills. I did wonder the same thing myself when you mentioned Horgan the first time: how come this jumped-up little turd from the city can come in and turn around a failing family business in a matter of months?'

'But it was the boom,' Mulcahy said. 'Everyone was

stuffing their pockets, weren't they? Especially in property. That's where all the money was.'

'Maybe. But to be making fortunes for everyone else around as well? Even taking the boom into account, he'd've had to be some quare kind of whizz kid to do that in the wilds of West Cork. Sounded more like Robin Hood than a feckin' estate agent.'

Mulcahy sat back and thought about it. 'But you checked out Horgan yourself. Whiter than white, you said.'

'And I also said too good to be true,' Ford said with some satisfaction. 'Anyway, who better to run a laundry? Don't forget the name of that record company Bingo set up – Klene. Jesus, it wouldn't surprise me if laundering was his specialist subject all those years and we didn't have a fucking clue. We should have guessed he'd stick to what he knew and just try to get better at it.'

'I don't think we need to beat ourselves up on that score,' Mulcahy said. 'We didn't even know he set up Klene Records until – when was it, yesterday? I don't think anyone could accuse us of dragging our heels.'

Mulcahy sat back and drained his pint.

'You are having another one, aren't you?' Ford said.

'Yeah, go on, then.'

Ford tutted. 'Jesus, you're worse than a bird you are: full of promises, but when it comes to the big pay-out . . . '

'Shit, sorry,' Mulcahy laughed, and signalled the barman for another couple of pints. Ford grunted, knocking back the remains of his own pint, and the two lapsed into a thoughtful, companionable silence as they waited for the drinks to come.

'You know, I'm still not sure I buy Horgan's involvement in all of this,' Mulcahy said, finally. 'Begley and Gemma Kearney? Okay, I can see that, no problem. There's the past relationship, and it sounds like the money she got to set up her practice came from nowhere, so why not from Begley? Maybe he even kept her going single-handedly, who knows? That's a nice little criminal enterprise. It might even explain why there wasn't much fuss from other clients when she disappeared. But Horgan? I'm not so sure you can get involved in all that shit and not leave a few skidmarks. Especially in a small town. People keep a careful eye on you when you're new. If you start making money like you're printing the stuff, someone'll notice. Someone's going to get jealous and put the bad word around.'

Ford held his hands up in mock surrender. 'Maybe Horgan just dipped in and out. Or maybe Kearney put a few things his way every now and again for old time's sake, and he didn't even realise he was being used as a sink.'

'That seems more likely,' Mulcahy agreed. 'Maybe he just dipped in the once and got so badly burnt he felt he had to go for the big dip, in the river.'

'Or maybe he got the big shove,' Ford said.

Mulcahy looked over at him and they both nodded in agreement. 'That would make the most sense, wouldn't it? Begley needs someone to cooper a big load of coke from a yacht off the Cork coast. He asks his best girl if she knows of anyone local, and she says she knows this fella who not only has access to boats but has been so hammered by the crash that he's absolutely desperate for cash, and, what's more, she can wrap him round her little finger. But it all goes wrong.

The coke's seized and Begley's left high and dry. He's going to be mighty pissed off. Even Cuypers said it was the guys in the rib who panicked and fucked it up.'

'So you reckon Bingo put the squeeze on Horgan?'

'Par for the course, I'd say,' Mulcahy said. 'Meanwhile some *muchacho* from the Cali Cartel spots their missing product on the news, puts two and two together and sends someone round to sort things out.'

'And the whole thing blows up when Ronson gets whacked and Bingo feels the need to go on the run. Only they caught up with him.'

'And maybe caught up with Gemma Kearney, too, do you think?' Mulcahy said. He sat forward in his chair, rubbed the back of his neck and shook his head ruefully. 'Murtagh wants me down in Cork tomorrow, to follow up on all this Horgan stuff in Skibbereen. I think it would be an idea if you came as well. While I'm out in Skibbereen, you can get the Cork lads to sort you out a warrant for Kearney's office, get in there and have a good root around. I have a feeling we're going to find a lot of answers in there.'

Friday

25

More than anything else it was the colour of the sky that swamped him with dread: blood-red gashes ripped across bunched black clouds massing in the west, the freezing air screaming in from across *Seaspray*'s stern and him alone at the tiller while his dad crawled forward, battling against the weather and the bucking boat to take in the sail. 'Keep her steady. Keep her steady,' his father was shouting, he knew, but he couldn't hear as the wind whipped the words from his lips and cast them out into the boiling sea. He battled to do as he was told, used every inch of his thin arms and bony chest to lever himself against the wooden shaft kicking against confinement like a wild creature, his father mouthing encouragement, struggling to tie in the sheet until a squalling gust ripped it from his hands and the sail went flying up and he saw his dad's face filled with fear for the first time ever and his own hands froze and he felt the boat shudder beneath him as the tiller jumped from his grasp with a rending, shrieking crack . . .

He woke with a start, sweat streaming down his face and

chest, disorientated, a lost and vulnerable child for the second or so it took him to realise it was the sound of his mobile that had woken him. He pulled an arm loose from the tangled duvet, fumbled towards the pulse of light and pulled it to his eyes, jolted into wakefulness by the name he saw lit up there, and the time: SIOBHAN FALLON, 4.30AM.

'Siobhan, Jesus, what's the matter?' he said, clamping the phone to a clammy ear and realising too late that his jaw was still half locked from sleep and his words were emerging in a moronic slo-mo mumble.

She didn't seem to notice. 'Sorry, Mulcahy. I'm sorry. I'm really sorry,' she said, sounding completely hyper. 'I just didn't know what else to do. I didn't want to get you into trouble, honestly, but it was my only way out. Those wankers held me for seven hours. Can you believe it? Seven hours. Even though they knew damn well I couldn't have had anything to do with it. But you know how it is – have a go at the hack every chance they get—'

'Hang on, Siobhan. Slow down, would you?' He was unable to pluck more than ten comprehensible words from the torrent gushing from her mouth. 'Where are you?'

'What do you mean, where am I? Skibbereen, of course. Where else would I be? You're supposed to be meeting me here in a few hours, remember?'

That at least slotted, or clunked rather, into place for him. 'Yeah, yeah, of course. Skibbereen. Sorry. So what's the panic?'

'The panic?' Her voice cracked in disbelief. 'The panic? Are you seriously telling me they didn't call you? The fucking tossers. I just don't believe that!'

None of that left him any the wiser, either, so he let her rant on until she had to pause for breath, then asked her to repeat everything she'd said to him already but more slowly. It took a minute or two for his sluggishness to disperse and her anger and agitation to diminish, but eventually they reached an equilibrium of sorts.

'So what actually happened, Siobhan?'

At last she made him understand that, at about 8.30 p.m. last night on returning to the B&B she had booked into on Bridge Street in Skibbereen, she had been intercepted at the door by two uniformed Gardai, one male, one female, and promptly detained for questioning. At first they wouldn't even tell her what it was about, just stuck her in a freezing-cold empty interview room and kept her waiting over an hour until eventually she kicked up so much of a stink that two plainclothes detectives came in and informed her that she was being interviewed in relation to the discovery of a dead body earlier that evening.

'A dead body?' Mulcahy said, fully alert now. 'What body?'

'They wouldn't tell me, just kept banging on about what I'd been doing in Glandore and who I'd been talking to. I honestly didn't have a clue what they were on about until I mentioned talking to this guy Hayes down at the harbour and I saw them share one of those ultra-dumb 'Oh yeah, now we've got her' looks. Then they buggered off again and didn't come back for another couple of hours. This time they had some real big cheese with them. Murtagh, he said his name was—'

'Donal Murtagh? The assistant commissioner?' Mulcahy broke in, trying to fit the other side of the picture together in his head. If Murtagh was there, it had to be to do with Rosscarbery Bay.

'Yeah, I'm sure he was at least that,' Siobhan said dismissively. 'He looked like he had that kind of clout, and he was a lot less of a dickhead than the others. Laid it all out for me: how Conor Hayes was found dead in the water down at the harbour at six o'clock or so. Jesus, I must've been one of the last people to talk to him, or even see him alive.'

'Conor Hayes is dead?' Mulcahy had only heard the man's name for the first time twelve hours earlier, but the significance of his death zapped into his central cortex like a shot of adrenaline to the heart. He threw the duvet back, swung his bare feet onto the cold, shiny fake-wood floor, held a hand to his mouth in the bleak dark of morning, goosebumps on his forearm, a chilly glissando running down his back. Ronson. Horgan. Begley. McTiernan. Now Hayes. When was it going to stop? But he knew the answer to that already: Kearney. An image of a tall, blond, tanned man squeezing a double trigger. Unless, of course, that act of vengeance had already been wrought, unknown, alone, elsewhere.

'How did the lads even know you were there?' Mulcahy asked, almost by way of distraction. 'I thought you said you were in Skibbereen.'

An audible intake of breath, followed by nothing. The tiredness would be getting to her by now, he thought.

'It wasn't you who told them?' She sounded genuinely confused by that. 'I thought it must've been you, after I spoke to you earlier.'

'No, I was tempted, but I thought it would make even more trouble.'

'Oh shit, Mulcahy,' she said. 'I'm really sorry. I think I might have really fucked things up for you. That guy Murtagh, he said he remembered my name from last year and the Priest and stuff, and he mentioned your name, and then he said he'd been speaking to you earlier about this case and I just assumed ...'

Even with the last stretch of the M8 open and the traffic thin in the early morning it took Mulcahy four hours to get there. Much of it in darkness. As the glare of his headlights picked out the names of the towns and villages he sped past – Newbridge, Kildare, Monasterevin, Abbeyleix, Durrow, Urlingford – it felt like he was leaving the dawn behind him rather than driving into the light of a new day. He remembered reading in the *Irish Times* about it being the autumn equinox that night, when the sun's power took its focus off the northern hemisphere for the year and tilted away to the south, when day and night fell into balance for a moment before darkness got the upper hand and winter fell. Equinox. Equal night and day. And he thought of the southern hemisphere, of a bright day drawing to a close on a city in South America just as the sun would be rising over Cork. As he sped along the high road past Cashel, the heavy clouds parted and he saw the harvest moon gleaming down on the Rock's towers and ancient buildings, and his heart lifted momentarily in awe. Then the sky closed up again and plunged him back into darkness.

It was ten past nine and the sun was well up by the time he cruised into Skibbereen, a bustling, prosperous little market town previously known only to Mulcahy for its touristic fame, and as the location of pits containing the bones of 10,000 victims of the Great Famine. He drove slowly past the old courthouse, looking for an empty space in the glut of Garda cars and media vans parked on the main road out front. He'd spoken briefly to Murtagh on the way down, knew he'd been due to hold a press conference there at half eight, and he was sure he spotted, as he passed, Siobhan's cropped black hair among the mob of reporters now streaming out from the tall double doors to film their spots or write up their copy. He found a parking place further down the road, past the hulking grey cathedral, and was walking back towards the courthouse when he saw her again, chatting to some plainclothes man, her reporter's notebook in hand, dashing down notes. He waited a moment, until the cop sensed his presence and looked over, annoyed by the intrusion, and only got more so when Siobhan, following the guy's line of sight, shut her notebook, thanked him quickly and walked straight over.

'Mulcahy,' she laughed, 'am I ever glad to see you.' She fell into step beside him, linking her arm into the crook of his elbow, and the zing of her touch pulsed through him. She seemed not even to notice, and the wide grin on her face utterly transformed her from the woman he'd met over the last couple of days. As if the anxiety she had given off then was just a skin to be shed and now, here she was, back to her old self completely.

'Your humour's improved,' Mulcahy said, finding it impossible not to let his own rise with it.

'Why wouldn't it? I'm already in the middle of a cracking murder story and now you're going to give me the inside track on it. Short of there being nuclear Armageddon tomorrow, I'm guaranteed the front page. What's not to be happy about?'

He resisted the urge to remind her of the early morning rant, and the massive bollocking he would inevitably get from Murtagh for involving her, but she seemed to interpret his silence only as hesitation.

'You are going to give me the inside track, aren't you?' she said, eyebrows arched reprovingly. 'You promised, Mulcahy.'

He pulled up, removed her arm from his and looked her in the eye.

'It's probably better if we're not seen getting too cosy together out here. I've got to go check in with Murtagh, which is going to take a while. Can we meet up in an hour or so, maybe? I'll give you everything I can then.'

'Everything you "can"? You said "everything you need" last night.'

'And that's what I meant, too, Siobhan, but there are limits to everything. I promise I'll give you more than enough, though, okay? Look, go and find somewhere we can talk privately and I'll meet you there as soon as I'm done, yeah?' He turned to go, but stopped. 'What the hell were you doing in Glandore yesterday, anyway? How did you even know about Hayes?'

'Someone in Skibbereen told me he ran a boating business with Horgan. I didn't remember seeing him at the funeral. I was just wondering why he didn't go. Looks like I was right to, doesn't it?'

It did, but that wasn't what Mulcahy had been getting at. 'I don't see why you were so interested in Horgan still. I thought it's Gemma Kearney you're looking for?'

'It is. But it's a kind of different story now, isn't it? I mean, even with the drugs run to Bristol, Horgan's story was blowing up, but with a murder involved now, I mean—'

'Hang on, Siobhan,' Mulcahy broke in, his voice a low whisper of disbelief. He put his hand on her upper arm and steered her into the doorway of the vacant shop they were outside, as if this would afford them some kind of auditory shelter. 'What are you talking about? What drugs run to Bristol?'

She looked up at him, whether trying to figure out how much he knew, or just amused that she knew something he didn't, he couldn't tell. 'Well, I don't know for certain that's what it was. I told you Horgan went to Amsterdam, didn't I?'

'Yes, but . . . ' He didn't even bother finishing the sentence.

She quickly outlined to him what she'd discovered about Horgan's flight to Amsterdam and subsequent overnight drive down to Calais and on to Bristol, with Mulcahy looking more exasperated with every detail.

'Why didn't you tell me about this before, Siobhan?'

'I tried,' she said indignantly. 'You were the one who told me I'd been given a bum steer and that I shouldn't go jumping to conclusions. Anyway, I wasn't sure what it meant myself until you told me about Gemma and this guy Begley being involved and then, well, you don't need to be a rocket scientist, do you?'

Mulcahy blew out his cheeks, ran both hands back over his head, then cupped them over his mouth as he tried to figure out how all this slotted into the investigation.

'Have you told anyone else about this?' he asked eventually.

She shook her head. 'Not a soul.'

'Not while you were being questioned last night?'

'Are you mad?' she said, giving him the look. 'And let those fuckers give it to some other reporter?'

She was so different to him, so sharp sometimes it hurt.

'Right, of course,' he said, still slightly thrown by how much she knew. He looked at his watch, remembering Murtagh. 'I've got to go. Look, we'll figure this out later, okay?'

'Absolutely,' she said. 'Just confirm one thing for now – you're working on the assumption that both Hayes and Horgan were involved in drugs smuggling, yes?'

'We're not sure of it yet.' He hesitated a moment. 'But that's part of it, yes.'

Now it was her eyes that were widening. She even licked her lips in anticipation. 'Part of it? You mean there's more?'

It was Mulcahy's turn to smile. 'You ought to have more faith in me, Siobhan. I told you it was a big story, didn't I?'

He made his way up the steps of the courthouse, a solid, stone-porticoed neoclassical heap that echoed inside with the sound of hurrying footsteps. There was a general air of energy and urgency he suspected wasn't the norm around there. He asked a uniform where the incident room had been set up, and was directed upstairs to a big, shabby, high-ceilinged meeting room that took up most of the upper floor. In the ceiling rows of dirt-streaked Victorian skylights let in a murky light that had to be supplemented by hanging pairs of harsh fluorescent tubes. Beneath he saw Murtagh standing at the centre of a huddle of uniforms and detectives, the shortest man there, but instantly identifiable as the most important.

Mulcahy hadn't even made it halfway across the room before the assistant commissioner spotted him and detached himself from the group, hand extended in greeting as ever. He was looking remarkably hale for a man who had been up most of the night, and the energy came off him in waves as Mulcahy shook his hand.

'You got here in good time,' Murtagh said, steering him over towards an area in which a number of freestanding whiteboards had been set up in a wide semicircle. Facing them were a couple of rows of desks, most as yet unoccupied, where a desktop computer network was still being organised by technicians from the IT Unit.

Murtagh pointed at the central whiteboard, which was already festooned in maps, scene-of-crime photos and other documents, as well as a list of names scrawled in marker pen. 'I want you to come down to Glandore with me in a minute,' he continued, 'but first take a look at these photos from the scene. The local lads fished your man Hayes out of the water last night – he was attracting quite a crowd – and we're expecting an initial assessment back from the state pathologist this morning. Not that there's much to assess. Half the man's head was missing from the blast. Tell me what you think.'

'Shotgun, obviously,' Mulcahy observed, studying one of the grim close-up photos that had been pinned up, its vivid colours and runnels and ridges of blasted flesh more like a violent expressionist painting than the remains of a human head. He knew there would be far worse in the folders lying on the nearest desk. They only ever pinned up the least offensive ones, for fear that someone unauthorised might wander unchallenged into the incident room.

'I'd say so,' Murtagh said, 'but too much damage for a sawn-off, we reckon, unless it was totally point blank. Looks like it was from behind, to the left. Even if he had more face on him, I'm sure we wouldn't see anything but surprise on it.'

Mulcahy turned his attention to another photograph, taken earlier, when the body was still in the water, floating face down, arms and legs spread out like a starfish, only the bloody red mush of the head and shoulder wound, and the slick of corporeal matter that had oozed from it, spoiling the picture's weird sense of tranquillity.

'Not much for the lads from Technical to get their teeth into,' Mulcahy said.

'No, not on the body,' Murtagh acknowledged, 'but he was up forward on his boat when it happened, so there's a fair bit of evidence to be collected from there. The boys think he didn't go straight into the water, but took it in the back on deck and then rolled over the side. C'mon, I'll take you down there now. There are a couple of other things I want to ask you about on the way.'

The huddle in the middle of the room had broken up after Murtagh abandoned it. Now he approached three men in crumpled suits who had continued in deep conversation and told them he was going over to Glandore again, with Mulcahy. The men gave Mulcahy an assessing glance and he recognised a couple of them from the video briefing he'd given the day before. They returned his nod perfunctorily, then assured Murtagh they'd call in the event of any developments.

Murtagh was eager to get going, so Mulcahy suggested they go in the Saab. The sun was high, the sky a storybook blue graced with an occasional cotton-ball cloud rolling in from the west. Once they turned off the main route to Cork and out towards Glandore, the road ran alongside a long sea-water inlet, narrow like a fjord, that glittered a dark sapphire blue in the sun. The steep land either side looked glorious, quilted in rich green vegetation, peat-brown earth and pale grey rock – with the road a darker shade of grey spreading out before them. Even Murtagh was temporarily quieted by it, although it didn't take long for him to get back to what he wanted: explanations.

'I know I said this earlier, Mike, but notwithstanding your tremendous help yesterday, that's some coincidence, you giving us the drop on a suspect who's never even blipped our radar before, and a couple of hours later he's dead. Especially when it's your lady friend who turns out to be the last person ever to see him alive. That's a hell of a tough one to swallow, you know?'

Mulcahy had already tried to explain it to him over the phone in the early hours after Siobhan called him, and would have tried again now if it hadn't been for his surprise.

'Does she know she was the last?' Mulcahy said.

'Maybe not,' Murtagh grunted. 'I doubt the lads who did the interview wanted to hand her another headline.'

Mulcahy nodded. That made sense.

'The thing is, we think she might have seen the killer, too.' Murtagh fixed him with a sidelong stare, as if suspecting Siobhan might have said something to him about it. 'I'm pretty sure she doesn't realise that, either, though.'

'Are you serious?' Mulcahy gasped, knowing she wouldn't have kept that to herself.

'She didn't say anything to you about it?'

Mulcahy glanced involuntarily at him, calculating the chances of Murtagh having seen them together on the street earlier, putting them at nil. He had to be referring to the early hours phone call, which had prompted Mulcahy's call to him.

'No, not a word. Why do you think she was?'

Murtagh shifted in his seat before replying. 'The killer struck less than half an hour after Fallon left Glandore. She told me she'd spoken to you on the phone and you told her to get out of there. Not the brightest thing to tell a journalist, Mike.' Murtagh gave him a disparaging glance before continuing. 'Needless to say, she went straight back to Hayes and started quizzing him again, which led to a stand-up row on the quay-side according to a couple of witnesses. I think she only left in the end out of frustration. We think the killer must have been sitting in his car all the while, watching and waiting for things to calm down again. It worked, to the extent that not a living soul saw the actual shooting, but we do have two people who say they saw a stranger sitting in a car down by the pier. A man in his late thirties with long, blond hair, one of them said—'

'Shit!' Mulcahy cursed, unable to stop himself. 'Was the car a pale blue or green Honda Jazz, something like that?'

Murtagh gave him a hard, suspicious look. 'An old-style VW Golf, we were told. Light green. How the hell would you know that?'

They were coming into Glandore now and Mulcahy pulled in at the first spot he could, opposite the harbour in the lea of what seemed to be a high old churchyard wall with a tall screen of yew behind. Across the road an ugly new-build hotel looked cramped and uneasy, hopelessly out of place, yet another testament to the greed of the boom years. Ahead of them, on a rise of land where the inlet opened out into a wide, tranquil bay, was the most picturesque location for murder Mulcahy had ever seen: a cluster of old white houses winding up the hill, the squat stone pier's protective sweep enfolding a scattering of small fishing boats and tenders to serve a flotilla of larger craft moored in the blue-green waters beyond.

Mulcahy switched off the engine, and putting a hand up to stave off the broadside that would inevitably follow, he told Murtagh everything he hadn't in the briefing the day before. About how Siobhan Fallon had approached him regarding Gemma Kearney. And more particularly about McTiernan's murder, and how a more dangerous killer than Murtagh imagined could well be on the loose.

'And are you seriously expecting me to believe that we could have a Colombian hit man running around here in West Cork?' Murtagh didn't so much ask the question as spit it.

'I'm not expecting you to believe anything,' Mulcahy said, 'but it's got to be worth considering. DI Brogan's witness said the killer was blond and driving a small green car. Commander Corbett said this guy's nickname is "the Blond". Yesterday those were just two possibly related facts. This morning they seem to be adding up to considerably more, don't you think?'

Mulcahy paused, tried to think of a way to set out his thoughts more coherently. 'Look, Donal, the fact is, everyone who's been rumoured to have any connection with this consignment of Colombian cocaine is either dead or missing now. I still don't understand how McTiernan got involved, but I'll say this: if the Cali Cartel is sending a message, it's a bloody effective one – don't fuck with us or we'll come and hunt you down. Even in the wilds of West Cork.'

Murtagh shook his head slowly and opened the car door. 'Come on, we'd better find O'Grady and fill him in on all this. Then I'll have to have a talk to this Inspector Brogan of yours and get her take on it.'

They walked along by the low harbour wall, over to the pier, ducking under the strips of blue and white Garda scene tape and making their way out along the pier towards a group of men and women in coveralls clustered on and around a small pleasure cruiser. Hayes's boat, Mulcahy surmised, noting the plastic sheet the team from Technical Bureau had fixed over the bow of the craft to secure the forensics evidence beneath. Squatting down and pointing out something to one of the technicians on the boat, Mulcahy recognised the broad shoulders and square jaw of Detective Superintendent Sean O'Grady and prayed he wouldn't make a meal of it when Murtagh gave him the bad news.

'Seems to me there's only one person who's had something to do with all of these people, now,' Murtagh said when they were halfway along the pier.

'And she's been missing for at least as long as Bingo's been dead,' Mulcahy said. 'I wouldn't hold out too much hope there.'

'I wasn't talking about Gemma Kearney. I was talking about your friend Siobhan Fallon.'

'No.' Mulcahy shook his head. 'She's just following the

story like we are. The only witness she's had any actual contact with is Conor Hayes, and it was just her bad luck that she got to him before we did.'

'Right, and ye've both still got questions to answer about that as far as I'm concerned,' Murtagh said gruffly. 'In the meantime I'll put out an alert on all flights and sailings out of Cork and Dublin tonight. Anyone with even a hint of a dodgy passport gets hauled in and questioned. I'm not having some Latin American cowboy thinking he can shoot all around him on my patch and get away with it.'

26

'Mulcahy, are you done there yet?' Siobhan's voice was a low, anxious whisper on the line.

He had dropped Murtagh off at the courthouse ten minutes previously and also checked in with Liam Ford on the way back, reassured to hear he had arrived in Cork and was about to execute the warrant to enter and search Kearney's office on Academy Street. Now Mulcahy was pulling up at a B&B place he'd spotted on the way in from Glandore, thinking he was probably going to be stuck in Skibbereen for one night at least.

'Yes, just finished. I can be with you in, say . . . ' He looked at his watch, figuring how long it would take, but she didn't give him a chance to finish the thought.

'No, there's been a change of plan,' she said urgently. 'Look, you've got to get over here to Drimoleague, right now. You've got to come. It's on the—'

'Drimoleague?' he cut in, the name sounding only vaguely familiar to him. 'What are you doing over there?'

'Just listen, would you,' Siobhan hissed, an edge of danger

in her voice now. 'I'm at a house called Culgreeny. It's a bungalow just outside Drimoleague, on the main road in from Skibbereen. You can't miss it. There's a long wooden fence and an ornamental windmill in the front garden. You've got to get over here quick. I'm serious, like, *now*.' She paused and her breath rasped in the earpiece. There was a sound like a door banging, then a muffled 'Shit, she's—' and the connection went dead in his hand.

Already the hairs were tingling like a burst of static on the back of his neck. Ever since Murtagh told him Siobhan might have seen the killer there had been a pinch of anxiety fretting away at the back of his mind. The killer had seen her arguing with Hayes, had possibly even been seen by her. Could she be in danger herself now?

He reached over and grabbed the road map, scanned a quick circle round Skibbereen and spotted Drimoleague about eight miles to the north. Seeing the name in print again, he remembered Siobhan telling him it was where Gemma Kearney had grown up. Could it be where her mother lived? His heart thumped as the crime-scene photos of Conor Hayes's corpse in the water came crowding back on him, along with the thought that the killer, shotgun in hand, might even now be stalking the Kearney house for Gemma. If he saw Siobhan there, wouldn't he take his chance, make sure?

Every instinct urged him to race off immediately, but instead he stepped out of the car and went round to the back, opened the boot and unlocked the small gun safe bolted to the chassis inside. He removed his official-issue handgun, a Sig Sauer P226, and inserted one of the two 9mm magazines, leaving the bulky regulation holster in the boot and slipping the weapon into a neat, hard plastic clip-on job he'd bought on the internet. Only then did he get back in the car and set off, a shower of loose gravel pelting the dry-stone wall by the roadside. Every junction he came to, he slowed just enough to check there was no danger of a collision, then shot through. In two minutes he was out on the main road, heading north at eighty, the fastest the Saab could cope with on the twisting, single-carriage road. The traffic was light, and overtaking wasn't a problem except once when, faced with a tractor holding up a queue of six or seven cars, he overtook the lot in one go, flashing his headlights, his fist on the horn, and raced away to a chorus of angry hoots from behind.

It couldn't have been more than ten minutes before he saw the six-foot black and white windmill in the garden of a low-slung property on the right-hand side ahead. The bungalow was set back twenty metres from the road on a rise, the sloping, well-manicured garden fenced all along the long road frontage by a wooden horse rail. On the driveway were two cars, a small new-looking Toyota and Siobhan's red Alfa, which he remembered all too well from the year before. He hit the brakes and drew to a stop on the roadside, not wanting to alert anyone to his presence by coming up the driveway in his car. He jumped out, clipped his weapon onto his belt under his jacket and approached the house cautiously.

He was halfway up the steeply sloping drive, feeling a little exposed, when the front door opened and he stopped. He was wondering whether to hold his ground or look for cover when he saw Siobhan coming backwards out of the door looking none too anxious about anything, as she was gabbing away animatedly to whoever was inside. She pulled the door to but not closed, then turned to face him, her eyes wide and a finger to her lips, the other hand making a cupping, come-hither motion.

'Come on, quickly,' she whispered at him. 'I'm not sure how long I can keep her talking.'

'Keep who talking?' Mulcahy said, annoyed. 'What the hell is going on here? I thought you were in trouble.'

'Trouble?' she said, searching him with her pale blue eyes like he was mad or something. 'No, look, I thought you'd want to hear this for yourself. You're not going to believe it.'

He breathed out heavily, trying to contain the pulse of frustration surging through him, thanking Christ he hadn't been spooked enough to actually draw his weapon. What the hell had he been thinking? But before he could put any of it into words, Siobhan grabbed his arm and, with a 'C'mon, hurry', pulled him in the door.

Inside was a small hallway, with a couple of rooms off it at the front and a corridor towards the back, leading to the kitchen and bedrooms, he assumed. The place reminded him of his parents' old house, having been furnished sometime in the 1980s and not updated since, although it was scrupulously clean and tidy. Siobhan led the way down the corridor and into the kitchen, a small room that also hadn't been redecorated in years, just regularly scrubbed into submission. Sitting at an abbreviated breakfast bar – the room wasn't wide enough to allow for more than one stool either side – was a thin, tired-looking woman with short, greying hair and green eyes, who looked up at him as he entered without

314

either greeting or warmth. She looked to be no more than in her late fifties, but already worn out by life.

'This is Mrs Kearney,' Siobhan said, giving him a little dig with her elbow. Then she addressed the woman, her voice slower, louder, like she was talking to a child or someone hard of hearing.

'Mrs K, this is the detective I was telling you about, from the Guards. His name is Inspector Mulcahy and he's completely trustworthy. I'm sure he'll be able to help us. All you have to do is tell him what you told me.'

At the words 'Guards' and 'inspector' Mrs Kearney's expression had become more animated. Her eyes ping-ponged anxiously from Siobhan to Mulcahy and back again, and when she spoke, her voice was shrill and breathy. 'I can't. You know I can't.'

She broke off as a bang from outside the house grabbed all their attention. Mulcahy put a hand up and in two strides was at the window over the sink, looking out across a wide back garden bordered by low shrubs and mostly laid to lawn. He saw nothing out of place other than a white plastic garden chair tipped over on the patio by a gust of wind, still rocking.

'It's nothing.' He turned back to the two women. 'What's going on here, Mrs Kearney?' He tried to catch her eye, to gain her trust, but her gaze eluded him, focused as it was on some fear locked away inside her. 'Whatever it is, I'm sure I can help, but not if you don't tell me what the problem is.'

'No, I promised her,' Mrs Kearney said cryptically, twisting her arms up in front of her chest, hugging her shoulders.

Finally Siobhan couldn't take any more and said it for her.

315

'It's about Gemma, Mrs K, isn't it? It's okay. Inspector Mulcahy knows all about her. I've told him everything you've told me, except ... ' She looked at the woman, encouraging her to complete the sentence for her, but all she got was another look of rising panic. Siobhan cursed under her breath and turned back to Mulcahy. 'I wanted her to tell you herself. Gemma called her last night.'

A kind of cold, post-nuclear hush fell over the room as the impact of her words was absorbed: Mrs Kearney's mouth opening in wordless fear and protest, Mulcahy struggling to suppress the genuine surge of surprise ripping through him that Gemma was alive at all.

'She phoned you, didn't she, Mrs K?' Siobhan said, eventually breaking the silence.

She didn't wait for confirmation but kept addressing herself to Mrs Kearney in slow, encouraging tones, although Mulcahy could see the message was entirely for him. 'And Gemma said she's okay. She's scared, but she's not hurt or anything. She just can't come home yet. Isn't that right, Mrs K?'

Mrs Kearney nodded, then slowly turned her face towards Mulcahy, a lifetime of maternal worry burning in her red-rimmed eyes. 'That's right,' she said, her voice a whisper. 'She said some fella was after her. That's all she said, but I could tell she was terrified. She sounded like she was in fear for her life. It was like the last time, with that other fella. She sounded so scared, my poor girl.'

The effort of holding in her worst nightmare finally got the better of Mrs Kearney and she seemed to collapse inwardly, bending at the waist as she raised her hands to her face and began to sob.

316

'Where is she, Mrs Kearney?' Mulcahy asked urgently, but he might as well have been talking to the wall.

He looked at Siobhan, whose upturned palms and blank expression told him she didn't have a clue, either. 'Gemma wouldn't tell her.'

It took a few minutes, but between them they managed to get Mrs Kearney calm again, their reassurances as strong and sugar-laden as the tea they made and gave her to drink. At the same time Mulcahy tried to extract some more details from Siobhan, but all she'd been able to glean was that Gemma had called her mother sometime the previous evening and made her promise she wouldn't tell anyone about the call. Gemma had explained her disappearance, apparently, by saying some people had been after her for money and she'd had to disappear for a while. That was all she had said, other than that she needed to stay out of circulation for a while longer and her mother shouldn't try to contact her or call her back.

On recalling that particular detail, Siobhan's face lit up and she turned to Mrs Kearney. 'Did anyone phone you since then, Mrs K? Obviously you called me this morning, but did you receive any other calls? About Gemma or anything else?'

Mrs Kearney had to think about it but said no, no one else had been in touch. Siobhan got up and went through the door into the living room, and emerged a moment later with a landline phone in her hand, clicking on the keypad. She held up the receiver towards Mulcahy, pointing at the number on its narrow screen.

'Last call received,' she said, and hit the redial button.

She kept the phone glued to her ear for well over a minute,

but eventually she shook her head and hung up. She hit the dial key again, waited, with the same result.

'No answer, no voicemail service. It just keeps ringing.'

'What's the number – land or mobile?' Mulcahy asked, putting his hand out.

'Mobile, I think,' Siobhan said, handing the phone to him. 'It's not the one I had for her before.'

'It looks like an Irish number, anyway.'

He turned again to Mrs Kearney. 'I know you said Gemma didn't tell you where she is, but was there anything that might give us a clue? You must have asked her?' He knew how difficult it is for people not to let something slip unconsciously about their whereabouts, especially when they're questioned directly. 'Did you even get any sense of where she was – here in Cork or somewhere else? Was there any kind of noise in the background, maybe?'

All Mrs Kearney could do was shake her head. If Gemma had left any clues, her mother hadn't picked up on them.

He turned back to Siobhan. 'If it is an Irish number and there's no answering service set up, there's a chance the phone's a pay-as-you-go and won't have roaming, either, in which case she'd only be able to use it for calls here in Ireland.'

'You think she might be back here?'

'Why not?' Mulcahy said, shrugging.

'You guys can track mobile phones, can't you?' she said excitedly. 'Pinpoint their locations?'

'Not without a court order,' Mulcahy said. 'And no way do we have grounds to get one.'

He cursed as his phone rang in his pocket, breaking his

concentration. Liam Ford's caller ID. He excused himself, walked to the back door and out into the garden.

'Liam, what's up?'

Ford was calling from Kearney's office, his voice heightened with excitement, his Cork accent noticeably more pronounced. 'This place is unbelievable, boss. She can't have been expecting to disappear. There's stuff out all over the place, to do with her businesses – "investment" companies and all sorts. They're nearly all hers, or else businesses she's actually running for other people. There's so much of it. There must be millions involved. It'll take us a while to go through it.'

'Us?' Mulcahy said.

'Yeah. Aidan called last night and asked if he could come along. He's going to be a big help here. He knows more about this kind of stuff than me. He's even got into her computer already. You should see the number of bank accounts she has access to.'

'That's great, Liam. Good work.' Mulcahy quickly explained to Ford what he'd heard from Siobhan and Mrs Kearney regarding Gemma's phone call the night before.

'Well, at least we know she's alive,' Ford said, 'if not exactly safe, given what happened to Hayes. Do you think that's why she called the ma?'

'I don't see how she could have heard about Hayes before she called. I didn't even find out about it till the early hours of this morning. But the mother did say she sounded terrified. In fear of her life, she said.'

Ford breathed heavily into his phone. 'It still could've been one of those "goodbye" calls.'

'Either that or she's somewhere that she thinks is secure

enough to risk a call from. Impossible to say, really, without knowing where she actually is.'

Mulcahy paused a moment, thinking it through. 'Do me a favour – and tell Aidan, too – when you're going through her stuff, keep a particular eye out for anything that might give us a clue about her whereabouts, and call me right away if you come across anything.' He stopped again a second, making sure he hadn't forgotten anything. 'Right, you get on with that. Did you at least leave Aisling in Dublin?'

Ford confirmed that he had. Mulcahy hung up and dialled her number, scraping impatiently at the grass with his shoe while he waited for her to pick up, at the same time trying to see in through the kitchen window but unable to because of the glare. A rustling noise from the shrubs behind startled him and he swivelled round to see a cat run out from cover at a small bird, which squawked shrilly and fluttered off just in time. He was breathing out a tense sigh of relief when Sweeney answered.

'Aisling, I need you to do something for me.'

It had been nagging him ever since Siobhan had told him of her suspicions that Horgan had been on a drugs run to Bristol. The ferry from France. The van. It had come to him as a stray thought that just clicked in his mind at the pier in Glandore. Ferries. There were at least three ferry ports with services to Ireland within a hundred miles of Bristol: Fishguard, Pembroke and, closest, Swansea, from where, significantly, the only ferry service to Cork had recently reopened. He asked Sweeney to contact the security chiefs at all Irish ferry ports, but in Cork and Rosslare particularly, and get them to run Kearney's name through their passenger lists for the past month as a matter of red-flag urgency. She sounded pleased not to be left out of the action altogether.

He hurried back into the kitchen, but only Mrs Kearney was sitting there, still nursing her cup of tea, looking just as shell-shocked as before. He put his head round the door of the living room – neat like the rest of the house, an old-fashioned three-piece suite, family photos on the sideboard, and empty. He heard Siobhan's voice towards the front of the house and walked back through the hall to the door, catching her in the front garden just as she was finishing a call on her mobile.

'Quick as you can, okay? I'm relying on you,' she was saying, her mobile tucked awkwardly between shoulder and ear with her chin, Mrs Kearney's phone in one hand, an open notebook in the other. She juggled the three to hang up and turned, looking surprised when she saw Mulcahy waiting in the doorway.

'You weren't supposed to hear that,' she said, flashing her pale blue eyes at him, a smile on her lips.

'Who was it?'

'A guy I know through work. Bit of an under-the-radar merchant. Calls himself a private detective but he just sits in front of a bank of computers all day, spying on people. He's going to run a GPS trace on that mobile number for me. If the phone is any kind of an up-to-date model, he reckons he can get it so long as it's switched on.'

Mulcahy stared down at her, the line between legality and expediency being fudged before his eyes. His own privacy was something he guarded jealously, but he knew too well how the laws surrounding privacy often only got in the way of doing the job. 'You don't get that kind of spookery for cheap.'

Siobhan looked pleased by his lack of explicit disapproval. 'He owes me the favour – I've put enough business his way over the years. And anyway, he won't charge if it doesn't work. If she's not in the country, I mean. And if she is, we'll know soon enough where, won't we?'

She looked over his shoulder to check that Mrs Kearney was nowhere within hearing distance. 'Do you seriously think someone's after her?'

'There's no way of knowing for sure, but someone thought Conor Hayes was worth taking out, and as far as we know, he was a hell of a smaller link in the chain than she is. I hope you're not in any danger yourself – after talking to Hayes, I mean.'

'Just for talking to the guy?' She gave him a sceptical glance. The thought that she could be in danger had never occurred to her. 'I think you're letting your imagination run away with you there, Inspector.'

'Did you notice anybody else down by the pier, maybe watching, or waiting?'

'Jesus, you're as bad as the others, Mulcahy,' she said, putting her hand on his forearm unconsciously, naturally. He might have thought it belonged there had it not been for the scar on the back of her hand. He tried not to look, but it made the breath stall in his chest from the burden of responsibility he felt for failing to prevent those injuries, for all she had suffered. His fault.

'I'm only thinking of your safety,' he said, conscious again of the weight of the weapon on his belt beneath his jacket.

'I'll be responsible for my own safety, thank you,' she said sternly, and stepped away from him, a scowl where the smile had been seconds earlier.

'Did Hayes even say anything interesting to you?' Mulcahy said.

'No. Like I said, the guy just looked totally scared out of his wits.'

'And what did he say about Horgan? Anything?'

'Nothing. I said I was surprised I didn't see him at the funeral, and when he asked me who I was, he got into a right state. Broke into a sweat on the spot, told me not to come anywhere near the boat. He got even weirder when I went back and asked him if he'd seen Gemma Kearney at all recently. He didn't even pretend not to know her. He just went apeshit. Started shouting at me to get away, that he'd have me done for trespass. I pointed out to him that I hadn't set foot on his stupid boat and that the pier was public property. In the end I just decided to walk away. I was thinking about going to the hotel for a drink, waiting around—' She broke off, chewed her lip for a second or two, then looked straight into his. 'I don't know. I just felt really knackered suddenly. It came over me, and all I wanted to do was get out of there.'

She grimaced unconsciously at the memory, her small white teeth clenched, the tendons in her neck standing proud, like she was deeply embarrassed by her lack of persistence.

'I think it's just as well you did.'

She shook her head ruefully. 'Sure, but look what I missed. "Eyewitness to Murder" – that would have been some headline.'

Mulcahy was about to point out that the headline could

323

have been far worse, but his mobile buzzed. It was Sweeney, and he turned away to take the call.

'Unbelievable, boss,' she said, her voice breathy with excitement. 'You got it bang on, first time. I rang the guys in Cork and they picked Kearney up on the very first sweep. She came in through the Ringaskiddy ferry terminal on the overnight sailing from Swansea only yesterday morning. The ferry docked at eight twenty-five a.m. They say she would have been disembarked and on the road by nine at the latest.'

Mulcahy wasn't sure whether to feel more relieved or worried by that information. Gemma Kearney, and more particularly her safety, was now very much his concern. 'What was she driving, did they say?'

'A Mercedes Vito van, apparently. With Dutch registration plates, weirdly. Do you have a pen? I'll give you the number.'

'No, but give it to me anyway.' He memorised it as she said it, then told her to get back on to the Cork port authorities and get any other information they might have on whether she was travelling alone or not, and where she might have been coming from. He hung up and was about to tell Siobhan when her phone rang.

She held up a palm to him, looked at the screen and mouthed, 'It's him ... Hi, Ray,' she said, followed by a string of 'Yeah' and 'No' and 'Hang on while I grab a pen', accompanied by an awkward but clearly well-practised scramble in her bag. There was a final 'Ah-ha' and 'Any idea where that is?' while she scribbled something in her notebook and hung up, with thanks.

'He could only pin it down to within a five-mile radius, because of the mountains.'

'Mountains?' Mulcahy frowned. 'Where the hell is she?'

'Not far. Dunmanway is the nearest town, Ray says. That's as close as he can get to it. I saw it myself on the road signs on the way over here. It can't be more than a few miles away.'

Dunmanway. The name was sparking connections in his mind. The trailer. That's what it was. Aisling had said, last night, the trailer company with the red 'H' logo was based in Dunmanway.

'What is it?' Siobhan asked him, seeing he'd made some connection, but he held a hand up to her, took out his phone and dialled.

'Liam, we've got a lead on her. Did you find anything?'

Ford said he'd found plenty, and that was the problem. Kearney's main holding company, Prolutum, which seemed to be jointly owned by a sleeping partner, had extensive holdings in holiday properties all along the southwest coast.

'And the partner would be Begley?'

'Absolutely,' Ford said. 'Aidan found his name on a few documents relating to Prolutum. He's got to be prime suspect for the sleeper. They were ploughing vast amounts of cash into property and construction for years. But that's not all. We're finding paperwork for all sorts of shite as well as the properties – art, antiques and so on – from auction houses and dealers all over the place. It looks like she was buying up half of feckin' Europe.'

Converting cash into consumables, the classic money launderer's ploy. But Mulcahy didn't even want to stop and think about that. All he could think of was getting to Kearney. They could think about the extent of her criminality later.

'Okay, look, we've just been told she's definitely in the area, so you can refine your search. Aim for anything within a few miles of Dunmanway. That's not tourist country, so it should stand out. For the moment just focus on that. I'm heading over that way now myself. Ring me the second you find anything, and I mean *anything*.'

He hung up, turned, saw Siobhan staring at him, her blue eyes brimming with anticipation.

'Are we going over there, then?'

'I think it's better if you stay here with Mrs Kearney,' he said, shaking his head, though in truth he wasn't even sure that was such a good idea. He'd have to make a call, get someone round from the local station, to be on the safe side.

Judging from the storm clouds in her expression, Siobhan wasn't exactly keen on the idea either.

'Better?' Better for who?' she snapped at him. 'Piss off, Mulcahy, would you? No way are you leaving me out of this. Gemma Kearney is *my* story.'

She paused, disbelief getting the better of her. It was something Mulcahy was struggling with just as violently. How could she even begin to think he'd allow her to accompany him?

'For Christ's sake, Siobhan. This isn't some stupid story. This is serious. There are people being murdered here. You know what happened to Conor Hayes last night and, for all we know, nearly happened to you. You can't just tag along on something like this. It's not some bloody game. It would be tantamount to reckless—'

He was about to say 'endangerment' but the palm of her small hand raised high in flat defiance in front of his face, the look of utter fury in her eyes, brought him to an abrupt halt.

'Don't you dare patronise me, Mulcahy,' she hissed at him, 'or belittle what I do. You wouldn't even *be* here if it wasn't for me. And you sure as fuck wouldn't have found out by your own lights that Gemma Kearney was in Dunmanway. So just get used to the idea. I'm coming with you. Even if I have to follow you in my own car. Even if I have to crawl there on my hands and knees, I'm coming. This is my story, and I'm staying on it – to the death.'

27

Five minutes later they were in the Saab and on their way, at speed, holding back only to make sure Mrs Kearney was okay and to tell her not to answer the door to anyone until they returned. Mulcahy was driving, Siobhan reading the road map, assuring him it was pretty much a straight road from Drimoleague to Dunmanway. He pointed at the glove-box, told her there was a portable sat nav in there and to get it out, ready for a call from Liam Ford, which he prayed would come sooner rather than later. As he negotiated the twisting route into Drimoleague and out onto the Dunmanway road, he did his best to bring her up to speed, in the briefest terms he could, on what Ford had told him about Gemma Kearney's ongoing business relationship with Begley.

'Jesus, after what he did to her,' Siobhan groaned. 'Whatever was between them, it must've gone a lot deeper than business, on her part at least.'

She was probably right about that, Mulcahy thought, and he tried to imagine what could be going through Gemma

Kearney's head right now. Her lover, if he was that, dead. And a killer on her trail, dogging her every step. Why was she risking her life to come home? To see her mother, maybe? One last time before she disappeared completely? Given what he'd heard of her already, it seemed pretty damn unlikely.

As it happened, it didn't take long for Ford's call to come through. Crooking his mobile under his chin, Mulcahy repeated the address – Blaggard Farm, Gortnakilla Road, Dunmanway – to Siobhan, who punched the details into the sat nav and waited for it to make a GPS match. In the meantime Mulcahy asked Ford the question he really wanted answered: 'So who owns the place now?'

Even above the rush of the car on the road Mulcahy could hear him working the keyboard, tapping the scroll bar impatiently rather than just holding it down. Then came a stream of muttered imprecation.

'Well, she didn't buy it through Horgan. Says here Blaggard Farm was seized by the Criminal Assets Bureau in 2003 from a company called Glanamh, as part of a long follow-up investigation into Klene Records. It seems Glanamh was also originally owned by one Declan J. Begley, esquire, gentleman fucking farmer.'

'"Glanamh" means "clean" in Irish, doesn't it?' Mulcahy said.

'Yeah, of course it does. Ah, Jesus, this is such a fuck-up.'

For a moment or two all Mulcahy heard on the line was Ford's laboured breathing and the thumping of big fingers on the keyboard.

'What've you got, Liam? Tell me.'

'You won't fucking believe this, boss. The CAB weren't

329

able to dispose of the farm until three years later, when the lawyers fighting its seizure suddenly withdrew their case. The property went to auction in May 2006, and listen to this – it was bought by some crowd called GemDec Associates. Gem, Dec – capital "G", capital "D". How the fuck could they have let that happen? The CAB let Begley buy back his own fucking land with dirty money.'

Mulcahy hung up and repeated the information to Siobhan, who laughed in bitter amusement. 'Cheeky bastards. They must've had a hoot over that one.'

'It cost them over a million euro,' Mulcahy said, 'so it must've meant a hell of a lot to them. What really kills me is the date they bought it. It means that Gemma Kearney and Declan Begley have been in business together for more than five years. Christ knows how much money they've laundered through her practice, and Horgans estate agents. It's probably in the tens of millions.'

A grim, purposeful silence invaded the car now as Siobhan began jotting some notes in her reporter's pad and Mulcahy put his foot down still harder and focused on the road ahead. Only a disembodied, mid-Atlantic, vaguely well-known female voice intruded on their thoughts: 'In five miles, turn left.'

28

Their route took them through the centre of Dunmanway, into the narrow, winding streets and prosperous market square, bustling with trade in the run-up to lunchtime, and on up a steep hill that, once crested, deposited them in noticeably less lovely countryside. It was as if the green, rolling landscape they'd been driving through for miles had simply run out of lushness and instantly become more jagged, grey and barren. The road was narrower, bordered not by fence and farmland now but by forest, scrub and bog. Even the farms they did pass had an air of neglect to them, the fields smaller, the barns rustier, the hedgerows untended and unkempt.

'Darkwood,' Siobhan snorted, looking up from the map. 'You'd think we were driving through Harry Potter country. There's another place further on called Coolmountain.'

'And where are we headed?' asked Mulcahy, who had been focused on following the sat nav's instructions.

'I'm not sure. I can't tell exactly where we are, but if I'm right, we've just passed through somewhere called Fernanes and we don't have much further to go.'

They were three or four miles beyond Dunmanway now, yet the land felt a hundred times more remote. To the north, a range of high, bare hills loomed, the 'mountains' Siobhan's call-tracer had mentioned, Mulcahy assumed, though he doubted it was easy to get a good signal anywhere around there. A minute later the voice told him to turn right onto a narrower road, a track really, graded but rarely used, a rib of shin-high grass running up the middle, which brushed noisily against the Saab's underbelly as he slowed to a crawl. Then he saw it: a decrepit gateway punctuating the overgrown hedge on his left. It was bracketed by two short, low stone walls with pillars at the entry, one of which had partly collapsed. A rusting iron gate, long torn off its hinges, leant drunkenly into the undergrowth on one side. A paint-peeled sign attached to it with coarse strands of wire was only barely legible: 'Blaggard Farm.'

'Fucking hell,' Siobhan said. 'Did you say they paid a million euro for this?'

'They must've wanted something here badly,' Mulcahy grunted, and turned the car into the entrance, the decaying tarmac of the overgrown drive crunching beneath the tyres. They rounded a corner and the scene opened out into a flat clearing of bracken-filled paddocks, fields almost entirely reclaimed by nature and a ramshackle cluster of barns and assorted farm buildings fronted by a squat, dilapidated-looking bungalow fifty yards or so ahead. An air of bleakness and long abandonment hung like a dank mist over everything.

Mulcahy drove slowly up to the house. Although the track led round the back, to where he presumed there was a farmyard, he pulled up in front of what must once have been a small lawn bordered by flowerbeds long gone to seed, and now swamped in coarse grass and a maze of brambles.

'You'd need a machete to get to that front door,' Mulcahy said, but Siobhan was already encouraging him to drive on, pointing urgently through the windscreen towards the muddy corner leading to the yard.

'I reckon somebody's been here pretty recently,' she said.

Now he saw what she'd seen: tyre tracks, and fresh-looking ones at that.

'C'mon,' she said. 'Let's go round the back and see if we can find her.'

Mulcahy took it slowly, turning the car cautiously into the yard, a ruinous arrangement of three large and variously crumbling barns, one completely open to the elements, and a few scattered, older stone outbuildings. The mud on the yard's split concrete and cobble surface showed a curve of tyre marks sweeping in towards a wide parking bay surrounded on three sides by a low breeze-block wall and steps up to a brick path leading to the back of the bungalow. Tyre tracks but no tyres. No vehicle of any kind save for a spooky, grime-covered green and cream caravan, which had collapsed on its axle and was, seemingly, decomposing slowly into the concrete beneath it.

Mulcahy pulled up on the far side of the caravan, looked around and lowered his window. There was no sign or sound of life whatsoever, not even the scurry of a rat in the barns to break the silence.

'Do you want to stay in the car while I check this out?' he said, pulling the door handle and putting a foot out on the

333

concrete before turning back to her. He'd intended it more as a question than an instruction, but, either way, he was met by a look of contempt from Siobhan.

'I've come this far,' she said. 'I'm not going to start taking a back seat now, am I?'

She stepped out into the muddy yard and together they made their way up a set of breeze-block steps to the back of the house. The walls had been whitewashed once, and the door varnished, but both were now weathered back to a flaky grey, streaked here and there with layers of the mottled green and black mould that seemed to cling to every external surface. Above the door the guttering bowed precariously, and the slate roof was host to broad colonies of dark green moss. Everything spoke of utter decay and neglect, except for one thing. Mulcahy tapped Siobhan on the arm and pointed: a new lock had been fitted to the door, the shiny brass flange surrounding the keyhole, the sole thing on the door not caked in the dirt of ages.

'Someone's put that in very recently,' he said. 'It looks like it hasn't been so much as rained on.'

He rapped his knuckles loudly on the wooden door and was met with a resounding silence. He tried again, this time calling out a hello, receiving only the same silence in reply. Meanwhile Siobhan had gone to the nearest window, to look inside, but gave up after a few seconds of failing to see anything through the grime.

'It's all dark in there, impenetrable,' she said, coming back, then stopped suddenly and pointed. 'Shit, Mulcahy, look at that. There is somebody here.'

He swung round, expecting to see a figure, but all he saw

was Siobhan hurrying down the steps and striding out across the yard. It wasn't until he was halfway down the steps himself that he saw what she was heading towards – just visible, the gleaming back end of a silver van poking out from the nearest barn.

It was more of a shed, really, laid out in stalls and open to the elements on the one side that wasn't clad in the same corrugated sheet metal as was used for the shallow sloping roof. Inside it was mostly bare, apart from a carpet of mud and empty plastic fertiliser bags, mouldering bits of broken machinery and rusting bales of barbed wire. Such was the general air of corrosion, the silver Mercedes Vito parked there might as well have been beamed in from another planet.

'Look, it's a Dutch registration,' Siobhan said, excited. Sure enough, there was a white 'NL' under the roundel of stars of the blue EU flag on the van's rear plate. The number matched the one Aisling had given him. Siobhan, meanwhile, was already up at the front of the van, peering on tiptoe through the driver's side window. Mulcahy tried the handle on the rear door, but it wouldn't budge. He shuffled past Siobhan and looked in the driver's window himself, saw nothing but the bare bench seat and a plywood panel behind blocking access to the cargo space behind.

'Nothing there,' he said, needlessly.

But Siobhan was gone. He looked around, could see her nowhere. He said her name. Listened. Nothing. He walked the length of the shed, checking each stall, calling her name more loudly each time, and got nothing but echoes bouncing off the metal siding. Thin air. Where the hell had she got to?

He was coming out into the yard again when a hollow

metallic rattle, the sound of an oil drum being knocked or something of the sort, caught his ear. He scanned the yard again and saw her, trying to pull open the tall, four-metre-high galvanised-metal door of the next barn along, the biggest one. She stopped trying when she saw him and instead gesticulated at him urgently.

'Mulcahy, over here,' she called, in a low whisper. 'Come and have a look at this.'

She was pointing at something inside, and stepped back as he reached her. 'It won't open any further,' she said. 'The door's chained up. I had trouble squeezing in there myself. But stick your head in. Go on – it's completely weird.'

He tried to tug the barn door open a bit wider, but she was right, it wouldn't budge. A heavy-duty steel chain was looped twice through a hole in each of the two sliding doors and secured with a hefty padlock. Like the lock on the house door, it looked new. He stuck his head and shoulders through the gap. It took a second or two for his eyes to adjust to the gloom, but when they did, what he beheld made them widen still further.

'What the hell is that?'

Of all the things Mulcahy would have expected to find inside a run-down, semi-derelict barn, the last was a house. He blinked again, to make sure he wasn't seeing things. But no, there it was sitting there, right in the middle of the floor of the barn, a small prefabricated bungalow with walls, windows fully glazed, even a front door with a letterbox in it. Everything, in fact, that you'd normally expect to see on a house, except rooftiles. Instead it was topped off with a mix of blue plastic sheeting, and more galvanised-metal sheets – whatever had come to hand, it seemed.

336

'It's a bit big for a Wendy house,' Siobhan said, pushing in beside him. 'What do you think it's for?'

Mulcahy wasn't sure what to think. The bungalow filled half the floor space of the barn and, from the condition of the windows, walls and front door, didn't look to be of recent construction. There was a wide space cleared around it on all sides, but the rest of the barn was filled with the rotting detritus of farm-labour past, obsolete machines for ploughing, planting and threshing, stacks of oil drums and tractor tyres, feed boxes and baling wire. In one corner, a tractor so old it could be a museum piece looked like it had actually taken root in the floor of the barn. Mulcahy stepped back and looked towards the van in the shed along the yard, feeling suddenly more uncomfortable about their situation than he had before.

'Well?' Siobhan was looking up at him like he was the one who was supposed to know.

'I saw photos of something like this, once before,' he said, the anxiety clear in his voice. 'Circulated after a raid over in England. Some London heavies bought an old farm in Suffolk, somewhere remote. The locals reckoned they were growing cannabis in the sheds, but when the police raided, they found a cabin like this inside one of the barns, wired up for electricity, heating, hot and cold water plumbed in and all. Even a satellite dish rigged on a fence outside.'

'What was it for?' Siobhan asked. 'Illegal immigrants or something?'

'No, it was far too comfortable,' he said. 'The gang said it was a safe house, for friends needing to disappear for a while. They could hole up in the cabin. All creature comforts.

337

Totally invisible. But the Brits thought they might have used it for other things, too: to hold kidnap victims, or make snuff movies, or just to keep someone captive in until they had screwed what they wanted out of them.'

'Why not use the farmhouse?' Siobhan said, grimacing at the idea.

'It's a double-bluff thing. The minders live in the farm-house to make the place seem occupied, legitimate, you know. Life goes on as normal. Nothing to make anyone sus-picious. The farm's a going concern. In theory nothing to make nosy neighbours suspicious, or get caught out by a sur-prise raid. In the minutes it takes to serve a warrant over at the farmhouse, anyone in here could be out the back and away across the fields.'

'Jesus, you think this is the same?' Siobhan cast a nervous glance back at the van in the shed, her thoughts exactly the same as Mulcahy's.

'I honestly don't know, but whatever it is, I don't think we should hang around to find out. This looks pretty heavy-duty to me. Let's just get out of here and call for some back-up, keep an eye on the place from a safe distance, down the road.'

She was definitely with him on that, but still found time to stick her phone through the gap in the barn door and take a couple of pictures. Mulcahy cursed and pulled her away. They were crossing the yard, halfway to the Saab, when the sound of another motor, other tyres crunching on the drive into the farm, reached their ears.

'Shit,' Mulcahy said. 'Whoever it is, they'll spot my car as soon as they turn in here. Come on.' He grabbed Siobhan by the arm and steered her back across the yard and into the gap between the two barns facing the rear of the house. That way, at least, they'd have a chance to see who it was coming in, before the driver could see the parked Saab and react.

As it happened, the battered old pale blue Golf that appeared seconds later didn't come all the way into the yard, but pulled up instead beside the caravan, from where the Saab was just out of sight.

Fuck, Mulcahy thought, a chill running down his spine at the sight of the car. Both Brogan's and Murtagh's witnesses had said a Golf. He turned to Siobhan, whispered urgently, 'Did you see that car down by the pier in Glandore yesterday?'

Siobhan took another look, made a meaningless expression. 'I don't think so. Why?'

He didn't dare answer as they heard the car door open and the driver stepped out. It was a woman.

'It's Gemma Kearney,' Siobhan whispered.

Mulcahy called to mind the mug shot Ford had shown him, and did a double take. Whatever he'd been expecting Gemma Kearney to look like now, this woman wasn't it. Short and quite heavily built, especially round the hips, her long, dark hair unwashed, wearing a wraparound brown cardigan over a tweedy brown skirt, she looked completely different from the willowy beauty arrested a decade before.

'Are you sure?'

'It's definitely her. There were photos of her on the sideboard in Mrs K's living room.' Siobhan opened her bag and removed a postcard-sized picture of an unsmiling dark-haired woman. 'See – here.'

Mulcahy looked down in disbelief. Siobhan must have

339

stolen the photo and he was shocked, even in this bizarre situation, by her brazenness. He shook the thought from his head and looked across the yard again. The woman in the picture and the one standing by the car removing a bag of groceries were undeniably one and the same. A few years older, but the same, right down to the beauty spot on her upper lip.

'Come on,' Siobhan said, stepping out into the yard and hailing the woman to Mulcahy's evident horror, but it was too late to stop her.

'Gemma? Gemma Kearney?' Siobhan shouted over at her. 'Hi. I was wondering if we could have a word.'

The look that appeared on the woman's face as she whipped her head round and gawped towards the barn and Siobhan was nothing short of terror. Mulcahy could see the blood draining from her face as she dropped the shopping bag with a crash and reeled a foot or two back, before being hemmed in by the car. It was clear from her expression that her first thought was to run, to try and escape, but there was nowhere to go: on one side the car, on the other the caravan, behind her the wall and in front of her Siobhan. The panic on her face only got wilder when she caught sight of Mulcahy's large frame emerging from the shadow of the barn and following in Siobhan's wake.

'It's okay. It's all right, Gemma. We're here to help,' Siobhan said, halting a couple of metres from the woman, flapping her palms to calm her.

Mulcahy came to a stop a few feet behind her. His main concern now was to keep an eye on the windows of the bungalow and on the outbuildings around, worried more

340

than ever about who else might be on the premises, and where.

The woman said nothing, still looked dumbstruck, her eyes swivelling anxiously back and forth between the two of them. As far as Siobhan was concerned, there was nothing for it but to try again.

'My name's Siobhan Fallon. Your mother said she mentioned me to you last night on the phone. I'm the reporter. She asked me to help find you. To help you, yeah? And this is Mike Mulcahy. He's a . . . eh, a friend. We're here to help, Gemma, honestly. There's no need to be afraid.'

At last the woman's face seemed to unfreeze a fraction, and she broke into a tiny, anxious smile. 'Oh, right. For a minute there I thought—' She broke off and the sentence went unfinished as she glanced nervously over towards the barn, then back at the grim-looking house. 'You'd better come in. Quickly,' she said, tilting her head towards the back door.

She all but pushed Siobhan up the steps to the house, then stood and waved Mulcahy forward, too. He stood there nonplussed. He had no desire to go inside, but he didn't want to stay out in the open arguing, either. He insisted she should go ahead, which she did, bending first to pick up the shopping bag where it had fallen. From a ring of keys she selected a shiny brass one and inserted it in the lock on the door. He wondered how it could have been fitted so quickly if she'd only returned yesterday, and might have asked her if Siobhan hadn't been rabbiting on about Gemma's mother, and how she'd been worried sick.

29

Inside, the house was a mess. The back door led straight into the kitchen, where every surface – floor, countertops, cupboard doors, furniture – was covered in a thick layer of dust and grime, except for the sink, a section of the old wooden draining board and the kitchen table, all of which had been wiped over with a cloth in recent days. Mulcahy noted that only one of the kitchen chairs stood away from the table, its seat alone in being free of dust. On the table, just one mug was sitting there, awaiting washing. On the draining board one plate, one knife and fork. Signs were, she was alone in the house. Hiding out.

Gemma Kearney didn't invite them to sit down, didn't offer them tea. She looked a little more self-possessed now, but was still breathing heavily, a hand held up to her chest, gripped by an anxiety that gave an aggressive edge to her next question.

'So how in Christ did you find me? My mother doesn't know about this place.' She paused, all her focus inward, then shook her head. 'Jesus, I didn't think anybody knew about it. That's the reason I'm here.'

'We figured it out ourselves,' Mulcahy said. 'Which means it isn't safe for you to be here. I think you should come with us, Gemma. Now.'

'Me? No, I'm all right. I'll be fine here.' Her gaze was steady as a rock and disconcertingly piercing.

'What are you so afraid of, then?' Mulcahy asked.

'Nothing. You guys just gave me a fright. I wasn't expecting anybody to turn up. Why would I? And who the hell are you to be asking, anyway?' She glared at him, then jerked her head towards Siobhan. 'I know what she's doing here, or what she says she's doing, on behalf of my forever interfering mother. But who the fuck are you? A reporter, too? You look more like a copper.'

'That's right.' Mulcahy smiled. It hadn't taken long for her to show her true colours. He was sure that his concern for her safety would never have extended to actually liking her, but he was glad now he wouldn't even have to try. 'You obviously know the type. My name's Detective Inspector Mulcahy.'

He watched her face closely as she took that in. Had she really expected to be right? But he saw no change in her expression.

'Look, it's okay,' she said, turning to Siobhan again now. 'You don't need to be here. Neither of you do. My mother doesn't need to worry. It was stupid of me to let her get concerned. I'll be fine on my own here, really.'

'We know that's not true, Gemma,' Siobhan said. 'Your mother said you told her someone was trying to kill you.'

'No, no, I just said someone was after me. Creditors, you know. I've just got to stay out of sight for a while.'

343

'There's no point lying,' Mulcahy said. 'We know about you and Declan Begley. The sooner we get out—'

Her face snapped back to him as soon as he said the name. 'Declan?' She gave a little laugh like she'd been caught out in a lie. 'You don't know anything.'

'We know that you and he owned this place, together,' Siobhan said, butting in again, 'and that you bought it back from the CAB for him.'

'We also know you were in Fuengirola when he was murdered, Gemma,' Mulcahy said. 'I'd really like to know what happened out there.'

Siobhan, who'd known nothing of this, was looking at him with an open mouth, but that was as nothing to the contempt on Gemma Kearney's face.

'Hang on a second,' Siobhan interrupted, giving him a look like she thought he was playing the game all wrong. 'I thought we were coming here to help Gemma.'

'She's the one claiming she doesn't need help,' Mulcahy said. 'And even if she doesn't, she still has some very serious questions to answer – about the conduct of her accountancy practice, her relationship with Horgans estate agents and her movements over the last three weeks, just for starters.'

He turned back to Gemma Kearney. 'I know you were in Spain, Gemma. I saw your name on the passenger manifest, flying into Malaga, from Bristol. On the same flight as Declan Begley. The day after your other ex-boyfriend, Cormac Horgan, died. What were the three of you doing in Bristol?'

Kearney said nothing for a moment, just absorbed it, expressionless. Then she turned on him, eyes blazing. 'Like I said, you haven't a fucking clue. If Cormac wanted to kill himself, that was up to him. Stupid fuckwit never could take the pressure. I made a multi-millionaire out of him, all the business I pushed his way, and what does he do? Loses the fucking lot. And when I offer him a way out of that, too, what happens? He goes and fucks that up as well. You know, I hope he screamed all the way down, 'cos he sure as hell fucked everything up for me and Declan. Everything would still be all right if it wasn't for Cormac.'

'That's bullshit,' Mulcahy said. 'You got greedy. You were both doing just fine. Begley must have had a hell of a stash put away and nobody even knew it – except you probably. Which one of you was it? Which one of you decided you could nick that consignment of cocaine in Amsterdam?'

She looked at him like she was both surprised and admiring that he knew about that. So much so she didn't even bother denying it. 'It was there for the taking. If we didn't, someone else would have eventually. A hundred million euro? That's an awful lot of future to leave lying in a container stack in Rotterdam.'

'Maybe, but at what price?' Mulcahy asked indignantly, knowing he shouldn't be debating it with her, but unwilling to let her get away with it. 'Not only did Bingo shaft Trevor Ronson, his best pal supposedly, he ended up getting himself killed over it, too. And how about you – didn't you stop at any stage to even consider the risks involved?'

'What would you know, in your stupid fucking job and with your shitty bloody salary?' Kearney's face was pure scorn now. 'The whole of life is a risk if you've got the balls to play for it.'

Mulcahy stepped back. It was the classic gangster whine of self-justification and it always irked the hell out of him because it was such a delusion. He waved a hand around the filthy kitchen. 'And what's this?' he snapped back at her. 'The big win? Sitting in some shithole in the middle of nowhere, your life in tatters, your boyfriend dead and you scared shitless the same guy's coming to kill you, too?'

Her response was the last one he'd expected. She burst out laughing. She sat on the chair in front of him, laughing so hard, so aggressively she broke into a coughing fit.

'Is that what you think happened?' she said, catching her breath. 'Jesus, you really are as thick as the rest of them, aren't you? Declan said it would fool the lot of you, and he was right as usual. That man's a genius, I always said so.' She laughed again and slapped the table with mirth.

'What are you talking about?' Mulcahy was beginning to wonder if the woman wasn't seriously unstable.

She didn't even respond to him, just nodded her head, laughing, but inwardly, more subdued now.

'This is pointless, Gemma,' Mulcahy insisted. 'Whether you like it or not, you're out of here. I'm taking you into custody. Come on, in the car, now.'

To his surprise she looked up at him with a strangely serene smile. 'Okay. I suppose you were never going to leave me alone after that lecture.' She smiled resignedly. 'But I have to take care of the dog first. She's out in the barn. I can't just leave her tied up out there.'

'I didn't see any dog,' Siobhan said, her eyes still out on stalks.

Neither had Mulcahy, nor heard one.

'Useless old mutt, she's deaf as a post. Probably fast asleep. I can't leave her without any food or water.' She stood up, went to the kitchen sink and filled a clear glass jug with water. 'Will you let me do that at least?'

Mulcahy hesitated. He didn't like the idea, but if it got them out of there without any more fuss.

'Okay, but you have to be quick about it.'

His anxiety returned as soon as they were out in the open again. The looming barns, the expanse of muddy concrete yard. Too many places to hide. Keeping behind the two women, he followed them over to the barn, the feeling of exposure gnawing away at him, the sense that someone else was there, watching them. As Kearney rattled the chain on the door and mused over which key on her bunch was the right one for the padlock, he was so tense he almost lost his life when his phone buzzed in his pocket.

'Hang on,' he said, just as Kearney started pulling the heavy chain free with an almighty clatter. He turned his back automatically, put a hand up to his ear, took the call.

It was Ford, sounding stressed. Or what he could hear of him was, the signal being so poor.

'Boss, thanks be to . . . sus . . . I've been trying . . . ugh . . . for ages.'

Mulcahy looked at the phone screen. Only one bar on the signal-strength icon. 'Yeah, hi, Liam. I'm out at Blaggard Farm. The signal's a bit crap here. What's the matter?'

But the signal was just too weak. All he heard was, 'Aisling got a ca . . . ano . . . passen . . . van.'

He moved forward a few paces, to get out of the shadow

347

of the barn. He looked over his shoulder. Kearney was heaving the door open. He tried to catch Siobhan's eye to tell her to wait, but she was pulling at it, too, and the screech of metal on metal as it shifted was such he had to turn away, squeeze his eyes shut to hear what Ford was saying, the sense of urgency the only thing clear in his voice. Something now about a call from the Spanish SIO, Chief Inspector Ferrer.

He took one more step forward and suddenly the reception was clear.

'... something about a technicians' strike in Spain,' Ford was saying, 'and the DNA on Begley not coming through. They never told us that, did they, boss? He never told you they hadn't got the DNA on Begley?'

In an instant the space in which Mulcahy existed condensed into a single pinpoint of star-bright understanding. He heard his own voice, a distant thing, say, 'What?' and then Ford's crackling response: 'Cunt says it wasn't him, boss. They're saying the guy in the dump wasn't Bingo. Did you get that?'

Mulcahy's thoughts were already expanding far beyond that now, and he was turning on his heel, and he was looking at a black empty space where Siobhan and Gemma Kearney had been standing only half a minute before. That realisation struck him like a punch. Of course there was no dog. How could there be? He had to take a step back to steady himself, and instantly the connection to Ford was gone.

He crushed the phone to his cheek, sorely tempted to dash the damn thing against the cobbles on the yard, but knowing that to do so would kill the one chance he might have to get help. He pushed the handset back against his ear, hoping against hope. 'Liam, I don't know if you can hear this – I think the signal's gone – but get on to Murtagh, get on to O'Grady, get an armed-response unit out here, quick as you can. I'm going to need some serious back-up.'

30

'Where the hell is he? How the fuck could you let him go like that?'

Gemma Kearney was standing a foot or two inside the barn door, looking out into the yard for any sign of movement, for any clue, in fact, of where the copper might have disappeared to. She turned quickly, angrily, to the man resting the barrel of his shotgun on Siobhan's shoulder, pressing the twin muzzles hard against the soft skin under her jaw, forcing her head over at a painful angle.

'I'm telling you, he was taking a phone call. I didn't want to spook him, Dec,' Kearney said in an angry, hissing whisper. 'Last time I looked, he was following us in. And why didn't you take him out yourself with that thing, seeing how you're so handy with it, and so full of foresight? It's not like you couldn't have managed her without it.'

Out of the side of her eye, Siobhan saw the man tense the forefinger he held poised across the double triggers at the end of the long, black barrel. Then she saw his thumb come up and decock each of the firing hammers in turn and felt the cold, hard weight of the gun barrel come off her neck, off her shoulder. She would have breathed a sigh of relief, but she wasn't feeling any. She couldn't see any real reason to be relieved. Her chief concern now was also theirs. Where the fuck had Mulcahy gone, and how the hell had he known what was awaiting them inside the barn?

'You, over there, move,' the man said to her. He jerked both his head and the shotgun in the same direction, towards the interior of the barn, towards the cabin. The thought of it made her stomach churn, but with disgust, not fear. For some reason she didn't seem to be feeling any fear. Annoyance, anger, caution, disgust? Yes. But not fear.

She did what he said, walking ahead of him, head down to seem more quiescent, her mind racing all the while. Gemma had called him Dec, which could only mean … But how? Did it matter? He was real enough for her not to have to go proving it to herself. When she got to the front door of the cabin, the man – Begley, she must start thinking of him as – pointed the gun at a shallow step in front of it.

'Sit down there. Keep your hands where I can see 'em.'

His accent was weird. Real hard-man Dublin, but like it had been ironed flat and lifeless. Must be all the time he'd been abroad. She looked up at him, this Begley, as he turned away to see what Kearney was doing, still at the door. Had he come over on the ferry with Gemma, in the van? Was that it? He was tall, a lithe six foot, the blond hair a bad dye job, the tan deep enough to have been built up over years. The hair. She remembered now. She *had* seen him down by the pier the evening before. She had walked past his car, seen through the windscreen his face turn away to avoid her eyes, fleetingly

351

pinned him as some shy farmer boy with a crap car and even worse hair. Christ, what a fool she was.

'He might have just gone to his car,' Kearney whispered back into the gloom. 'I can't see it from here. The caravan's in the way. Will I go out and have a look?'

'Is he carrying?' Begley said. It took Siobhan a couple of seconds to realise he was talking to her. She looked up at him blankly.

'Has he got a fucking gun?' he hissed at her.

Mulcahy, a gun? She knew some detectives did, but not all the time. She'd never seen him with one. Was that the right answer?

'Does he or not?' Begley's face was down near hers now, glaring, spitting at her. She felt nothing but disgust. Shook her head. No, no gun.

'He probably wouldn't shoot a woman, anyway. Or a helpless animal,' Kearney sneered. 'He has that old-fashioned look about him, doesn't he, Siobhan?'

Kearney was coming over to them now, quickly, looking over her shoulder all the time. 'Here, give me that,' she said, pointing at Begley's shotgun. 'I'll have a better chance with that. You have this.'

For the first time Siobhan noticed Kearney also had a gun in her hand, a small automatic pistol, which she proffered to Begley now, pulling the shotgun from his grip. As he let it go, almost meekly, Siobhan saw with a stab of understanding right into the heart of their relationship. Kearney was the one taking charge. She was the more dangerous of the two.

'You take care of her inside,' Kearney said to Begley. 'Come out after me when you're done.'

There you are at last, my old familiar, Siobhan thought, as fear sank its claw into her gut and twisted hard.

Through the tiny rust hole in the galvanised-metal sheeting, he could just about see the three indistinct figures inside the barn, like ghosts in the dim light. The splodge of blue, seated, quiet, was Siobhan. The other two were standing, floating, wavering, pacing. One squat and brown by the flare of light that was the barn door: Kearney. The other taller, all in black, topped with a mane of dull gold: Declan Begley. Of course it was. Who else could it bloody be?

Mulcahy cursed himself for the thousandth time for not having figured it out earlier. He should have guessed, the minute he saw that cabin in the barn, that there was something not right about the situation. He should have known for sure when he saw the new lock, and when he saw Kearney arrive in that pale blue car, that there had to be two of them staying at the farm.

But most of all he cursed himself for not working out, the very second he heard about McTiernan's murder, that poor Eddie could never have been the target of some vengeful Colombian hit man. Because there was no Colombian hit man. Or if there had been, then it was almost certainly his corpse that had been found on the dump in Fuengirola. Outsmarted, somehow, by Declan Begley, when he came to look for him, and killed. With Kearney's more than willing help, no doubt. No wonder El Güero hadn't turned up back in Colombia, or that the guys in SOCA hadn't been able to pick up his trail. And Begley, ever the opportunist, had seen his chance to continue doing what he did best: cleaning, washing, erasing traces. This time cleaning up after himself, and on a grand and murderous scale, making sure that everyone who knew of his involvement in the cocaine theft, even Conor Hayes, would never get a chance to tell anyone.

Except for Gemma Kearney, of course. What had been their plan? To jet off into the sunset together, armed with clean, new identities and enough drugs money to do them for ten lifetimes? And now there was only him, Mike Mulcahy, left to stop them.

Mulcahy held that thought bright at the forefront of his mind, right beside the fear, as he forced himself to focus on how exactly he was going to do that. He had found himself a useful hiding place, but he knew that Begley and Kearney would soon decide they had to come after him. They would figure out that, being a cop, he probably wouldn't just run off and abandon Siobhan to her fate, and they would reckon Siobhan herself would be their best hope of flushing him out, of drawing him into a trap. What he had to decide now was whether to play a waiting game or try to move so fast they wouldn't see him coming. He watched the figure in brown walk inside, take something from Begley and then head back towards the barn door and out. Right, he thought, this could well be the best chance he would get.

Moving with all the agility a man of his size could muster, he picked his way carefully through the stacks of rubbish and loose detritus that littered the passageway between the two barns. Behind him, he could hear Kearney in the yard calling for him, her voice soft in fake entreaty. He had a couple of minutes at most, he reckoned. In his mind's eye he recalled the police photos of the farm in Suffolk where that other safe house had been, a gaping panel at the back of the barn to allow easy escape. Or access, of course. There had to be a way in there. A couple of minutes. If he didn't get in by then, both he and Siobhan would die and Begley and Kearney would be home free. He wasn't going to let that happen. He wasn't going to die for them.

'Get up. Come on, in there,' Begley growled at her, waving the pistol at the open door behind.

Keep them talking, Siobhan thought. That's what they always say.

'What are you going to do with us?' she said as she struggled to stand up. Her legs had ceased to function normally, and she was aware now of a tremor in her voice.

The look Begley gave her seemed to be one of genuine disbelief.

'What the fuck do you think we're going to do? Apart from her out there, you two are the only people on the planet who know I'm still alive.'

'We don't have to tell anyone.'

He didn't even bother to laugh at that. 'A reporter and a cop? Yeah, I mean, who would you tell? Fuck off.'

'But we won't know where you're going, who you're going to be. You don't have to hurt us. You could just leave us here and go. I could make a legend of you, Declan. Think of the headlines.'

It was pathetic, even she could see that, but it was the best she could come up with.

'There'll be headlines all right, but it's not me'll be in

them.' Begley shook his head, gave a short, horse-like snort. 'You're all the fuckin' same – think all people want is to be famous. Not me. I'm happy as I am, so long as I have money to back it up.'

'But—'

'Shut up talking, would you. Now get the fuck in there.' His anger was real now. If her hair had been longer, he would have caught her by it. Instead he seized her by the neck and pushed. She fell back awkwardly against the door jamb, felt the ache of its sharp, hard edge connect with the back of her skull and then her knees went from under her.

She squeezed her eyes shut as she slid down, trying to block it out, determined not to give in to the fear. If she gave in to it, she would have no chance. Then, as she opened them again, looking up at Begley bending over her, snarling, his hand out to drag her to her feet again, from the corner of her eye she saw it, a wisp of shadow moving, gliding through the darkness behind him, and felt the claw in her belly grip so tight she just couldn't keep it in any more . . .

Had she done it deliberately? He could have sworn she caught sight of him just before he got there. He almost quailed, stalled, made a misstep, for fear that Begley would see it in her eyes. But then she made that moan and Begley got too stoked up on her terror, too focused on bending down to pick her up, to hurt her some more, the rush of blood deafening him to what was coming up behind him. The man didn't have a chance, bent over like that, his neck exposed.

'Easy there, big man,' Mulcahy whispered. 'Don't move a

muscle, now. One twitch from you and your brains will be going through that door without you.'

Mulcahy accompanied the threat with the sound of his thumb cocking the hammer on the Sig, snapping it into place with a hard metallic click. Begley froze. Mulcahy pushed the muzzle still deeper into Begley's neck, hoping it hurt, and patted his hand down along Begley's arm until he came to the gun. *Never take your eyes off the face*, he heard an old instructor echo across time.

'I'll be having that,' he said, prising Begley's pistol from his open fingers and slipping it into his own jacket pocket. Then, with a vicious sweep of his boot, he scooped Begley's feet out from under him. Mulcahy watched Begley topple, flail uselessly for support, and hit the ground with a loud curse.

'Shut the fuck up, Bingo,' Mulcahy said, reaching forward now and pulling Siobhan to her feet by her outstretched arm, pulling her back behind him. She looked dazed, ashen-faced, but alert enough to do what he needed her to do.

'Are you okay?'

She nodded, not snapped out of it yet.

Out in the yard, Mulcahy heard Kearney shout for him again, all pretence of care gone. She'd be back in again any second, that shotgun in her hand.

'See that bit of baling twine over there?' he said to Siobhan, pointing at a scrap of filthy green string lying on the floor a few metres away. 'Go get it for me, yeah?'

She nodded slowly, understanding what he was saying, and went to get it, making a wide arc round Begley, who was staring up at Mulcahy, a frown of recognition diluting the contempt in his expression.

357

'Jesus, is it yourself?' Begley laughed, pulling himself up into a sitting position. 'Together again after all these years. Fuck's sake. And there was me thinking that Colombian cunt was the worst we'd have to deal with. Looks like the missus'll have to take another scalp, eh?' Begley rubbed his dyed blond hair mockingly. If he was worried, he sure as hell wasn't showing it. With his other hand he slapped the side of his thigh, laughing at some private joke, the arrogance alive in his eyes. 'Thought I was a gonner there in the doorway, y'know, but he only nicked me. Then I saw her coming up behind. Ka-boom! She's got a taste for it now. You'll fuckin' see.'

'Shut up, I said,' Mulcahy growled, refusing to be spooked. 'If you bring her back in here, it'll be my pleasure to put a bullet in both of you. Now, turn around, on your knees, hands behind your back.' Mulcahy backed up a step, his gun arm straight, aiming at the centre of Begley's forehead, knowing in his soul if it came to it, he wouldn't hesitate to pull the trigger, and take the consequences later.

Begley got the message. The smile vanished and he twisted himself round onto his knees, turning away from Mulcahy, arms behind, palms out, as Siobhan came back. She proffered the filthy piece of twine to Mulcahy, but he shook his head and instead raised his gun, flat in the palm of his hand, and brought it down with a vicious crack on the back of Begley's skull. The man slumped forward, expelling a low groan as he sprawled unconscious on the floor. Mulcahy moved quickly, sinking his knee into the small of Begley's back, pulling the limp arms and wrists together, gesturing for Siobhan to hand him the twine now.

'Jesus, I thought we were done for there,' she whispered,

shocked by his sudden violence but shaking with excitement again now, not fear. 'Is he all right?'

Mulcahy stared back at her, something blank and intransigent in his eyes, something she'd never seen in them before. 'He'll live. Come on, we've got to get him in there, into the cabin, while he's out cold.'

He stood up, pushed his hand into Begley's armpit and pulled him up, indicating to Siobhan that she should do the same. Between them they hauled Begley through the door of the cabin and into what appeared to be a luxuriously appointed living room, laid out like a studio apartment with a single bed to one side, a sitting area with table, chairs, armchairs and a flatscreen TV to the other, and what looked like a fully equipped kitchen and bathroom towards the back. There was only one real incongruity – a wide rectangular hole in the middle of the floor, its steel hatch lying open.

'Jesus,' Siobhan said. 'You could hide out in here for weeks.'

Mulcahy didn't really have time to take it in. Already Begley was beginning to come round, his eyes rolling under the lids, his breath coming in short, rasping gasps. Mulcahy looked into the hatch in the floor, saw a pit with a set of wooden stairs leading down to what looked like a steel door. Dragging Begley the rest of the way himself, he dumped him unceremoniously down the steps, crashing the hatch closed on top of him.

'Let's go,' he said, holding a hand out to Siobhan.

31

They should have run out of the back of the barn, and away across the fields. But if only they could get to the car, Mulcahy thought, he'd be able to get Siobhan properly away. Even in the fraction of a second it took to hesitate, his ears became attuned to a new sound, that of an engine, another set of tyres crunching into the farmyard outside.

He stood stock still, his hand gripping Siobhan's, returning her stare of puzzlement, of fresh anxiety. Who the hell could this be?

A second later they got their answer. A car door opening, a male voice shouting, a thick accent. 'Hello there, now. Garda Siochana. Do you need some help there?'

An ecstasy of relief was breaking out on Siobhan's face.

Had Ford heard him after all? But Mulcahy knew that couldn't be right. There was no way an armed-response unit could have got out there so quickly, not from Skibbereen or Cork, which meant Ford must have phoned the local Garda station, got a patrol car to come out. Jesus, if they were uniforms, they wouldn't even be armed.

He pulled Siobhan round to the side of the cabin. 'Let me go see first. Can you stay here and make sure Begley doesn't get out?' he said, pulling Begley's pistol from his pocket. 'Do you know how to use one of these?'

As he handed the gun to her, she took it without a hint of the tentativeness with which most people handle a firearm. Her hands were shaking, but she knew what to do with them. 'My dad was in the army for a while,' she said. 'He showed me how. It's been a few years, but . . . ' She turned the small Beretta over in her hand, checked the safety, pulled the slide back along the barrel and showed Mulcahy the chambered round before easing it back again. 'Like riding a bicycle.'

He didn't even stop to smile at her. Instead he turned and ran, holding his own weapon straight down by his side, thinking only of Gemma Kearney and that shotgun. Maybe she'd try to brazen it out, like she had with him. There was no way she could know Begley wasn't still in charge inside . . . The first shot rang out before he was even halfway to the barn door, the unmistakeable crump of a shotgun blast. Mulcahy cursed, ducking down instinctively into a crouch, flattening himself against the metal door when he got to it.

Outside, in the middle of the yard, he could see a blue and white patrol car, its blues flashing silently on the roof, both the driver's and passenger doors wide open. Hearing no more firing, he inched his face out of the door, could hardly believe what met his eyes: a tall stripling of a Garda, carrot-haired, freckle-faced, no more than twenty years old, reeling in silent, disbelieving agony across the yard, clutching a wound like a shark-bite ripped from the side of his uniform between ribs and hip.

Even as Mulcahy searched to see where the shot had come from, he heard another blast. He turned towards the sound, watched in horror as a second Garda staggered out from the far side of the patrol car, clutching a ragged, spurting wound to his leg, and collapsed to the ground, screaming. That's when he saw Kearney emerging from behind the caravan, a baleful expression on her face, breeching the shotgun, reloading and raising it to fire again.

Half mesmerised by blood and horror, Mulcahy knew only that he had to stop her. He shouted out her name and ran into the yard holding his Sig in a straight-arm, two-hand grip in front of him, aiming squarely at her chest, focusing on the two white dots of the sights.

'Don't kill him, Gemma,' he shouted, trying to make it sound authoritative. 'You don't have to. He's no threat to you now. Put the shotgun down.'

She didn't even seem to see the weapon in his hand, just swung round with a look of titanic fury, the barrel of the shotgun following her eyeline. Mulcahy dived to his right just as the flame blossomed from the barrel, and he was still falling when he heard the rattle and ding of the shot on the metal door behind him, followed instantly by a shredding pain all along the left side of his face. But it was nothing compared to the screaming agony that, a fraction of a second later, hurricaned through his entire body when he slammed, shoulder first, into the concrete breeze block lying where he landed. The shoulder socket he'd done so much damage to fourteen months before cracked like an egg. His gun spun out of his

362

grip, a tidal wave of shock consuming every thought like a savage at a feast. For a moment there was nothing but pain, howling through him. By the time that horror had eased, and he remembered to open his lungs and eyes and ears again, another had joined it: a shotgun barrel poking into his chest and a deranged Gemma Kearney screaming at him to get up or she'd kill him right there on the ground.

'Where the fuck is Declan? Where is he?'

Somehow, he found a way – with his good arm, his knees, his feet – to scramble into a slumped position against a rusting oil barrel. It was difficult to keep his eyes open through the pain, but even as another wave peaked, it seemed to bring a kind of numbness in its wake. Which was just as well, as Gemma Kearney wanted him up on his feet and was jabbing the barrel at his face now.

'Where's that reporter bitch?' she was screaming at him. 'Has she got him?'

Suddenly an image crystallised in his head: Siobhan wrapping her hand round the Beretta. Where was she?

He turned towards the barn, felt blood trickling down his face and inside his collar. He must've been caught by two or three pellets at least, though he felt nothing, just the atom-splitting pulse of pain in what used to be his shoulder.

'If you don't come out, I'll take his head off,' Gemma screamed through the barn door. But he knew she wouldn't shoot him, not yet, when she began prodding him again with the gun barrel, forcing him to get to his feet.

He'd just about managed to stand up when they heard a pistol shot crack out hollowly from inside the barn. Kearney flinched. Mulcahy didn't have the energy even for that, but they both held still as the report echoed hollowly down to a silence broken by the ragged moans of one of the wounded Gardai behind them. Then came the screams – a man's screams – from inside the barn.

Begley had taken a hit.

Kearney stepped back and poked Mulcahy savagely in the kidneys with the shotgun. On the scale of pain it registered no more than a nudge.

'We're going in there,' she said, 'and you're going ahead of me, now.'

Bracing his damaged arm with his right hand to limit the pain of movement, Mulcahy shuffled forward towards the wooden barn door. Inside, the first thing he saw was Begley lying in front of the cabin door, desperately trying to staunch the flow of blood coming from a wound in his upper left thigh.

'The bitch shot me. She shot me,' he shrieked at them, holding his hands round his thigh in a kind of manual tourniquet. Mulcahy saw the length of baling twine trailing from one wrist – he must have worked it loose and made his way out of the cabin, only to encounter Siobhan outside. But there was no sign of her anywhere now. Where the hell had she got to?

'Get over here, would you,' Begley roared at Gemma. 'Can't you see I'm bleeding out? Do something, for fuck's sake. Help me.'

But Gemma didn't drop her guard. Pushing Mulcahy forwards with the gun, ensuring she stayed well in his shadow, they ventured further into the barn.

'Hang on, Declan. You'll be okay,' Gemma said levelly,

almost chidingly. 'Tell me where she is first. Did you see where she went?'

Begley, however, was succumbing to the effects of shock. All the blood from his leg seemed to have drained directly from his face, which was crumpling with emotion. He shook his head in answer to her. 'I don't know,' he whimpered, and repeated the phrase over and over again.

Mulcahy, barely managing to focus himself, heard Gemma curse behind him. He could sense her grip on the situation, her taste for the fight, beginning to go. She was muttering to herself, unsure what to do. Then, making an abrupt decision, she stepped out from behind and turned to face him, the shotgun pointing at his gut.

'Come out, Siobhan, or I'll finish off this fucker,' she shouted at the emptiness, at the piles of old tyres, the heaped coils of barbed wire, the empty diesel drums and fertiliser sacks, at the unresponsive silence.

'Come on,' she shouted again. 'This is your last chance.'

Nothing.

Kearney shifted her trigger hand to get a better grip on the stock, raised the barrel towards Mulcahy's chest, on her face a look like death. 'Looks like she ran out on you,' she said. 'So you're no use to me—'

A sharp report rang out from the far end of the barn to their right. Mulcahy swivelled round at the same time as Kearney, watching as she raised the gun to her shoulder to track a shadow scuttling past a pile of tyres. Gemma was in front of him now, her back turned to him, and through the fog of pain behind his eyes he recognised what would probably be the last chance he'd have to save his life. In a slow-motion blur he watched Kearney draw her shoulder back to fire, and, with all the energy he could summon, he lifted his right foot as high as he could and lashed out at the back of her knees with it.

It wasn't pretty, it wasn't even accurate, but he was a big man with a big shoe size and the heel of his boot sank into her thigh with such force she went flying to the ground, the shotgun going off in her hands with a deafening roar. Without stopping to think, he hurled himself lengthwise after her, blanking out the certainty of still more excoriating pain by bellowing out as he fell on her, pinning her down.

'Come on, Siobhan, come out. She can't move. The shotgun's empty.'

When he opened his eyes next, Siobhan was there above him, anger bright red on her cheeks, the Beretta digging into the side of Kearney's face.

'Let go of the shotgun,' Siobhan hissed at her. 'Let go of it or I'll do you. I swear I'll do you.'

'Watch out for Begley,' Mulcahy wheezed, trying to breathe through the pain. Siobhan looked down at him, an infinity of emotion charging across the space between their eyes.

'I don't think he's going to be doing much of anything,' she said quietly, lowering herself to the floor, keeping the gun trained on Kearney, her legs starting to shake uncontrollably.

Mulcahy did his best to turn his head to see what Siobhan was talking about, understanding what she meant at exactly the same moment as Gemma Kearney did. His ears were rent by Kearney's howl of anguish. Declan Begley, or what remained of him, was lying slumped against the cabin wall, his chest caked in blood, the lower half of his face entirely missing. Kearney's last blast had taken him out, permanently.

Epilogue

Mulcahy remembered nothing more of the events of that day. He had to rely on Siobhan's account, related to him and the rest of Ireland across an eight-page spread in the *Sunday Herald* two days later. From his hospital bed he read how he and Siobhan had not had to restrain Gemma Kearney after her realisation that Declan Begley was dead. There had been no need: all she'd done was crawl across the floor to the bloodied corpse she'd made of her lover, and weep uncontrollably over him.

Mulcahy had no recollection whatever of insisting, despite his own injuries – thirteen shotgun pellets to his face and neck, a shattered collarbone and shoulder socket, torn ligaments – that he and Siobhan should make their way out of the barn to the yard to see what they could do for the two injured uniforms outside. Back-up was already on its way by then, with Murtagh and O'Grady leading the posse of six cars that raced up the track to Blaggard Farm fifteen minutes later and slewed to a halt just outside the yard, the silence seeming even heavier as they fanned out, weapons drawn, and one by one stopped to take in the bloody scene before them. Both of the uniforms survived, just about; the younger was still fighting for his life in the intensive-care unit at Cork University Hospital, where he had been helicoptered within half an hour of being discovered.

Mulcahy skipped over the stuff that made him out to be a hero. He knew that was just Siobhan being a hack. All he'd done was try to survive. He knew all too well that if Siobhan hadn't held her nerve and outsmarted Gemma Kearney in those final crucial minutes in the barn, they'd both be dead by now and Kearney and Begley would already be out of the country with new identities and wholly untroubled consciences. Of more interest to him by far was a short follow-up report on the body found in Fuengirola, originally thought to be Begley's. The piece echoed his own suspicions that Begley and Kearney had lured an assassin into a trap and turned the tables on him, planting Begley's ID on his body before the couple embarked on their own clean-up spree. The report was largely speculative, but carried a strong sense that a well-informed insider, Murtagh maybe, or Ford, had guided it along. As for Cormac Horgan, there was talk of the police in Bristol reopening the investigation into his death but Mulcahy doubted whether, short of a confession from Gemma Kearney, anyone would ever get a definitive answer to what had happened up on the Clifton Suspension Bridge that night.

The pages that bemused Mulcahy most were the ones devoted to what was called, in a blaring headline, THE HIDE – WHAT THEY FOUND IN THE BLAGGARD FARM STASH. Beneath the cabin in the barn, in the cellar where he'd tried to confine Begley, a bizarre strongroom had been found, containing a huge assortment of Irish art works, antiques and other precious objects. The term 'Aladdin's cave' featured heavily in the coverage. An offshoot of Begley and Kearney's other money-laundering activities, its combined worth was in the millions, but there was no obvious rationale to the collection other than cash conversion: paintings by Le Brocquy, Middleton, Dillon and Swanzy stored side by side with Georgian silver sauce boats, antique clocks and mirrors, porcelain, gold, loose gems and jewellery of every kind. And ten bales of Colombian cocaine, weighing in at ten kilos each, the twine with which they were tied identifying them as probably the last of the Rotterdam consignment.

As ever, Mulcahy wasn't so much shocked by the extent of Begley and Kearney's criminality, as baffled by it. What could stealing that cocaine possibly have brought them that they didn't have already? Greed that raw was something, he knew, he would never get his head around. He wasn't sure he would want to either. If it weren't for that gulf in understanding, or in empathy at least, there would be no point in him being in the job.

Mulcahy lay back motionless in the bed, the strapping on his shoulder and chest making any but the smallest movements difficult without assistance. He closed his eyes, saw a byline swimming in an ocean of newsprint, words and ink slowly melding and morphing into short black hair as soft as cashmere, slipping through his fingers like ripples on a beach. At the diamond-shaped pane of glass in the door, Siobhan Fallon's face appeared, decided he was sleeping, and turned away.

Acknowledgements

More than ever, enormous thanks to my agent Broo Doherty; to David Shelley, Daniel Mallory, Thalia Proctor, Kirsteen Astor, Laura Collins and all at Little, Brown UK; and to Breda Purdue and Margaret Daly at Hachette Ireland. Many thanks also to Andy Hamilton of the Bristol Coroner's Office; the ever-generous D.P. Lyle for his medical and forensics advice; to my fellow writers at Criminal Classes: Kathryn Skoyles, Richard Holt, Elena Forbes, Keith Mullins, Cass Bonner and Nicola Williams, and our wise friends Margaret Kinsman, Chris Sykes and Peter Guttridge; to Andrew Pettie and the team at the Telegraph; to the staff at the Garda Press Office and all the other members of the Garda Siochana who helped me in the writing of this book. As always, a lifetime's gratitude to my mother, Jo; to Noelle, Carmel, Billy, Tony, Clare, Gill and Alison; and, most of all, to my gorgeous wife, Angela.

www.gerard-odonovan.com